THE
KING'S
JEWEL

ELIZABETH
CHADWICK

SPHERE

SPHERE

First published in Great Britain in 2023 by Sphere

1 3 5 7 9 10 8 6 4 2

Copyright © 2023 by Elizabeth Chadwick
Map artwork by Stephen Dew

The moral right of the author has been asserted.

A CIP catalogue record for this book is available from the British Library.

Hardback ISBN 978-0-7515-7760-0
Trade paperback ISBN 978-0-7515-7761-7

Typeset in BT Baskerville by Palimpsest Book Production Ltd, Falkirk, Stirlingshire
Printed and bound in Great Britain by Clays Ltd, Elcograf S.p.A

Papers used by Sphere are from well-managed forests and other responsible sources.

Sphere
An imprint of
Little, Brown Book Group
Carmelite House
50 Victoria Embankment
London EC4Y 0DZ

An Hachette UK Company
www.hachette.co.uk

www.littlebrown.co.uk

For my readers, each and every one of you

A Cast of Characters

Persons marked with an asterisk are recorded in history

The Welsh (in order of appearance)

Nesta ferch Rhys
Daughter of Rhys ap Tewdr, Prince of Dyfed, Lord of Carew*

Dewi ap Einan
An experienced, loyal groom in the service of Nesta's family

Morgan
Dewi's son, a young but experienced soldier

Geraint
Dewi's other son, Morgan's brother and also an experienced soldier

Gwladus
Nesta's mother*

Gruffydd ap Rhys
Nesta's brother*

Ifan
A scout and informer to Gerald of Windsor

Rutherk ap Tewdr
Nesta's uncle*

Eleri
Nesta's senior maid

Wilfrid
Bishop of St David's*

Owain ap Cadwgan
Handsome, charismatic warrior prince, eldest son of Cadwgan ap Bleddyn*

Ceridwen
Nesta's junior maid

Madog ap Rhyrid
Owain's volatile, self-seeking cousin*

Cadwgan ap Bleddyn
Prince of Powys, Owain's father, a survivor of many skirmishes and wars*

Rhian
Another maid of Nesta's

Rhodri
Ifan's son

The Normans, English, Flemish and others (in order of appearance)

Gerald FitzWalter of Windsor
Younger son of the Constable of Windsor Castle, a talented, ambitious hearth knight*

Arnulf de Montgomery
Son of Roger de Montgomery, Earl of Shrewsbury, an accomplished military commander and Gerald's lord*

Hugh de Montgomery
Oldest son of the Earl of Shrewsbury*

Adele Corbet
Robert Corbet's wife (her Christian name is not known to history)*

Roger de Montgomery
The powerful Earl of Shrewsbury*

Robert Corbet
A Marcher lord, subordinate to the Montgomery family*

Richard de Belmeis
A deacon in the service of the Montgomery family, later the Bishop of London, and viceroy in the Welsh Marches*

Sybilla Corbet
Adele's small daughter*

Yolanda
Gerald's mistress (her name and circumstances are unknown, but she existed)*

William Hait
A Flemish knight, Gerald's second in command at Pembroke*

Brian
Squire to the knight Jordan de Mara

Jordan de Mara
A Montgomery knight

William Rufus
Son of William the Conqueror, King of England from 1089 to 1100*

Henry I
Ambitious, womanising younger brother to William Rufus, King of England from 1100 to 1135*

Robert de Belleme
Another of the Montgomery brothers, breeder of fine horses*

Madame Beatrice
The lady in charge of the women's chamber at Woodstock

Ede
One of the mistresses of Henry I and possible mother to his son Robert*

Robert de Caen
Eldest bastard son of Henry I*

Annora
One of Henry I's mistresses domiciled at Woodstock*

Walter FitzOdo
Constable of Windsor Castle and Gerald's father*

William FitzWalter
Gerald's older brother and future Constable of Windsor Castle*

Odo de Barry
Friend of Gerald and Lord of Manorbier*

Marguerite de Barry
Odo's wife (her Christian name is unknown to history)*

Emma de Sai
Daughter of Picot de Sai and wife of Cadwgan ap Bleddyn (her Christian name is unknown to history)*

William of Brabant
A Brabançon settler in South Wales, an important merchant and community leader*

Matthew de Reivers
A Norman soldier of the Cenarth Bychan garrison

Juel
A Flemish soldier of the Cenarth Bychan garrison

Magnus Sigurdsson
Hiberno-Norse trader in legitimate goods and less legitimate plunder and people

Einar Yellowbeard
Hiberno-Norse mercenary and trader

Queen Matilda (Edith)
Henry I's wife*

Nesta and Gerald's children

Walter
Gerald's son by an unknown woman (in this novel, Yolanda)*

Henry
Nesta's son by King Henry I*

Gwilym
Nesta and Gerald's eldest son*

Angharad
Nesta and Gerald's firstborn daughter*

Dafydd
Nesta and Gerald's second son, later Bishop of St David's*

Maurice
Nesta and Gerald's third son*

Gwladus
Nesta and Gerald's second daughter*

A Note on Pronunciation

For those fortunate enough to speak the beautiful Welsh language, pronunciation of the names will come as a matter of course. For those unfamiliar, here is a brief guide to pronouncing those names that might look a bit more unusual or less obvious.

Cadwgan ap Bleddyn – Caduggan ap Blethin
Dafydd – David, rhyming with the word 'avid'
Dewi – Dough-wee
Dyfed – Duvvid
Gruffydd – Griffith
Gwladus – Gladys
Madog ap Rhyrid – Madoc ap Rhirid
Owain – O-wine
Tewdr – Tudor
Tymestl – Tim-*estel*

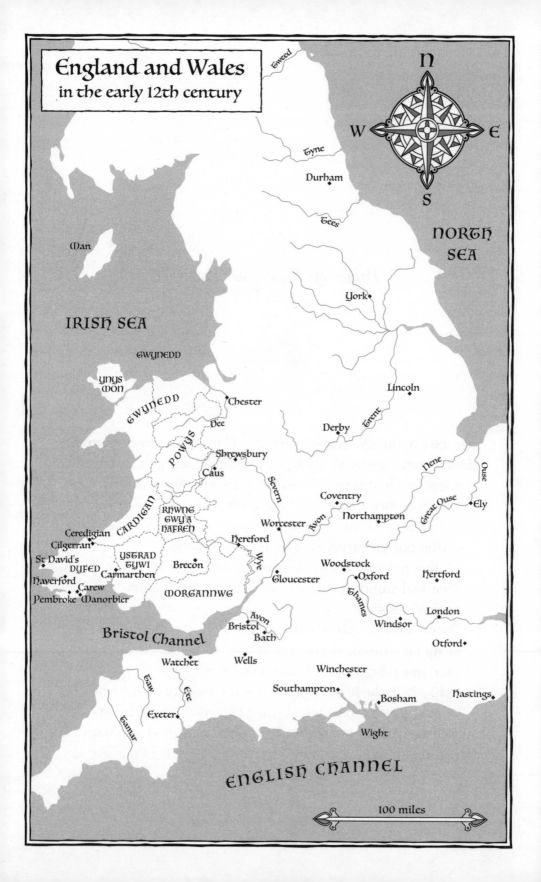

1

Palace of Carew, South Wales,
April 1093

Nesta was in the stables greeting Hera's new foal when her father came home. Wet with birthing fluid, the colt struggled to his feet and immediately tumbled back into the straw. The mare whickered encouragement and licked him with long strokes of her tongue until he tried again, this time surging to all fours, swaying but precariously upright.

'A fine future warhorse for your father,' said Dewi the groom as the foal wobbled into the shelter of Hera's flank. 'He's the image of his sire.'

Nesta smiled with wonder and delight, for the foal did look exactly like Taran, champion of the royal stud at Carew. Her father was riding him on campaign, three days' journey to the north, where the hated Normans were building another of their castles at Brecon, pushing ever further into Welsh territory. The peace agreement her father had made with King William the Bastard had died with him, and under the new rule of his son,

William Rufus, the Norman border barons had turned their avaricious gaze westwards, viewing the principalities of Wales as ripe for their picking. Ten days ago, news had come to Carew that the Normans had allied with her father's old and bitter enemy in Powys, Cadwgan of the house of Bleddyn, and her father had ridden out with his warband to put a stop to the incursions.

Legs splayed like a drunkard, the foal sought the mare's udder.

'What shall he be called then, young mistress?' Dewi asked, his eyes twinkling.

Nesta tilted her head. 'Tymestl,' she said. Tempest, son of Thunder. Her heart always leaped when she watched her father's stud herd galloping together, manes and tails streaming with their speed. Taran, with his arched crest and high-stepping pride, was her favourite, but she loved the sleek mares with their sun-polished coats, and the leggy foals dancing at their heels. The storm-horses of Carew were renowned and coveted throughout Wales.

'A fine choice,' Dewi said. 'Your father will approve.'

Nesta hugged herself at the praise. Pray God her father returned soon; she wanted to be first to show him the new arrival. Her stomach growled. On waking, she had thrown on her clothes, braided her hair and raced to the stables, knowing the birth was imminent. Now, although ravenous, she was reluctant to leave the mare and foal. For a few precious moments this wonderful event was hers and Dewi's alone.

Giving her a knowing grin, the groom unfolded the napkin containing his breakfast of bakestone bread and fat bacon. 'You are welcome to share, young mistress.'

Nesta dipped her head, affecting gracious dignity. She was the Prince's daughter, and there were boundaries, but she had known Dewi since he had first held her on a pony as a chubby infant, and by mutual assent they had made their own rules of hierarchy. She was fond of him, and he cherished her, for he only had sons – grown men away with Lord Rhys and the warband.

Nesta bit into the bread, flat and chewy from the bakestone, but flavoursome, and the perfect accompaniment to the thinly sliced fat bacon, tasting of hearth smoke and herbs. Having taken his first drink, the foal curled in the straw to sleep and Hera stood over him, absorbing his scent and nudging him softly with her nose. The spring sun was climbing in the sky and the morning was going to be fine and clear. Not a day for spinning in her mother's chamber with her four-year-old brother Gruffydd under her feet, but for riding along the river bank or over to Manorbier to watch the waves roll white-maned to the shore.

The lookout guard shouted from the palisade, and a horn blew the sequence Nesta knew by heart, heralding her father's return. Brushing crumbs from her gown, she dashed into the compound, her breathing swift with anticipation as the great wooden gates swung open.

As the first men straggled through the entrance in exhausted disarray, her eyes widened at the sight of her father's formerly proud and vibrant warband returning in disorganised clots of wounded and beaten men. She searched with growing panic for a prancing stallion with a hide of twilit gold, and a raven-haired man in a sweeping red cloak, and saw neither. Nor was her father's brother, her uncle Rutherk, among the men.

Dewi's sons Morgan and Geraint rode through the gateway, Morgan leading a brown gelding with a body lumped across the saddle. Nesta's breath jammed in her chest for the corpse's hair was midnight-black and its red cloak was heavily stained with blotches of darker rusty-brown.

Dewi had run out of the stables after her, and the other

servants were gathering in a huddle, eyes staring, hands to mouths.

'Montgomery is coming, with Cadwgan and his warband behind him,' Morgan announced grimly. 'We have a few hours at most – we have ridden ourselves into the ground to get here, and we are spent. Too many are dead and not enough of us to defend Carew from attack.'

'Where is the lord Rutherk?' Dewi demanded.

Geraint's face contorted with disgust: 'He yielded his sword to the Normans and swore allegiance to save his own hide. Do not look to him for help.'

Nesta heard the exchange but it meant nothing. Her father would come and make everything right. He couldn't be dead; that was not his body draped over the horse. How could it be, when it wasn't Taran? How could it be when he was so big and strong? He would never leave his people leaderless and unprotected.

Taking her arm, Dewi turned her towards the hall. 'Child, go to your mother, we have to leave.' She resisted him, needing to see the face of the man hanging over the brown horse to make sure it wasn't her father, but Dewi's grip tightened. 'There will be time for other things later,' he said with increased urgency, 'but now we must run for our lives. Quickly, go now!'

The mingling of hardness and compassion in his gaze ripped into her and, crying out, she tore from his grasp and fled from the shocking sight of her father's shattered warband.

Time became a blur, as slow as riding in fog and as fast as water in spate. Nesta packed her jewels, her rich clothes and ribbons – the items of her status as the cherished daughter of the High Prince of Dyfed. This was a dream, and in a moment she would wake up safe in her bed. She pinched herself hard enough to bruise the skin, but the nightmare remained the reality.

Her mother, Gwladus, grimly bundled her little brother Gruffydd into a cloak and knelt before him to fasten the pin. 'Be a good, brave boy for me,' she said, a quiver in her voice. 'Do as you are told and I will come to you as soon as I can.'

He nodded solemnly, round-eyed, bewildered and on the verge of tears as she hurried him outside and handed him to Dewi's sons who were waiting with fresh horses. 'Do not stop for anything,' she said. 'Get him safely away. Here are his clothes and money for your needs.'

'We shall protect him with our lives, Lady Gwladus,' Morgan replied, lifting Gruffydd in his strong arms while Geraint took care of the bundle and the bag of coins.

The last Nesta saw of her little brother was his frightened face and big eyes as Morgan lifted him onto his saddle and reined about. And then they were gone at a pounding trot.

'Please God they reach the coast in time,' her mother whispered, crossing herself. She drew a shuddering breath and turned to Nesta. 'We must hasten too – are your things ready?'

'Yes, Mama.' Nesta pointed to her own bundle. Four years ago, during a period of strife with Cadwgan of Powys, they had been forced into Irish exile for a time, and they were always ready, but this was different: the Normans had a terrifying reputation, and her father was . . . could not lead them.

'Good. Put on your cloak and cover your hair – quickly now.'

Nesta swallowed. 'Mama . . .' she said, and then stopped, because the words were stuck in her throat.

'Ah, child . . .' Gwladus draped Nesta's cloak around her shoulders, fussed it into place as she had done with Gruffydd, and pinned it with her favourite silver and garnet brooch. 'None of that. Be brave as your father would expect and command.'

Nesta swallowed hard, nodding to show that she understood, even while her world fragmented into jagged pieces. Her mother hugged her fiercely, and together they stepped outside, leaving a life that only an hour ago had been routine and secure, but was now gone for ever, like a candle snuffed in a puff of wind.

By late morning they had arrived at the stone watchtower on the estuary three miles from the settlement at Pembroke, and here they pitched their tents and shelters close to the shore. The watchtower guardian, a dour, balding man of middle years, relayed the message that Morgan and Geraint had secured passage with Gruffydd on a vessel headed to Ireland with a cargo of wool, and had sailed two hours ago, bound for the court of Diarmait MacEnna, King of Leinster. More ships were expected, but not before the return of the tide, many hours hence.

Three of Lord Rhys's warband took his body gently down from the horse and placed it on a board, hands crossed upon his breast. Standing beside her mother, Nesta gazed at her father's body. His face was undamaged, the chiselled features still beautiful even though there was no breath in him. She wanted his chest to rise, to see him open his eyes, smile at her and tell her it was all a ruse. If she believed she was dreaming, she could live from moment to moment, knowing she would eventually wake up, and everything would return to how it was. How could her handsome, vibrant father be lost to all sense and feeling? No longer to sit in the hall with his silver rod of office, drinking mead from the Prince's horn. It couldn't be true.

With rigid control, her mother approached her husband's body and leaned over to kiss his brow. 'God keep your soul, my fair husband,' she whispered. 'You will be avenged, I swear it. Your son is gone to safety across the sea, and he will return when the time is right, and strike blow for blow. This is not the end – never the end.'

Nesta clenched her fists until her fingernails bit her palms.

Even if her brother did return and avenge their father's murder, for now Gruffydd was only four years old and it was a long, long time to wait.

Her mother called for water to wash the body, and a linen sheet from the baggage to make a shroud, while the men dug a grave, and their chaplain said prayers. Nesta knelt to help her mother, and wiped one of her father's hands, dissolving away the blood rimming his fingernails, holding the cold, unresponsive hand that had once patted her head. And still it wasn't true because it was too enormous to contemplate.

The three shames of a corpse are asking, 'Who killed this one?' and 'Whose is this bier?' and 'Whose is this fresh grave?' So said the law of her great-great-grandsire Hywel Dda who had set down the rules by which the people of the Cymru should live. But how would anyone know in the days and years to come when all that remained was dust and the family scattered?

Her mother's grief was as hard and glassy as stone. Her own was made of fog.

Gerald FitzWalter tossed another branch onto the fire and watched it settle amid the greying coals with their hot red underbelly. Sparks snapped free, shooting bright dashes into the darkness, making him think fancifully of Welsh dragons – a notion he would never admit to any of the men gathered around the camp fire.

The Norman host of Arnulf de Montgomery had arrived at Carew at dusk to find it deserted, with signs of a hasty retreat. The hearth in the hall had retained a vestigial heat and stray hens had been pecking in the compound, one of which had served Gerald and his serjeant for their evening meal, although it had been as tough as his winter boots, and Gerald was still picking rags of meat from between his teeth.

They had spent three days pursuing the remnants of Rhys

ap Tewdr's warband southwards, but the Welsh had slipped through the trees and from their grasp, swift and light as wraiths. He did not trust their guide an inch, even if Rutherk was Rhys ap Tewdr's brother and desired to ingratiate himself with his new allies. Gerald suspected that Rutherk hoped to rule Dyfed, and that meant ensuring Rhys's wife and children were dealt with, especially the boy. Rutherk had not been happy to find Carew deserted, but it had been too late to press on and the horses needed to rest.

Gerald reached for his cup but flashed his hand to his knife instead and cursed in surprise as a figure materialised at the guard fire – a slender Welshman of indeterminate years, wearing a rough sheepskin hood and a tunic mid-way between olive and grey. Ifan was one of their scouts, valuable because he spoke the Norman tongue – atrociously it was true, but better than Gerald's command of Welsh, although he was improving.

The scout's eyes squeezed together in amusement at Gerald's discomfiture. 'Be not so fast to draw steel, my fine lord,' he lilted. 'I bring news.'

Gerald cautiously withdrew his hand from his knife hilt. Stealthy as wolves, the Welsh scouts knew the terrain intimately, but despite their love of silver, their loyalty was fickle and could not be bought – only their service. Gerald's lord, Arnulf de Montgomery, paid them well but withheld his trust. 'And what news would that be?'

The Welshman licked his lips and eyed Gerald's cup. Sourly amused, Gerald handed it to him and sloshed in some wine. It was one Norman import the Welsh never scorned.

Ifan drank, smacking his lips with relish, then said, 'They are at the watchtower on the estuary beyond Pembroke, hoping to take ship for Ireland before you arrive to prevent them.' He shrugged. 'Whether they escape or you take them matters not.

Prince Rhys is dead and no one to fill his place. Rutherk ap Tewdr might fancy himself Lord of Dyfed, but he lacks the strength to sit in his brother's chair.'

Gerald rasped his palm over his chin stubble. 'Then who will they follow?'

'That is not for me to say, my lord.' Ifan took another drink, swilling the wine around his cheeks to savour before swallowing.

'Perhaps not, but I am asking you.'

'You should watch the lord Cadwgan. He has long desired this territory, and he and Prince Rhys have fought over it bitterly before. Last time, the lord Rhys cut down two of Cadwgan's brothers. He will be seeking scraps at the least and his heir, Owain, is coming into his strength too.'

'Interesting.' Gerald held out his hand for the return of his cup. It would not be the first to go missing and he was wise now. 'I will bring you to my lord – he will want to hear your report for himself.' He paid the scout with a silver penny, minted with the head of King William Rufus.

Ifan squirrelled the coin into a drawstring bag tied to his trews. 'Perhaps a fine Norman lord might decide to take his chance in Dyfed?' His eyes glinted with mockery.

Gerald gave him a hard look. 'Do not go too far.'

Ifan continued to smile. 'Only ever as far as I need, *fy arglwydd*,' he said, mockingly addressing Gerald as his lord.

Ignoring his impudence, Gerald escorted Ifan from the watch fire to the hall where Arnulf de Montgomery, his brother Hugh, and the Welsh noble Rutherk ap Tewdr were sitting by the hearth deep in conversation, Rutherk using an interpreter.

Arnulf de Montgomery looked up, his fox-brown eyes immediately alert. He was as lean as a fox too. His brother, in contrast, was wide-shouldered, with a paunch drooping over his belt.

'They're on the coast beyond Pembroke, by a watchtower,

waiting for an Irish ship,' Gerald said. 'It's our luck against theirs.'

'What about the boy?' Rutherk asked through the interpreter, his handsome face creased with anxiety. Gerald disliked him on principle; a man who would sell his own brother rather than stand hard was unworthy of respect – although disposing of rival relatives was a particular and complex feature of Welsh ruling families.

'The whole court is there, *fy arglwydd*,' Ifan said. 'I saw the daughter with her mother, and I saw the body of the lord Rhys laid upon the ground. If the boy was with them, he was not in sight. Perhaps twenty warriors and as many servants.'

Hugh de Montgomery folded his arms across his belly. 'We should leave at first light; it would be a waste to pursue our quarry all this way for nothing.'

Arnulf turned to Gerald. 'Have the men ready.'

'Sire.' Gerald bowed, kindled a lantern at the fire, and returned outside to check the guard posts and walk the boundaries, pausing at the various fires to speak to the soldiers and warn them of an early start. He carried out Arnulf's orders with meticulous efficiency, leaving nothing to chance. Promotion would only come from proving his worth. Wales was a land of opportunity, far more than England where, as a younger son of his father's hearth, his prospects were limited. And beyond ambition, something about Wales had stitched itself into his being, a thin golden thread that embellished his soul.

Humming to himself, he arrived at the stables – his final visit on his rounds. A cat slunk away on the edge of the light, a young rat in its mouth. The Welsh had left straw and some feed in their haste to depart. He checked his own horses, ensuring his squire had bedded them down properly. Brun, his warhorse, pricked his ears and Gerald paused to scratch the stallion's thick crest and speak softly to him, before moving on to his palfrey and baggage horse.

Moving further along, he came to the Montgomery warhorses. Another of Arnulf's brothers, Robert, had bred them – fabulous greys, powerful, full of stamina and fleet as the wind through grass. Wistful desire swelled in Gerald's breast, for their price lay in the realm of kings and earls, not young hearth knights who had to eke out their wages.

Beyond the greys stood Arnulf de Montgomery's latest acquisition – Prince Rhys's stallion, seized during the battle. In his young prime, the horse was a beauty, with a coat that glistened like storm-washed shingle. Gerald stood to one side, allowing him to breathe in his scent before quietly putting his hand on the smooth, arched neck. The horse stamped and tossed his head, but permitted Gerald's admiring touch.

'His name is Taran,' Ifan said, silently materialising at his side. 'It means Thunder. I do not think your lord will allow Rutherk ap Tewdr to have him as booty – far too valuable. The storm-horses of Carew are worth a king's ransom in silver. They go back to the stallions ridden by the great Hywel Dda.'

Gerald concealed his irritation at the scout's ability to creep up so silently. Arnulf would not permit Rutherk anything beyond his life and a few manors on which to live in service to his new Norman overlords. A prince was dead and he was not going to set another in his place. That part was done. 'Tell me his name again.'

'Taran,' Ifan repeated. 'Thunder.'

Gerald said the word, committing it to memory. Piece by piece he was learning to speak Welsh rather than relying on interpreters who could skew the details as they chose. The language intrigued him too with its poetic lilt and resonance.

'Why do you scout for us?' he asked Ifan. 'Beyond the money. What makes you serve a Norman lord?'

The scout shrugged his fleece-clad shoulders. 'Whatever we do, you will overrun this land, as you have overrun England, that much I have seen, so why should I swim against the tide and die when I can live and be paid?' He stepped suddenly into the full pool of lantern light and bared his throat, causing Gerald to start. 'See. These are the marks of a collar put upon me by my own people.'

Gerald gazed at the pale scars, barely visible, but still indelible for life. He knew that in warfare, Welsh lords would capture men, women and children from the lands of their enemies and ship them in fetters across the Hibernian Sea to be sold in the Dublin slave market. The Church condemned such activity, but it continued, for it was too lucrative to give up.

'I was a slave for three years to Cadwgan ap Bleddyn,' Ifan said. 'My young wife and son were sold in Ireland and died there but I escaped. You Normans, you are hard masters, and we suffer under your hands. I do not love you, but you pay my wages and give me opportunities for revenge.'

A glimmer of unease stirred in Gerald's breast at the feral gleam in Ifan's eyes. 'Thank you. I will not mention this to anyone else.'

'It is no secret,' Ifan said with angry pride. 'I have another wife and small son now, but I remember my first family every day.'

Behind them, the storm-coloured stallion snorted and pawed the straw. Gerald turned to calm him and when he looked round again, Ifan had melted into the darkness.

Deep in thought, Gerald returned to the hall and laid out his bed pallet at the side of the room. The three lords and the interpreter were still talking quietly at the hearth, but he did not join them, just nodded his head and exchanged a glance with Arnulf to indicate he had completed his duties.

He drank two full horns of water – enough to wake him in the early hours with a full bladder and be ready to rouse the men – and then rolled himself in his cloak, his sword at his side, and closed his eyes.

The Normans rode into the Welsh camp like a thunderous waterfall, scattering all before them, cutting down any who stood in their way. Nesta was standing on the shore, wrapped in her cloak, watching the tiny dot of a ship making for the harbour when she heard the screams and the clash and clamour of fighting. Whirling, she stared in shock at the soldiers descending on them with weapons brandished.

Her uncle drew rein in front of her in a shower of stones, blocking her path. 'Where is Gruffydd?' he shouted at her. 'Where is your brother?'

'Gone where you cannot reach him!' If only she had a blade to cut out his treacherous heart. She gathered a ball of saliva in her mouth and spat at his feet.

'This is my brother's daughter,' Rutherk told another Welshman who had joined him. 'Tell the Normans she says the boy has escaped to Ireland, but you should search for him anyway.'

'Already being done,' the man replied. 'Lord Arnulf has the mother and her women. He's taking them to Pembroke and we'll move from there.'

Nesta burned with loathing for both men. The sea wind stung her eyes and tears spilled down her cheeks, but she was not weeping; she never would in front of these cowards.

They brought saddled horses and her mother was dragged forward, resisting. A soldier shoved her to hasten her pace and she stumbled. Nesta's hatred increased until acid vomit burned her throat. A Norman shoved Nesta towards the horses, and squeezed her buttocks, making a lewd comment to his companions and laughing. Immediately, a knight astride a stocky brown stallion snapped a rebuke and the man dropped back. His smirk lingered until wiped from his face by another warning, icier than the first.

The knight turned to Nesta. 'You will not be harmed – you have my word,' he said in heavily mangled Welsh.

Dear God, she thought, they even murdered the language. The middle of his face was concealed behind the dull iron nasal bar of his helm, but his eyes were the same cold grey as the sea bursting on the shore.

'You killed my father; I have no faith in your word,' she spat with sick revulsion.

'Even so, you should take it, for it is all you have.' He gestured to the waiting horses. 'Better to mount of your own accord than have us force you.'

Tight-lipped, trembling, she allowed Dewi to help her into the saddle. His face was swollen from a blow, and dark blood clotted one nostril. 'Courage, my young mistress,' he said gruffly, his head turned away so the Normans would not hear. 'You and your mother are safe because they need you. Keep your head down; do as they say.'

'As you did?'

Dewi grimaced. 'That was your uncle Rutherk's man, searching for your brother. Your uncle's sour because Gruffydd has escaped his clutches, but the Normans will take everything anyway. Best to stay on their good side.' He left her to help her mother to the saddle.

'Tell them nothing,' Gwladus commanded. 'Never forgive, never forget – that is your vow.'

'Never, Mother,' Nesta replied, her body taut with contempt and grief. Seeing Taran among the Norman horses, she bit the inside of her cheek as she faced the reality that her father was never coming back. She and her mother were at the mercy of these hard-armoured strangers. She was no longer the beloved, pampered daughter, but a beast trussed for sale in the market, for slaughter or the breeding pen.

Passing the bodies of the men who had been killed as the Normans rode in, she neither flinched nor looked away, but acknowledged and marked them, giving them respect and silently promising revenge.

A short ride brought them to the settlement at Pembroke, where the women were thrust into a small room halfway up a stone lookout tower. A soldier tossed in their baggage, ransacked of all jewellery, fabric and trinkets. Straw pallets and coarse woollen blankets were thrown down for their slumber. The only light in the dismal chamber came from a slit of a window open to the air, and cresset lamps, burning smokily, sputtering tallow fat. The soldier returned, bringing bowls of barley broth and coarse bread, and then departed, closing and barring the door.

Nesta gazed at their bleak surroundings with a horrible, hollow sensation in her stomach. Two nights ago she had slept in a feather bed with fresh linen sheets and soft furs. She had enjoyed the clean, sweet light of beeswax candles and had washed her hands and face with rose water. She had belongings, wealth and status. Any man daring to fondle her haunch and laugh about it would have lost his hand for the insult.

'What will happen to us?' she asked her mother who was staring at the pallets in disgust.

'If they had wanted to kill us, they would have done so by now,' Gwladus said with a shrug. 'I do not matter, unless I happen to be carrying another child, which I know I am not, but you are your father's daughter, and that makes you valuable.'

Nesta folded her arms and shivered.

'You had your first bleed at Christmas, and you are of an age to wed. Any of those Normans could take you to wife and lay claim to your father's lands by their laws. You are not a hostage for your people, but a girl who brings with her the gift of stolen territory.'

Nesta went rigid. 'I would never marry one of them – never!'

Gwladus shook her head. 'What you want does not matter to them, but they cannot take what you already are inside. Hold your head high and remember your heritage. You are a pattern for others to emulate for courage and loyalty.' She took three steps to Nesta and touched her cheek. 'I am depending on you to carry this burden for your family's pride.'

'I won't let you down.' Nesta's voice quivered for, despite her defiant words, she felt small, afraid and overwhelmed.

'Oh, my beautiful girl.' Gwladus hugged her hard and tears squeezed out from between her closed eyelids. 'I know you will not. And you shall always have my love – always, whatever happens.'

Nesta drew in the familiar scent of her mother's skin, seeking comfort. 'I want it all to go away,' she whispered.

'I know you do, I know.' Gwladus rocked her back and forth and kissed her cheek. 'So do I. Dear Holy Virgin, so do I.'

Accompanying with the Montgomery brothers Arnulf and Hugh, Gerald stood on the lookout platform at the top of the stone watchtower, receiving a gull's-eye view of their surroundings. The estuary wind was cold, but not unpleasant, and the clouds were breaking up to reveal underskirts of palest blue, embroidered with sunlight.

'I want you to stay here and supervise the building of a fortress,' Arnulf told him. 'We need one here to control the Welsh if we are to govern the region, and increase trade with Ireland.'

Excitement flashed through Gerald, but he maintained a neutral expression. Being entrusted with the project was a huge promotion for him, even if it meant being left in this hostile corner of South Wales to fend for himself. 'Sire, thank you. I will not let you down.'

Arnulf de Montgomery eyed him shrewdly. 'We shall provide you with men and resources – I shall send some men from Brecon to start the work. Do this well and I shall make you constable. You are ambitious I know, and this is a chance to prove yourself.'

'Sire, I am honoured and grateful.' More than grateful.

Arnulf pivoted to face the land to the west. 'I want the keep sited there.' He pointed. 'You have water on three sides and control of any shipping coming up the river – it is the best defensive position.'

'I thought that too, sire. I shall begin organising the work immediately.' Gerald could control his voice and his expression, but not the flush that burnished his face.

'Good.' Arnulf nodded brusquely. 'I shall take the hostages north-east tomorrow. Better to have them within our own territory; we do not want them attracting the jackals down here. Cadwgan of Powys and his son would dearly love to steal them from us, and the girl is a marriage prize worth a risk.'

Gerald felt a surge of relief. Thank Christ he would not have to keep the women safe. He had already had to discipline one soldier for acting out of turn with the daughter – had docked him a day's pay and threatened to stripe his back with a whip. With her lustrous black hair and magnificent dark eyes, the girl was already a beauty even though not fully grown. He had been touched by the way she bore herself trying to mask her fear with scorn and haughtiness. 'And Rutherk ap Tewdr? What of him?'

'He comes with us. He may think he is in line to rule Dyfed, but he is untrustworthy and he will not stand firm if he is challenged by the men of Powys. The King will find him some reward or other, but he is a means to an end. Without power he is powerless, but he may prove useful for other projects.'

The scorn in Arnulf's voice was a timely reminder to Gerald that all men were a means to an end for the Montgomery lords. He turned his attention again to the prospect before him. A few fishermen's houses and hovels would have to be torn down but it was a perfect site for a fortress as demonstrated by the remains of ancient rampart lines. And it was his to build and to command.

He cleared his throat. 'The Welsh have a mare with a new foal. It will be a long journey for them. I could keep them here . . .'

'I am sending them to run with my own stud herd,' Arnulf said smoothly, giving him a knowing look. 'The dun stallion too. I have seen you eyeing him. I shall put him to a couple of my mares and see what he breeds. Making yourself successful here is reward enough for now I think.'

Gerald dipped his head and concealed his disappointment. Keeping the mare and foal would have been the cream on top of the milk and it had been worth asking. The Montgomery brothers would give him the resources to build this castle because they wanted him to succeed, but extra trimmings such as fine horses were no part of the bargain – not yet, anyway.

Arnulf and Hugh made their way back down the tower, but Gerald remained a little longer, imagining a castle and himself its lord, here on the edge of the world.

2

Shrewsbury Castle, Shropshire,
May 1093

Nesta surfaced from fitful slumber to the sound of whispered conversation beyond the door. Light shone through a crack in the shutters and touched the edge of the bed on which she lay. Her face was tight and sore from the tears she had wept and her stomach was hollow with grief, not hunger.

Slowly she pushed herself upright, her body aching from her anguish and from the long days in the saddle as the Normans abducted her from her homeland and brought her into their stolen territory far to the north-east. The paths and the greenery had changed little as they travelled inland, but she had lost the salt tang of the sea and all of her bearings. Yesterday morning, reaching a crossroads, they had separated her from her mother and the rest of the household. She had clung fiercely to Gwladus, who in turn had fought tooth and nail to hold on to her daughter, but they had been torn away from each other by the brutal strength of the soldiers, dragged in their different directions, kicking and screaming until they were tied up and slapped to silence.

She had arrived here at twilight, pulled down from her mount and locked up in this small chamber. She did not know where she was, only that it was some kind of fortress in a town larger than any she had seen in her life. They had brought her some savoury pottage with shreds of pork in it and a jug of water but she had touched neither. There was a pail for a latrine, and this bed. In a way she had been glad of the solitude, for she had been able to release the storm of emotion she had dammed up since fleeing Carew. All the grief, all the terror, rage and hatred had poured from her in thrashing screams and tears until she was deflated and empty. She might as well be dead – what did it matter?

The whispers ceased and the door opened with a soft creak. Nesta braced herself, clenched with fear, but instead of a rough-handed man with a sword, a woman entered the room. She was slightly younger than her mother and wearing an apple-green gown with crimson sleeve linings. A wimple of soft pale silk framed her face.

'You poor girl!' she declared in fluent but heavily accented Welsh. Sitting down on the bed, she extended her hand as if to a wounded dog. Nesta flinched and recoiled. A clean smell of herbs wafted from the woman's beautiful garments. Her eyes were moss-hazel, the pupils ringed with amber. 'Do not be afraid; you are safe now.'

Nesta didn't believe her. 'Where am I?'

'You are in Shrewsbury, at the castle,' the woman said. 'I am Adele Corbet, wife of Robert Corbet of Caus, and I am going to look after you for the time being at least.'

'Where is my mother?' Nesta wrapped her arms tightly around her body. 'I want to see my mother.'

Adele Corbet rose, went to the window and unlatched the shutters to let the morning light stream into the chamber. 'I believe she has been taken to the nunnery at Wilton.'

'Why have we been separated?' Nesta dug her fingers into her armpits. 'Why could I not go there too?'

Adele looked round with sympathy in her gaze, but sharpness too. 'I do not know why; it is not my decision. The nuns will take care of your mother, do not fear.'

'I am not afraid.' Nesta jutted her chin.

Adele pursed her lips at the untouched food and drink. Going to the door, she summoned a maid to remove it, ordering her to bring fresh victuals, and water for washing. 'I understand how angry and distraught you are just now,' she said, turning back to Nesta. 'I would be the same.'

Nesta pressed her lips together. This woman was obviously here to cajole her into compliance and she was not about to give her that satisfaction. Besides, how could she know what it felt like? How dare she say she understood.

The maid returned with fresh bread, a dish of honey, and a small earthenware jug of buttermilk. Behind her a second woman arrived with a bowl of warm water and a towel. Adele directed the women to leave the items on a low trestle near the window, and dismissed them.

'You must be hungry,' she said to Nesta. 'Come, eat.'

Nesta turned her head away. 'I do not want any of it.'

Adele sighed. 'Listen. You have been brought here against your will and I am sorry for it, but it is what men do, and nothing can turn back that moment or make it right. I am not here to force you, but if you fight and make trouble, then others will deal with you in my stead, and they will not be merciful.'

Nesta looked dully at Adele, still feeling defiant, but the woman's expression was open, without hostility, even if irritation marked the space between her brows. She had no interest in pleasing her, but Adele was her only source of succour. While resenting her words, Nesta understood her, and she had a duty to live and avenge what had been done to her family.

'I need to wash before I can eat,' she said with dignity.

'Yes, of course. I will find you a maid who speaks Welsh, but I shall help you for now.' Adele went to Nesta's baggage bundle and found a clean chemise and a blue gown decorated with red and white braid. 'This is pretty,' she said.

Nesta shrugged. The gown belonged to another life. One where she had sat at her father's feet as a princess and sung for him. She didn't want to wear it, but the one she had on was a travel-muddied rag.

Adele helped her to remove the soiled gown and her sweat-stained shift. Shivering, Nesta washed her hands, face and underarms in the water bowl, feeling embarrassed by the woman's scrutiny. She tried to cover her barely formed breasts with her hands. With a sympathetic murmur, Adele draped a towel around her shoulders, patted her dry, and helped her into the fresh chemise. Nesta inhaled the smell of summer and sea and home in the sun-bleached linen and her aching heart wanted to disappear into the garment for ever.

Adele found a comb and gently untangled Nesta's hair, murmuring a compliment about how thick and shiny it was. Nesta endured her deft and delicate ministrations, until a sudden memory of her mother doing the same thing made her pull sharply away from the comb's seduction. She jerkily braided her hair herself, then took the gown and drew it over her head, shunning assistance.

'You need a brooch,' Adele said neutrally.

'They stole my jewels,' Nesta replied. 'I have nothing save the pin from my cloak.'

Adele's eyes narrowed at that information. 'No matter, I will find you one of mine, and I shall speak to my husband. Come, eat.' To encourage Nesta, she tore a piece of bread from one of the two small loaves, dipped it in the honey and ate it herself.

Nesta's mouth watered. Reluctantly she followed Adele's example. The bread was fluffy and soft and the honey as sweet as summer. She realised as she chewed and swallowed how ravenous she was, and had to make a conscious effort to take small bites and appear indifferent.

'Is that better?' Adele asked with a half smile.

Nesta nodded grudgingly.

Adele briefly left the room and Nesta devoured the bread and honey with gusto, immediately ceasing as Adele returned.

'Here, use this to close your gown and chemise.' Adele gave Nesta a round silver brooch and added two rings for her fingers. 'If you look like a lady, you will be treated as one. Come, they are waiting for you.'

'Who?' Nesta looked up from securing the brooch.

'The Earl of Shrewsbury, and his sons – and my husband who is their vassal and who will be responsible for your care.'

Nesta's stomach threatened to void the bread and honey at the thought of being brought before these men, who had murdered her father and ripped her from her mother. 'No!' She shuddered. 'I refuse!'

'I know it is hard, and I am sorry, but the Earl insists on seeing you, and his sons are present to make their report.'

Nesta gulped and pressed the back of her hand against her mouth. 'No.'

'I will stay with you, I will not let them harm you, I promise.'

Nesta shook her head, not believing her. They would not stop for the word of a woman.

Adele took Nesta by the shoulders and lightly shook her. 'I

know what it is to be a pawn in the games of men. I was betrothed and married outside my will and the only way I make my life bearable is by using my wits. I counsel you to use yours if you want to survive.'

Nesta looked into Adele's eyes. 'Then help me, in God's name,' she whispered.

'I have said I will, and I mean it. Come.'

Trembling, Nesta followed Adele out of the chamber and across a courtyard to another building, accessed by an outer set of timber stairs leading to the doorway of the great hall. Here she froze, and Adele gently tugged her arm. 'Just a little further. You can sit with my ladies in a moment.'

Being in the same room as her father's killers filled Nesta with terror and revulsion, but without escape, her best hope was to follow the woman's lead and obey her.

The room was similar in size to the one at Carew, and well appointed with limewashed walls and fresh rushes covering the floor. Veils of fine smoke wreathed towards the roof louvres over the central hearth where Arnulf and Hugh de Montgomery sat either side of an older, balding man. An embroidered tunic strained over the latter's paunch, and many rings adorned his thick fingers. A fourth man sat with them, his gaze shifting between them in a way that suggested he was a subordinate. There was also a well-fed cleric in his twenties with shrewd eyes. Uncle Rutherk, thank God, was not among their company.

The men spoke rapidly to each other in Norman French of which Nesta understood not a word. The bald one rubbed his grizzled jawline and regarded her with hard eyes. The whites were tinged with yellow, giving him a demonic aspect. He snapped a question to Adele.

'Earl Roger is asking how old you are and if you have bled yet,' Adele translated, and Nesta started to shake. The man repeated the question and leaned forward, stabbing his forefinger at her, and she shook her head, wild-eyed.

Adele quickly stepped in front of her and spoke rapidly to the men. The Earl grunted and made a short answer, but Adele persisted, never raising her voice, but making her point. The cleric, who had been sitting back, hands folded over his comfortable stomach, cleared his throat and said something, gesturing in Nesta's direction. Eventually the Earl nodded and gruffly addressed Adele, before waving a dismissal.

Nesta had understood nothing of the exchange but relief swept through her as Adele dipped her head to the men and, curling her arm protectively around her shoulders, led her out of the hall. They walked a few steps to an adjoining building, once more accessed by stairs and leading to a spinning gallery and a chamber for the castle's women, who were busy about various textile crafts. A nurse sat rocking a cradle, and a little girl with long dark braids was leaning over to look at the baby.

Adele clapped her hands for silence and spoke to the women in the Norman tongue. Nesta heard her name spoken and guessed that she was being introduced. Adele then drew her to a sunlit cushioned bench and bade her sit. 'I told my ladies who you were,' she said in Welsh, 'and that you are here to learn our ways and our language to prepare for your future. I have also told them you are a princess of your people and they are to treat you with the care and kindness we would extend to a guest, and at the Earl's command.'

'The Earl . . . he was the bald one?' Nesta grimaced. He had not sounded as if he cared about treating her with care and kindness.

Adele patted Nesta's hand. 'Yes, Earl Roger. He is a soldier with a soldier's concerns and little time for women, but he understands practical matters when they are pointed out to him.

I told him I would look after you so that he would not be troubled, and that caring for you now would reap reward in the future. Deacon Richard agreed with me, and as a cleric his word carries weight. Do not think on it for now, just rest and settle down.'

Nesta silently nodded, twisted the silver rings on her fingers, and felt numb.

Adele sent for the castle physician who opined that Nesta's humours were unbalanced and that she was suffering from a surfeit of melancholy and damp. 'Such conditions are hard to treat,' he said sombrely. 'You must keep her dry and warm near the fire, and you must not allow her to sink any further, or her malady may become untreatable.'

'She is valuable to the Earl, and needs to be cured, if possible,' Adele said.

The physician looked doubtful. 'I shall prepare a nostrum, but in the meantime, keep her quiet and warm, and continue as you are doing. I trust to your good sense, my lady, but do not expect miracles.'

For the rest of the day Nesta sat with Adele's women while their chatter flew over her head, like a flock of small birds on the wing. Adele gave her some fleece to spin – a task she could do without having to think. She could just watch the thread twirl out of the cloud of wool and be in the moment as she spun and wound in constant rhythm.

A wet nurse lifted the baby from the cradle and put him to suckle. Nesta blinked back tears, for the atmosphere was so enclosed and domestic that it could have been her life at home in her mother's bower – but it wasn't. These people had stolen that from her and she was bereft. She desperately needed the comfort, but not from this source, and between her need and her denial she was torn in two. Neither fleece nor thread.

One of the women took up a harp and sang for the ladies as they worked. The song was in the Norman tongue, but reminded Nesta of her own family's songs and how they would never be sung again. She stared at the spinning until her eyes burned. She would not cry in front of these women and she would learn their language and know what they were saying.

The ladies dined at noon in their own hall and did not join the men. Profoundly glad, Nesta ate the chicken in spicy cumin sauce and more of the fine white bread, but could barely swallow with everyone watching her while pretending not to watch. Although many ladies smiled, she saw their wariness and speculation. A few spoke Welsh, but when they addressed her, Nesta replied in monosyllables to discourage them.

At the day's end, Adele showed Nesta to a bed in the chamber, consisting of a mattress on the floor the same as the other women's, but it was well stuffed and smelled fragrantly of dried lavender. There was also a good linen sheet and a plain but clean blanket. Adele gave Nesta a cup of dark-coloured medicine prepared by the physician. The sweet, thick texture made her gag, but Adele coaxed her. 'Come, it will help you settle. The Earl's physician is highly skilled. I know I am not the person you want, but I will sit with you and be your comfort.' She stroked Nesta's hair and hummed a quiet, repetitive tune.

Nesta's eyelids started to droop and she fought the waves of slumber until she could fight no longer as the drugged tisane did its work.

'Poor child,' she heard Adele say in Welsh. 'May God bring you peace.'

The darkness pulled Nesta deeper. She saw her father standing before her, caked in dried blood, and his eyes were burning coals as he spoke to her. 'I cannot be with you to care for you, daughter, but know that I fly above you like a seagull and protect you in spirit if not in flesh. Do not let them take your soul.'

She struggled towards the surface, but she was fathoms away from the light, from the cry of gulls. The nightmare for her was that her father was not present in the flesh, and what use was the spirit to her now?

'Hush, child, hush.' Adele's voice washed over Nesta and the darkness enveloped her.

In the morning Nesta struggled to wake up, feeling disorientated and lethargic. A freckled young woman with dark-auburn hair sat beside her pallet, spinning, but when Nesta opened her eyes she set her spindle aside and rose to curtsey. 'I am to serve you,' she said in Welsh. 'My name is Eleri. My lady says you are to break your fast and join her.'

Gingerly Nesta sat up, and Eleri fetched a bowl of warm water and helped her to tidy her hair and dress in yesterday's gown. She brought her bread and cheese with buttermilk to drink, and when Nesta had picked at it and pushed it aside, she led her out to the spinning gallery where the women were sitting in the sun working on their textiles.

Nesta was greeted, given more fleece to spin and a place in the sun. The women chattered among themselves, mostly in Norman with a few interspersions of Welsh. Now and again Eleri would translate a word or a phrase for Nesta, but mostly she was left to herself under Lady Adele's watchful eye.

Later in the morning, the wet nurse gave Nesta the baby to hold, snuggled and secure in his swaddling. Gazing down into the little face, a storm of conflicting emotions swept through her. She could not hate a baby, but one day he would be a man and wear a sword and come against her people.

Adele's small daughter Sybilla wriggled onto the bench beside her and regarded Nesta out of wide hazel eyes like her mother's. 'Have you come to live with us?'

Eleri translated, smiling.

'It would seem so,' Nesta replied.

'Nesta is here to learn our ways, and she is our guest,' Eleri said, first in Norman, then in Welsh.

Sybilla swung her legs while she absorbed the information. 'Will you play with me?'

'Not now,' Eleri said gently. 'Nesta is not well. But later perhaps.'

'I do not mind,' Nesta said after Eleri had translated. 'Of course I will play with you.'

Sybilla beamed and skipped off to fetch her doll.

'I have a brother of about her age,' she told Eleri. *Who I might never see again.* Nesta swallowed the ache in her throat. She did not want to learn Norman ways, she would rather throw them over a cliff, but knowledge was power.

She returned the baby to the wet nurse, and when Sybilla came back with her doll, asked her its name, and began the process of learning the new Norman words. Who better than an infant to begin her education?

3

Pembroke Castle, South Wales, Spring 1094

Awake, Gerald leaned up on his elbow and watched the woman dressing in the early morning light. The sun streaming through the window highlighted her hair with hues of honey and bronze. As she turned sideways to him, her belly showed the swell of a developing pregnancy. Yolanda's husband had been a Flemish serjeant, part of the contingent sent by the Earl of Shrewsbury to garrison the castle, but he had died of fever a week after the troop arrived. Yolanda had remained under Gerald's protection, tending to the domestic quarters. Loneliness on his part and dependency on hers, coupled with a night of too much wine, had led them to his chamber and matters had developed from there. His initial shock at the news of impending fatherhood had turned to pride and anxiety. He was willing to acknowledge and provide for the child, and care for Yolanda, but it was a deviation from the path he had mapped for himself.

'He is busy today,' Yolanda said, stroking her womb. 'But at least he sleeps at night.'

Gerald smiled. 'God grant that he does not cause too many sleepless nights after he is born.'

'Oh, males always do,' she retorted impishly.

He gave a grunt of amusement, sought his clothes, and once dressed, kissed her and went out to patrol the domain.

His chamber was one of several timber buildings he had built inside the compound. Pembroke being an outpost to Norman domination, the first defences had been raised swiftly and crudely, but were effective. A stout palisade girdled the top of the slope with a strongly defended gatehouse and a tower for retreat in the centre of the compound with a clear killing ground for the archers in front of it. Anyone breaching the palisade would immediately be shot down. The Welsh were ill equipped and inexperienced when it came to siege warfare against Norman fortresses but Gerald was not complacent and kept everything tight and organised, leaving nothing to chance.

He paused at the bakery and collected a loaf of bread, filled his flask with ale, and climbed to the palisade walk. The lookouts on duty stood to attention, making Gerald quietly pleased. They had quickly learned that he would brook no slacking.

Gulls wheeled and screamed above the timber walk and the morning sun threw a sparkle of linked stars onto the water below. A supply ship had recently docked and also a barge laden with timbers, giving Gerald a warm feeling of achievement. A year ago, this site had been nothing but a windswept promontory. Now there was a palisade, a tower, and a growing community. It was still basic, but it functioned effectively, and in time he would embellish and improve both the defences and the domestic quarters.

Arnulf de Montgomery had kept his word and sent him men and supplies, with sufficient funds to pay them, and work had commenced at a driven pace. Gerald had not scorned to join the toil, stripping to his braies in the summer heat to help pound in the posts and build the walkway. With each blow of the mallet he was putting his own roots into the soil, his sweat and effort and blood becoming a part of this place.

The garrison consisted of a backbone of Flemings, displaced from their own lands by war and flood, and eager to settle here, and a small group of Irish mercenaries who were cheerful as long as they were paid. Most of the Normans sent to him by Roger de Montgomery were decent soldiers, but a few were envious of his promotion, and some were disgruntled at being posted to a frontier of hard work and peril far removed from the convivial taverns of Shrewsbury and Hereford.

Gerald ate the bread and washed it down with the ale while walking along the palisade. He took a progress report from his second in command, a young, sandy-haired Fleming called William Hait, and then returned to the courtyard where he found Ifan waiting to speak with him. The scout's hood was down, exposing his curly brown hair, wired with silver. He was shrewdly assessing the defences, with hands on hips, but when he saw Gerald he dropped the pose and swept a bow. Gerald was not entirely sure if the gesture was respect or mockery; with Ifan he could never tell. The Welshman would probably not bite the hand that fed him, but there was always a chance.

'I assume you have news.'

'News you will hear soon enough from other sources, *fy arglwydd*,' Ifan replied, 'but I arrived first. It is good that you have strengthened your defences. If I were you, I would do so again, for Roger de Montgomery is dead.'

Gerald's focus sharpened. 'In battle?'

Ifan shook his head, his eyes gleaming with sardonic humour. 'Not unless you count it as a battle against his gut. He rose from his dinner and dropped from a seizure in the middle of the great hall – died the next day.'

Gerald concealed a grimace. Roger's son Hugh would become Earl of Shrewsbury, and he lacked his father's strength. The North was already unsettled, and this news might just cause a revolt. At least the chain of command still existed even if Hugh was not of his father's mettle. Arnulf would provide support and backbone. He gnawed his thumbnail. In this far corner of Dyfed, his best chance lay in using his wits and keeping men like Ifan in his employ. He was damned if he would abandon everything he had built at Pembroke and let it all go to ruin.

He nodded to Ifan. 'You have brought me hard tidings, but I thank you for giving me time to prepare.'

'You are staying then?' Ifan perused the defences again.

Gerald snorted. 'Why would I abandon what I have made here? If I am ordered back to Shrewsbury then I shall go, but I doubt it will happen. My duty is to hold this place, and I have never shirked an order.' He clapped Ifan's shoulder. 'Find out who is likely to come against me. Keep an eye on the lie of the land and report as often as you can.'

'As you wish, *fy arglwydd*.' Ifan swept him another of his ambiguous bows.

Gerald presented the scout with a ring tugged from his little finger. 'Find messire William and give him this. Tell him by this token he is to pay you a week's wages and travelling expenses.'

Ifan departed, his stride jaunty. Gerald sighed. Pray God the little scout was trustworthy. At least armed with information he could make a start on strengthening the defences, and stock-piling his supplies.

'You are going to be taller than half of the men here,' Adele said as the seamstress finished adjusting the hem of Nesta's new gown. In the year since she had been seized from Carew, and forced to live as a hostage in the household of Robert Corbet, she had grown a hand's length taller and developed curves. Still willowy and fine, she was no longer a child, although not yet a woman. Her height, and the way she bore herself, made her seem older than fourteen years.

Raising her chin, she struck a haughty pose. 'I care not if I grow taller than all of the men,' she said in fluent but accented French. Because then she could look down her nose at them. She knew from what others said, and from the evidence of Lady Adele's hand mirror, that she was beautiful and she was learning that presence, beauty and clothes all helped to project an aura of confidence and power. Lady Adele said she had to value herself in order for others to value her too. Maintaining her shield for long periods was exhausting, although becoming easier, especially here at Caus in Lady Adele's household where she was now an accepted member of a familiar small circle. It was different in Shrewsbury. To the new Earl and his brother, she was a valuable commodity, but little more than meat on a butcher's counter to be bought and sold for profit. They paid for her fine clothes and treated her well because of her exploit-able lineage, whereas at Caus she was almost a surrogate daughter to Lady Adele. She never forgot or forgave that she was their prisoner, but she had learned to adapt and even to laugh and find small moments of joy, including the dark delight of hearing that Roger de Montgomery had keeled over in his dinner and died.

'You would not want to be as tall as Sir Adam and bang your head on every door lintel,' Adele said with amusement, referring to a knight of the household who towered above everyone else and walked with a stooped back because of it, and sometimes sported bruises on his skull when he forgot to duck when drunk.

Nesta dismissed the point with a wave, and twisted and turned to enjoy the swish of the fabric around her long legs. Lady Adele's terrier, Monty, danced with her, yapping, until Nesta laughed and picked him up and cuddled him, while he wriggled and tried frantically to lick her face. Her father had had dogs – sleek gazehounds for hunting and to enhance his prestige, but no pet for the chamber. He would have considered it a soft indulgence, and a waste of time.

'Come, come,' Adele said. 'Change your gown before you cover it in dog hair!'

Nesta sighed but did as she was bidden and reluctantly returned the gown to the seamstress, replacing it with her everyday green one. Three months ago the hem had touched the floor and had even swept up dust as she walked; now it ended just above her heels and was tight across the chest. She walked out onto the balcony where the women sat to spin in fine weather, and, leaning on the rail, saw a messenger arrive on a lathered horse, dismounting even as he drew rein. Leaving his mount to a groom, he ran into the castle.

Nesta turned back into the room. 'Something has happened.' She told the others what she had seen. Perhaps Earl Hugh had followed his father into hell. She hoped so.

Lady Adele calmly continued her sewing. 'If it is that import-ant, and if it concerns us, we shall know in due course. Come, sit with me and wind this wool. You must not see excitement and grand news in every messenger who rides in.'

Suppressing another sigh, Nesta sat down beside Adele, picked up the wool winder and started transferring the spun thread onto it. At first the daily round of textile work had been soothing, but as she acclimatised to her new situation she had grown bored. She imagined taking a horse and making her escape, but where would she go? Even if she did reach the coast and find a ship to take her to Ireland, she would still have to travel through hostile territory with neither friends nor funds, and beyond her imagination it was not viable. If she ran to her mother at Wilton, they would only come for her and lock her up.

Adele finished her sewing. Having bidden the women continue their work, she quietly left the room. Nesta knew she was going to find out what news the messenger had brought. There was one rule for the ladies of the bower and a different one for its mistress.

When Adele returned a short while later her expression was serious, and clearly the news was of import, for she stood up straight and clapped her hands.

'I want you all to listen. The Welsh have taken Ceredigion and burned Brecnoc. My lord will be joining Earl Hugh in the field and word has been sent to the King.' She raised her hand at the gasps of alarm and dismay. 'A strong garrison will stay here, but we are to pack our baggage and retire to Shrewsbury as a precaution.'

Nesta experienced a surge of fierce exultation mixed with a little fear. She wanted to ask who the leaders were, but bit her tongue. She was a hostage, and they might turn on her for being Welsh. Whoever it was, let them come to Caus and Shrewsbury, and raze them to the ground.

Adele commanded the women to leave their work and begin packing. One of the other ladies asked the question burning inside Nesta.

'Cadwgan ap Bleddyn and others,' Adele replied. 'What does it matter? They think they can take advantage with Earl Roger gone, but they will find to their cost that we are not weak.'

Nesta dropped her gaze as she put away her spinning and tidied the fleece into its sack. Her father had always said that Cadwgan of Powys was a viper in the grass; he had long been one of her father's rivals for power. She would be glad if he took down the Normans, but she felt no shining joy at the prospect. The Normans were all bastards, but so was Cadwgan, and if he gained control she would still be a pawn in his game, and her brother would not be safe in Ireland.

Shrewsbury Castle was packed to the rafters with soldiers and camp followers. The news that the timber border castle at Montgomery had been razed to the ground had sent a wave of shock rippling through the Norman community and everyone was looking to Earl Hugh to resolve the problem.

Nesta fervently hoped the Welsh would continue their success, even if it was Cadwgan. Following Adele across the compound to their temporary lodging, her gaze chanced upon a group of saddled horses being led away to the stables and a jolt shot through her. 'Taran!' she gasped, and Dewi, who was leading the stallion, looked up and met her eyes. Given the circumstances, they could not engage, but Nesta stood rooted to the spot as Dewi dropped his regard and continued towards the stables with his charge. One of the other ladies nudged her and castigated her for stopping, and she was bustled off in the direction of the Corbet lodgings.

Nesta spent the rest of the day in fidgety preoccupation, plotting how to escape and speak with Dewi.

'What is wrong with you?' Adele demanded. 'Your mind is so full of wool today, I could mistake you for a sheep!'

The other ladies laughed behind their hands, and Nesta mumbled an apology and retired to a corner where she continued to plan. Her opportunity finally arrived when the women were summoned to the hall to make their obeisance to Earl Hugh who was presiding over the gathering from the centre of the high table. Having received their curtseys and greetings, he dismissed the women to a side table. Nesta swept her gaze around the hall and at last located Dewi at the far end among other grooms and stable lads. She caught his eye and slightly tilted her head before turning to Adele and murmuring that she felt unwell and thought her flux was upon her.

Adele touched her arm in sympathy, and looked almost relieved. 'I wondered why you were not yourself earlier. Yes, you may retire and see to yourself.'

Head bowed, the image of modest decorum, Nesta unobtrusively made her way out of the hall. A moment later, Dewi joined her, bowing and standing a suitable distance away. She clenched her hands at her waist and controlled the impulse to throw her arms around him and burst into tears.

'We have both survived,' she said tremulously.

Dewi bobbed his head. 'Yes, mistress.'

'I saw Taran saddled as a Norman warhorse.'

'The new Earl is riding him,' he answered, grimacing. 'He employs me as Taran's groom because I know the horse better than any other. I would never have chosen to serve the Earl, but I do it for Taran and deal with the rest as best I may.' He twitched his shoulders as if ridding them of an irritation. 'And you, young mistress, how is it with you?'

'I hate them,' she said savagely. 'I am being trained to make an obedient bride for one of them when the time comes, but I would rather salt such a husband's pottage with hemlock than submit to him. Adele Corbet is kind, but she is grooming me, even as a horse is groomed for its rider. I have no wish to be a brood mare for Norman children!'

Dewi looked round and lowered his voice. 'The lords are greatly alarmed because Montgomery's castle has been razed, and other strongholds too, but they still have resources to call upon. Their king will come if the need is great enough, and he has all of England and Normandy at his command, including men like the Montgomerys, hungry for power. All we Cymraeg can do is raid and burn and cause them aggravation and then retreat into the hills.' He spread his hands. 'I have seen and suffered their strength – as have you. It will not be easy.'

Hearing his doubt, she changed the subject. 'I want to see Taran.'

Dewi shook his head and looked round again, his body stiff with tension. 'It is not safe, young mistress.'

She tossed her head. 'What have I to lose? He was my father's horse and I will see him – for I shall never see my father again.'

Dewi remained reluctant, but took Nesta to the stables and brought her to Taran's stall. The stallion was in magnificent condition, his hide shining like sunlit shingle. He pricked his ears and nickered at Dewi, demanding a treat. The groom presented him with a wizened apple on the palm of his hand and the stallion lipped it delicately into his mouth and crunched with enjoyment.

A wave of conflicting emotions surged through her. Taran had been her father's pride and joy and the Normans had defiled her memories by stealing him. However, he was well cared for, even to having Dewi retained as his groom. She patted the stallion's arched neck, suffering tightening her throat. 'I am glad to see him looking so fine, but I cannot bear it.'

'My lady, I know your suffering,' Dewi said gruffly. 'Taran is what matters to me, and he keeps me whole.'

'And how shall I keep myself whole?' Nesta asked desolately. 'I do not have a horse like you. I have nothing by which to remember my father.'

'You have the courage of his blood,' Dewi said with compassion. 'You are a princess of Dyfed – they can never take that from you. You are worthy of both your parents, and you stand in their stead.'

Nesta gave a single sob and now she did fling her arms around Dewi, hugging him swiftly and fiercely before stepping back, wiping her eyes. 'Look after Taran,' she said. 'He is precious.'

'Until my last breath, *fy arglwyddes*. Hera and Tymestl are safe too with the Earl's stud herd and I hope you will see them again.'

'I hope so too.' She sniffed and stood tall. 'I must go. Lady Adele thinks I have gone to lie down in my chamber because I am unwell – but thank you, thank you!'

'Young mistress, I am yours to command.' He bowed to her.

She gave him a watery smile and took her leave. Hurrying back to her quarters, her heart felt lighter and fiercer, like a blade that had been through a second forging. Once in the chamber she lay down on her pallet and drew her knees towards her stomach as though nursing her cramps. Her flux was not due for another week, but she could always blame the pains on wind.

When the ladies returned, they enquired after the state of her health and Nesta replied diffidently that she was all right. Adele brought her a soothing tisane and sat down on a low stool at her side. 'Where did you go?' she asked in a soft voice that did not carry beyond the air between them. 'I know you did not come straight back here.'

Shocked, Nesta clenched her fists against her stomach. 'I . . .'

'Do not lie to me,' Adele said sharply. 'Where I do not see, others do. My duty is to keep you safe, and following a man into the stables is one of the worst things you could ever do.'

Nesta knew she could refuse to tell her and test her own strength, but she needed Adele for an ally. 'He was my father's groom,' she said. 'I have known him since I was born. He is caring for my father's stallion that the Montgomerys took on the day he died in battle. The Earl now rides him to war. I wanted . . . no, I needed to see them.'

'Then you should have asked me first.'

'Would you have allowed it?' Nesta said bitterly. 'Perhaps you would, but you would have made me bring a maid and a guard, and it would have been different.'

Adele tightened her lips.

'This was for myself.' Nesta pressed her fist to her heart. 'It might be wrong to you, but it is not wrong to me – and I would do it again.'

Adele sighed and touched Nesta's braid. 'I understand, child, but you should not take risks. If you had come to me first, we would have found a way.'

She had found her own way, and it was better; however, she gave Adele a nod of appeasement.

'Well, no harm done this time, and in future you must ask for your own sake – and for mine, for I too am accountable to others, and it would not just be you who received punishment.' Adele stood up. 'This is your life now and you must accept it,' she said firmly. 'No good will come from looking back.'

Nesta dropped her gaze. 'I was not looking back – or only to say farewell and to promise I would not forget.' *And never, never forgive.*

Satisfied, Adele left her. Nesta closed her eyes to shut out the room and tried to ignore the sound of the women's chatter. There was indeed a pang in her stomach – a deep longing for Wales and home. At least in looking back she could find the taste of what happiness had been.

4

Pembroke Castle,
late Summer 1096

Sitting with his back against the palisade, facing the compound, his food protected from marauding gulls, Gerald worked his jaw on the stale bread spread with slightly rancid pig fat, which given the current state of their rations was almost a feast.

The last lot of arrows had sailed over the palisade several hours ago, but their besiegers kept them constantly on alert by their utter unpredictability. Three weeks ago the Welsh had arrived at Pembroke, surrounded the perimeter palisade and since then had kept up a barrage of assorted missiles. A couple of direct assaults during the second week had failed, but the efforts had been about testing how strong the defences were and how prepared the garrison. Gerald had left them in no doubt about the stoutness of both. The Welsh, led by Cadwgan ap Bleddyn, Prince of Powys, and his son Owain, had settled to besiege the castle, evidently believing they could successfully starve them out. Gerald eyed the last mouthful of bread and grease before he ate it. If this continued for much longer, the Welsh might just obtain their wish.

Relief from the Montgomerys was unlikely. Of the embryo chain of castles they had built between here and Brecon, only Rhodigros and Pembroke still stood following almost two years of sporadic fighting, that was fiercely intense during execution and ominously quiet between.

Discovering that Montgomery itself had been razed had been a blow to the gut, but he had taken it and stood firm. The Welsh were unlikely to break through the physical defences at Pembroke, but food was becoming an issue, and one or two agitators among his own men were not keen on tightening their bellies.

His Flemish constable William Hait approached him with his deliberate, solid tread and Gerald dusted his hands and rose to his feet.

'I have checked the stores as you asked, sire.'

'And?' Gerald braced himself.

Philip cleared his throat. 'We are down to five bacon flitches and the same number of sacks of flour. Three wheels of cheese. There's enough stockfish for one more week and the same for fodder for the horses.'

As he had thought.

William stood quietly, legs planted slightly apart, waiting. Like Gerald, he was a seasoned soldier and a younger son. Gerald liked him, for he was solid, reliable and unfazed by difficulty.

'Then we have a week left to us.' Not a week to decide what to do – that decision must be made today because a week hence it would be too late. The Welsh would not offer terms for they had come to burn and slaughter. He stroked his chin stubble. There was always a way, he just had to find it. 'Leave this with me; I will hold a meeting at sunset.'

'Sire.'

Gerald started to speak again, but stopped as he saw a small cluster of people approaching the castle. Flanked by two monks and two Welsh soldiers, an elderly man wearing embroidered robes was making slow progress towards them, leaning heavily on his staff of office. At his side, shortening his pace to accommodate that of his infirm companion, was a wide-shouldered Welsh lord, garbed in a red tunic that was a deliberate provocation and made him a perfect target for Pembroke's archers.

William raised his brows in question and Gerald shook his head. 'It would be dishonourable to take down a man walking beside the Bishop of St David's and intent on parley. Let us see what they have to say.'

He eyed the churchman as the group drew nearer and stopped a short distance from the outer defences. Bishop Wilfrid, whom Gerald had encountered on several occasions, had no love for Normans but regarded it as his duty to negotiate between the two sides. Gerald reciprocated the Bishop's antipathy, but he was pragmatic. The red-clad Welshman was an interesting development. It wasn't Cadwgan, who was older, but possibly the son, Owain.

'Find Father Samson, and we shall go down and see what they want,' he said. 'We are covered by our archers and they are in more danger than we are. How much wine do we have left?'

'A hogshead of ordinary and half a barrel of the best.'

'Good. Then have a trestle set up and serve the best wine and wafers. Let the cook use the good flour and any decent fat he has remaining, not the rancid stuff.'

'Sire.' William's brows rose higher still.

Gerald sent him a sardonic smile. 'They will be checking our morale and observing all we do while we are at parley, so let us, as good hosts, give them crisp wafers and fine wine.'

An intermittent tick twitched beneath Bishop Wilfrid's right eye. He was gaunt and ageing, although not yet in his dotage. Silvery curls poked out from under his cap, and his knotty hand clutched an embellished, ivory-headed crozier. Gerald greeted him properly by kneeling to kiss his ring.

The Welshman did indeed turn out to be Owain ap Cadwgan, eldest son and heir of Cadwgan ap Bleddyn, the latter having sent him to the parley rather than come himself. Owain's eyes were as dark as peat-water, and his hair so black it had a bluish sheen in the sunlight. He was no taller than Gerald, but his breadth and attitude made him seem much larger as he responded to Gerald's overtures with an air of amused superiority, cut with just enough charm to avoid insult.

Gerald gestured to the trestle and benches that had been carried out to the parley, and the Bishop sat down ponderously to rest his arthritic hip. Owain remained standing, but accepted a cup of wine, narrowing his eyes as Gerald made the offer in fluent Welsh. He took a swallow, wiped his moustache, then helped himself to a steaming wafer.

'You Normans eat daintily I see,' he said.

'Indeed, we enjoy plenteous food at our hearth,' Gerald replied, 'but when it comes to fighting, we are not so dainty.'

Owain showed his teeth in a white smile. 'That remains to be seen. It seems to us that you are in difficult straits, far removed from the support of your masters and with your supplies running out.'

Gerald drank his own wine and took time to eat and relish the wafer before answering. 'You should change your informers. As you see, we have ample provisions and we can outlast you.

How long can you keep your own men loyal and in the field? How many will slip away to their homes and their sweethearts? Mine cannot do that, for their only safety lies behind this palisade. A few of my soldiers are veterans of the great battle that took down Harold King of the English, but they still have their strength for they were young men then. You might match us in the woods, but not when it comes to a siege. Better to retreat while you are still intact.'

Fire flashed in Owain's eyes. 'Ah, but you are encroaching into lands that are not yours, and you are a small and isolated group. Whatever your prowess, you cannot hold out for ever.'

Gerald smiled. 'What makes you say that? I have enough to last me until my lord sends relief, and he will.'

'I do not believe anything you say,' Owain snorted.

'Well then, what is the point of this parley?' Gerald spread his hands. 'Are you not yourself encroaching on lands that do not belong to you, like a kite following a wolf-pack's kill?'

Owain's nostrils flared. 'The point is to give you the chance to leave now, while you still have the opportunity.'

'You should listen to the lord Owain,' Bishop Wilfrid spoke up. 'You will save many lives if you do.'

Gerald turned to the old man. 'I do listen to the lord Owain, and I shall treat his words with the same consideration he treats mine. I shall of course consult with my men, but for now there is nothing more to say. You are welcome to take the rest of the wine if you wish, and the wafers.'

Owain's smile was savage. 'Keep them; your need is greater than ours. If you do not yield, your days are numbered.'

Gerald shrugged. 'If you want to waste more time around our defences and die of boredom, that is your choice.'

'You have had your warning. On your own head be your death.'

Owain departed, stalking off like a prize stag. Bishop Wilfrid prepared to leave, leaning on his crozier to push himself to his feet. 'I counsel you to think again,' he warned. 'You have women and children in your camp and even if they are spared they will be sold for slaves in Ireland; and the same will happen to their husbands, and to your warriors if any survive.'

A pang close to fear flashed up Gerald's spine, but the Bishop's words only hardened his resolve. 'I know full well what the Welsh will do if they take Pembroke, but they shall not prevail. I thank you for your advice, but I trust my instincts on this.'

'Then there is nothing more to say and I shall pray for your soul.' The Bishop thumped his staff on the ground to terminate the conversation, and turned to make his slow way back to the Welsh camp.

Gerald walked back to the keep, leaving the servants to bring the wine and wafers, which he told them to share between themselves. He diverted to make his own prayers on the matter, seeking a moment of solitude in the fortress chapel. The Welsh had the advantage of Bishop Wilfrid on their side and might claim a closer intercession with God, but surely God would not bestow such favour on him and then desert him in his hour of need. He vowed to the cross that he would make an offering of his sword's weight in wax for altar candles if only he was allowed to prevail, and felt uneasy as he imagined Owain making a similar petition in his camp. Even God had to choose.

Leaving the chapel, he visited Yolanda and his son. She was sitting with the other women, but had put her spinning aside to bounce little Walter on her knee. At two years old, he was a sturdy, bright-eyed infant with Yolanda's fair hair, red-tinted in some lights, and a beaming smile. 'See,' Yolanda said, 'here is your father.'

Gerald stooped and lifted his son in his arms. Infants were a mystery to him but he felt a fierce sense of protection for this helpless creature, born of his seed. The thought of him being sold with his mother on the Dublin auction block to some Norse pirate sickened him.

'Is all well?' Yolanda said anxiously. 'I heard about the parley.'

Gerald kissed Walter's rosy cheek and gave him back to her. 'You have nothing to worry about.' He projected the words with the confidence he needed to feel. 'I will keep you safe. The Welsh are growing tired of waiting, so I say let them grow so tired that they leave. Soon the weather will turn, and hardy as they are, they will not want to huddle outside our defences in the autumn rain.' He kissed her cheek too, and went outside. A tenuous idea had begun to grow, but he needed to think and turn its vaporous form to solid reality.

He retired to his chamber, and picking up his harp, set about tuning it while he pondered. Gelert, his grey gazehound, settled down at his feet, nose to tail, graceful limbs folded. Gerald plotted, his lips forming silent words. He had learned to play the instrument in childhood and music was his solace, his inspiration and his retreat. His plan unfolded with the notes, becoming a definite tune, certain and simple, but with elegant undernotes. If his gamble did not pay off, they would be in a worse case than now, but better the risk than allowing the situation to become desperate.

Gelert raised his head sharply at a knock on the door, ears pricked. A growl rumbled in his throat.

'Come.' Gerald set the harp down and it resonated softly.

William Hait entered, ushering a squire before him, and swiftly closed the door.

Gerald frowned. 'What's all this?' The young man was pale and swallowing. 'Brian, is it not?' Squire to one of the Montgomery knights, Jordan de Mara.

'Yes, sire.' The youth looked down at his shoes, lank brown hair flopping over his brow.

'De Mara and three others are planning to abandon us,' William said grimly. 'Tell him, Brian; you are not in any trouble.'

'Indeed not,' Gerald said, 'but look at me not your feet when you speak.'

Brian raised his head and swallowed again. 'They're going to take a boat when it is their turn for guard duty and everyone is asleep.' He squared his shoulders. 'I know I should follow my lord and obey him, but when he chooses dishonour for himself then it becomes my dishonour too. I could not let him do this, and I could not be a part of it myself.'

Gerald studied the young man. 'It must have been hard to make such a choice, but I am glad you did. You shall have a place at my hearth as one of my own for your courage, and I shall give you arms, horses and a knighthood at the appropriate time.'

The squire's face turned a dusky red. 'I did not do this for reward, sire!'

'I know, and that is why you receive it.'

'Some of the others are not happy either.'

'If they do not wish to leave, they are welcome to remain. Speak with those you trust, for I have my own trust in your judgement.' Gerald clapped the youth on the shoulder. 'You have done the right thing in coming to me; never doubt it.'

Over the youth's head, he exchanged a look with William Hait.

Long after midnight, by the light of a fitful moon, the four deserters crept from their posts and set about unmooring a fishing boat from the landing stage at the foot of the rock. Brian and two other squires who did not wish to accompany their lords had remained with the party, to avoid suspicion.

Gerald waited in the darkness, listening to the soft commands and the lumbering noises of a boat being readied to depart under oar. Once it could not be mistaken that the men were intent on absconding, he stepped from the shadows with William and the Flemings in the garrison, torches kindled and arrows knocked.

The shock on the faces of the deserters filled Gerald with bitter satisfaction. The men were seized and stripped of their weapons and baggage, including flasks of wine and bread, cheese and bacon stolen from the near-empty stores. The purloined provisions were piled in a heap before them to illustrate their shame.

'My lords, you are going nowhere this night beyond a dungeon,' Gerald said grimly. 'You have deserted your duty and mired yourselves in dishonour.'

Jordan de Mara bared his teeth at Gerald. 'There is a difference between dishonour and madness. You cannot hold this place against the Welsh. You might want to end your life on one of their spears or with a slave collar around your neck, but others have more sense. There is no food and we are finished.' Raising his voice, he addressed the soldiers gathered in the torchlight. 'Listen to me! Make your escape while you still can! Come with us, now!'

Gerald drew back his fist and punched de Mara full in the mouth, snapping the knight's head back. 'You are a coward!' he cried for all to hear. 'I can and I will hold this place against all comers. I do not doubt myself and neither do these men at my side. You have desecrated your honour and you shall lose your lands. The Earl of Shrewsbury shall know of your betrayal.' He turned to his men. 'Throw them in the cells and shackle them. Let them have water – we have an abundance – but no food for three days. Their weapons and rations shall be distributed among those who have the spines to stand firm.'

Once the deserters had been dragged away to their fate, Gerald turned to the rest of the garrison. 'Some of you may harbour concerns about what is going to happen, but I promise you that this siege will soon be over. If the Welsh have not marched away within ten days, I give you permission to hurl my body over the walls yourselves. We are still standing at Pembroke when everyone else has gone down, and we shall still be standing when the tide turns. Messire William will organise some of you to stand night duty to replace our false absconders, and the rest of you, back to your beds, and we shall see what the morning brings.'

As the gathering broke up, Gerald called William back. 'After morning mass, I want you to bring the bacon flitches from the stores. Cut them in pieces and throw them over the palisade. Sling them as close to the Welsh as you can.'

'Yes, sire.' William looked at him askance, but did not query the order.

'I'll want to see Father Samson first thing in the morning too, and the scribe. I have an important letter to write.'

Owain ap Cadogan looked up as Bishop Wilfrid entered his tent. It was raining hard and the cold wind carried flurries of the first brown leaves, making Owain wish he had never come to this place. He hated sitting on his backside for longer than the time it took to eat a meal and the siege had been dragging on for ever. Other places had capitulated swiftly and the Normans had either been killed, captured or had run away with their fortresses alight behind them. But Pembroke continued to resist like an abscessed tooth with deep roots. A week ago, his father had returned home, leaving him to oversee operations, and Owain was sick of it all. What had seemed like a fine notion in the late summer warmth had lost its appeal.

He dearly wanted to thrust a spear down Gerald FitzWalter's gullet, especially after that stunt with the bacon flitches. Some of the pieces had even borne messages carved into the rinds, bidding the Welsh to '*Cnoi are hyn*' – 'Chew on this'. He had ordered the men to throw the flitches back in case they were poisoned, but the Normans had merely shot them back, and the grisly game had been going on for a week now, with ever more ragged and greening pieces of meat thunking into the muddy grass.

The arrival of the Bishop deepened Owain's irritation. They had nothing in common save their hatred of the Normans. Wilfrid's voice grated on him like a double saw through a tree trunk.

'My lord Bishop,' he said, 'I did not expect to see you today.'

Wilfrid leaned his crozier against the table, shook water from his cloak, and from his satchel produced a letter with a broken seal. 'This was found not far from my chambers, dropped by FitzWalter's chaplain.'

Owain took it and opened it out. His lips slowly formed the Latin words. He both spoke and read the language – his father had insisted on it – but it did not come easily to him. As a child he would always be shirking his lessons in order to go out riding with his friends. As he stumbled over the words, Wilfrid said impatiently, 'He says to Montgomery that he has another four months' worth of supplies and that he can hold out until Christmas at least.'

'He's lying.' Owain tossed the letter on the table in contempt, but his inner thoughts were less certain. All this bacon throwing, all the fine wine and wafers, and now this letter – it might be a ruse, but he could not sit in this tent and wait the bastard out for weeks on end to find out. The men were as tired of this as he was, and talking of all the raids they were missing, squatting here like broody hens, waiting on a clutch that might never hatch out.

Wilfrid sniffed and rubbed the back of his hand across his

red nose. 'Perhaps, and perhaps not. It could be genuine; it could have been dropped on purpose.'

Owain growled in frustration. Sweeping his cloak around his body, he stalked from the tent. The rain lashed down in face-stinging needles as he tried to focus on Pembroke's defences. They had no chance of making an assault today and the oak palisade stakes were so sodden, even the fires of hell would not burn them down. He glowered at the fortress, unwilling to concede defeat but equally unwilling to sit it out when he could be raiding to much better gain. His gut told him Gerald of Windsor was lying, but he knew that given his circumstances, the bastard would fight to the death, and the cost of defeating him would far outweigh the gain.

'May you be cursed for the rest of your life,' Owain muttered. 'I will have the better of you yet, I swear it.'

Head down, he returned to the tent and sent for his senior men.

On the ninth morning since sending the note, Gerald woke to the sound of rain drumming on the wooden roof shingles. It had not ceased in four days, and walking between the buildings was like wading through brown pottage. He had had the men throw down boards and straw, but it made little difference. At least it was keeping the palisades wet and slippery. The Welsh, camped out, were suffering their own tented misery. His empty belly ached with wind. They were scraping the barrel and everyone was on short rations. Someone had suggested killing a horse but Gerald had refused to countenance it. They would stand fast and everyone apart from the last four hens would survive.

His boots were still unpleasantly damp as he pushed his feet into them and his cloak smelled powerfully of woodsmoke from the fire where he had hung it to dry, reminding him of smoked herring until his mouth watered. It might come to eating the garment yet. He fastened the pin, left his quarters and squelched up the stairs to the palisade walk. The morning mizzle cast a grey veil over the landscape, blurring and fading the detail. Gerald narrowed his eyes and then turned and shouted down to Brian who was carrying the piss pot to empty. Setting it down, the lad ran up the steps and joined him.

'What do you see?' Gerald asked.

Brian followed Gerald's pointing finger and narrowed his eyes. 'They have gone, sire,' he said. 'The Welsh have gone!'

Gerald clapped the lad's shoulder. 'Go and find messire William and bring him to me – quickly!'

Within the next few minutes, what Gerald had dared not hope for became confirmed reality. Still cautious of ambush, he rode out with a contingent of men to examine the camp and the terrain. The Welsh had indeed departed in the night, leaving behind the soggy ashes of their camp fires and a few pieces of broken equipment. They might return with reinforcements or it could be a ruse, but he thought not. They had cut their losses and gone. His gamble had paid off and they had survived. Now he must send another letter to Montgomery, informing him that Pembroke had successfully resisted the Welsh but needed restocking as a matter of urgency. In the meantime, they would forage what they could from the sea and the hinterland – and keep watch.

'You must be mightily relieved, sire,' William said with a glint in his eyes.

Gerald regarded him quizzically.

'Well, one more day and we would have had to throw you over the battlements the same as those flitches, sire.'

Gerald snorted with dark amusement. 'I never had any doubts, or I would not have given you that permission in the first place,' he retorted.

5

Hereford Castle, Welsh Marches, May 1097

'Let me look at you.' A forefinger pressed to her lips, Adele stepped back.

Nesta was wearing her gown of cherry-red wool with a new trim of Italian damask. She had grown again, and all her hems had had either to be let down or borders added. Laced at the sides, the gown enhanced Nesta's figure showing the swell of breast and curve of hip, but in a subtle not suggestive way. Her belt was weighted with bronze strap-ends, and glints of gold sparkled in the ribbons woven through her braids.

'Truly a princess,' Adele said admiringly. 'You are beautiful indeed.'

Nesta lifted her head proudly. In the four years she had been forced to live among the Normans she had developed her own means of survival and identity, albeit moulded and guided by Adele Corbet. She spoke French fluently now and had learned how to make a single look serve for a hundred words. She was a competent seamstress; she could pour wine, and make conversation. She knew the lore of the hawk and the hound – everything that a man might wish to talk about when at leisure. If he did not wish to talk, then she was skilled in singing and telling stories and playing different board games from merels to chess. And beneath the smiling compliance and downswept eyelids, her hatred smouldered with the quiet intensity of a hot coal. One day it would be different, and even if that one day did not come and her death overtook the waiting, she would keep that fire alive until her breath was gone.

The King had arrived in Hereford, and was dining in the hall with his younger brother, Henry. The women were not attending the feast, for the King had no wife and it was purely an affair of men. Instead, they were eating separately and were to be presented to the royal entourage later. Nesta rolled her eyes in irritation at some of the women who were twittering with excitement at the thought of meeting the King and his brother. Nesta's own reaction was one of resentment and distaste; relief too, that the ladies had not been called upon to dine in the royal presence. William Rufus was here to make further depredations into Wales. She fervently hoped that he choked on his meat.

Watching from the women's gallery earlier, she had seen him and his brother arrive with their entourage of courtiers and soldiers. William Rufus was broad-shouldered with a solid belly and a stubby neck. His fleshy cheeks were as scarlet as rosehips, and his light blond hair carried an insipid tinge of flame. He had dismounted from his horse with a grunt and stumped into the hall, bow-legged and spread-armed with surplus flesh. Henry, younger by ten years, had hair as dark as oak-gall ink, and although he was stocky, he was taller than Rufus and more limber, walking with a lion's tread rather than a bull's. Pausing on his way into the hall, he glanced up and half smiled at the sight of the women watching from the gallery, eliciting giggles and blushes. Nesta immediately withdrew into the background, for he looked like a predator eyeing up its prey.

An usher arrived to fetch the women from their quarters to the King's Hall, and with more giggling and swift adjustments of skirts, belts and headdresses, the ladies assembled. The afternoon sun beat down on their heads as the group crossed the courtyard, Nesta hiding in the middle, apprehensive about being noticed. It was one thing to enjoy dressing up in front of other women, quite a different prospect to face a masculine oppressor.

As the ladies entered the hall, a courtier who had been standing near the door stepped aside and bowed. His hose were grey and his tunic the colour of a blue-tit's wing. He had rich-brown hair and ordinary features given presence by intelligent sea-grey eyes. Nesta thought she knew him from somewhere but the impression was fleeting.

The usher escorted the ladies to the high table, there to kneel before the King and his brother. Hugh and Arnulf de Montgomery were also present at the long, cloth-covered board, as was Roger Corbet and sundry officials and barons.

King William Rufus regarded the women out of light hazel eyes, heavy-lidded and fringed with white lashes. Copious amounts of wine had flushed his already ruddy complexion and given his cheeks a purple tinge. Grease stains blotched the embroidered front of his silk tunic.

After one swift glance, Nesta looked down, conveying modesty to the outside world while she burned with anger that such a disgusting, vulgar buffoon should hold the power of life and death over her person.

Hugh de Montgomery leaned in to the King. 'The young woman in the red gown is the daughter of Rhys ap Tewdr of Dyfed,' he said. 'She has been in our wardship for four years ever since her father's death in battle. Lady Corbet has been caring for her and educating her. She has learned our tongue and I believe she will make a useful bridge between us and the Welsh if wed to the right husband.'

Nesta listened as her hopes of being overlooked were dashed to pieces. Risking another upward glance, she saw the King eyeing her and tugging his chin.

'What lands does she have?' he asked. 'And remind me, is there a male heir?'

'Her father was Prince of Dyfed in the south, sire.' Hugh de Montgomery proceeded to list her father's territories. 'There is a male heir, but he is a child and exiled in Ireland. The mother is at Wilton Priory and will not wed again. Prince Rhys has a brother, but he is no threat and has no power to challenge. My man Gerald FitzWalter administers the lands from Pembroke – Walter of Windsor's youngest. He saw off the Welsh when they besieged him by hurling bacon flitches over the palisade walls and telling them he had enough food for months.'

He beckoned, and Nesta saw the courtier who had bowed to them at the door leave a group of other men, approach the dais, and bend his knee. Now she knew him. He had been among the Normans who had come down on them at the shoreline when they were waiting for a ship to take them to Ireland.

'You are to be commended,' William Rufus said. 'I like a man who stands his ground and uses his initiative.'

'Sire, my wits were all that stood between me and certain death,' FitzWalter replied smoothly. 'And, of course, my duty.'

'Without your stout defence, we would have lost our foothold. See my chancellor and he shall give you a gift from me of five marks and I shall instruct my marshal to bestow you a palfrey and saddle in gratitude.'

Gerald FitzWalter flushed. 'Sire, you are generous.'

'I know.' William Rufus beamed, and his wide cheeks dimpled.

The knight bowed and moved away, flicking a glance at the women. Nesta ignored him, but was still aware of his swift appraisal and wished him to perdition.

The King's brother had been observing the proceedings with keen eyes, and now, fixing them on Nesta, leaned over to murmur in the King's ear.

Rufus listened, raised his brows, and then he too stared at Nesta. She willed herself to become invisible. Rufus said something to Henry, half smiling, and invited the women to places at a trestle table to watch the entertainment.

Nesta could feel the royal brothers watching her as she sat with the other women. Rufus more resembled a louche innkeeper than a king, and she disliked him on principle. His brother, however, frightened her for he seemed the true predator in the room.

The entertainment consisted of acrobats and jugglers, skilled and amusing. One, a woman, was so flexible and limber that she turned somersaults one after the other across the open space before the dais. There was a man with a little performing brown dog that made Nesta laugh and forget her fear as it jumped through hoops, begged and rolled over.

A squire from the high table approached and bowed before the women, and then specifically to Nesta. 'The lord Henry wishes to speak with you,' he said.

Nesta's heart started to pound. 'With me?'

'Yes, my lady. I am to escort you.'

Flustered, Nesta turned to Lady Adele for guidance, but Adele's expression was tight and closed, although her cheeks had reddened. 'Do as you are bidden,' she said. 'Remember everything I have taught you. You have courage and strength. Let those guide you now.'

Nesta's stomach tightened with fear for Adele would not look at her. She stood up, her face burning. The King and his brother were conversing and neither man was looking her way. She could not imagine what the lord Henry wanted to say to her. She took a step towards them, but the squire touched her elbow and turned her in the opposite direction. 'The lord Henry wishes to speak with you in private,' he said. 'You are to wait for him in his chamber.'

Nesta swallowed. 'What about my maid?'

'She will be summoned in due course.'

The squire gestured again, a trifle impatiently, and she had no choice but to follow him from the convivial atmosphere of the hall to another chamber with a trestle and benches, and a large bed.

'Wait here,' the squire said. 'My lord will come to you when he is ready.'

Nesta gazed around. The sun had passed its zenith and late golden light spilled through the open window, gilding the floor, the bed curtains and covers. Various people were going about their business. Two scribes were at work, writing letters. Another man was cleaning mud from a cloak with a damp cloth, and a youth was preparing a table with wine and bread.

'Where shall I go?' Nesta asked.

The squire pointed at the bed. 'You may sit there,' he said with a slight smirk. Nesta looked at him and he stared back, his young eyes hard and knowing. 'You have to stay until my lord arrives. I shall be outside the door if there is anything you require.' He set his hand to the hilt of his knife, making her understand that if she tried to leave, she would be prevented.

He departed, and Nesta pressed her hands together, feeling them clammy and cold with fear. She knew the most obvious thing Henry might want from her, because it was what men always wanted. He was the King's brother, and she was in his power; a caged bird with no way out.

She went to the window and looked out, instinctively seeking an escape, but the aperture was too narrow and the room too high up. The setting sun flowed over her gown, washing the red with a sheen of gold. She lifted her head and sought the courage of which Adele had spoken, but she was very scared.

The sun sank lower, and as the light left the window the servant who had been setting out the food and drink draped a cloth over it and lit the candles. The scribes ceased their work, gathered up their equipment, and left the chamber. Nesta considered going to the flagon and drinking until she was insensible, but the thought remained in her mind. A sheathed sword was propped against one wall. She could draw the blade and defend herself. Going to the weapon, she touched the hilt, then drew back, for the caretaker servant was still present.

Drawn by a horrible fascination, daring her fear, she climbed onto the bed and smoothed one hand over the embroidered silk coverlet, wishing that her father had returned victorious from battle and that she was still living in privilege at Carew, wishing that she had never heard of the Normans.

The door opened and she stifled a scream. The King's brother, Henry, entered the room, his way lit by a squire bearing a lantern. Henry was deep in conversation with Arnulf de Montgomery and Gerald FitzWalter, talking over his shoulder to them. A scribe followed on their heels, clutching his work satchel. Nesta shrank back, wishing that like a snail she could retreat into a shell.

Henry glanced her way briefly but then, ignoring her, went to the lecterns where the scribes had been working earlier. He sorted through some sealed parchments on a small table, and handed a couple to Montgomery and another to Gerald

FitzWalter. Nesta listened to them discussing tactics for their own defence, including rebuilding the castles recently destroyed, and plans for further invasions of Welsh territory, and wished that a thunderbolt would strike them all where they stood.

'What of Rhys ap Tewdr's daughter?' Arnulf enquired. 'Is she to stay with the Corbets?'

They all turned to look at her. 'I think she is safer in my custody for now,' Henry said smoothly. 'It might be wise to remove her from Wales altogether until she has a husband, but of course that will be for the King to decide.'

The men departed, the scribe following in their wake, leaving Nesta alone with Henry. He did not approach her immediately but busied himself at the lectern, checking what the scribes had been doing and making a few notes of his own on a wax tablet. She was intensely aware of his presence, sensitive to his every movement.

At length he poured a cup of wine from the flagon, and came to the bed to look at her. 'You were a delectable surprise when I saw you in the hall,' he said. 'Who would have thought to find such a jewel amid all that common straw.'

Nesta's throat was so tight she could not answer – probably was not supposed to.

He finished the wine, set his cup aside, and climbed onto the bed beside her. She flinched and pulled back.

'Look at me.'

She raised her eyes, and he nodded at some private satisfaction.

'You know I am the King's brother.'

She could smell the wine on his breath. 'Yes, sire,' she whispered.

'I have the power to be generous to those who please me and obey my will. I also have the power to punish and destroy those who do not. I make it simple for people to understand, and I always keep my word, be it to man, woman or beast. Which is it to be for you, my dear?' He ran his finger up her throat and tipped up her chin. 'Be good, and you shall have a new silk gown and a brooch of gold. You shall have rose water and musk to perfume that delectable body.'

Nesta was holding herself so rigidly that she was shaking.

'You need not fear me, providing you do as I say,' he continued. 'But do not fight me, for it will not end well. Now, take off your clothes.'

Her mind was reeling, but the urge to survive made her reach for and fumble with the laces of her gown; her fingers were trembling too much to unfasten them.

Henry watched her avidly, and then muttered an oath and drew his dagger. Nesta gasped and writhed backwards on the bed.

'Hold still,' Henry snapped, 'or you will indeed be hurt.'

He used the knife to cut the laces with short, swift flicks, and then he pulled the gown off himself, followed by her under-dress and chemise until she was shivering and naked save for her knee-length hose. She made to cover herself, but Henry stopped her with the terse command, 'Now, let me see you.'

He leaned over her, and grasping her arms, forced them above her head. His breathing was harsh, and his pupils dilated. 'Am I the first?' he demanded. 'Have you ever known a man before?'

Nesta gasped and shook her head. Dear God, this was not happening.

Henry licked his lips and smiled. 'Well then, it shall be my pleasure indeed, and you are greatly honoured to have a prince take your virginity. No man of any higher rank will ever enter your body and sow his seed.' He began kissing and licking her, like a lion about to feed, before moving over her and forcing her legs apart.

Nesta took herself far away into numbness as the English king's brother had his way. The pain when he gave a final push and grunted and shuddered on top of her was too much for the barrier she had raised, but she bit her lip and stifled her scream. He slumped on her, and she felt his ribs flexing in and out with each harsh breath, and his belly pressing down on hers. When he withdrew from her, the pain made her arch her spine. She half sat up clutching her stomach, silent tears running down her face.

Flushed and heavy-eyed, Henry looked at her. 'There is no need to cry. You did very well for your first time.' He turned her face to his and kissed her mouth, then, drawing back, he wiped away her tears with a hard stroke of his thumb. 'No weeping; it is done, and you are mine.'

Nesta gulped, trying not to retch. She could feel him and taste him in her mouth, and the place between her legs where he had intruded burned like fire.

'You can go now,' he said. 'I have no more need of you tonight.' Leaving the bed, he adjusted his garments and smugly regarded the red smear on the sheet.

Nesta put on her shift and her undergown with shaking hands. The dress lacings were broken, and anyway, she was incapable of tying them. Her braid was coming loose and her veil lay on the coverlet, like a wisp of her life from an hour ago. A woman without a veil, a woman with her laces undone, was a whore, and that was what he had made her.

Ignoring her, Henry went to the lectern and began looking through the parchments awaiting his attention. Nesta took her veil, staggered to the door and into the vestibule, where she leaned against the wall for support, feeling as though she had been killed, even if she was not dead.

The squire was sitting on a stool and another squire had

joined him at a low table to play dice and share a jug of wine. When Nesta emerged from the King's chamber, they looked up, and the one who had brought her to Henry smirked.

Nesta did not know where the words came from, or the ability to pull herself together to address the youth, but she fixed him with a look that wiped some of the leer from his face. 'Go and fetch my maid, and bid her bring my cloak,' she said. 'And then you will escort us back to my chamber, or the Prince will know about it.'

He rose to his feet and slouched off. The other squire said nothing and poured himself more wine. Nesta waited and endured what seemed like an eternity until the first youth returned with Eleri, Nesta's cloak folded over her arm.

'Oh, my lady!' Eleri gasped, her eyes growing wide with shock. 'What has happened to you?'

'I do not wish to speak of it. Give me my cloak.' Nesta grabbed the garment, drew it around her body and stood tall, armoured in icy dignity. 'Now you may escort us back to the ladies' chamber,' she told the squire.

He scowled at her, but Nesta looked pointedly at the door behind them, intimating that she would walk in there and complain to Henry. With a snort of disdain, the youth took up the lantern again and in tight-lipped silence led her and Eleri to the women's quarters.

Once inside, Nesta drew a deep breath and walked over to her bed, but remained standing. 'I need to wash,' she said to Eleri, 'all over.'

Adele hurried over to her and shooed the other ladies away. 'Oh, my dear!' She took Nesta in her arms and tried to hug her, but Nesta stood rigid, refusing to let Adele's sympathetic tone undo her. Adele was complicit. She could have protected her and she hadn't.

'I need to wash,' she said again with flat composure.

'Of course,' Adele replied, shame-faced. 'And you shall have a proper tub.'

She clapped her hands and issued instructions and a partition curtain was drawn around the bed space to lend a modicum of privacy. Two serving women manoeuvred a wooden tub between the curtains and filled it from pails of warm water and a scattering of herbs. Nesta removed her cloak and Adele gasped as she saw the ruined laces.

'I was too slow to unfasten them,' Nesta said. 'He was impatient, so he used his knife, and he used it also because he could. I am beginning to understand now.'

'Understand what?' Adele asked.

'Why the Normans take what they want – for this is their exemplar.'

Adele shook her head. 'No, it is because it is men who rule, not just Norman ones, and we deal with it as best we may. Come, undress and bathe. Your gown can be repaired, it just needs new laces.'

'I wish I could be repaired as easily,' Nesta said blankly.

Making sympathetic sounds, Adele helped Nesta into the tub, giving her a soft cloth to wash herself. 'I shall find you some salve to ease the pain,' she said. 'It will be useful to keep in your personal coffer.'

Nesta nodded without speaking. The part of her that was not numb with shock was hardening to vengeful determination. No one would pity her. She would clean her body of Henry's touch, use Adele's salve, and she would survive.

'I am sorry for what has been done to you,' Adele said later once Nesta was robed in fresh garments and had anointed herself with the soothing salve. 'But we must be practical. It has happened once and will do so again now that you have caught the Prince's eye.'

Nesta had refused to sit, preferring to stand with her back to the wall because it felt safer. Now she pressed her hands against the cold plaster as realisation dawned. The salve was not just to soothe her now, but because she would be called upon to repeat the experience. 'No.' She shook her head from side to side. 'No!'

'You have no choice,' Adele said. 'You must play to your advantage. You may think you are powerless, but if you please him, you have much to gain. He is the King's brother, and he will give you gowns and jewels and all manner of riches and comforts.'

Nesta curled her lip. 'I want nothing from him!'

'Even if you do not want it, you should take it,' Adele insisted. 'Make of it what you can. Royal favour is an especially valuable coin to possess, but a fickle one.'

Nesta said nothing, but a tentative thread created by Adele's words was weaving through her revulsion. She would remain dignified and proud, and let the shame be on them. She would find out all she could about the King's brother. If the Normans were going to use her, she would reciprocate with all her might and use them too.

'You are right,' she said to Adele flatly. 'Please, I would like to sleep now.'

Adele leaned forward and kissed her brow. 'I am sorry,' she said again, and with a look of shame on her face, took her leave, making sure the curtains were closed. Nesta lay down on her bed, curled up her knees, and closed her eyes.

Two nights later, Henry summoned her to his chamber again, by which time Nesta had learned from Adele and the others that he was a man of appetites with a field of women already behind him and a propensity for moving to pastures new as soon as the most recent conquest lost her appeal and freshness.

He had several bastard children by different mothers, and was not faithful to any one mistress. However, he still took an interest in former concubines and their children, and saw to their welfare, like a farmer tending cattle. The mothers were often married to loyal supporters who were keen to have that link with his influence – it was an advantage and a privilege for a man to have a wife of proven fertility, favoured by the King's brother.

'With the King not yet wed – and perhaps he never will – his brothers are his heirs,' Adele said to Nesta. 'The older one, Robert, is fighting in Outremer, and that leaves Henry only a step from the throne. Who knows what will happen; you may yet be mistress to the King of England.' She spoke as if that was a wonderful thing, but it made no difference to Nesta's contempt. She desperately hoped she had not conceived. Her flux was due by the end of the week, and she would know soon enough. The lore said that a woman would not conceive unless she had experienced pleasure during intercourse, the pleasurable sensations being caused by the ripples of her body releasing her seed to meet the man's. Nesta strongly doubted the theory. Enough women were despoiled against their will and still bore children of the event.

'But if I do not want to bear a child, what should I do?' she asked Adele in a whisper. 'Is there a salve for that?'

Adele picked away at her sewing for several stitches without speaking, but having looked around, said softly, 'You should take a piece of fleece soaked in sour milk or vinegar, and insert it up inside yourself to protect you from the man's essence, and then remove it when you are alone and drop it down the latrine shaft. It does not always work and the man may be angered if he discovers what you are doing, but it offers some protection – so I am told.' It was a hastily added qualifier. 'But you should consider that bearing a child to a man of Prince Henry's rank is of no small account when it comes to his obligation towards you.'

Nesta shuddered; she could think of nothing worse. 'Why would the King of England never marry?' she asked.

Adele gave her a sidelong look. 'Because he does not wish to.'

'Does he have mistresses?'

Adele shook her head. 'His preferences lie in other directions, which is why I say that his brother may one day be king. Accede to the lord Henry's wishes. Do not resist him, and be willing. Use the salve, and use the wool if you must, and keep your eye on the reward, not the sacrifice.'

So this time Nesta was better prepared. She wore a different gown, a looser green one without laces. She anointed the place between her legs with the salve and made use of fleece from the spinning basket, dipped in vinegar and inserted into the part of her she had barely known existed a week ago.

The squire escorted her to Henry's chamber again and left her there, closing the door on his way out. Nesta suppressed the urge to cower in a corner and advanced into the room. This was business and she must help herself, for no one was coming to her rescue.

Henry was busy at a lectern, studying some pieces of parchment by the evening light and rubbing his forehead. She had learned from the women that Henry never stopped, and even when he appeared to be at leisure the cogs of his mind were still turning briskly. He was meticulous, determined, and driven.

'Sire.' She curtseyed.

He glanced up, grunted, and pointed to the bed. She walked to it with dignity, making the point that she was a lady of high birth, and sat down on the edge. Having removed her shoes, she swung her legs gracefully onto the coverlet and folded her cloak around her shoulders, for warmth. She dreaded what was to come, but at least she knew what to expect now.

He continued to work, still rubbing his forehead, now and again muttering under his breath. She rearranged her skirts, partly exposing one of her legs to mid-calf. She might as well comply and take an active part in the matter for, as Adele had said, it was better to obey and be valued.

'Stop fidgeting,' Henry snapped, glaring from the lectern. 'How am I supposed to work?'

'I am sorry, sire.'

Frowning, he bent over the parchments, but she could feel his tension and his awareness. Her breathing shallow and soft, her stomach taut, she did not move an inch. Henry muttered another oath and, pushing his work aside, rose and stamped over to the bed, unfastening the cord on his braies, already erect. This time he did not order her to undress, just pushed up her skirts and thrust into her.

It was over in seconds, and this time it was bearable, for the salve had eased the passage. He was heavy though and she struggled to breathe as he slumped on her. Eventually he moved, lifting himself off and flopping onto his stomach with a groan. Nesta lay still, wondering what to do, and at last plucked up courage to gently touch his ear and the side of his head.

'Sire,' she said softly.

'I have such a headache,' he muttered.

'You work too hard, sire.'

He did not rebuff her so she continued to stroke his head. She hummed a gentle Welsh lullaby just as if he was a sick child. Taking her cloak, she drew it lightly over his shoulders and Henry fell asleep with his mouth open, emitting soft snores.

She studied his features. He was handsome in a way that would raise mild interest but not turn heads. With his fierce stare banished and that hard mouth slack, he was just young and ordinary. She could take his eating knife and murder him as he slept. It would mean her own death, but it would not be so bad a price to pay perhaps. Except first she would have to reach the knife, and she just knew he would wake up. Perhaps next time she could bring one concealed about her person. Even a cloak pin driven through the eye would have the desired result. An intense feeling gathered in her belly as she imagined doing the deed, while she continued to stroke his hair.

As the light faded she started to ease away from him, but he set his arm across her body. 'You are not to go,' he said. 'You shall stay with me until I give you permission.'

Nesta lay back, feeling queasy.

'Sing to me again,' he murmured. 'Soft and low.'

Nesta complied, and he went back to sleep under the influence of her smoothing hands and her voice, while the room darkened into nightfall. Unable to sit up straight or lie down flat, Nesta endured the discomfort and dozed through the night with the weight of his arm across her stomach.

At sunrise, Henry stirred and at last allowed her to leave the bed. She went to the flagon, poured wine and brought it to him, holding it ready. Slowly he sat up and took the drink. His hair stood up in dishevelled spikes, and rough stubble outlined his hard mouth and jaw.

'You have been here all night,' he said.

'Yes, sire. You bade me stay with you.'

'I did, didn't I.' He looked both wry and thoughtful.

'Has your headache eased now, sire?'

He nodded assent. 'Yes. I needed to sleep, and I do not sleep well usually – but I seem to have done so this time. You are a good girl, Nesta.' He patted the covers. 'Come back to bed.'

Her heart sank. 'Sire, it is late . . .'

'Not too late,' he said, smiling, but with an edge.

Sensing that another protest would bring censure, she

concealed her revulsion and complied. This time Henry was more leisurely about his business, and although she closed her eyes and endured for the time it took for him to reach his release, the experience was bearable. What was it that drove men to want so badly to do this?

By the time he had finished he was late and the sounds from without the chamber door were becoming noticeable. Cleared throats, louder voices.

'Begone,' Henry said to her, as if his tardiness was her fault. He sat on the edge of the bed. 'But make sure you are ready again tonight.' He patted her bottom through the shift.

Nesta set her teeth, but when she turned at the door to give him a last look, she smiled shyly. When she left the room the smile remained, becoming enigmatic and feline. The courtiers awaiting Henry's attention might be resentful, but they were wary because she clearly had the Prince's favour for now. The duty squire fetched Eleri with more alacrity than last time, and Nesta returned to the women, walking with her head carried high.

In the courtyard, Gerald FitzWalter was preparing to leave with his retinue and was taking some last orders from Arnulf de Montgomery. Both men looked her way, and Nesta haughtily ignored them, walking regally like a young queen.

Adele welcomed her with concern, but Nesta shook it off and asked for food and a bath. While the former was being brought, she washed herself again, but in a business-like manner without distress, and carefully eased the fleece from within her body. 'I have heeded what you said to me,' she told Adele. 'I will do what I must and I will rise above it and prosper. It is not my shame after all.'

When the food arrived, she devoured it, partly because she was hungry, and partly to fill the terrible hollow inside her. She had Eleri comb and braid her hair, using rose water on the tines of the comb, and then rubbed scented unguent into her hands and feet. If this was to be her lot, then she would make the most of her assets.

'He wants me again tonight,' she said. 'I need to lie down, for I barely slept between dusk and dawn.'

Adele's eyes opened wide with astonishment but Nesta did not elaborate. Let her think like everyone else that Henry was in thrall. If this was what it took, she would do it.

'You *have* changed indeed!' Adele said, eyeing her with surprise, not altogether approving.

'It is a necessity of warfare,' Nesta said coldly as she went to lie down. 'I won't go to mass.' She turned towards the wall and plumped her pillow. 'I am not in a place to commune with God.'

As Nesta had crossed the courtyard, escorted by Henry's squire and her maid, Gerald had stared, entranced, for the young woman carried herself with such dignity, as though all were beneath her notice and only worth her contempt. She had power where there had been no power before.

'The King's little brother knows how to pick his bedmates, I will say that for him,' Arnulf remarked with a knowing chuckle. 'Who would have thought?'

Gerald agreed. It was like seeing a caterpillar become a butterfly overnight. 'What will happen to her?'

'Who knows, but I doubt she'll be returning to Caus, or that she will be given anywhere in marriage until either he's had his fill or got a child on her.'

Gerald set his foot in the stirrup and mounted his palfrey. He had been listening to a translated Welsh poem round the fire last night, and the words returned to him as he rode through the gate and set out on his return to Pembroke.

Black is her hair,
As thick as a forest,
Shiny as jet, or a blackbird's wing,
Darkest eyes, flawless my praise.

The wild hawk came and made his kill,
A blackbird in the snow,
Smoothed as a heaped snowdrift.
The bird's blood, red upon white,
Black wings spread, and still her flight.

Gerald sang the words to himself, changing them, honing and turning. He did not think he had ever seen anything look so beautiful, so haughty – or so doomed.

Nesta was roused from her slumber by the excited exclamations of the women. Adele swept aside the bed curtain and gestured Eleri to lay a pile of items on the coverlet.

'Come, wake up! See what the lord Henry has sent you!' Adele cried.

Still fuddled by sleep, Nesta gazed at the bounty Eleri was spreading before her, including a new undergown of saffron silk – silk! – and an over-dress of mulberry damask sewn with pearls. There were ribbons and veils and gold laces, and a belt decorated with silver wire; pendants and embroidered bands, and rings for fingers – none ornate, but of precious metal nonetheless. Some knee-length hose too, of delicate white silk with red ribbon garters.

'I do not know what you did last night, but you have truly won his favour!' Adele said, marvelling.

Nesta blushed. 'I did nothing. I sang for him, and soothed his headache, that is all . . . and the other thing,' she added, her blush intensifying. 'But that didn't take very long.'

'Well, do not spread that one abroad,' Adele said with a wry smile. 'Men prefer to brag about their stamina. Whatever you did, clearly you have the lord Henry's approval, and just reward.'

Nesta tried on the gowns and jewels, enjoying the feel of the rich fabrics and the looks of the other women, both admiring and envious. The gifts would never compensate for what Henry had done to her, but they were nice things to have and increased her status and her power. She had gained Henry's protection beyond the bedchamber and that was not to be scorned.

That night he summoned her again, and she sat on the bed and waited while he worked. And then he came to her, and took his release. When he was finished, even though he disgusted her, she stroked his hair and thanked him for the gifts, mindful of the advice Adele had given her.

'You please me,' he said, 'and that is why I reward you.' He raised himself up on his elbow and gave her a hard stare. 'I warn you: I am ruthless, but I am always fair and I always pay my debts – remember it well.'

'I shall, my lord.' She smiled at him innocently, concealing the flash of fear at the implied threat. Her contempt too. 'Do you wish for some wine?'

'Why not?' he said.

She went to the flagon standing beside the chess board.

'Do you know the game?'

'I do, sire. My father taught me, and I play often with the lady Adele and others.'

He eyed her with intrigued amusement. 'Well then, let us discover how good you are. Bring light.'

Nesta fetched a lamp from the bedside and set it by the table and Henry called for more wine and sweet wafers. Arriving with the refreshments, Henry's squire stared at his master sitting across from Nesta, the lamp creating an intimate glow between them. She shot the youth a narrow, triumphant look, and he exited the chamber looking pensive. Nesta smiled and lowered her gaze. The Prince had a new favourite and people would have to watch themselves.

While admiring the carved ivory pieces, she grimaced at the ferocious expression on the face of the King, scowling on his throne. 'Why do men want to be kings?' she asked. 'It does not seem to make them happy.'

Henry looked at her intently. 'They are born into the role,' he said. 'It is their task. Each piece has its place, and what happens to it is then decided by its own actions.'

'Not the will of God?'

Henry picked up two bone dice from the bottom of the chess-piece box and threw them onto the board where they fell as a six and a one. 'There is the will of God – thrown by my hand, but I have no say in how those numbers land. But when I move a piece on the board, it is by my mind and my will.' He tapped the side of his head.

'But is not your will God-given?'

He wagged his finger. 'Do not be too clever,' he said, his amusement tinged with warning.

Nesta looked down, affecting modesty, but sent him a glance through half-lowered eyelids. 'But not foolish either, sire.'

A thin smile curved his lips. 'It would seem not.'

Henry won the game fairly, although she gave him a hard battle and learned more about him. He had a fierce concentration and was always thinking several moves ahead. He was swift and decisive but never rash, and he was without mercy.

He kissed her and gave her another ring to wear, set with a large purple amethyst that could not be mistaken as anything other than a mark of great favour. When she left, he went to the door himself and ordered his squire to fetch Eleri to escort her back to the women. 'I have work to do,' he told her. 'Tomorrow we leave Hereford, but you shall join my retinue – you and your maid. Pack what you need tonight and be ready at dawn.' He tipped up her chin on his forefinger. 'You have my protection and you shall lack for nothing.'

'Thank you, sire.' Nesta lowered her lids, concealing her turbulent emotions. Her importance to him filled her with triumph, but she was angry and frightened too. In the four years she had dwelt in the Corbet household she had grown very attached to Adele in lieu of her mother. To leave it all behind would be like stepping out from safety onto a ledge with a long way to fall if she put one step wrong, and no one to save her. For now, she intrigued Henry, but it would not pertain for ever, and he was without compassion.

Eleri arrived and the subdued squire escorted Nesta back to the women's domicile, where she immediately sought Adele. Telling her the news, tears filled her eyes. 'I do not want to leave,' she said, her throat tight.

'Oh, come now, child.' Adele drew Nesta into a maternal embrace. 'I do not want you to leave either, but this is a rare opportunity.' She drew back, and wiped her own eyes on her sleeve. 'Look at me, as foolish as you, and after all I have taught you.' She noticed the ring shining on Nesta's finger. 'What is this?'

'We played chess, and he gave me this and said I was to go with him tomorrow.'

'Then you *are* greatly favoured, for this is far more than a trinket.' Adele looked impressed and a little awestruck. 'It's a jewel fit for a queen. My dear, you have outgrown this household. You are clearly far more than a chance comfort on the Prince's road.'

Nesta smiled bitterly. 'I am honoured by his dishonour.' She turned away to start packing her belongings. 'I am sorry,' she said to Eleri. 'I do not suppose you wish to go either, but you as much as I have no say.'

Eleri shook her head. 'It does not matter, mistress,' she replied with her customary cheerfulness. 'I have no family, and if I care for you, then you will care for me. It is the way of the world.'

Nesta sighed, wondering what the way of the world would bring her next, when it had brought her so much already.

On a pearlescent early morning, Nesta bade farewell to the ladies of Caus, and it was strange to be leaving a group of mostly Norman women and thinking of them as family. She had to wipe away her tears several times, and there were many hugs, embraces and little gifts of embroidery, trinkets and food for the journey.

'Go with God, daughter,' said Adele, eyes brimming. 'I wish you well, and I will pray for you every day.'

Nesta embraced her. 'I am grateful for all you have taught me, and I shall miss your kindness and wisdom.'

The King arrived in the courtyard with Henry at his side. Pulling on his riding gloves, Rufus glanced at the women and spoke over his shoulder to Henry who shrugged and made a reply that caused the King to laugh and give him a hefty shoulder-whack. Henry laughed too, but as soon as Rufus turned away the humour dropped from his face like a stone.

Nesta's mount was a placid grey cob, with a similar brown one for Eleri, and a sumpter horse to carry their baggage. A spotty junior groom had responsibility for their accoutrements.

Henry spared Nesta a single look before mounting his own richly caparisoned palfrey and riding off to join his brother, leaving her to travel in the supply train with the portable furniture, the cooking pots, the laundresses and chamber servants. It was a swift reminder of the ambivalence of her position. She might share Henry's chamber, he might give her fine clothes and jewels, but she was still a hostage riding in the baggage cart with all the others who saw to his comfort at his command. She smiled for him, and beneath that smile her hatred burned.

6

Palace of Westminster, London, May 1099

Eleri fastened the side lacings of Nesta's ruby silk gown, making a ruched effect, emphasising the slenderness of her waist, although the maid had to adjust the ties considerably and Nesta stifled a gasp at the painful pull across her breasts.

Having finished, Eleri stood back. 'Truly all will look at you, mistress, you are so beautiful,' she said with admiration.

Nesta turned, and the sunshine through the window shimmered on the gown, enhancing the colour to blood-red. Her lustrous hair fell in two thick braids to her waist, wound with narrow golden ribbons with extension pieces at the end, weighted with gold fillets. A light veil covered the top of her head, secured by a thin gold circlet set with pearls. Nesta checked the latter with a swift touch. Her power lay in her beauty, in her clothes, her willowy height. She had learned how to turn men's heads and then rebuff them with a single smile, and had refined her art in castle and camp, following Henry through England and across the sea to Normandy. She had seen the impregnable stone border castles of his ancestral lands with their thick walls and small arched windows, had dwelt in their towers. Feeling their dominant energy, she had understood why these insatiable people had overrun her homeland. Wales could never command the kind of resources they had at their beck and call.

Henry had enjoyed showing her the massive Norman donjons, and she had been suitably awed, but although these great stone fortresses offered comfort and security, they were oppressive and lonely, especially when Henry was in the field, and she was essentially a prisoner, walled up in a foreign land. Sometimes other women kept her company, but many were not disposed to be kind to a young and beautiful royal concubine. They were like hens with a pecking order rife with spite and jealousy towards an outsider.

She knew Henry was unfaithful, and only minded because of the threat to her influence over him. She worked hard to keep his favour even while hating him. A couple of women had vied for his attention in Normandy, but neither had lasted beyond the novelty of their deflowering.

Nesta had been at his side for two years and the wool and the wine had done their work and her flux had come regularly, until three months ago; now her breasts were sore, and the constant fatigue and nausea told their tale. She had been sick three times on the return crossing from Normandy to England, but had blamed it on the rough sea. A small space of time remained for a false alarm. She would keep it to herself until she had no choice, for once it was known, everything would change, and she dreaded what the future might hold. Only Eleri knew of her predicament, but she was utterly trustworthy.

Henry's squire came to escort her to the King's new Great Hall, which was supposedly the largest in Christendom, intended for business and banquet alike – a grand space, reflecting the prestige of the King of England and Duke of Normandy. The sheer size of it stretching away to the arched windows above the dais took her breath. It resembled a gigantic barn enriched with expensive textiles and gilding. Today it was packed with England's Norman nobility, parading in their rich robes and furs.

A few ladies were present – wives and daughters of the barons – but the King was a bachelor and the only women regularly at court were the concubines and whores who lurked on the perimeters. The noble ladies were ambivalent towards Nesta's presence and kept their distance. She might be a princess, but to them Wales was a backward land and Nesta, although favoured by the King's powerful brother, was still a concubine.

Nesta sat with Eleri on a bench at the side of the room and kept her own counsel with stiff dignity until Henry left his conversation with a group of men and joined her.

'What a magnificent hall, sire,' she said as he raised her to her feet and people stared while pretending not to stare.

He cocked his head. 'Yet I receive the impression you disapprove?'

'It is not something I could ever imagine for Wales, where the greatness of a man's hall is measured by the songs sung in it,' she replied. 'But I suppose it has grandeur and imposition.'

'You have the truth of it,' he said with a flat smile. 'My brother wanted it to be the largest in Christendom, but his nature is inclined to grandiose spectacles.'

During the time she had spent as Henry's concubine, she had come to appreciate Henry's contempt for Rufus. Once, when he had drunk too much wine and they were alone, Henry had told her he would make a far better king than either of his brothers.

Walking at his side, she felt the stares and the speculation. He was showing her off to his nobles in the same way he might flaunt a favourite hawk or hound – to display his taste and his power and spark the envy of other men. However, she sensed a different nuance too, as if he was parading her like a choice mount at a horse fair. Only one rider, and the saddle already warmed. Some of the lords to whom he introduced her were unwed, and a couple had interests in Wales.

He presented her to a dark-haired, handsome man with aquiline features and a cruel, thin mouth. Robert de Belleme was the new Earl of Shrewsbury since his brother Hugh had died last year. She had seen him from a distance and knew who he was, but this was the first time at closer quarters.

De Belleme regarded her as though she was a succulent morsel on his trencher. 'I have a Welsh grey-dun mare,' he said. 'My brother Arnulf acquired her from your father's stable at Carew a few years ago. She has bred some fine foals when put to my stallion.'

Her stomach clenched at his innuendo, but she knew he was speaking of Hera.

'I have a colt of hers that is making an excellent warhorse,' he continued. 'It is all in the mastery, no?'

Nesta looked down, declining to answer. The colt must be Tymestl, whose birth she had witnessed on the day everything had changed.

'Women, horses, dogs, they are all the same,' de Belleme remarked, smiling at Henry. 'Rule them, or be ruled.'

'Indeed, my lord,' Henry replied, and moved on. Nesta walked blindly at his side and could not prevent a shudder. 'Robert de Belleme is dangerous, but useful,' Henry said. 'Always rub shoulders with men you can use, but on whom you need to keep an eye, for you ignore them at your peril. He is right. It is all in the mastery.' He glanced at her. 'We are leaving tomorrow, so make sure you are ready for the dawn.'

'Where are we going?'

'To the hunting lodge at Woodstock. You will like it. There are other ladies there and it is comfortable.'

'Is it near Wales?' She experienced a wash of homesickness. All of these places were nothing to her. A series of bedchambers and social gatherings surrounded by cold stone walls, and this particular gathering in the midst of a pack of predators was the frayed end of too much.

He shook his head. 'It lies not far from Oxford. Two days' ride – three in a cart.' He pinched her cheek, and she tried not to recoil. 'I promise you shall see Wales again in good time.'

Henry did not visit her that night and she was glad, for she was tired and out of sorts. Asking about Wales had made her think about Wales and how she wanted to go home. She did not know if her mother or her little brother were still alive, had not seen them now in six years. No news came to her of her homeland and the only Welsh she heard was in conversation with Eleri. Sometimes she feared she was losing her own language and culture to the inexorable Norman subjugation.

'Pack the baggage,' Nesta told Eleri. 'We are leaving at dawn with the court.'

'Yes, mistress,' Eleri said. 'Will you tell him about the baby then?'

'I shall tell him when I must,' she replied, and then had to rush to the chamber pot, overwhelmed by a wave of nausea. How long did she have? A couple of months at most. She did not have to face it tonight, or tomorrow, or the day after. She would think no further than that. It was pointless when life's certainties could be destroyed in a single heartbeat.

* * *

Woodstock was three days' ride from Westminster. Henry had told her it was a hunting lodge, but that did not begin to describe the assortment of spacious timber buildings set amid gardens and an extensive park. The place had been built for royal entertainment and pleasure rather than defence.

Nesta and Eleri were escorted to the women's complex which Nesta found similar to the arrangements in other places, with a sleeping chamber and a long open gallery for spinning and textile work, positioned to catch the best of the light. A female chamberlain, Madame Beatrice, oversaw the running of the women's area, with a coterie of servants under her instruction. Several other women dwelt here, as well as children and nursemaids. Nesta noticed a robust boy of about eight years with dark hair, vivid blue eyes and a strong resemblance to Henry. There were two fair-haired girls of a similar age to the boy, and another little boy somewhere between two and three years old, all of them marked with their father's stamp.

Madame Beatrice showed Nesta to an alcove with a bed and space for her chests and belongings, and introduced her to the other women. Most were polite but cautious. However, one named Ede, who had thick golden hair and the same intelligent blue eyes as the oldest boy, welcomed her warmly and made room for her on the bench at her side.

'This is my son, Robert.'

She beckoned him to come and make his obeisance. He bowed beautifully and studied Nesta curiously. Nesta reciprocated with a dip of her head, and the boy went back to what he had been doing.

'His father will want to see him and judge his progress I do not doubt,' Ede said.

'His father . . .'

'Henry, the lord King's brother.' Ede faced her. 'I think it best that everything is said now, at the beginning, so that there are no misunderstandings later; I want us to be on good terms if we are to spend time together here.'

Nesta nodded warily. 'Of course.'

'Good. You should know that all these children are the lord Henry's. My Robert is his firstborn son. Matilda and Sybil are his daughters – they belong to Annora and Edith.' She indicated two of the other young women. 'The little one is Sara's.' She gestured towards a girl with brown hair and full pink lips.

Nesta looked at the women, not knowing what to think. 'And you all live here?'

'Most of the time, or until we leave – sometimes to a convent, mostly to marriage – but this is . . .' She paused while she sought the words to explain. 'The King and his guests come to Woodstock to hunt, to discuss business and to take their leisure and pleasure. A household and comforts must be provided for them. It is the lord Henry's favourite residence and a home, inasmuch as a prince can have a home.'

'I see.' Nesta looked down at the rings adorning her fingers, including the big amethyst jewel.

'No, you do not as yet, but you will in time,' Ede said, smiling. 'If, of course, you stay with us.'

Dear God! She didn't want to live in this domicile for cast-off mistresses. She wanted to go home to Wales. Henry had bedded all these women for these children to exist, but whether he still did, and whether they were expected to 'entertain' the male guests at Woodstock, she dared not ask, even if Ede was prepared to be open.

'You will come to know us, as we shall come to know you,' Ede said, setting her hand over Nesta's. 'We are sisters here.'

Over the next few days, Nesta became accustomed to the routines and atmosphere at Woodstock. The park and gardens clothed in early summer green were delightful, and she loved the intricately carved timbers over the porches and doorways. Every room was well appointed and comfortable, with cushions and colourful hangings and furniture.

The men spent most of their time deep in political talk, some of it conducted while hunting, which they did voraciously with hawk and hound. The women kept to themselves, engaged in textile work, which explained to Nesta why there was so much of it displayed round the lodge, but there were gardens in which to stroll and for the children to play, and they could ride escorted around the inner part of the park.

Meals were mostly segregated and the men dined alone, but there were occasional feasts where both sexes mingled with dancing and entertainment. One night a Welsh harpist played and sang for them. Hearing a voice from her homeland raised in song, Nesta fled the feast and found a corner to weep, feeling homesick and desolate.

On the fifth night, Henry sent for her. Nesta swept a light wrap about her shoulders and prepared to join the squire, who was standing at the doorway holding a lantern. Ede lightly touched her arm. 'Have you told him about the child?'

'How do you . . .'

'I have watched you trying to hide your sickness,' Ede said softly. 'I have seen how you pick at your food and fall asleep over your needlework. You have all the signs for those who know.'

Nesta shook her head. 'I have not told him . . . I am still not sure.'

Ede removed her hand. 'I wish you well,' she said compassionately, 'but you have little time remaining for uncertainty.'

* * *

Nesta found Henry busy with his scribes and a knight named Walter Tyrel who had followed him back from Normandy and become a particular companion. She adopted the usual routine of removing her shoes and curling up on the bed to wait for him. At length Tyrel departed, sauntering to the door and saluting Nesta on his way. She looked down, feigning modesty, avoiding the fox-gleam in his eyes.

Henry dismissed the scribes, poured himself a fresh cup of wine, and joined her. 'Ah, it's good to be here,' he said, stretching out, 'even if not for long.'

'It is very beautiful,' she said dutifully.

'Yes, a haven.' He chucked her under the chin. 'I would spend more time if I could but there is always too much to do. Rufus prefers London and the New Forest for hunting, but I would always choose Woodstock.' He set the wine aside, knelt over her and began kissing her, squeezing her breasts through her gown. They were so tender and sore that Nesta gasped, and flinched.

Henry drew back, narrowing his eyes.

'It is nothing,' Nesta said quickly.

'Take off your clothes,' he said, ignoring her words.

Nesta turned away from the light to conceal herself, but he turned her back with a firm grip on her shoulder and looked her up and down.

'You are with child.'

Nesta swallowed. 'I am not certain, sire. I may be.'

Henry hissed through his teeth and sat back. He studied her more closely now and ran his hand over her belly. Her muscles were strong and there was nothing to see, but there was no denying the change in her breasts. 'I think you do know very well, and given the time you have been with me, I would be surprised if you were not. No matter. I shall care for you as I have cared for the others, and the child will not lack for anything.' He gestured to her garments. 'Get dressed.'

Nesta fumbled her way back into her chemise and gown, feeling sick.

Henry left the bed and sat in his chair by the chess board. 'It is fine timing that we are at Woodstock. You can stay here with the other ladies and bear the child in safety.'

Nesta swallowed bile. She would be buried alive. Shut up for months on end, and the only way out would be to marry someone Henry wanted to favour – a Norman lord with a swagger and a belly. It would be a demotion too. She had tasted the power of being the mistress of the heir to the throne but what need would he have to buy her clothes and jewels and pamper her now?

Henry's expression was heavy and almost sad. 'You should return to the other ladies, and spend your night in peace.'

Nesta rose to her feet and faced him with dignity, although inside she was crumbling. 'Sire, if you have ever appreciated me, I ask you to grant me one boon.'

A wary look crossed his face but he inclined his head. 'Name it and we shall see.'

She drew a deep breath. 'I pine for my homeland. After the child is born, I ask that you consider my welfare kindly if you give me in marriage.'

Henry pursed his lips and studied her thoughtfully.

'I also ask that if my mother still lives, you permit me to visit her. If she does not live, then tell me. I am to become a mother myself, and it pains me to think of my own.'

'I shall consider it,' Henry said, 'but I promise nothing.' He rose from the chair and summoned his squire to return Nesta to the women's quarters. On the threshold, seeing her out, he kissed her cheek, a farewell peck. 'I shall not forget you, never think that.'

As Nesta followed the squire back down the torchlit corridors, unbidden tears rolled down her face. She reviled Henry for what he had done to her, but she had come to enjoy the clothes, the status, the small moments of power. Those would diminish now that he was setting her aside. She should be overjoyed at her release, but it just felt like entering another prison.

By the time she reached the women's chamber she had wiped her tears away, and when she walked into the room her dignity was regal and contained.

Henry rode out two days later. Sitting in a cart, among a pile of baggage, was an elfin young woman with silvery-fair braids and wide blue eyes set in a pale, frightened face. Nesta stood with the other ladies to wave the entourage on its way and felt sick. She didn't want to make her life here with Henry's other former concubines. She was desperately sorry for the wan young woman in the cart, but so envious too, and that emotion sickened her.

Ede put a compassionate arm around Nesta's shoulder. 'Come. Much better to be comfortable here than on the road with a child in your belly. At least with us you are safe and so is your baby. You have plenty of time before the birth and you can be happy if you set your mind to it. You shall have the best of care, which you would not receive anywhere else.'

But it was still a cage. 'Are you happy here?' Nesta asked pointedly.

Ede looked taken aback, but then the practised smile appeared. 'I am comfortable and cared for. My son is the son of a prince and will have a finer future than any he could have had from being sired by a different father. One day he will be an earl. Yes, there is a price to pay, but I am well recompensed for the bargain I have struck, and I am content.'

Nesta grimaced. Ede said she had struck a bargain, but it wasn't true because none of them was in a position to bargain with Henry. He gave the order, as if he was God, and they had no choice but to live as he dictated. Woodstock was a beautiful prison and the only way she would leave was through marriage, and that would be a step down from her once high position as Henry's favoured mistress. Her only influence rested on the child growing in her womb.

'What if he chooses to marry you to someone else?'

Ede shook her head. 'That will not happen, for I am the mother of his firstborn son and the ties remain strong between us. My place is assured, but even if it were not, what use is there in worrying about what cannot be changed? The future will be what it will be. That is perhaps the greatest lesson I have learned. I pray you have the wisdom to learn it too.'

7

*Palace of Woodstock, Oxfordshire,
November 1099*

On a cold winter evening in late November, Nesta's birth pangs began. She felt as large as the whale she had once seen washed up on the Pembroke coastline. The labour was painful, with strong contractions, but nothing was amiss, and as dawn broke, her son arrived bawling into the world.

His cries were just another sound as Nesta slumped on the pillows, exhausted from pushing. But once the midwife had washed him and brought him to her wrapped in a blanket, emotion stirred as she held him. Her family had been torn apart, but here was this baby that belonged to her, blood and bone, because he had come from her body, even if he had been conceived in coercion. He had damp black hair, and tiny little fists. She could clearly see Henry in him, but she could see herself too.

'Is he not beautiful?' Ede asked, and touched the baby's cheek with her forefinger so that he turned towards it, working his lips. 'You have done so well. I shall send a messenger to Henry immediately. He will be greatly pleased!'

Nesta said nothing. She did not care whether Henry was pleased or not. She kissed the baby's forehead and a surge of protective love washed over her. 'You are mine,' she said fiercely. 'None but mine.'

Nesta woke several hours later to find Henry standing at the bedside, watching her and the baby. She scrambled to sit up and he extended his hand in a calming gesture. 'Lie still,' he said. 'I am only here to see my new son – and his mother of course,' he added, almost as an afterthought.

My son, Nesta thought. Henry had not had the burden of growing and carrying the child. His part had been over in an instant, and this infant was not going to grow up to be like him.

'Are you well?'

'Quite well, sire,' she answered, and then pressed her lips together to stop them trembling.

'I am glad. This little fellow shall have my name, for he looks like me and it is a good way of acknowledging him. I shall take him to the font and have him christened this very day.'

Panic jolted through her. 'But you will return him straight away?'

'Of course I shall,' Henry said with amused scorn. 'For the time being his place is with you. Do you truly think me an ogre that I would separate a newborn baby from its mother?'

Nesta did indeed think him an ogre; Henry would do as he saw fit and have no qualms about any of it.

'Speaking of mothers,' he said, casually, 'your own still lives in the care of the nuns at Wilton. She is not well in mind and body, but I shall arrange for you to see her when you are recovered from the birth.'

Stunned by the force of the emotions tearing through her, Nesta stared at him. If he was waiting for her to thank him, he would wait for ever.

After a long silence, he placed his forefinger under her chin and raised her face. 'I see you are too overwhelmed to show gratitude, but no matter; I will make allowances, and my permission is a gift. I will have the letter of safe conduct written.' He kissed her cheek. 'I will send for my son later when the chaplain is ready.'

When he had gone, Nesta lifted the baby from his cradle and cuddled him, her heart tender and sore with love for her child, and hatred for his father.

Six weeks later, on an icy morning in early January, her breath frosting the air, Nesta stepped out of the cart at the convent of Wilton with a dry mouth and a churning stomach. The last time she had seen her mother had been at their traumatic separation on the road almost seven years ago.

She had not seen Henry since the day he had come to look at the baby, but apparently he was now in Normandy. He had kept his word though, and his clerks had issued her a safe conduct to visit Wilton with her son. Fierce as a lioness, she had insisted on feeding him herself, despite shocked protests that he should have a wet nurse. Ede had spoken up in her favour, declaring that she too had nourished her son for the first months of his life. After that, Nesta had been left alone, despite looks askance, and she had heard someone say 'She's Welsh' as if it explained everything.

Nesta and Eleri were taken to the convent's guest house and shown to a small chamber with benches and a table. A servant brought a charcoal brazier to warm the room, but Nesta's breath still emerged on a frosty swirl. Moments later, a stooped elderly-looking woman entered the chamber. Her cloak was of a sombre dark-brown wool, and a thick white wimple covered her hair. Her cheekbones were blades with hollows beneath, and her mouth was a tight line, not much thicker than sewing thread.

Nesta stared at her in shocked dismay. 'Mother?'

'Nesta.' Her mother's voice emerged with a cracked, dry sound as if she seldom used it. Instead of opening her arms, she folded them around her body in a defensive gesture and drew back, her eyes glazed with pain.

'Dear God, what have they done to you?'

Her mother made her way to the bench and, with an effort, eased down on it. 'They care for me after a fashion, but I am not well,' she said. 'Soon, praise God, they will cover me with earth, and I shall go to join your father, and I shall be glad. My heart and soul are already in the grave; it only awaits my body, and that is failing as you can see.'

Baby Henry's hungry wail filled the void after her words. Nesta took him from Eleri and kissed his face. 'This is my son,' she said, 'your grandson. My father's grandson too.'

Her mother looked at the baby, then turned her head aside. 'Is it true that his father is the King of England's brother?'

'Yes, it is,' Nesta said defensively, 'but I love and cherish him because he is mine.'

'From what I hear, you are his concubine. How your father would turn in his grave to know such a thing.'

'Do you think I have chosen this path?' Nesta said bitterly. 'I was forced against my will! I have nothing but loathing for the man who begot this child.'

'And yet you have been well rewarded to look at you,' her mother replied, rocking back and forth, arms folded about her midriff. 'Is that silk you are wearing? And gold in your hair?'

'Would you have me dress in sackcloth and ashes? Would you

have me tear my hair and lie down and die as you are doing, Mother? Whatever they do, they will not take my pride or my dignity. Even if I am trodden under their feet, they still shall not have me.'

Her mother looked at her then and the dull expression had left her eyes, replaced by a bright anger. 'But at what price? I have lost my husband, my children, my land – even my descendants.'

'You do not have to lose me, or this child,' Nesta said. 'That is of your choosing.'

She sat down to suckle the baby, who hungrily latched onto her breast. Her mother watched with a tense expression on her face that was almost worse than looking away.

'He is an innocent child,' Nesta said. 'I speak to him in Welsh as I am speaking to you. His lullabies are Welsh. I refused to give him up to a wet nurse so that his nourishment might be Welsh too, through his mother's milk. Somehow, I will return to our homeland, and I will ensure that our dynasty lives on – this I swear on my soul.'

Tears magnified in her mother's eyes, and in a long pause between words, the baby continued to suckle vigorously.

'I do not want to lose you,' Gwladus whispered at last. 'Every moment of every day since we parted it has been my dearest wish and heartsick longing to see you. I have worried about you and worn my knees to the bone praying that you were alive, that you were safe. They told me you had become a concubine in the entourage of the King's brother and one of his favourites.'

Nesta lifted her chin. 'I had no choice, so instead I have used what they have set upon me. I have silk gowns and jewels and gold in my hair, and it is a way of fighting back and gaining recompense.' Her voice trembled with the anger of speaking her condition aloud. 'I am only here because they allowed me, and I can tell you that I have come through the fire and I have survived. I shall not yield, however it seems on the outside. You spoke from your pain, and I know it comes from the deepest part of you, even as it comes from me.'

She gently removed the sated baby from her breast, gave him to Eleri, and adjusted her gown.

Tears glistened on her mother's cheeks. 'I do not ask forgiveness for what I have said, because it is too great a thing to forgive.'

'No forgiveness is needed,' Nesta said, tears in her own eyes.

She took her mother in her arms, and this time Gwladus allowed her in and embraced her, sobbing harshly.

'I have tried to pray, but my supplications go nowhere, while all the Normans' prayers are answered,' she wept. 'I have received no news of your brother – I know not whether he is alive. You are all I have, and I am dying!' She drew back to touch her breast. 'I have a lump here, and it grows daily. I do not have long to live and I am glad. But I am glad too that you have come to me in time.'

Nesta looked at her mother, once the spirited Lady of Carew, now a wizened shadow with only fading glimmers around the edges that told of who and what she had been. 'I am glad too.' She forced a smile, behind which all her rage and grief simmered. 'And I ask you for your blessing.'

Her mother shook her head. 'I am not worthy to give it. Let me have yours instead.'

Nesta took her son from Eleri. 'Gladly, if you will hold your grandson for a moment. He has my father's eyes.'

Her mother hesitated, but then held out her arms for the baby. 'I still wish that my first grandson had a different sire,' she said tremulously, 'but you are right. He also has your eyes, for they are your father's too.' She kissed the infant's brow and held him for a long moment before returning him to Nesta.

Some of the damage had been healed but it was fragile and still in many places broken beyond repair. She would never tell her mother the full tale of her life since their separation, and she could see that Gwladus had come to the end of her words.

'I would like to pray with you,' she said. 'Together.'

'That would be my wish too, daughter.' And from somewhere her mother found the remnant of what had once been her beautiful smile.

Nesta sat on the floor, playing with her son. At nine months old he was an expert crawler and had begun to pull himself upright on low stools and benches. She had to watch him constantly around the fire for which he had a fascination, although fortunately, today was hot and the hearth was swept and bare. He was playing with a coloured ball of wool, throwing it to her with his chubby hand and laughing as she threw it back. She told him the name for ball in Welsh and that he was a clever boy. '*Am fachgen clyfar!*' She clapped her hands and he copied her.

Ede flurried into the room, interrupting their play, her usual air of unflappable calm abandoned. 'There is news!' She pressed her hand to her chest and sought her breath. 'The King is dead and the lord Henry has claimed the crown!'

Nesta gazed at her in speechless astonishment.

'In a hunting accident near Winchester. An arrow went astray and struck the King in the chest and he died instantly. Henry was with him, but rode to Winchester to gain control of the treasury and claim the throne. He dared not leave it to chance lest the country fall into turmoil.'

Nesta shook her head, too stunned to reply.

'I do not know when Henry will be coming to Woodstock again,' Ede said. 'He will have much to do over the next few months.' She was speaking quickly, shock making her garrulous. 'I expect he will send for Robert because he is of an age to join the royal household. Of course, now Henry is king, he will be looking to a wife and legitimate heirs, although it will not change our lives here.'

The other women had come from their tasks to listen to Ede, their expressions wondering and anxious. 'Surely matters will change here if there is a new queen?' said Annora, mother of one of the girls.

Ede shook her head. 'Henry will still come to Woodstock to shed his burdens. The Queen will only be part of his life. He will visit often, even if not for a little while at first, while he does what he must to rule the kingdom.'

Nesta wondered if Ede was trying to comfort and convince herself, but then Ede had known Henry longer than any of them – truly known him, had been the first to bear him a son. Of course he would still visit Woodstock.

Henry had been born to wear a crown. Her time as his favourite concubine had shown her his talent, his desire to rule and his ruthlessness. He was far more suited to the task than William Rufus. What his brother Robert would think of it when he returned from the Holy Land – apparently, he was on his way – was another matter. She looked at her baby son, mouthing the ball of felted wool, holding it away, looking at it, and putting it to his soft little lips again. Between one moment and the next, he had gone from being the son of a prince to the son of a king, and for all that she loathed Henry, what a formidable king he would be.

8

*Windsor Castle, Berkshire,
January 1102*

Gerald sat before the fire in Windsor's great hall, with his father and oldest brother, his feet pointed towards the warmth of the flames, and a cup of wine resting on his belly. Three of his father's gazehounds were piled upside down at his feet. Outside the winter dusk had turned into a moon-silvered night, the eaves already spined with hoar frost.

'How is Wales?' Gerald's father gestured his squire to replenish the jug. Walter FitzOdo was a gaunt but still handsome man with an age-leathered complexion and a head of vigorous frost-white hair. As Constable of Windsor Castle he was a senior administrative cog in the wheel of royal government and a trusted servant of the crown – Henry I, who had been king for almost a year and a half following William Rufus's unfortunate demise.

Gerald sat up straight and cleared his throat. He respected his father, and could hold his own, but always felt on edge nevertheless. As a younger son who had had to make his own way in the world, he was often aware of trying too hard to please and still not measuring up. His father and brother did not understand his feelings for Wales, for they were utterly pragmatic. His mother would have done, but she had passed away before he was barely a knight. 'Pembroke is flourishing,' he said. 'I have been reinforcing it, but no one has troubled me since I resisted that siege. There were a few skirmishes about that time with followers of Cadwgan ap Bleddyn and his son, but nothing recently.'

'You speak the name like a true Welshman,' his brother William teased. He was tall and broad, with lighter hair than Gerald's and a cleft, forceful chin. He was following in their father's footsteps at Windsor and already performing many deputised tasks.

'The more I know, the better informed I am,' Gerald said defensively.

His father nodded sagely. 'There were times I thought you too tied to the bower and the softness of women, but you have proven me wrong. You have a fine soldier's mind, and as you say, knowledge is power.'

Gerald flushed at the rather back-handed compliment.

'Is it true you threw your last four bacon flitches over the palisade during that siege and told the Bishop of St David's you had a winter's worth of supplies?' William asked with a grin.

Gerald shrugged. 'I am still here, so it must be. I had run out of choices and it was either surrender or die, and I was not prepared to do either.'

'You are a survivor, that much is clear,' Walter said. 'Indeed, we all are, and that is why we are here to decide what to do now, because the wrong choice will bring us down.'

A pause lingered between the men – the hesitation of choosing between two bridges across a chasm, neither of them secure. Gerald's summons to Windsor had been caused by the return of Henry's older brother Robert from crusade, complete with a wife and child – a male heir, thereby making Henry's place on the throne precarious.

By the time Gerald had heard of Rufus's death, a fortnight had passed since the event, and Henry had firmly seized the throne. The new King was like a solid tree with many branches that an ambitious man could climb, providing he was not afraid to fall. However, now Henry's brother was demanding his portion of the inheritance, and this meeting at Windsor was to decide whether Robert was enough of a threat to the tree.

Henry's brother was a powerful soldier, genial and popular. Less calculating and ruthless than Henry, he had been making inroads into the loyalties of some of the barons, especially in Normandy, although England and the Welsh borders were not immune either. The Montgomerys, including Gerald's immediate lord, Arnulf, had chosen to side with Robert. Gerald was left in the unenviable position of rebelling either against his lord or his king – who might not be his king in a few months' time if Robert prevailed. And whichever way it went, he was in danger of losing Pembroke.

'I am Constable of Windsor,' Walter said. 'My loyalty has always lain with the crown and the King. I served King William faithfully, then Rufus, and now Henry, and I shall remain faithful. My loyalty is tied to my honour. It is also true that in my opinion Henry will be a better ruler than Robert. He has the steady purpose the other lacks.' He fixed his gaze on Gerald. 'But where do you stand on this, my son? Will you continue to govern Pembroke for Montgomery or will you hold for Henry?'

One of the dogs stretched and yawned. Gerald looked at its long forelegs and dark pads, and drew a deep breath. 'I owe a debt of gratitude and allegiance to Arnulf de Montgomery,' he said, thinking his way as he spoke. 'He trained me as his squire, then household knight, and gave me the opportunity to rise high above that, and I am indebted to him. But even if he gave me those opportunities, I have had to make them happen, and now I must choose. I have no wish to see Robert Curthose take England's throne. Even if I am sworn to the lords of Montgomery, how much more am I sworn to honour my father and my own kin, and indeed the King, to whom my lord knelt and vowed allegiance before he changed his mind?'

'I am glad we see matters the same way, my son,' Walter said, with relief in his eyes.

'But if I am loyal to the King, and renounce my oath to the house of Montgomery, I shall need recompense and support. Arnulf supplies Pembroke, and he has recently taken an Irish wife, which means he has access to mercenaries and resources from across the Hibernian Sea, and they are as great a threat to Pembroke as the Welsh. I do not know which way Cadwgan ap Bleddyn will jump, but he will seize advantage if he can. I need to provision for a siege and I need Henry to know the risk and sacrifice I am making in swearing for him.'

'If you do not swear, the King will not forgive and forget,' Walter warned.

'I know that, sire, and as I have said, I shall do so, but I need the means to hold out at Pembroke – and more securely than last time when we were almost overrun. If you can ensure I receive the necessary supplies, then I will be indebted.'

His father clenched his fists on his chair arms. 'You shall have all the help you need. I will make sure this comes to the King's immediate attention, and deal with it myself.'

'Then thank you, we are as one.' Gerald paused and drew breath. 'There is something else too.'

Walter lifted his brows.

Gerald hesitated. The idea had been growing for some time, but now it came to the crux, he was reluctant, lest it be rejected by laughter, or comments that it was impossible; that he was aiming too high. Approaching the King on his own behalf was not appropriate. It had to come from an intermediary, and there was no one more suited than his father or brother.

'If I am to strengthen my hand in the south of Wales, I need a lever to increase my authority, especially among the Welsh. Arnulf de Montgomery felled Rhys ap Tewdr, Prince of Dyfed, in battle. Rhys has a brother, whose claim will never be recognised, and a son who is in exile in Ireland and still a boy. He will not be capable of challenging for the territory for years to come. But Rhys also has a daughter – Nesta. She is a grown woman now, but still young . . .'

'Go on.' Walter pursed his lips.

'Arnulf de Montgomery took her hostage but she caught the King's eye when he came to Wales with Rufus. He made her his concubine and she has borne him a son, but now she dwells at Woodstock with the child and the King has moved on, as he does. He will doubtless wed her to one of his supporters in due course – and why should it not be me when I govern the territory that was her father's? Under Welsh law she has no right to the lands, but under Norman law she can bring them to me, and to our heirs.' He felt heat rising into his face as he spoke.

Walter folded his arms. 'You have been thinking about this for some time?'

'Yes, sire.'

His brother grinned. 'Hah – you have a fancy to her? Is she beautiful? You've gone red!' William had always enjoyed baiting him from his position of firstborn son, secure as the heir to the family's lands. He had not had to fight and toil for every reward and privilege.

'She is indeed beautiful, and accomplished,' Gerald responded calmly. 'She has borne Henry a son, so she is fertile, and any child I get on her will be half sibling to Henry's own heirs. She is a Welsh princess, so I attain my desire of being more firmly tied to the Welsh, for my children will be half of that blood, and royalty too.'

'You have thought it through indeed,' his father said gruffly with an upward lift of his mouth.

'Yes, sire, I have.' Every night. Testing, imagining, refining.

'I think it a sound notion, and I shall make overtures on your behalf to the King. You are right that it will benefit our family.' Walter smiled wryly. 'I remember when you first came to Wales with the King's father, and how taken you were – I should have realised even then that it was your destiny.' Rising stiffly to his feet, he clapped Gerald's shoulder. 'Let us see what we can accomplish between us, eh?'

'Yes, sire.'

Hope burned through Gerald's body, as did a small, shameful thread of fear, like a thorn caught on the underside of a magnificent cloak. He was reaching at full stretch and it was a long way to fall if he failed. And Nesta herself – how was he to gentle her and make her a willing partner in his dreams of dynasty? Wanting did not always mean obtaining, even if a thing was placed in your hand.

The King's chamber was appointed with the portable furniture from his baggage train, including the large bed with its coverlet of silk and fur. Following the usher into the room, Gerald noticed a woman sitting upon it – not the Queen and not one of the usual coterie of young mistresses Henry had on hand to slake his lust. This was a mature and dignified woman who gave off a subtle air of being here by choice, rather than Henry's prey. Henry had married Edith, daughter of Malcolm of Scotland, just four months after his coronation and was now the father of an infant daughter, Matilda, but it had not stopped him from enjoying other women as regularly as eating his dinner.

Gerald knelt at Henry's feet and bowed his head. 'You wanted to see me, sire.'

'Get up.'

Henry directed him to a bench opposite his own chair. The woman left the bed to pour wine for both of them. An expensive scent of musk and roses wafted from her garments which were of silk and richly embroidered. Plainly she was going to be a party to their exchange.

Gerald had been in the field with Henry since the early spring when Arnulf de Montgomery had pre-empted his return from Windsor by ousting him from Pembroke during his absence, and putting in a different constable. Gerald had joined Henry's entourage and had fought with him against his former lords, for his hand had been well and truly forced. Eventually a truce had been brokered and the royal brothers had reached an uneasy agreement, one of the clauses being that those who had fomented the trouble were either to submit to Henry's rule or leave England. Arnulf de Montgomery had chosen the latter, together with his older brother Robert de Belleme, and was preparing even now to depart.

Henry took a swallow of wine and set down his cup. The woman retired to the bed and picked up her sewing.

'It would seem that Pembroke is in need of a new constable,' Henry said. 'As its builder and recent former custodian, I think you may be the person to fulfil the task.'

'Sire, I would be honoured to resume the post.' Gerald's heart leaped. He had been hoping for this outcome, but Henry could be unpredictable and harsh. He would always do what was best for himself and without leeway.

'You shall pledge your oath to me before witnesses in the hall,' Henry said, 'but I summoned you here for more than that. I need faithful and intelligent men to guard my borders, able to think for themselves but of unquestioning loyalty. Sometimes men who think for themselves think their way into betrayal.'

'I would not do that, sire,' Gerald said stoutly.

'Would you not? Every man has his price, and no man is beyond temptation.'

'Sire, I hope never to find either my price or my honour compromised to the point where I would soil myself.'

Henry arched a sceptical eyebrow. He glanced at the woman who paused her sewing and gave a slight nod.

Henry ran his tongue around the inside of his mouth. 'You have expressed an interest through your father and your brother, pursuant to my ward, Nesta, daughter of Rhys ap Tewdr.'

Gerald felt a betraying flush rise up his neck and into his face. 'Sire, yes. I spoke of the matter to my family.'

'No doubt when considering your price,' Henry said pointedly.

'I will not deny that it crossed my mind as it would cross anyone's. Sire, I have seen the lady on occasion and have thought her gracious and beautiful. I would hope that such a match would bring unity to Pembroke and the wider perimeter.'

'A diplomatic answer,' Henry said judiciously. 'I have been considering where to cast Nesta to my best advantage for a while now. I am told that she pines to return to her homeland. You know the place and the people better than anyone else I could place there, so I am willing to agree to your suit. My scribes shall draw up a contract.'

Although Gerald had been hoping for the King's consent,

shock at the speed with which it had been granted rendered him speechless. 'As you wish, sire,' he stammered. 'Thank you.'

Henry smiled. 'You will find Nesta possesses hidden depths – she is a skilled chess player, and swift to learn. I want you to return to Wales and assume your position immediately. Nesta shall follow you in due course – better if you wed on Welsh soil to increase your authority.'

Gerald bowed deeply, still reeling.

'I am entrusting Nesta to you and also entrusting my son. I shall provide an allowance for him but your duty will be to keep him safe and raise him until I deem him of an age to leave his mother and come to me for training.'

'Sire, it will be my privilege.' Gerald was gradually recovering his wits and starting to think. 'Will you permit me to visit the lady Nesta before I return to Wales?'

Henry inclined his head and indicated the woman sitting on the bed. 'You may escort Lady Ede back to Woodstock at the same time.'

'Madam.' Gerald bowed in her direction, still wondering who she was.

'Then it is settled. My clerk will write the details.'

Gerald cleared his throat, and mustered his courage for a final push. 'Sire, you have given me much, but there is an especial boon I would ask of you.'

Henry's gaze sharpened. 'You are bold, with the contract not yet written.'

'Sire, I know this, but if I do not speak now, it may be too late, and I do not mean it as a gift for me – although it might be seen that way – but as a gift to my future wife.'

Henry's expression changed to one of intrigued amusement. 'Name it then and let us see how far you are prepared to try me.'

Gerald stood upright. 'Sire, Hugh de Montgomery had a stallion that belonged to Rhys ap Tewdr, the lady Nesta's father. I believe that the horse and its original Welsh groom are in the possession of Robert de Belleme, as are some other horses from the former stud at Carew. I ask that they be restored to the lady Nesta's estate as part of the contract. The groom and stallion are here in Shrewsbury. The others are running on de Belleme's Shropshire lands, although I know they will be moved to Normandy unless you intervene.'

Henry gave him a hard look. 'You are asking for several extremely valuable horses as well as to govern from Pembroke and take a woman of Welsh royal blood to wife? You are audacious indeed!'

'They are her family's horses, sire,' Gerald replied, and then swallowed.

'I think you can spare them as a gesture of goodwill, sire,' the woman intervened, her voice warm and melodious.

He looked round at her. 'Do you indeed?'

'Yes, my lord, although of course it is your decision and I would never presume.' She lowered her eyes.

'No more than he does,' Henry said, but his lips twitched. He turned back to Gerald. 'Very well then, but I shall have the next foal you breed from the mare as tribute. Now go, before I lose patience with your impertinence.'

'Sire.'

Gerald bowed and almost stumbled from the chamber, his heart thundering in his chest. Success! He had emerged with not only a wife but wider lands and magnificent horses – the stuff of dreams had become reality. Feeling as weak as a soldier in the aftermath of battle, he staggered to the castle chapel to light a candle and give due thanks to God. Tears of gratitude blurred his vision, and he had to cuff his eyes and swallow hard.

Entering the chapel, he found Arnulf de Montgomery kneeling at the altar and his stomach twisted. He was unarmed, and his former lord might be disposed to turn on him.

Montgomery made the sign of the cross on his breast and glowered at Gerald as he knelt. 'Well,' his voice grated through the silence. 'You have made your choice as I have made mine, but be careful what you wish for when it is facilitated by Henry of England, for it will return to bite you – nothing is more certain.'

Gerald settled down. Arnulf's expression was bitter and there was even some rancour, but no violence. 'You left me no choice when you took Pembroke from me,' he said. 'And you were right to do so, for I could not have followed you, or the seigneur de Belleme.' Indeed, he would rather have ridden in the entourage of the devil himself.

Arnulf exhaled hard. 'Well, Christ knows what kind of life you will have, but you have made your choice.'

'I am to wed Rhys ap Tewdr's daughter,' Gerald said. Arnulf would hear the news soon enough, but better to be honourable and tell him in person.

Arnulf gave a bark of grim laughter. 'Dear God. I always knew you were ambitious but you have truly excelled yourself.' He clapped Gerald's shoulder as hard as a blow. 'On your head be it, but do not say I did not warn you.'

Leaving the chapel, Gerald sought the groom Dewi in the stables, and found him sitting on a stool, plaiting some hemp fibre into rope. A dull red stripe resembling the mark of a whip branded his left cheek, perhaps a couple of days old. On seeing Gerald, he sprang to his feet, eyes wary. The golden-grey stallion tethered behind him pricked his ears towards Gerald and tested his scent with flaring nostrils.

'Be still,' Gerald said. 'Dewi, isn't it?'

'Yes, sire.' The groom gripped the rope in his hands.

'I thought so; I like to remember names.' Gerald stepped up to the stallion, but stood to one side rather than head-on so that the horse could see him. 'And this is Taran,' he added softly, and joy expanded within him like a sunburst. 'I have held him in my memory for nine years.'

'He'll be leaving tomorrow, my lord – Arnulf de Montgomery is taking him to Normandy, and I am to go with him.'

'Not so, and the reason I am here. You and the horse are mine, granted by the King. I shall have written authority before curfew tonight.' He rubbed the stallion's powerful cheek and scratched the star-twirl of hair between his eyes. 'Best to move him now to make certain. He will indeed be leaving in the morning, but not for Normandy. You and the horse are returning to Dyfed with me.'

Dewi's eyes widened with astonishment and hope. 'To Dyfed, sire?'

'We have a couple of detours to make, but you shall be home within the fortnight. Take the horse to the King's stable and pack your belongings.' He gestured at Dewi's face. 'You will find me a better lord than Robert de Belleme. I expect your service and loyalty, but I do not habitually whip my servants or my horses – and not because I am soft. If anyone gives you trouble, come straight to me.' Gerald paused, his hand on the stallion's muzzle. 'On second thoughts I shall accompany you, and that way no one shall be in any doubt – no one.' Almost queasy with tension and triumph, Gerald attached a halter to Taran's head-stall and handed it to the dazed groom. 'Lead him out,' he said.

In the morning Gerald set out for Woodstock with the lady Ede. By judicious enquiry he had discovered that she had been the

King's first mistress and the only one to have retained his attention beyond childbirth. She had brought her son Robert to begin
his training at court, as a page in the royal household. Now he
knew her identity, Gerald was respectful and thoughtful, for this
woman had been a fixture in the King's firmament for more
than ten years, and he had seen the way Henry listened to her
opinions and even deferred to them, which was astounding,
given what he knew of Henry's character. This was indeed silk
over steel.

He escorted her at first in courteous silence, and he had plenty
to think about while becoming acclimatised to his new horse.
Taran was of a mature and settled nature, but still possessed
fire. Gerald had been entertained to discover that he understood
verbal commands in both French and Welsh. He responded
swiftly to a touch on the reins or pressure from Gerald's leg,
and had obviously received extensive training while in the possession of the Montgomerys – and unlike his groom, had not been
ill treated.

Henry's chancellor had given Gerald a list of the lands that
would come under his jurisdiction when he married Nesta. He
had no authority over the estates himself – he was still the King's
constable – but if Nesta bore him sons, their claim would become
hereditary on the Carew estates, and others. Not *if* he had sons,
he corrected, but when, God willing. Nesta had borne a boy to
Henry and he himself had a son, so that might reasonably
indicate a predisposition. Yolanda had died the year before from
the stiffening sickness after treading on a horseshoe nail, leaving
little Walter motherless at seven years old. Gerald had employed
a nurse to care for him, and was doing his best to ensure the
boy was properly raised; however, he missed Yolanda with a dull
ache, and had genuinely grieved her death.

He imagined facing Nesta with a marriage contract in his

hand. It mattered not how she responded, for although he had to make a formal request, Henry had decreed it would happen. She was the path to legitimising his rule in South Wales and a means to an end. But he harboured a longing for it to be more than a cold political union. In a way, it was a symbol of his wider yearning for Wales, and he feared rejection.

'Deep thoughts, messire?' said Lady Ede with a smile.

He turned a little in the saddle. 'May I ask if you know the lady Nesta well?'

Her eyelids crinkled with warm amusement. 'I know her, but whether you would consider it well or not is another matter. Like all of us, she is careful about what she shows to others.'

Gerald plucked a stray leaf from Taran's dark mane. 'I do not want to force her; I want us to be amicable, but I must be secure in my tenure and I will have her to wife.'

'I can see you have many requirements working against each other, messire,' Ede said, her amusement fading. 'If a forced woman is amicable, it is not out of love but because she fears you or wants something from you. Who is going to hear her if she protests? If she has the will to survive, then she will adapt, but do not expect love and amity above resentment.'

Gerald frowned, reaching for words and feelings he did not know how to express. 'I will not abuse her,' he said. 'My mother taught me kindness to women. She may have of me what she desires for the asking.'

'Then tell her this, and it may smooth the path, but do not look for miracles. I hope, too, that you are a man of your word.'

'I am a man of my honour,' he said stiffly. 'And whatever I am given to protect and care for, I do so with diligence. You will never see me with stained clothes or armour, never see me whip a horse – or a servant, or a woman.'

'That is commendable, messire, and unusual . . .'

'I find that a look or a word is sufficient,' he said quietly. 'I am not Robert de Belleme.'

Her lip curled. 'I am glad to hear it.'

They rode in silence for a little longer, and he thought Lady Ede had finished speaking, but then she looked at him and said, 'My advice to you is to think even more gently about Nesta while still being true to your manhood. Before she became a hostage – a prisoner even – she was, and still is, a princess of her people. She is proud and courageous – and bitter. She has neither forgiven nor forgotten what has been done to her in the time since her father was killed, and that is why I say be cautious. She has been snatched from her home and family, trained to please her captors and has borne the King a child – none at her own will. Now she faces a marriage arranged by the King that for her will be just another part of the same rut.'

Gerald concentrated on his riding while he digested her words. He lived in a world of simple rules where man was the rightful master and had dominion over all. If everyone did as they were bidden and did it well, everything would fall into place. But women complicated matters. It was like the difference between stitching a series of straight rows and trying to untangle a mass of knotted but gloriously colourful embroidery silks. Unravelling them called for a very different set of skills.

'I would hope to do that,' he said, 'but I know it will be difficult.'

She returned his look with compassion but also judgement. 'Do not just say the words but hear them and listen to what she says in return.'

'I love Wales,' he said. 'It calls to me in ways that nowhere else has ever done.' He strengthened his voice as he strove to make her understand. 'It is more than ambition. I want to make my life there for the rest of my days, and wedding Nesta ferch Rhys is a part of that.'

Ede inclined her head, intrigued at the juxtaposition of the romantic and pragmatic within him. Like most men, Gerald FitzWalter was concerned with himself, his own wants and needs and perspectives, and he was looking at the best way of making Nesta comply without considering what Nesta might want from the match. But Nesta could do much worse for herself, and anyway, she had no choice and would have to make the best of what she had. There were compensations, providing she played the game with skill.

'All I can advise you is to give her time and stability. The rest is up to Nesta and God.' She looked at him curiously. 'How did you come to love Wales?'

He smiled and shook his head. 'It was with my father shortly before I joined the Montgomery household as a squire. The King's own father came to Wales, to St David's on pilgrimage, and made treaties with the Welsh lords including Rhys ap Tewdr.' He picked at a mark on the rein leather. 'I remember standing on a hill as a lookout, and gazing over the landscape until it stole my breath. I had to beat on a drum to alert everyone if I saw anything, and I was the first to see the Welsh soldiers coming to the parley. When I beat out their coming on my drum, I heard it echo in the hills. When I heard the Welsh speak, I wanted to learn the language, and when their bards sang their tales, I wanted to be a part of that too.' He gave her a swift look from under his brows and understood more of the power of this woman, for he had never told anyone the tale before. 'I have many memories tied up in that journey; it was a turning point in my life. When the opportunity came to live there, I seized it.'

'And you oversaw the building of a fortress I understand?'

'Yes, my lady, at Pembroke.'

'And withstood a siege with cunning and fortitude.' Her eyes twinkled.

'I survived.' He shrugged. 'If I had not held Pembroke I would either be dead or dishonoured.'

'And now you have your just reward and will build more fortresses and fill them with sons.'

'God willing.' His face grew hot.

'The King has put his faith in you and entrusted you with his son, and with Nesta – and he does not lightly give his trust to any man, or woman. He sees something in you, and it is your duty to live up to his expectations. Just remember that it is for longer than tomorrow and the day after.'

Gerald nodded. 'It is *am byth*.'

'*Am byth*?'

'It is Welsh,' he said. 'It means it is for ever.'

9

Palace of Woodstock,
August 1102

Nesta was telling a story to little Henry when Ede returned –
about how his grandfather had been a mighty prince who rode
a magnificent storm-horse called Taran that could fly like the
wind and was so named because his hooves sounded like thunder
when he galloped. All Nesta's tales were about her son's Welsh
heritage and kin. He would learn enough and too much from
others about the Norman side and she had no intention of
polishing that reputation for him.

The servants bore Ede's baggage into the chamber and the
other women hurried to welcome her home, fussing like poultry
in the yard, while Ede laughingly embraced them as though she
was the mother hen and they her chicks.

'See,' said Nesta to her son who would soon be three. 'Here
is the lady Ede back from her visit.'

Henry smiled. He loved the lady Ede, who gave him sweetmeats and cuddled him and told him what a big strong boy he was. After his mother, she was his favourite person.

Nesta rose to make her own greeting and Ede left the other women and came over to her.

'Oh, it is so good to be home!' She hugged Nesta. 'Much as I enjoy my visits to court, I would rather be here.' She ruffled little Henry's hair. 'My, you have grown again and I have only been gone a few weeks!'

'I'm a big boy now.' Henry stretched onto his tip-toes.

'And what a fine, tall knight you will be.' Ede gave him the wooden horse she had been concealing under her cloak. 'This is from your father,' she said, 'for you to play with.' The carving was beautifully wrought and the horse had a harness made from leather and cloth.

'Taran!' Henry cried with excitement. 'See, Mama, Taran!'

Nesta swallowed her antipathy that the gift was from Henry and that her son had immediately named it after her father's stallion. 'Yes.' She forced a smile. 'Say thank you to the lady Ede.'

Henry bowed to her most properly, and received a warm hug and kiss in response. Ede watched him fondly as he swooped the toy in his hands, pretending to make it gallop, and said quietly: 'Nesta, have Henry go to his nurse. You have a visitor waiting in the guest chamber.'

Nesta stiffened, immediately on her guard. 'Who?'

'How well are you acquainted with Gerald FitzWalter of Windsor?'

'Not at all,' she said, 'or not beyond seeing him at the Montgomery table when making a report – I know he has won acclaim as a soldier.' *Against the Welsh.* 'Why?'

'He escorted me from Shrewsbury, and he wishes to speak with you.' Ede took Nesta's hand. 'It concerns your future and

your son's. The time has come for you to return to your homeland, as you have long desired.'

Nesta swallowed panic, for this could only mean one thing.
'What if I do not wish to speak with him?'

'It would make no difference, and it is best that you do – for
your sake,' Ede said, her tone gently implacable.

Nesta looked down at Ede's hand on hers, strong but fine
with manicured nails. She was wearing a ring Nesta had not
seen before, rubbled with pearls. Ede had been her champion
ever since her arrival at Woodstock. She had defended her
against the other ladies and educated her well beyond the lessons
she had learned from Adele at Caus, but Ede was also pragmatic
and politically astute, and would never go against her own
interests, or Henry's.

'Come, he is waiting. We can talk again afterwards.'

Her delight at Ede's return evaporated. She tried to conjure
the face of Gerald of Windsor in her mind's eye as they made
their way to the guest hall, but it had been several years since
she had seen him and all she had was a vague recollection of
a steady sea-grey stare.

Ede held her arm in a light, supportive grip, although Nesta
thought it might tighten in an instant to prevent her from running
away.

A page sat outside the door on usher duty, but stood to attention and admitted them to the chamber. A man was standing
in the light from the window arches, his back to the door, his
stance one of quiet self-possession. Turning at the sound of their
entry, his eyes alighted on the women, and his complexion flushed
with colour, giving the lie to his air of containment.

He walked over to them, bowed, and straightened. Nesta looked
down while Ede made the formal introduction. The words went
over her head and her courteous response was by rote.

Ede stepped back, giving the illusion of privacy, but still within hearing distance.

Gerald cleared his throat and came straight to the point. 'My lady, I think you know why I am here.'

Nesta continued to look down. His boots were of fine tan leather with tassels on the laces and he must have changed for his hose was not garb for riding but of costly deep-blue wool, and the hem of his robe was embroidered. Her eye for stylishness picked up on the details and even appreciated them, although without delight. Wrapping something unpleasant in fine textiles did not make the item any less distasteful. 'I think I do, sire.'

'Then will you look at me?'

Reluctantly she raised her head. Apart from the steady sea-grey eyes, his features were commonplace and would not mark him out in a crowd. He was lithe and well proportioned and a little above average height. Everything about him was neat and orderly – and ordinary.

'The King has given me the task of governing the part of Wales that was ruled by your father, and of holding it safe and protecting it and administering it,' he said.

She lifted her chin. 'I do not know what to say about that, sire. I have been absent from my homeland for many years – ever since my father was killed.'

'It is a time to heal such things now.'

'Some things can never be healed,' Nesta answered, and saw Ede make a sharp gesture of warning.

'And never will unless the effort is made.' He held her with that stare. 'The King has granted me the right to sue for your hand in marriage. It will be my honour to be your husband as you shall be my wife – if you will consent. That is what I have come to ask, before I return to Wales to govern for the King.'

Nesta's distaste intensified, as did her anger, but her mind had started to clear. She could not avoid this match. In order to survive and have her advantage, she would have to work with it as she had done when she was Henry's unwilling mistress. No man could be worse than that. If she could come to know this one and his ways, she could spin him like thread. After all, she thought with bitter cynicism, what had all this training been for if not to please a Norman man? It did not mean she had lost herself, and if she could control him by subtle means, she could have her way.

'You do me honour in asking,' she lied. 'I have an obligation to consent, and I do so, sire.' She clasped her hands. 'This has come as a surprise, indeed a shock, so I ask you to allow me time to grow accustomed.'

'Of course.' He bowed. 'I am leaving tomorrow for Wales with orders from the King, and I understand you will follow within the month. This will give you time to prepare. We shall be wed at Carew. The King has had his clerics draw up contracts, and I will have a copy sent to your chamber.'

Nesta nodded wordlessly. A hundred years would not be time enough for this.

When she did not speak, he added, 'Although this has been dropped upon you, I hope you will come to see the match as advantageous for all.'

Nesta swallowed. 'Indeed,' she said, because it was the simplest word with many nuances. 'If you will excuse me, sire, I need to retire and recover myself.'

'Of course.' Gerald bowed and stepped back. The sun slanting through the window touched his brown hair with glints of chestnut.

Nesta departed the chamber; her head was buzzing and Ede had to take a firm hold of her arm and help her. Reaching the ladies' chamber, she went to her bed and sat down, trembling. Ede shooed away the other women and brought her a cup of wine. Nesta sipped and set it aside. No amount of wine would make this any better.

'So, the King decrees that I must marry one of his foot soldiers.'

'When my lord chooses men, he selects the best for the task,' Ede said. Her brows drew together in a light frown.

'Henry's recommendations would seem to be the criteria for all of us – unfortunately,' Nesta spat.

'Now, now,' Ede reproved. 'All is not lost. He is not disagreeable to look upon. He dresses well and someone has taught him courtesy to women – most likely his mother, and that is a good sign. You will be returning to the land of your birth and in the fullness of time you will have children who you can raise to be yours. There are far worse fates, my dear.'

Her stomach curdled. 'But I shall have to lie with him in order to beget those children, and they will be half of him and that means half not Welsh. The lands are mine but they will not be mine.'

'Yes,' Ede said calmly, 'but that is how women have always had to deal. I have grown fond of you and I will be sad to see you leave Woodstock, but you are a fish out of water, and it is time you returned to your own stream. Take what is offered and find the good things, for otherwise your life will have been wasted.'

Nesta closed her eyes.

'Use what you have,' Ede urged fiercely. 'You are returning to Wales as you desired, and it is your task to weave the thread and make your own pictures. You will be in a position to help your people and to have influence over your husband if you are clever. You know this.' She emphasised the last three words.

Nesta managed to nod through her revulsion. 'I hear you, and I understand. If I must, I will live the lie and make it so convincing that it becomes the truth.'

'Just so,' Ede said.

In the morning, Nesta went for a walk in the garden attached to the ladies' apartments. Birds were singing their hearts out and the household was stirring about its business. The heat of the day had yet to gather strength, and the perfume of roses and honeysuckle from the arbours was still subtle and delicate.

A gardener was weeding one of the beds on his knees, accompanied by an opportunistic robin, and Nesta smiled to see the small bird flick and flirt its tail, waiting impatiently for the next worm.

At a cleared throat behind her, she whirled, and found Gerald FitzWalter standing a few feet away, his fine blue hose encased now in over-hose of leather for riding and his gloves folded through his belt.

'I am leaving now,' he said. 'But I shall see you again soon for our wedding.'

'Then I wish you Godspeed on your journey and I will not keep you from it, my lord,' she replied, wishing him already gone.

'I did not want to go without bidding you the courtesy of a farewell.' He fixed her with his calm stare. 'I want you to know I am not the kind of man who will neglect or mistreat you. You need not fear.'

She regarded him without favour. 'Norman men have "cared" for me before, and I have every cause for fear given what has happened to me since my father died by their swords.'

He took his gloves from his belt without dropping his gaze. 'My word is my oath. You shall have as much time as you need.

I shall treat you as the royalty you are, and hope you will see beyond our differences to the partnership we could make for the good of all.' He bowed to her again. 'Until our wedding.'

She watched him leave. His spine was straight and strong and his head was up, the departing hero. She had her desire – a return to Wales, to Carew, and a man who swore he would honour her – but it was wrong, because he was a Norman and because she was being forced into a marriage she did not want. She had vowed never to wed a Norman, and now here she was on the cusp of doing that very thing because once again she had no choice.

She left the garden and returned to the ladies' chamber, for she had baggage to pack and possessions to sort out. Pausing at the window that looked out on the courtyard, she saw Gerald feeding his horse a titbit from the palm of his hand. The animal's coat was the colour of wet shingle, and he had a white splash on his muzzle. 'Taran!' she cried, and her sense of betrayal increased as she saw Dewi among the servants in the baggage train.

'What is it, my dear?' Ede came to her side and touched her arm.

'That horse he has,' Nesta said, tears in her eyes. 'My father was riding him on the day the Normans murdered him. Gerald FitzWalter has no right to him, and never will! It's a desecration!'

'Gerald FitzWalter will become your husband, and govern your lands even as any Welsh husband would do,' Ede said, impatient now. 'Perhaps God is giving you a sign – have you thought of that? The horse is not resisting him, is he? Indeed, they seem to me to be in perfect accord.'

Nesta watched Gerald swing smoothly into the saddle and clap the stallion's neck companionably before gathering the reins, his actions similar to those she had seen her father perform. 'I cannot bear it,' she whispered. 'I hate him.'

'That is nonsense,' Ede said briskly. 'You can bear it because you must, whatever you feel inside. You will not break; I did not break, and you are just as strong as I am. Would you rather have had Robert de Belleme take that horse back to Normandy, for that is what would have happened without Gerald FitzWalter's intervention. I was there when your future husband requested that stallion from Henry, and he did it from a love of good horseflesh, not to rub salt into your wounds. He wanted the horses for you as well as himself.' She pointed to a wooden jewel coffer carved with intricate figures. 'There is a different story on each side of that box, and only what your eye sees on the outside. Then there are all the jewels within. Are you going to discard the whole thing just because there is a small piece broken on the edge? Are you? If so, you are more foolish than I thought.'

Nesta watched Gerald ride out, and shook her head. 'No,' she said, and sat down heavily on the window bench. 'You give me good counsel.' But although she took Ede's advice into her mind, her heart remained hot with anger and grief.

10

Palace of Carew, August 1102

Nesta approached Carew with her entourage on a bright morning in late August having set out from Woodstock over two weeks earlier, pausing each night at various abbeys and castles along the way. Henry had provided an escort of serjeants and two of Gerald's soldiers were also part of the group. For the first week the people with whom she interacted along the way had spoken French and English, but now the language was frequently Welsh and music of the soul to Nesta's ears, although strange and nostalgic too, almost dissonant, for she had not heard its full tide for almost ten years. Returning to the home she had fled in terror, her world in tatters, was deeply unsettling.

Her son slept against her side, tucked in a fold of her cloak, his little face flushed and dewy. He was already becoming a rumbustious little boy, always wanting to play-fight and yell, although for now he was a slumbering, cherished angel. Nesta stroked his tousled black curls. She had no one to rely on for her own comfort and succour; she had left all that behind at Woodstock when she had bidden the lady Ede a tearful farewell. Ede, like Adele earlier, had taught her to survive in the Norman world, but now she was bereft of female support and had no one in whom to confide apart from Eleri, and that was a different kind of relationship.

She was coming to the moment at the end of her journey when she would have to meet and engage with Gerald of Windsor. She could no longer ignore the reality that she was travelling to her marriage with him. She kept telling herself she would be lady of her own hall with authority and status. It was not freedom, but her chain would be longer, allowing more movement, and the key to that allowance was Gerald. But every time she thought of him riding Taran, she recoiled.

Cuddling her son, she whispered to him to wake up. He stirred slowly, and came round, warm with sleep, and rubbing his eyes. 'See,' she said. 'We have arrived.'

Carew's gates were open, allowing her a view into the court-yard. Externally, little had changed. The same palisade, the same hall, basking in the August sun, woodsmoke twirling in a transparent thread from the roof louvres. Deceptively sleepy and peaceful.

Observing the guards on the palisade walk and standing at the gate, she shivered. Once she had passed through the entrance, she was trapped. Carew might be strongly defended, but could as easily be a prison as a place of security.

Once the cart had rumbled into the courtyard, she stepped down, shook out her gown, and then lifted Henry out and set him to stand at her side.

Gerald FitzWalter hurried over to greet her and she raised her chin and stood tall to face him.

'My lady.' He dipped his head.

If he expected her to curtsey, he would wait for ever; but she inclined her own head in reply.

He took her response in his stride although his complexion reddened. 'I bid you welcome after your long journey, my lady. May I escort you inside and offer you hospitality?'

'You may,' she answered neutrally. It was not lost on her that he was inviting her into her own home. 'Come, Henry.'

Gerald crouched to the child's level and smiled. 'And welcome, sire, to your new abode.'

Henry looked up to Nesta for reassurance and she smiled and gently squeezed his hand. Gerald was gazing at her too, but she did not smile for him. He rose and held out his arm, and she allowed him to lead her towards the hall. Walking through the dust that was still settling from the arrival of the carts, she shivered as she trod the familiar but irrevocably changed ground.

'Is there something amiss?' he asked, swift to note her reaction.

Nesta shook her head. 'It has been a long journey. Is there a chamber where I may rest and wash away the dust of travel?'

'Of course. I have had the women's hall swept out and made ready, but I have not long arrived myself and it is not furnished. I thought you might wish to do so as Lady of Carew.'

She could not think of him as Lord of Carew in place of her father or her brother estranged in Ireland, but at least she had somewhere to retreat. 'Thank you,' she said, managing to be gracious.

Gerald escorted her to the timber building that had once been her mother's realm, opened the door, then stood aside. 'This is your domain,' he said. 'I shall not enter until I have a husband's right, and I shall always do you the courtesy of asking first.'

She repeated her appreciation, hating to be beholden to him, thinking him unctuous; but if she was to win his favour and bend him to her will, she had to be courteous and compliant.

'I will leave you then,' he said. 'We shall eat in the hall later and I will send a squire to escort you.'

Relieved to see him go, Nesta entered the women's hall and found it bare of everything but a few tables and benches. The hearth in the centre of the room was swept but cold. Dust motes danced in the light raying through the warped shutters and the room smelled of neglect. The Normans might have seized this place but they had made little use of it; it had certainly not been a woman's space for a long time.

Servants delivered the baggage from the carts and pack horses and in the disturbed air the dust flecks spun and glittered. How many particles of her past danced here? Nesta wondered if she could capture any of those momentary sparkles and draw them inside herself for solace.

A youth arrived from the kitchens, a white apron tucked into his belt, the tray he carried occupied by a jug of mead and some crumbly honey cakes hot off the griddle. Another servant followed with warm water, a brass bowl and a towel. Nesta took a cake and bit into it. The taste of honey filled her mouth and she closed her eyes, savouring it. It had been for ever since she had eaten one of these and the experience added to the weight of her return. So much sweetness layered upon sorrow, and an unsettling awareness that Gerald had ordered them for her. She broke a piece off the cake and gave it to Henry and indicated that everyone else should eat too.

The servants started setting up the furniture she had brought from Woodstock, including a bed that Ede had given her as a wedding gift, complete with a mattress and covers. She would not dwell on the fact that the money had come indirectly from Henry, but think of it as a gift from a wise woman to a friend. She could obtain different textiles and a new mattress once she had settled in. For now, the linen sheets were fine and soft, and the intricate embroidery on the coverlet spoke of wealth and status.

Having eaten, she washed her hands and face and changed her travelling gown for one of embroidered blue wool and an embellished belt. She covered her hair with a light linen veil and a silver circlet decorated with enamelled speedwell flowers. There was rose oil for her wrists and throat and a light powdering of expensive nutmeg for her braids, so that when she walked, the air around her was suffused with a subtle aroma of flowers and spice. She would attract Gerald like a bee to blossom. No matter her personal thoughts, she must become a beguiling, sophisticated creature and Gerald's *raison d'être*.

Gerald's squire arrived to escort her to the public hall for a formal meal and she walked across the compound before hesitating to gather her courage. Here was another barrier to cross, entering the chamber where her father had held court, feasted his warriors, dispensed justice, and thrown silver to his bard.

'My lady?' the squire said politely.

She did not reply, for the youth was insignificant, and he understood none of this – how could he? Inhaling deeply, she stepped over the threshold into the candle and firelight and the cry went up, making her start.

'Make way, make way for the Lady of Carew!'

The announcement, first in Norman, was echoed in Welsh from the side of the room by a group of archers. And then Gerald was at her side, taking her arm, and benches were scraped back as the men got to their feet and stood to honour her.

'My lady,' he said, and escorted her up the long hall to the dais at the far end and the place where her father had once sat. He assisted her to a chair at his side at a table spread with a fine white cloth. An embroidered hanging draped the wall behind her chair, and as she took her place she knew everyone was watching her. She protected herself behind gracious dignity, and a carefully judged smile. She was introduced to Gerald's older brother William, who was broader than Gerald with fair hair and shrewd eyes of lighter grey.

'Fortune has smiled on my youngest brother,' he said. 'I am delighted to welcome you to our family and call you sister.'

Nesta murmured a polite reply and lowered her eyes.

Further introductions to Gerald's senior knights and their wives followed, and she responded with more polite platitudes while her stomach churned.

'My lady, you grace my table, as I hope you will do evermore,' Gerald told her after his chaplain had blessed the food and they settled to dine. 'Whatever you wish of me, you may have for the asking.'

Nesta raised her brows. She could see from the look Gerald's brother was giving him that William of Windsor thought the offer a bad idea. 'I had not taken you for a man who makes rash statements,' she said with a half smile.

'I am not, because I judge you a woman of sense when it comes to what you ask for.' He neatly divided up the roast chicken that had been placed before them. 'May I serve you with a portion?'

Nesta accepted with a nod, but rejected the accompanying spiced sauce.

'You do not care for cameline sauce?'

'It is not to my taste, my lord.' Indeed it revolted her because it was a favourite of Henry's, especially with lampreys, and the smell was forever connected to those nights in his chamber. She swallowed hard.

'Then I will see that you are not served it again,' he said, continuing after a moment, 'Once we are wed, I want to go on a progress of the lands with you and explore the people and boundaries. We can come to know each other better in that time.'

'If it is your wish,' Nesta said, avoiding his gaze.

'It is, for our lives will be easier if we are familiar with each other. This match has been made by the King to give me increased authority and sanction in Dyfed. I know it is less to your taste than mine, but we can make it magnificent if we cooperate.'

She nodded by way of answer, then raised her head and said abruptly, because the issue was still agitating within her, 'When you left Woodstock, you were riding a horse that once belonged to my father, and you had my father's groom with you.'

'Yes, Taran.'

His smile made her want to throw the contents of her goblet across his face. 'How did you come by him?'

'I asked the King to give him to me when he banished the Montgomerys from England, and he agreed. Your father was truly a skilled horse breeder.'

'The last time I saw my father was when he rode out from those gates on Taran and he did not return,' she said with quiet intensity, and now she did look at him, with anger in her eyes. 'I have since seen men riding him who were my father's sworn enemies. I am to wed you in two days' time, yet my father would have considered you his enemy too. I am his beloved daughter, and what has happened to me since his death has been shameful. As you say, we must both deal in the world and go forward. I shall not oppose you, for it would avail me nothing. I have my wish to return to Dyfed and at least I can walk the paths of my old life and hear my own language, spoken by my own people. I shall be a wife to you in partnership, but I need time. When I saw you riding my father's horse . . . ah, I have said too much.' She reached for her cup.

'I have told you I shall give you time, and I keep my word – as I expect you to keep yours,' he said, his mouth tight at the edges and controlled. He turned to talk to one of the men sharing their board, a neighbour, Odo de Barry who had a fortified manor on the coast at Manorbier.

Nesta clenched her fists.

Odo's wife, Marguerite, was a small woman, red-cheeked and pleasant, with sparkling blue eyes and keen perception. She spoke to Nesta of Manorbier, inviting her to visit, then talked of ordinary, inconsequential things. Her voice was soothing, like cool water, giving Nesta time to recover, although later she was to recall little of what Marguerite had said.

As soon as it was polite, she begged leave to retire, citing the exhaustion of the journey.

Gerald rose and assisted her to her feet. 'I shall escort you to your quarters, my lady.'

'There is no need, sire.' She was desperate to escape, but Gerald was not dissuaded.

'Not everything has to be done because of need,' he replied, and having bade the guests continue without him for a moment, he escorted her from the hall, leaving his brother wryly shaking his head.

Instead of leading her to her chamber, he took her to the stables. 'The horses are bedded down for the night, but I thought you would like to see Taran and have a word with the groom.' He shouted, and Dewi emerged from his lantern-lit hut.

Having bowed to Gerald, Dewi greeted Nesta by going down on one knee. 'Welcome, my lady, daughter of our prince,' he said in Welsh.

Nesta gestured him to his feet, swallowing tears. If Gerald had not been present, she would have flung her arms around him and sobbed.

'We have come to see Taran,' Gerald said.

'Of course, my lord.'

Dewi picked up a lantern and took them to where the stallion was dozing, resting on one hip. Nesta cuffed her eyes, and swallowed. The horse snorted, nostrils flaring, his eyes liquid obsidian, his coat shining like wet sand under moonlight.

She fed him a honey cake that Dewi gave her and he quested for it on her flat hand with his whiskery muzzle. Then he turned towards Gerald and butted him with his nose, seeking more, just as he had once done with her father. A sense of burning betrayal filled Nesta at the sight, but through it she realised that Gerald knew how to handle horses and she could not lay any accusations of neglect or bad management at his door.

'We cannot live in the past, we have to go on,' he said, running one hand over the horse's gleaming neck. 'I shall not ride him except around the demesne. He will never again go to battle, but I shall put him to pasture with my mares and breed fine foals. On my way here I visited the former lands of Robert de Belleme and with the King's permission took a mare that had also belonged to your father and her foal, as well as a few other horses you might recognise from the Carew stud.'

'My lady, the mare is Hera,' Dewi said. 'The foal she bore on the day we left Carew is the lord's new warhorse, but he is stabled at Pembroke.'

Nesta shivered, feeling physically unwell. Her new life would be surrounded with these familiar objects, animals and people. She should be glad, it was what she had longed for, but dealing with the memories they raised had cast her mind into turmoil. 'Please,' she said to Gerald, 'I need to go to my chamber.'

Dewi bowed again and retreated into his dwelling.

'I know this is difficult,' Gerald said as he escorted her from the stables. 'I hope it will grow better in time.'

She said nothing, unable to speak. When they reached her door he saw her within, took her hand and bowed over it. She managed to curtsey and not snatch her hand from his grasp but remove it smoothly. Having closed the door, she leaned against the wood and took a deep breath of the dusty air, wondering if she was capable of maintaining this courteous, neutral façade. She had to separate Gerald the man from Gerald the Norman warrior, and the past that had brought each of them into this marriage, and knew it might prove an impossible task.

11

Palace of Carew,
August 1102

Nesta went to her marriage at the small Church of St John, a short distance from the homestead at Carew. She stepped from the ladies' hall gowned in red damask, trimmed with gold silk, her black braids twined with ribbons. Eleri followed, holding little Henry's hand, and he skipped and danced excitedly at her side. Marguerite of Manorbier walked with Nesta, acting as her chamber lady together with the wife of Tancred de Rhos, commander of Haverford.

Dewi was waiting in the courtyard with Hera. Gerald was already mounted on Taran who had been groomed until his golden-grey coat gleamed like twilit sand. Silver bells jingled on the harness and had been plaited into his mane. Gerald too was clad in finery – tawny hose, blue tunic, fur-edged cloak and shoes with thread of gold lacings. His brother William sat beside him on a handsome black palfrey.

Nesta approached the mare and stroked her face before accepting Dewi's assistance into the saddle.

Gerald rode over to her. 'Your beauty takes my breath,' he said. 'I am the most fortunate of men.'

She lifted her head and gathered the reins. 'You look fine also, my lord,' she replied, for she had to reciprocate at least a little, and it was true.

'Are you ready?'

'As I shall ever be.' Which was never.

'Well then, let us ride to our marriage.'

He turned the horse, but paused and beckoned to a freckled fair-haired boy of about eight years who was sitting on a glossy brown pony among the entourage.

'This is my son, Walter,' he said. 'He is my page and part of my household. I hope you will accept him into yours when occasion demands.'

Nesta's eyebrows shot up. To present the boy as they set out to their marriage was clumsy, but she supposed that the longer he left it, the more difficult it would have become, and given the circumstances now, she could not make a fuss.

'His mother died last year and he is my only one, but I do my best for him. I will not have him disparaged for his birth. His mother was a good woman and he is my responsibility. Come, Walter, greet my new lady.'

A little sheepishly the lad nudged his pony forward and folded in a bow to Nesta. She replied with a nod of acknowledgement. 'I am sure we shall do well together,' she said formally, and saw the flicker of relief on Gerald's face. He nodded to the boy, who returned to the ranks, also looking as if he had been let off a hook.

'He will be no trouble to you,' Gerald said. 'He's a good boy.'

'As long as he respects my position, I shall respect his,' Nesta answered. 'It is not as though such situations are rare after all, is it?' She glanced at her own son.

'There will be no others,' Gerald said, flushing. 'Only those of our marriage. This I vow.'

Since it was good weather, with barely a breath of wind, the wedding feast following the marriage was held outdoors with trestle tables set out to accommodate the guests. Roasting hogs glistened with fat over rosy coals. The kitchen attendants, under the cook's gimlet-eyed direction, had been busy since before dawn. There was salmon with green sauce, plentiful bread, cheeses, fruit and wine, mead as well, and griddle cakes flavoured with honey and spices.

Gerald assisted Nesta to a decorated seat at the head of the main table and the other guests took their places. She waited for the priest to bless the food, then rose to her feet before the meal could commence. Raising her mead cup in toast she addressed the gathering. 'I thank everyone who has come to celebrate and bear witness to this wedding today, and especially those who have laboured so hard to provide our feast. I hope I shall be as good a lady to Carew as my mother was, and that I may follow in my father's footsteps in doing justice when it is asked of me. Let us make changes for the good of all, and especially for Dyfed!' Triumph coursed through her veins. Even if she must pay for it later, she exulted now.

Gerald had looked a little taken aback at the lead she had taken, but smiled as he rose beside her. Taking the cup from her hand, he raised his own toast. 'May I echo the wise words of my bride, for she is Lady of Carew and I shun her advice at my peril. I swear to govern fairly and firmly. There is no reason why we cannot live in amity. I am of Norman blood, I serve King Henry, but I have loved Wales since I was a boy, and I shall continue to do so, through my wife, through these lands, and through the children that God will hopefully grant us to raise among you. A toast, the first of many, to my lady wife –

long may she dwell here and lend us her wisdom, beauty and grace!' He drank from the cup, and as people cheered he presented it to her so that she had to drink too. He then repeated the words in fluent Welsh, and finished with an exhortation for everyone to eat, drink and celebrate.

'That was well done,' he said, sitting down at her side, smiling.

She was surprised, for she had expected him to be annoyed. She had dared him to the edge of the line, but he seemed unfazed.

'You were like a queen when you spoke, and people will now see in us the beginnings of a dynasty.' He raised a personal toast. 'I salute you and your courage. May you pass it to the many sons you will bear for me.'

Nesta's cheeks burned and she realised that his measured response did not mean he was going to ignore her behaviour either. Her stomach churned with tension, part of which was the excitement of rising to the challenge.

Everyone feasted until their bellies were bursting. Little Henry was carried off to bed in an exhausted stupor following a fractious tantrum. There was dancing and singing. Gerald's brother juggled five leather balls at once without dropping a single one. There were contests for the men of wrestling and throwing the stone, to see who could hurl a small boulder the furthest. Nesta watched Gerald step and twist and fling his stone out into the night to strike the turf with a soft thud several yards away. He didn't win, there were others with more expertise, but he acquitted himself well, and smiled as he presented the prize of a silver cup to the winner, Odo de Barry, with a clap on the shoulder. There were archery and spear-throwing contests, won by two young Welshmen, and Nesta bestowed twelve silver pennies on each of them, and felt immensely proud. No one could shoot an arrow or throw a spear better than the men of Dyfed.

The knife-throwing contest was won by a small, unobtrusive Welshman with a puckered leathery face and something of the weasel about his eyes. He bowed deeply to Gerald and then boldly to her, and she received the impression that although they shared a language, he was not necessarily her ally.

'You have great skill with a knife,' she said.

His face creased with what passed for a smile. 'It is my trade, my lady. I leave the fancy swords to others.' He waggled his eyebrows suggestively at Gerald.

Mouth twitching with amusement, Gerald handed him a fat pouch of silver. 'We shall talk later, and you can bring me abreast of news.'

'Sire.' He bowed deeply. 'May I wish you both felicitations on your marriage day.' And then he was gone, weaving between the guests, and in a moment Nesta lost him from her sight.

The hair prickled on the nape of her neck. 'Who was that?'

Gerald shrugged. 'One of my scouts. A scoundrel, but useful.'

'And his trade is the knife?'

'In the dark,' he said. 'Ifan hears and sees everything and he is loyal to me because I pay him well and we have an understanding.'

Nesta hid her distaste, that one of her countrymen would spy for the Normans, although it happened often enough. 'How did he come into your pay?'

'Of his own accord, and he had his reasons.' Gerald changed the subject. 'Come, we should dance.'

He rose from the table and, taking her hand, led her to the open ground in the centre of the trestles. The musicians struck up a tune with a steady beat of drum, and he circled with her, one hand on his hip. Nimble and precise, having had plenty of practice at Norman court dances, Nesta matched her step to his, even experiencing a slight frisson as their hands touched. A circle dance followed with everyone involved and Nesta lost herself in the motion because while moving there was no time to think.

When the dancing ended, she begged leave to retire to prepare herself.

'Certainly,' Gerald replied. 'I have a few people to talk with, and it will give me that chance.'

He started to summon the ladies, but Nesta shook her head. 'I need a moment to myself, if you will.'

He summoned an older knight instead to escort her quietly, without fanfare, lest people think the bedding ceremony was about to commence. Again, she had cause to thank him, but she was unsettled. Gerald constantly bucked her expectation. He was nothing like Henry, who was forceful and ruthless, nor her father, who had indulged her but whose word had still been a sharp command that ended all discourse. Gerald was supposedly a warlord of high repute, pragmatic and steely, but not in a mould she recognised. Indeed, all she knew about him thus far added up only to a great deal of unknowing.

Entering his chamber, she stopped in the doorway and looked around. Everything was neat and tidy. His clothes were all either folded over a pole or hung on hooks. The floor was cleanly swept, with sheepskins at the bedside for bare feet. An intricately carved small Welsh harp stood on a stool. She plucked a note from it, and listened until the resonance faded.

Nesta wandered over to a low table where gaming pieces and dice awaited players. She shook the dice in their horn cup and tipped them out, throwing a six and a one. All or nothing. Smiling bleakly at the irony, she approached the bed. The sheets, straight and smooth, smelled of clean, sun-dried linen and a slightly astringent herbal perfume. The coverlet was linen too, but two layers and filled with feathers, stitched into place by embroidery of white on white. A weapon chest stood under the window. Knowing it would hold his sword and accoutrements of war, she left it well alone. His shield was propped against the wall and she avoided that too.

Some of her own items had been brought earlier – clothing for the morrow, a white chemise for sleeping, together with her combs and unguents. A fresh flagon of mead stood on a low table by the bed, and she poured some into a cup. Did she want to be aware or insensible tonight? To have her wits or be witless? Grimacing, she took a single sip and set the cup aside. This would not do at all. She took off her wedding gown and chemise, and put on the loose linen night gown. Having unbraided her hair, she combed it until it hung in a black skein to her waist. A dab of rose oil on each wrist and behind her ears, and she was ready. She curled up on the bed and waited as she had so often waited for Henry, and shivered at the prospect of what was to come.

Gerald's brother appraised him with new respect as they sat together in the hall, finishing their wine. 'You have fallen on your feet, I will say that for you,' he said. 'A Welsh princess and her lands.'

'Part of her lands,' Gerald qualified, 'and I shall spend a great deal of time defending them.'

'But you say it in the manner of a cat washing its paws after it has gorged in the dairy.'

'Do I?' Gerald smiled wryly. He had often envied William his relatively safe position at Windsor. Not a guaranteed post but close to being hereditary, and controlling one of England's major strongholds. Now, by his own perseverance and diligence he had won a piece of South Wales and a dazzlingly beautiful wife of royal blood, and perhaps William was the one to be envious. 'Many will not rejoice at this match, and I must prove my ability to the King. The Welsh lords around me are persistent. The best I can hope for is a truce. Cadwgan of Powys supported

Robert de Belleme, but he has made his peace with the King and taken a Norman wife – Picot de Sai's daughter.' He took a swallow of his wine and did not add the detail to his brother that Emma de Sai had been another of Henry's conquests, although in her case she had been an overnight comfort rather than a long-term concubine. 'Cadwgan's eldest son is a trouble-maker. He besieged me at Pembroke a few years ago and will bear watching – as will Cadwgan despite his new wife.'

William grunted. 'Rather you than me, but the King obviously trusts you to control the region, otherwise he would not have given you this marriage.'

'We shall see. I do not fear my opponents and rivals, but I need to keep them in my sight.'

'You always were one to quietly evaluate and work your way to where you wanted to be – and you have your reward. Many will wish themselves in your place tonight.'

Gerald finished his wine. 'I hope you will give our father a positive report of my wife.'

'I shall indeed. Although I will say to you, little brother, by way of advice, do not let her charms seduce you beyond reason. She is very, very beautiful.'

'That will not happen,' Gerald said shortly, defensive because there was some truth in the statement, and also because William was back on his superior horse again.

'I am pleased to hear it.' William set down his empty cup, slapped his knees and stood up. 'Time to go and pay your bride some proper attention and show her who is master then, eh?' he said with a grin. 'Perhaps nine months from now she will bear you a strapping son if you plough the furrow well.'

William set off to organise the escort to Gerald's chamber. He collected the priest and assembled the knights and serjeants into a walkway of lit torches for Gerald to pass down on his way to the door. The ladies had been swiftly sent on ahead, and when Gerald arrived, Eleri opened the door to his knock and he entered, followed by a procession of guests.

Nesta was sitting on the bed, but rose as he entered with the well-wishers. Wrapping her cloak around her shoulders, she stood regally to greet him, her face taut and her complexion almost as pale as the chemise.

Gerald's squire helped him remove his belt and tunic, but Gerald held up his hand to prevent any further undressing and faced the expectant guests. 'I thank you all for your good wishes, and attendance at our wedding feast,' he said. 'Pray depart and celebrate some more or retire as you wish. I only ask the good priest to bless our union and that we may then be left in peace to become better acquainted.'

Someone guffawed. Someone else shouted out, demanding to know about the danger of repudiation. Welsh law declared that should a man not be satisfied with his wife he had the right to renounce her in front of everyone – providing he did so that very night with his penis standing to attention as proof of his ability to pierce her.

'I have no intention of repudiating this marriage under either Welsh or Norman law, and I am aware of both,' Gerald responded steadily. 'I promise you shall see neither of us again until dawn – and I am sure that my wife concurs.' He turned to Nesta, who made a gesture of assent, her cheeks flaming.

'My husband speaks truly,' she said.

The priest blessed the bed, sprinkling the white quilt with holy water from an aspergillum. He sprinkled Nesta and Gerald liberally too, exhorting them to be fruitful. William and Odo de Barry, at a nod from Gerald, began ushering people from the room. One or two had to be persuaded, but Odo and William were a formidable team, and eventually the last person lurched out on drink-sodden feet, and Gerald was able to put the bar across the door and face his new wife. His brother had been right to warn him, because he knew how susceptible he was. His dream was that she might one day love him, but he knew it wasn't hers.

Nesta stared back at Gerald, and with trepidation saw the hunger in his eyes, the same hunger that had always been in Henry's in the early days. She still remembered those occasions vividly; the fear, the pain, the revulsion. She had subsumed those reactions in order to survive and now must do so again.

Going to the flagon on the chest, he poured mead for both of them. 'To our marriage.' He handed her the cup.

Nesta drank because it was expected, but could not bring herself to answer the toast. She glanced surreptitiously at his groin but there was no eager tent within his braies quite yet. Henry had been brusque and quick to his business, and she had often been sore for hours afterwards. Tonight, she had anointed herself with the salve in anticipation of what would probably happen. She had no expectation of pleasure, but at least she knew what to do.

Gerald finished the mead, put his cup aside and removed his shirt. He was well made with a taut, flat stomach and good muscles; indeed, he had a better physique than Henry. Nesta looked and then looked away as he sat on the bed to take off his hose and braies. He beckoned her to join him, and she did so reluctantly.

'I will be gentle,' he said. 'You will take no harm from me. This is our wedding night, and should set the seal on all our nights to come. I know what has gone before, but it is in the past.'

It was easy for him to say, and although he said he knew what had gone before, he truly had no notion. He had not been there with her each time Henry sent for her to pleasure him. It could never be in her past, but at least Henry had taught her about male pleasure and in her own interests she had learned how to bring it about swiftly.

'Take off your chemise,' he said softly.

She slowly pulled the garment over her head and pushed out her breasts, and heard his soft intake of breath as he gazed at her in the light from the lamp. He drew her down to his side and pulled the cover over them, then kissed her eyes, her cheeks, her throat, and finally her lips. He stroked her body, cupped and kissed her breasts. Hearing his breathing change, she shifted her body under his, and parted her thighs. He muttered against her throat, telling her she was beautiful, and that he would care for her for all his days and that he honoured her with his body. But as she steeled herself to take him inside her, he slowed, and drew back to look into her eyes. 'I mean every word. This is *am byth*. This is for ever.'

Despite her misgivings, Nesta was moved, and surprised that he had not just attended to business. At the outset she had hoped he would, the sooner to be left alone, but now she felt on the verge of knowing something greater. She touched his face and felt his skin, the slight prick of stubble, the softness of his close-cropped beard.

'It is all right,' she said. 'I am ready.'

Nesta lay in the aftermath of their mating and pondered the experience with perplexity. It had been so different from her encounters with Henry. Gerald had been eager, especially at the end, but not rough or over-forceful. Now he held her in his arms, stroking her body, kissing her tenderly, and she had no compass to know her direction. Henry, even when in a good mood, had always used her as the object of his release without consideration or thought for her wellbeing. This was new, and it was difficult to assimilate. It would have been much easier to cope with if he had been like Henry.

Eventually he kissed her shoulder a final time and fell asleep, as men always did after they had had a drink and gained release. That at least was the same. Once his breathing had become regular and settled, Nesta stealthily left the bed. Quietly pacing the room, she tried to think, but her mind lacked clarity. She paused at the window and gazed at the shutters barred against the night and wished they were open, so that like a bird she could take wing and leave everything behind. But she wasn't a bird, she was earthbound, with a sheepskin rug curling between her toes and the sound of Gerald's breathing winding through the air between them like a thread of possession. The thought that this was 'for ever' terrified her. Two men she had lain with in her life, neither of whom were of her choosing. One had forced her, the other she had accepted in resignation, and he had a husband's right to claim the marriage debt. She looked over her shoulder at his mounded form beneath the bedclothes. Henry had taken what he wanted by force, Gerald by fair words and courtesy. She remembered the thoughts she had once entertained about killing Henry and briefly considered the same for the man sleeping in the home he had usurped, but it was a momentary flare like a kindled spill that burned down in the fingers and went out.

Eventually she returned to the bed and climbed in beside him. Her action disturbed him and his eyelids fluttered. 'Sshhh, go to sleep,' she whispered. She inhaled his scent – slightly herbal from the bath he had taken before the wedding, but otherwise neutral, neither disagreeable nor evocative. She leaned over to blow out the lamp and then curled up, putting space between them, and went to sleep with her back turned.

In the morning when she awoke, Gerald was already dressed, and as she stirred he came to the bed and stooped to kiss her.

'Take your rest,' he said. 'I have always been an early riser. I will send your maid in to tend you.'

As he left the room, she heard him telling Eleri to be gentle with her, and wondered why he would say that. She was hardly a virgin, and he had been considerate well beyond her experience. Indeed, it had not hurt at all. And then she realised with a blush that perhaps he was hoping she had conceived.

Eleri entered, bringing a bowl of warm water for her to wash. Another maid arrived with bread, honey and buttermilk. Nesta told her to open the shutters and sat down at a small table to eat and drink. The morning was fine and clear with a sky as blue as pigment. Sunlight streamed in a bright ray onto the bed where she and Gerald had lain. She looked at it, and then away.

Having broken her fast, she washed thoroughly, and Eleri helped her dress in a gown of forest-green silk with gold laces, and a white veil decorated with a band of pearls and green glass stones. As Eleri was applying the finishing touches, Gerald returned and bowed an apology to the women.

'I forgot my hat,' he said, going to a folded pile of his clothes and plucking a cap off the top.

Caught off guard, Nesta experienced a soft lurch in the pit of her stomach.

'You look very beautiful,' he said. 'Be sure to rest today.'

'I shall, my lord.'

She looked down modestly until he had gone, and then breathed out her tension. It was strange to feel warmth in her solar plexus. If she kept him satisfied, she would have the security of a high position and acceptance – things she had not possessed since childhood; and she could start to make plans.

12

Palace of Carew,
August 1102

Two days later, Nesta and Gerald set out for Pembroke. Nine years ago, she and her mother had been seized from here by Arnulf de Montgomery, so Nesta experienced feelings of dissonance, for the ride was pleasant, the weather was fine and the atmosphere one of celebration, even if the men were watchful.

Gerald had been unfailingly courteous and considerate. He had not pressured her into bedding with him again and was treating her like a queen, showing her off proudly to his guests. She had embraced the role with alacrity, for who would not be a queen? The frisson between them, though, was a constant tension. He watched her with hungry eyes even while he held back; she refused to encourage him and remained modest and demure. Let the approach be his.

Arriving at Pembroke, he drew rein before the gates and turned to her. 'You are mistress here too, although it is only a soldiers' garrison and your home will be at Carew. But you may make your chamber as comfortable as you desire for the times you do stay.' He reached across their horses to cover her hand with his. 'This marriage must work for both Norman and Welsh, we must be united. If there is anything that upsets you, tell me, and I shall do my best to set it right. I want you to be happy.'

Nesta looked down at his hand over hers. While she could be satisfied, she doubted that she could ever be happy. He might frame his words in terms of concern for her wellbeing, but his interest was in managing these lands. He could do nothing to set right the wrongs from nine years ago, and this fortress in front of her was part of that wrong. Gently she removed her hand from under his, but smiled at him, playing the game.

That night, when they were alone, he took his harp and played for her. He was not as talented as her father's bard but he had some skill and his fingers were delicate and sure. He sang to her – a hymn in Latin that stirred her emotions. French was the language of the conqueror and she would have resented him stealing her own tongue and using Welsh, but Latin was safe territory, and his voice was glorious and many-toned, and soothed the rough spots within her.

They made love, and again it was a gentle thing that was almost a poem. His slow touch was erotic and almost pleasurable, but disturbing too. She refused to have warm feelings for this man whom she had intended to manipulate and who, instead, seemed to be moulding her like warm wax. She put her fingers in his hair and wove the strands between them. If Gerald were Welsh, not Norman, it would be different, but she could not forget that he had ridden with Arnulf de Montgomery at the time of her father's death.

They departed Pembroke, leaving it in the care of its constable, and made slow progress through Dyfed, visiting the towns and

villages where they received a mixed response. Some Welsh celebrated the return of the lord Rhys's daughter and the survival of
the ruling bloodline, but others viewed the match as a sign of the
increasing weight of the Norman yoke and the stealing of a Welsh
highborn woman, and muttered behind their hands.

At St David's the Bishop welcomed them – not warmly, but
enough to preserve the civilities, and Gerald was civil in his
turn, for he and Wilfrid had to work with each other.

That night, lying at Nesta's side in the guest house, Gerald spoke
to her of his plans for the children they would have. 'A son and
heir for Carew to follow my sword, and another in case of mishap.'
He ran his forefinger up and down her spine, making her shiver
with the deliciousness of the sensation despite her determination
to remain indifferent. 'And one for the Church to serve in the
cathedral here. It would be fine to have the rule of Carew and St
David's. We shall have a dynasty of Church and state.'

His breath was in her ear, against her neck, and she turned
over to him, jolted by the way he was planning what their children as yet unconceived would do, and the positions they would
hold in society. For certain she had still only encountered the
shallows of this man. 'You are ambitious,' she said. 'What if I
do not bear you children? What if I give you only daughters?'

'I do not dream of doubt,' he replied. 'The future is God's
will and I shall do His bidding, but I may still carry my ladder
of dreams and climb them one rung at a time, never looking
down.'

Nesta did not speak, for what was she to say of her own
ladder of dreams? That it had been chopped off at the base?
That what remained was mutilated and unsteady?

She felt him absorb her silence. He rolled onto his back. 'I
would hope for daughters too,' he said. 'As beautiful as their
mother.'

Because daughters made fine profits in the marriage market. Daughters to be sold. Daughters subject to the rules and cruelties of men. And while he had the pleasure of sowing the seed, she had the travail of bearing, and to what end?

When again she did not answer, he sighed. 'While we are here, I have asked the Bishop to dedicate a mass for your father's soul, and I wish to give an endowment to the cathedral for his honour and salvation. If in time a God-granted son of ours should come to St David's to serve, then he too shall praise his fallen kin and pray for the redemption of all.'

Nesta's eyes started to prickle and she blinked hard. His words were like a hand held out to pull her onto his ladder and all she had to do was reach. That he would honour her father moved her, but brought her pain into sharper focus. 'I would like that,' she said in a tight whisper. When he drew breath to say more, she covered his mouth. 'No more for now. You have laid a surfeit before me and I cannot think.'

He took the hand she had laid across his lips and kissed the fingers. 'You are right, it is late for talk. But I meant what I said. You and I shall leave our mark on the world in our children and our children's children, and beyond.' He drew the covers over both of them, and rolled onto his side. Nesta lay staring up into the darkness and felt the tear tracks drying stiffly on her face.

The following day, Gerald saw to the business of committing the endowment to St David's to parchment, and then took Nesta for a walk along the coastal path. He needed to feel God in the great sweep of nature unfettered by the cathedral's solid walls, and he wanted to share it with his wife and make her understand his love for Wales.

A strong breeze was blowing the tops off the white wave

crests. The sea reflected the sky but in deeper blue, and although the wind was cold, the early September sun was a benediction. 'On a day like this, I feel as if I could take off and fly like a bird!' He gestured at the gulls riding the layers of wind.

Nesta laughed, surprised. 'You are not meant to be a seagull. God made you a man to walk upon the land.'

'Ah, but God also made me an imagination to take flight and see what there is, beyond the ship and over the horizon.' He looked up and, drawing a deep breath, started to sing, because he needed to.

Nesta shivered at the strength and purity of his voice. She had heard him sing before in hall and chamber, and he had been good, but this was baring his soul. While he used his own breath to praise God, her own was locked in her chest. He was ordinary to look upon, steady of purpose and exuded an air of calm determination, but without charisma – nothing that would shine in a crowd. But the voice was that of an earthbound angel.

He ended on a sustained note with a triumphant uplift, arms extended. The resonation became part of the sea wind, and like the sun on a cloudy day, the dazzle was suddenly gone. He dropped his arms and once again was ordinary Gerald.

'That was beautiful.' She swallowed, for tears were not far away.

'It is for God and comes from God,' he answered simply. 'But I wanted to share it with you – for you to know.'

'And I thank you that you did.' Her emotions continued to churn. She didn't want to soften towards this man.

He kissed her and turned, with his arm around her waist, to look out to sea.

Drawing herself together, she followed his gaze. 'My little brother is somewhere across there in Ireland. Perhaps not so little now, for he will be thirteen years old. Last time I saw him he was being rushed from Carew to avoid being captured by Arnulf de Montgomery.' She moved away from the shelter of his embrace and wrapped her arms around her body, for he had been part of Montgomery's entourage. 'I have had no contact with him since. I do not know if he still lives, although surely he must for bad news always travels swiftly.'

'I could send a messenger to find out,' Gerald offered. 'The merchant ships run between here and Ireland except in the worst weather.'

She wondered how much she could trust him. Those who spoke of his reputation said he was a formidable soldier and a cunning fox. Finding Gruffydd might be a prelude to removing him. 'Would you do that for me, or for yourself?'

Gerald glanced at her. 'Your brother is not yet a man, and I have enough enemies to deal with without making more trouble for the future. I have able people I could send to seek him out, but I would look to make alliances, not stir up trouble.'

'Or you could have him killed,' she said bluntly.

'Do you really think that of me?'

Her anger stirred. 'I know what happened to my father, to my mother and to me at the hands of Normans. I have a child as a constant reminder. I cannot fault your generosity and concern for my welfare, but I am the means to your end and the vessel by which to bear more children to hold this land in thrall. You are a soldier. You have built a fortress at Pembroke and stamped your authority on all of us. You get what you want, Gerald, by whatever means it takes.' She had not meant to say as much, but it was like relieving the pressure on a sore.

His eyes grew bright and stone-hard. 'Do you think that sending someone to murder your brother would be in my best interests when you are my wife and I need your cooperation to grow my influence here? Do you think I could conceal such a deed from your knowledge? If you believe I would do such a thing, then where do we stand?'

'We stand in honesty. I do not know what you would do, my lord, because I do not know you.'

'Then know this,' he said coldly. 'When I give my word and my oath, I do not go back on it – ever.' He turned round and began walking back towards the grooms, his shoulders set and stiff.

They returned to St David's without speaking and he stalked off to the stables, to the horses, leaving her in the guest house with Eleri and Ceridwen, a new maid Nesta had employed from among the young women at Carew.

Nesta sat down at her weaving. A half-finished piece of braid waited on her narrow loom. The pattern was intricate and required concentration that she did not have, and she could only stare at it. How she missed another woman to talk with. Ede would have helped her unravel her thoughts and given her perspective. Sometimes she would speak to Eleri, but their different rank created barriers. She had begun a rapport with Marguerite de Barry before the progress, but it was a fledgling friendship and Marguerite wasn't here now. She could only fall back on her own resources, and wonder how the pragmatic Adele would respond to the situation.

A short while later, Gerald entered the guest house. He had washed, for his hair was damp around the edges, and he had changed his tunic. 'Madam, I would speak with you,' he said with cold formality. 'Will you ask your ladies to leave us?'

Her stomach lurched but she dismissed them, for what choice did she have?

He walked over to the weaving frame and studied the length of braid on which she had been working, with the pattern twists like incoming waves. 'I used to watch my mother do this,' he said. 'Sometimes she would allow me to put in a few turns for luck.'

Nesta waited tensely. If he touched the work, she would not finish it; she would rather throw it away.

He looked up and fixed her with a steady stare. 'What we said just now on the cliffs. I swear on my soul and the souls of my unborn children that I will never intentionally threaten your brother's life. If that is not enough for you to believe me, then I can do no more.' He opened his hands to emphasise his words.

'You say that, but he is your rival – even if not now, then in the fullness of time. He is the heir to all that you govern and one day he will come for that land. You can see why I might doubt your word.'

He hooked up a stool with his foot and sat down with a sigh. 'I would hope to broker a truce with him. Yes, I govern here for the King, and Pembroke has been situated to defend against attacks from Ireland and to protect and control the surrounding land. I intend building further up the coast on our boundary with Powys too, to consolidate my border. That is my intent and the patrimony I shall build for our sons. The lords of Powys, Cadwgan and Owain, would take it from me if they could. They have long had their gaze on these territories. Cadwgan has a Norman wife and has made peace with King Henry but that will not stop him from taking from his neighbours – it has always been the way, even before the Normans arrived.

'Your brother, when the time comes, can challenge Powys for the lands on which they have encroached, and we can establish a strong border between us. Better to have your brother for an ally. I cannot retreat or yield my own position – I have lived here for almost ten years and the land has been in my heart since my youth.' He struck his chest to make his point. 'That I have a Welsh wife with a Welsh brother and that our children will have that golden thread in their veins lights me with joy. You doubt me. You wonder if I speak untruths, but I will prove myself to you as many times as I must. I will wait as long as the mountains for you, if that is what it takes.'

His words were the stuff of dreams, but Nesta did not want to walk inside them when her own dreams had been turned to nightmares by the men he served.

He left the stool and joined her on the bench. 'We should not argue – we have no cause to do so. Send messengers to enquire how your brother fares, but let him dwell in Ireland for a while longer. He is not yet a man, and when he returns he will attract attention from others who have more reason to want him dead. Indeed, I would have to protect and defend him with my sword.'

He was right about Gruffydd's age, and Gruffydd was indeed safer in Ireland for now. She had always considered herself the custodian of her brother's right to rule Dyfed, but now, thinking about the sons she might bear, that had changed. Perhaps it would be better in partnership, as Gerald said.

'What do you say?' he asked. 'Are you willing to take me on trust?'

She arched her brow, but showed him her amusement. 'You told me you would wait as long as the mountains, and you are asking me again within moments?'

'I said that I would wait, I mentioned nothing about how often I would ask.' He drew her towards him.

Nesta pulled back to look at him. 'What I think is that I shall reserve my judgement,' she said, but forced a smile to deflate the tension, and when he kissed her, she leaned into the embrace.

13

Palace of Carew,
July 1103

Soft sounds from the cradle at her bedside woke Nesta from a heavy slumber. Opening her eyes she gazed round the chamber, while she returned to the world. A broad beam of sunlight stole across the floor and glanced on the edge of her clothing chest at the foot of the bed.

Her ladies were busy on the other side of the chamber and Nesta pushed aside the bedclothes, eased to her feet, and went to lift her new son from his cradle. He had been born yesterday evening at sunset following a swift, uncomplicated labour. There was no mistaking Gerald's siring in the miniature version of his features, showing proof of his strong seed. She had fulfilled her duty and borne him a lusty son and heir. Her ambivalence about bearing another child to a Norman father had evaporated as she held him in her arms after the birth, and she had loved him straight away. Little Henry had been mildly interested, but his sights were already set on the pursuits of bigger boys and he had taken a quick look then run off to play with his toy sword.

Gerald had yet to see his new son. He had been busy at Pembroke and would not have received news of the birth until late last night. Their relationship had travelled a steady course in the first year of their marriage, each of them performing their duties with courteous civility and presenting a united front – Gerald because it was his nature, and Nesta for the moment taking the path of least resistance. She was still acclimatising to her life as the wife of a Norman administrator and warlord, and constantly struggled with the discord between that and her own heritage and earlier experiences.

Gerald had been true to his word, though, and on their return from St David's had not stood in the way of her sending a messenger to Ireland, enquiring after her brother. The reply had arrived a couple of months later via a trading ship, that he was well and dwelling at the court of Donnchadh MacMurchada, King of Leinster, with other Welsh exiles. One day, if God was good, he would return to Wales and he and Nesta would be reunited. The reply, rather than the words of a thirteen-year-old boy, had been penned by one of Donnchadh MacMurchada's scribes. However, Gruffydd had enclosed a small silver brooch that had belonged to their mother, and that, as much as the formal letter, had made Nesta cry. She wore it every day, using it as a closure for her chemise.

The baby's snuffles turned to a hungry complaint, and Nesta parted her chemise and put him to suckle.

As the baby latched onto her nipple and began to tug with a will, Marguerite de Barry came over from the fire to give her a warm tisane. Marguerite had been horrified when Nesta had insisted on feeding the baby herself instead of employing a wet nurse. Nesta had replied that it was customary in the royal household of Dyfed. It wasn't, but it was more diplomatic than saying that nourishing her children with the milk of their Welsh-born mother would increase their ties to Wales and tip the balance when it came to their identity.

'You should not be out of bed yet,' Marguerite admonished. 'Lie and rest and let us tend you.'

Nesta tossed her head. 'The farmer's and fishermen's wives are up and working as soon as they give birth. I am well enough to leave my bed and be about my own chamber. Pass me my bed robe.'

Marguerite rolled her eyes but handed her the loose gown Nesta had designed to wear over her chemise, which fastened at the front with ribbons. Marguerite had been intrigued by the garment, and was now busy making one for herself. 'Even so, you need to heal, and you should be careful of the milk fever. I was sick almost to the day of churching after I bore my own son.'

Nesta puffed out her cheeks and almost rolled her eyes. She enjoyed being cosseted and having the leisure to lie in bed but preferred to savour it as a choice rather than having it forced upon her. Now her son was born, she wanted to be slim again, dressed in her silk gowns, and busy as Carew's lady. Marguerite meant well and Nesta had grown fond of her, but frequently their viewpoints diverged.

Eleri returned from an errand to fetch some eggs for coddling over the fire. 'Your lord has just arrived,' she announced. 'I saw him riding in.'

The baby had finished at her breast so Nesta dabbed his lips with a napkin and gave him to Ceridwen to change his clouts. Feeding him was one thing, but she was perfectly content to have someone else deal with what emerged from the other end.

Marguerite helped her back into bed, and combed and braided

Nesta's hair into a lustrous plait with nimble fingers. 'You have done so well,' she said as she worked. 'You make sure he knows it too. It's not men that have the work of pushing their heirs from a small hole in their bodies. All they do is put it in there for us to do the work, and the minute we're churched, they want to put it in all over again!'

Nesta bit back laughter at her friend's candid remarks. 'I shall make very sure. There will be no "putting in" until I am ready, I promise that.'

Marguerite gave an approving nod and smoothed Nesta's braid under her hand in an almost tender gesture, then turned to Eleri. 'Is he changed? Good, give him to your mistress. Quickly now, I hear footsteps, and they're not a woman's!'

Eleri placed the clean and swaddled baby in Nesta's arms, and as she was doing so there was a rap on the door. Marguerite hurried to open it to Gerald who formally craved admittance, all the while peering past her into the chamber.

'My lord, you are welcome,' Nesta called from the bed.

Marguerite stepped aside to usher him in. 'You have a fine, healthy son, and a recovering wife. Do not tire her.' She took the maids away, leaving Nesta and Gerald alone.

Nesta watched Gerald come to her, a broad smile on his face. He stooped and kissed her cheek, but his eyes were drawn to the sleeping baby. 'Are you well, my love?'

'Yes, I am well.' She returned his smile and did not have to force herself. 'I have borne us a strong, healthy son. It was no small task to bear him, but as you can see, I am being zealously cared for. Woe betide you if you fall foul of Marguerite de Barry!'

He cast his glance heavenwards, and they shared a moment of mutual, genuine amusement.

She held out the baby to him. 'Your son, my lord.'

Gerald awkwardly took the little parcel in his arms and experienced an unexpected tenderness and tug on his heartstrings. Babies were soft, vulnerable creatures, barely formed, and belonged to the realm of women. They screwed up their faces and screamed at all hours and soiled their swaddling. He had not had much ado with them before, even with Walter – not until he became a personality in his own right. But this was his heir, to follow in his line, and born of a royal Welsh woman. He raised his head to Nesta. 'You are the cleverest, most courageous woman I know,' he said, and his eyes were liquid.

Nesta preened, taking the compliment as her due, but nevertheless she was touched.

'This is our firstborn son, and he must have a name to follow in my stead.' His tears had gone, replaced by the determined look with which she had grown familiar in the months since their marriage. Although he was a Welsh prince, her son would not be granted a Welsh name.

'Not Henry,' she said with a curl of her lip, showing her emotion now.

He flushed. 'Credit me with some tact. Let him be called William, after my mother's father of whom I was fond as a child, and let him be known for his birthplace and his heritage – as William of Carew.'

She inclined her head, not overjoyed but satisfied that it was at least fitting. She would call him by the Welsh version – Gwilym.

'I shall see to his baptism this very morning.' Gerald stroked the baby's cheek, kissed his forehead softly, and placed him in the cradle, then, turning back, presented Nesta with a small, embroidered cloth bag. 'This is for you. Of course you shall have a new gown and belt for your churching, but this is for now – family rings given to a wife when she bears a child.'

Nesta took the little silk bag from him and tipped three gold rings onto her palm – two of beaded gold, and another set with a cabochon ruby that would go perfectly with her crimson gown. When she put them on, they fitted her fingers perfectly.

'What of your older brother?' she asked. 'Should not these go to him?'

Gerald shrugged. 'He has some of his own for his wife. These were given to my mother at my own birth. They are family jewels, bought by my father from a London goldsmith – *not* taken in raiding and plunder.'

Nesta rubbed her forefinger over the blood-red stone and felt relieved. 'I will treasure them,' she said. 'Thank you.'

He looked over his shoulder as Marguerite de Barry entered with a folded pile of linen. The severe look she sent him brought him to his feet. 'I shall leave you to rest, before I am thrown out,' he said wryly. 'If there is anything you need, you have only to ask, and it shall be yours.' He leaned over to kiss her lips before gently lifting the swaddled baby from the cradle to take him away to his baptism.

Nesta watched him carry their son out of the room. The way he paused on the threshold and gazed at him with such pride and tenderness caused a sudden, painful swoop in her heart that was like hitting a barrier and rebounding, and made her want to cry.

Marguerite's expression softened. 'As far as men go, I would say you had a good one there,' she said. 'You count your blessings, and let him count his.'

Nesta looked down at her three new rings. 'Yes,' she said, blinking.

Following the baby's baptism, ensuring that tiny William of Carew's soul was now secured a place in heaven rather than purgatory should he suddenly die, Gerald returned him to Nesta.

Although keen to see her again, he knew not to chance his luck with Marguerite a second time. She received the baby at the chamber door, and although refusing him entry, saying that Nesta was asleep and that a birthing chamber was no place for men, gave him a smile, her eyes twinkling.

Gerald left and went to dictate a letter to his father at Windsor, that he had a new grandson, a veritable Welsh prince. Then he joined his soldiers, broached a barrel of wine from the stores and applied himself to the business of celebrating his son's birth. However, drinking toast after toast was not one of Gerald's strengths. Wine always made him maudlin. Sitting at the board, he rested his head on his arms, feeling dizzy and overwhelmed. He had to wipe tears from his eyes, for it would not do for his men to see him weeping. Eventually he stumbled from the hall, going outside, away from everyone. He climbed the stairs to the palisade walk and stood under the summer stars, letting his breath tear and sob in his throat. He had so much good fortune. A son of royal Welsh blood and a wife who had survived the bearing. A wife of his dreams. He had estates to govern, castles to build and a dynasty to forge. He had a stud of magnificent horses with foals already at foot. It was as though God had piled his trencher with so much largesse that he could not do justice on his part to the blessings he had received. He had everything he desired, more than everything, and he was afraid. Having climbed to the top, it was a long way to fall.

Closing his eyes, he let his mind fill with words. *All that God has made me for, and all that I have made for God. All come together now in this moment, in this ground, in this woman and child, and my life. The breath in my body, the air that fills my lungs. The fair firmament, and the sky. I cannot think, I cannot pray, but I am at one with God.* The words in his head took him to stillness. He stood a while longer on the palisade, swaying on his feet with the effects of drink and emotion, but at last turned and stumbled down the steps, not back to the celebration but rather to his own bed.

A week after her churching, Gerald having returned to Pembroke, Nesta was sitting in her hall watching over the baby, wondering what colour his eyes were going to be, when a youth came rushing from the gates with a message from the guards. 'Madam, we have guests,' he announced. 'The Lady of Powys is here.'

Nesta stared at him blankly, wondering what he was talking about.

'The lady Emma, wife of the lord Cadwgan ap Bleddyn,' the lad qualified.

Nesta recovered enough wit to tell the guard to admit the visitor and bring her to the ladies' hall. 'And send word to Pembroke, to my husband,' she added.

There was no time to change her gown, it would have to do. Muttering under her breath, she chivvied the servants to plump cushions and smooth coverlets, and sent for refreshments. Cadwgan ap Bleddyn had prospered under the Normans as a carrion-picker, swooping on their leavings with voracious opportunism, and he and her father had been enemies more often than allies. After her father's death he had invaded Dyfed, slaughtering and plundering. He had allied with the Montgomery faction against Henry, but then changed sides when he saw which way the conflict was going. Henry had brokered a marriage between Cadwgan and Emma, the daughter of Picot de Sai of Clun. He had also granted Cadwgan the town and port of Ceredigion, which had once been part of her father's territory. Nesta despised Cadwgan, but she did not underestimate him. But just what was his Norman wife doing here?

The woman ushered into Nesta's chamber was as thin and straight as a spear, with fine narrow features and a small, pursed mouth. She had sharp cheekbones and glassy green-blue eyes that busily assessed her surroundings. Nestling in her fur-lined cloak with its ornate metal clasps was a fluffy white dog with shiny jet eyes and a quivering nose.

Nesta rose from her seat. A moment of awkward etiquette ensued, for the lady Emma was wed to a Welsh prince but of lower status herself, and Nesta was of Welsh royal blood but with a husband of lower rank than Cadwgan. Eventually both women curtseyed to the other at the same time.

'Welcome to Carew,' Nesta said. 'Will you sit and take refreshment?'

'Thank you.' Emma handed her cloak to a servant, while keeping a tight hold on her little dog. She pressed a kiss to the top of its mop-fur head. 'This is Treasure,' she announced. 'He was a gift from my husband. He comes from an island far south of Rome – he's very rare.'

'How sweet.' Nesta knew how valuable these little dogs were. Lady Adele had possessed one. This one, trembling like a leaf, wore a blue collar with a silver bell. 'Would he like a dish of scraps?'

Emma's nostrils flared as if Nesta had insulted her. 'He eats from my own dish.' She sat down on a bench, placing the dog beside her, before gathering her skirts and swirling them for effect as she arranged them.

Nesta bit back the remark that she could provide Emma with a dish of scraps for her own use. 'What beautiful fabric,' she said instead.

Emma preened. 'My husband had it brought from Flanders.' She gazed round at the walls with a slight wrinkle of her nose. 'He gave me a Flemish hanging too – it covers one wall of our private chamber from side to side. If you come to Ceredigion, I will show you. There are compensations in any marriage, and Cadwgan is, after all, a prince.'

Nesta's fingers curled into claws at the woman's sweetly corrosive tone – it was like pouring honey over a toothache. 'It is a pity I cannot introduce you to my lord husband,' she said, 'but he is absent about his duties.'

'As is mine. But I did not come to visit your husband, I came to see you.'

Nesta raised her brows, but before she could enquire further the refreshments arrived in the form of a flagon of wine, cheese wafers and honey tarts.

Emma fed the little dog morsels of wafer from her dish. 'I heard you had borne your husband a fine son, so I came to express my felicitations. I know how important the birth of a male child is in a woman's life.'

'It is kind of you to come so far to do such a thing.' Nesta bade Eleri fetch Gwilym. 'Do you have sons?'

'One thus far – Henry – but he is at home with my women. My husband has older sons from his first wife of course, but mine will have a Norman patrimony from me.' She spoke of the older ones as if they were something undesirable, and Nesta pressed her lips together in suppressed irritation.

Eleri placed Gwilym in Nesta's arms and he showed her his new gummy smile. Emma de Sai murmured approving platitudes but Nesta could tell she was not really interested, paying more attention to her dog.

'There are other children too?' Emma said, clearly aware, but looking for Nesta to comment on them. Her gaze was needle-bright.

'Yes, the King's son is here, and my husband has a son from before we were married.'

'Ah,' said Emma. 'Does Welsh law pertain? Does your husband's firstborn have any claim to an inheritance here?' She fed the dog another piece of wafer.

'Indeed not!' Nesta could not keep the indignation from her tone even though she knew Emma was goading her to it. 'The land is passed on in my bloodline, not Gerald's. His son shall have whatever his father can spare for him, but it will not be any of mine.'

'Of course, and as it should be.' Emma's smile was tight and forced. 'I understand you still have a brother in Ireland?'

Nesta was at a loss with the woman. Her questions verged on rudeness and she had a way about her that made Nesta want to kick her out into the courtyard, preferably in the vicinity of a midden puddle, but there had to be something she was missing. 'Yes, although I have not seen him for many years.'

'But you hope you may do so again, I expect?'

'That will be as God wills,' Nesta replied tautly.

'Indeed . . . Forgive me for asking so many questions, but women in our position are gatherers of information and peace weavers, and we must do our part.'

'What sort of information do you want from me?'

Emma beckoned to her maid. 'I have brought you a gift which I hope you will accept in a spirit of alliance and peace.'

The maid knelt before Nesta and held out a package wrapped in a piece of linen secured with braid. Nesta accepted it and untied the linen to reveal a bolt of wool, dyed the deep red of a garnet stone. She recognised the quality of the dye, and that there was enough for a gown. 'How beautiful!' She was genuinely delighted, but still wary. 'Thank you, my lady. This is a generous gift.'

Her guest looked smug. 'I knew you would recognise fine cloth. We have a few things in common at least. I came to visit you because I was curious to see Carew and its lady. We have heard much in Ceredigion, but you can never trust rumour and gossip.'

Nesta raised her chin. She could feel the other woman's claws. 'But surely you are not here merely to satisfy your curiosity about rumours?'

Emma sniffed. 'Indeed not, and I had not finished speaking. I was going to say that I am here to extend peaceful greetings to you and your lord. You might ask why my husband has not come himself, but this is by way of a preliminary overture. As I said, we women are peace weavers and it is in both our interests that peace should indeed prevail. I hope we may become allies.'

Nesta suppressed a shudder, knowing a rejection would be foolish. Plainly Emma de Sai felt the meeting was necessary, even if her attitude did her no favours. From Cadwgan's point of view it was probably a good idea to send his wife to do his foraging. 'I hope so too,' she said with courtesy but no warmth. 'Of course, our husbands will have their own thoughts on the matter. Our marriages bind our lords to England's king and Gerald's loyalties are as solid as stone. Providing your own lord does not encroach beyond his boundaries, we shall remain neighbours in friendship, I am sure.'

'That is good to know, and your own lord the same.'

Emma de Sai departed soon after, leaving Nesta to puzzle. As her guest had said, women were the peace weavers, but Emma had definitely been reconnoitring and fishing for detail – perhaps even assessing how well defended Carew was, hence arriving without prior warning.

Gerald arrived from Pembroke in response to her message not long after Emma had gone on her way. 'Cadwgan's wife,' he said, looking surprised and thoughtful.

Nesta brought him a cup of wine. 'I did not warm to her. She was taking note of everything in order to report back.'

'I am sure you are right. You know she was one of Henry's concubines before she wed Cadwgan?'

Nesta stared at him. 'No, I did not! How do you know?'

He shrugged. 'It was gossip when I was at the Montgomerys' hearth. It would have happened shortly before you came to his attention. It was a brief affair, a matter of days, and he did not take her with him or send her to Woodstock, but it put de Sai in good standing with the King.'

In her mind's eye Nesta replayed all the nuances of Emma de Sai's expressions and words. Now she better understood the glimmers of tension and the undercurrents that were more than just fishing for details. They certainly had more in common than she had thought. Emma's son was called Henry, and Nesta counted up the months, but swiftly concluded that the child was Cadwgan's, but named to curry favour.

'If Cadwgan is searching out weaknesses or places to probe then we shall give him none,' Gerald said.

'He has several older sons, and is Lord of Ceredigion – he would have all of this area if he could.'

Gerald cupped his chin. 'I had dealings with his son Owain at the Pembroke siege, and I know all about Cadwgan's slipperiness. I am prepared to maintain a truce with him providing he keeps to his own lands. I am going to build a castle to guard my border with Ceredigion. When I go to plan the site, you can visit with the lady Emma again. There is no harm in cultivating Cadwgan's wife.'

Nesta concealed a grimace. She had better ways to spend her time than socialising with Emma de Sai, even if it was politically useful. 'She had a little white dog with her, so small she could hide it up her sleeve. She told me they come from overseas and are very rare and costly, but Cadwgan had managed to obtain one for her.'

Gerald grunted. 'Indeed,' he said without enthusiasm.

Nesta watched him to see if he had taken the hint, and thought that despite his apparent indifference he had. 'He was very sweet. She fed him from her own dish.'

Gerald snorted, and Nesta smiled to herself. She wasn't finished with him yet. After they had eaten and she was sitting at her sewing while Gerald mended a piece of harness, she said: 'That space along the wall by the window. It needs a proper hanging and a frieze painting above it. The lady Emma says that Cadwgan had one brought all the way from Flanders for her.'

Gerald eyed her sidelong, thinking that perhaps having Nesta cultivate Cadwgan's wife might not be such a good thing after all. A fluffy white lap dog and a Flemish wall hanging were no small undertakings in terms of cost and effort to obtain – especially the latter, and the hanging would have to be better than Cadwgan's or he would never hear the end of it. He received the distinct impression that Nesta was deliberately baiting him and that Emma's visit had left her like a cat with ruffled fur. She gave him a melting look, but he saw through it to the steel beneath. His first instinct was to ignore her remarks, but on the other hand he wanted her to be content, because then he could be content. Besides, she was part of his status, and ultimately the prestige of living as Welsh royalty came at a price. The more he paid, the more it was worth in the eyes of others. If Cadwgan had a Flemish wall hanging at Ceredigion, then they would have a greater one at Carew.

'I shall see what can be done,' he said. 'I said at our marriage you could have anything of me for the asking and I will keep that vow. You shall have a dog for your chamber companion, and you shall have a wall hanging from Flanders.'

Leaving her frame, she came and sat in his lap and folded

her arms around his neck. 'Thank you, husband.' She gave him a dazzling smile. 'You are so good to me!'

She kissed him warmly and his heart twisted. To have her embrace him of her own accord was worth a hundred dogs and wall hangings. He knew she did not reciprocate his feelings, but he held on to the hope that one day she might. He just needed patience – or bottomless pockets. When she looked at him like this, or thanked him with joy, his heart became a sun, and for now it was enough.

14

Fortress of Cenarth Bychan, near Cardigan,
Spring 1107

Gerald dismounted from Taran in the inner ward of his new fortification and, looking round at the work, sighed with satisfaction. Cenarth Bychan stood on a rocky promontory high above the river Teifi. The building work had commenced last autumn with a winter lay-off, but now the ditches were dug, the palisade was in place, and the timber gatehouse almost complete. The new fortress stood four miles south-east of Ceredigion, hard on the edge of Cadwgan's current territory. Gerald intended to remind his neighbour of exactly where the border between them stood. It was a statement of solidity and strength, and that Gerald was no weakling to be overrun, and possessed a base from which to make swift retaliation for any raids and infractions.

Cenarth was almost impregnable from the north with its steep, rocky gorge, and the river was sufficiently deep for good-sized supply ships to run upriver from the coast and dock. Gerald was established and secure – a player in the world. He had continued to strengthen Pembroke and improve Carew, turning it into a beautiful home and setting for Nesta, his jewel. Carew had two Flemish hangings to adorn the walls, exceeding her expectations, and she had her fluffy white dog. He was not so sure about its name, since she had insisted on calling it after him – Geri for short – but he had managed to regard it with a measure of amusement rather than insult.

His compensation was a blossoming of the domestic harmony he so valued, leading to the birth of a daughter a week ago. As soon as he was finished here he would return to Carew to see Nesta and the baby. His visit to Cenarth had coincided with her confinement and she had been unable to travel with him. Ideally he would have liked a second son to secure the dynasty, but there was time enough for that. A daughter would be useful for making marriage alliances, and he had already pondered the matter of a match with de Barry at Manorbier, or perhaps one of the Flemish families who had recently arrived to settle on lands in South Wales. Disastrous floods in Flanders had caused a displacement of people from their waterlogged homes and King Henry had offered them succour. He had commanded Gerald to settle some of them around Pembroke, and he had done so, although it had caused some friction with the local Welsh, and Nesta had been disgruntled. Her confinement meant he had not yet had an opportunity to speak to her. The decision was economically sound for the region, and an order from the King could not be defied. He was not looking forward to the conversation with his wife though, for Nesta was fiery and stubborn when roused, especially if she thought he was acting against Welsh advantage.

Dewi took Taran away to the stables and Gerald entered the private dwelling to wash his hands and face and change his riding clothes before going to dine. He was wiping his lips on a napkin when a guard came to tell him that a troop of Welsh had arrived and were requesting to speak with him. 'A hunting party, sire,' the soldier said. 'Ten men with spears and dogs. Their leader asks you to receive him as a courtesy to a neighbour – it's Owain ap Cadwgan.'

Putting his napkin down, Gerald stood up, ready to deny them entry, because never mind hunting, this was clearly a fishing expedition; but then he decided to play them on his own line and observe. 'Admit them,' he said. 'Serve them bread and cheese, and enough wine for two cups each, no more. A pity they were not on the way home from a hunt – they might have had some good venison to contribute.'

More than ten years had passed since Gerald had faced him at Pembroke but Owain ap Cadwgan's swagger remained the same and his charisma was a hot coal, brighter than before if anything. The wide sable collar of his cloak emphasised his broad shoulders. His hair shone like raven feathers and his eyes were a brown so dark that the pupil barely showed at the centre. Before, his skin had been smooth and taut with an oily bloom of youth. Now, fine lines etched the eye corners and creased the cheeks, but had not yet developed into full score lines. Two sleek gazehounds padded at his side, long-muzzled and copper-eyed.

'Thank you for offering your hospitality, my lord,' Owain said, bowing. He spoke passable Norman French these days, with a lilting accent. 'I am visiting my father before attending to other business and the hunt brought me close to this new castle of yours.' His white-toothed smile was wolfish.

Gerald gestured to a trestle for his men and had his squires pour wine and serve the bread and cheese. One of the Welsh, thin and muscular with untidy fair hair, cast sneering looks at Gerald's attendants and made a disparaging jest in Welsh about being served by Normans.

Gerald arched his brow.

Owain made a sign to his companion indicating in no uncertain terms that he was to keep his mouth shut, to which the man responded with a shrug and an unapologetic grin.

'My cousin, Madog,' Owain said. 'He has no manners, but he is a fearless huntsman so I tolerate him.'

'I am not sure your tolerance commends you,' Gerald replied, 'but enough of that. We all know people who will deliberately cross a line to see what will happen.' He showed Owain to a seat at the high table. 'At least your father is courteous to send his greetings, unless of course you are here of your own volition.'

Owain sat down, and spread his legs in a masculine gesture of domination. 'A little of both. I told him I might ride this way and he said that if so, I was to offer you our felicitations should you be in residence.' He raised his cup and took a hearty swallow of wine that removed half the contents in one go. 'Good wine.'

Gerald forbore to remark that if such was the case, Owain should take his time to savour it. 'The last time we had an encounter, I recall that I was feeding you and your companions with bacon flitches.'

Owain's laugh, warm and rich, rose from deep in his chest. 'Ah yes, indeed. You even carved messages in the rind encouraging us to feast. Had we known they were the last of your supplies the outcome would have been very different, I promise you.'

Gerald shrugged. 'We use the wits that God has given us.' Despite his determination to remain detached, he was almost warming to Owain even while alert to danger. He noted how Owain's men were looking intently round the hall, absorbing every detail, and he made a silent note to double the guard and be extra vigilant. 'Your stepmother paid us a visit a while back at Carew,' he said conversationally. 'My wife has stayed in contact with her and exchanged messages and gifts.'

Owain's amiable expression closed down. 'I do not often see my stepmother,' he said flatly. 'We do not cross each other's paths other than at certain family gatherings. I usually busy myself elsewhere.'

'Well, give the lady Emma my regards if you do see her. And perhaps tell her and your father that my own lady has been safely delivered of a daughter.'

'Congratulations to you and the lady Nesta.' Owain raised his cup in toast. 'I hope you will both visit our court at Ceredigion on another occasion.' He finished his wine and rose from the board. 'We will keep you no longer, but I am glad to have had this opportunity to meet again.'

Gerald smiled tightly. The 'opportunity to meet again' was Owain's way of staring his enemy in the eyes, and a declaration of a continuing power struggle. He returned Owain's look calmly, facing out the fire and glitter. 'I am glad to have met you also. Tales are often told around the hearth, but when a face is put to them, it colours the knowledge. Of course, I have yet to meet your father.'

'He is nothing like me.' Owain's smile flashed again. 'But we swim in the same sea and we have the same allies, enemies and ambitions. I thank you for your hospitality. Perhaps I shall repay it one day, although not in bacon flitches.'

He gestured to his party and they rose from the trestle table, cramming last pieces of bread into their mouths and gulping down their drinks. Owain's cousin openly stuffed a loaf inside his jerkin and fixed Gerald with an insolent stare, which Gerald marked but ignored.

When the gate had closed behind the hunting party, he summoned Ifan to his side and asked the scout what he had heard about Owain of late.

Ifan hitched his belt and drank the mead Gerald gave him. 'He's grown since he besieged you at Pembroke,' he said. 'From what I hear, he desires to rule in his father's stead, although they remain united for now. He knows how to bring men to his banner. He promises them all the booty, women and food they desire.' A grimace deepened the weather seams surrounding his eyes. 'He raids the lands of his enemies and trades his plunder in Dublin, and he makes plenty of money selling slaves to the Norse and Irish.' He touched his throat and the scars from the iron collar. Unbidden, he helped himself to more mead. 'Owain ap Cadwgan is a powerful man who attracts yet more power, but he has a tendency to be reckless and he squanders it in rashness. He talks up a blaze that he cannot sustain, and that cousin of his throws on furze and twigs and makes it brighter while it lasts. Father and son are like fire, but Cadwgan is contained and burns under a low flame; he is wily and cunning and uses his power to navigate dangerous straits, picking up morsels as he goes. Owain is a furnace so hot that eventually he will destroy himself and everything he touches, but men are still attracted to the blaze.'

'And men who play with fire always get burned.'

Ifan shrugged. 'Men who are the fire cannot sustain it without destroying that on which they feed.'

'If Cadwgan and Owain are coals, what then am I?' Gerald asked, curious as to his scout's reply.

Ifan finished his second cup and wiped his lips. 'You are the enemy of fire,' he said in his sing-song story-teller's voice. 'You are the river to quench it. But it is not a given, for if there is too much fire it will burn the water away, and if there is too much water it will flood the land, and how then shall an ordinary man kindle his hearth and his woman tend it?'

'Wise as ever,' Gerald said wryly, and Ifan responded with an acerbic smile.

* * *

Standing in the window-light, Gerald cradled his new daughter in his arms and watched her purse her lips and make small kissing noises at him. She had been baptised in his absence and as agreed with Nesta had been given the Welsh name of Angharad, meaning 'beloved'. The tenderness in his heart was very different from that of receiving his son nearly four years ago, but no less intense and perhaps even more protective. A daughter would further his dynasty in a different way, through marriage, and was as precious as a son.

Returning to the bedside, he sat down beside Nesta, who was still in confinement ten days after the birth, although eager to be up and about. 'My clever wife. We have two beautiful children, one of each. God is smiling on us indeed.'

She returned his smile, but it was superficial, and he wondered what was amiss. She had her wall hangings, her dog, a new baby christened with a Welsh name, and some beautiful tawny silk to make into a churching gown. He was home, and all was well with the world.

He began telling her about Cenarth Bychan and the progress he had made. 'I shall take you to see it when you have fully recovered. There is some excellent hunting nearby too, which reminds me.' He told her about Owain ap Cadwgan's visit and she sat up, alert now.

'I know he was bringing his warband for a good look around,' Gerald said. 'He said they were going hunting, and so they were, but it was not their only motive.'

'The house of Powys has long had its eye on Dyfed,' she said. 'They have Ceredigion, and they will be looking to expand their influence. I know Cadwgan has been setting his feet under the table at Shrewsbury with Richard de Belmeis.'

'Cadwgan is shrewd and wily,' Gerald answered. 'He has his area of influence and now has bought peace with a Norman wife and gained Ceredigion; he will be cautious in what he does. Owain is the one to set the fires – he is restless and ambitious. He's encouraged by his kin too: his cousin Madog struck me as someone who would light a fire just to watch trees burn – or homesteads. The situation will bear watching, and I shall send a report to de Belmeis.'

The chill returned to Nesta's expression. 'Yes, you should write to de Belmeis, and when you do, you should mention the Flemings. While you have been at Cenarth, more have arrived under his safe conduct.'

From the spark in her eyes, he realised that her irritation was caused by the issue of the Flemish refugees who had to be found land on which to settle – Welsh land. 'Surely it is no bad thing to have the expertise of Flemish weavers? They can make fine cloth on our doorstep, and everyone will prosper.'

'Except for the Welsh,' she snapped. 'These people are being settled here on the English king's order, under your direction. What of my people? Are they to become foreigners in their own land?'

'Of course not! They will farm the sheep and the Flemish will weave the wool. It will be good for both communities. I see no reason why you should object.'

Nesta pressed her lips together. That he saw no reason for her objection rubbed salt into her wounds and made her furious. These changes were being forced on her without a say. The Flemings would owe no allegiance to her or her bloodline and they would have no welcome for her brother when he returned as rightful ruler. Gerald would not see it in those terms, indeed would be horrified, she suspected; she could tell from the set of his jaw that whatever she said, he would ignore her. She could have anything she wanted providing it was about fabric and decoration, dogs and fripperies and giving a daughter a Welsh name. And while such things all added to her status as Lady of Carew, they did nothing to address the political will of her family.

'Because you give me no say. You married me to strengthen your presence here, but what have I had from it? What have my family had except to be burdened under your Norman yoke and ignored?'

'You have your inheritance,' he countered with a frown. 'I have not interfered with how you run Carew. I have given you a son to follow in your stead, a son from your womb who claims royal Welsh blood. Your line will continue in strength in our children.'

'But I had no choice in the say of their father!' The words blazed out of her before she could think better of them.

Very carefully, Gerald returned Angharad to her cradle. 'Your circumstances could be far worse. I suggest you look to what you do have, madam. I had no choice either, even though I admit you were my dream. I try to see everything I am given as something to be cared for and cherished and made better. I should go. I have work to do and, as you say, Flemings to deal with.'

As he closed the door behind him with exaggerated care, Nesta seized her cup from the bedside and hurled it at the wood, then put her face in her hands and wept, while her ladies watched her wide-eyed. Dear God, just now she hated Gerald and she hated herself. He was so calm, so reasonable, even when she pushed him. He always had an answer, and most of the time he was right, and that made it worse. He would walk out rather than argue with her, and then go his own way whatever she said, leaving her impotent and fuming.

Angharad's birth had been hard on her in ways beyond the body. Bearing her had been easier than either of her sons, but she feared for her daughter's future and how she was going to protect her from the ways of men. She had thought to be in a better position of power as a married woman with possessions, but the past was always with her, sharp as a thorn in her side, and however she moved, it dug ever more deeply into her flesh.

Sighing heavily, Gerald sat down on a stool in the small chamber used by the scribes and palmed his face, at a loss, his hurt all the sharper because he had believed until now that he and Nesta had reached an understanding. She seemed to enjoy her daily life with him. They would go out riding and walking, or play chess and dice in the hall. She would listen to him sing and play the harp. Sometimes she would even sit in his lap and stroke his hair.

He had his areas of work and she had hers. He would no more expect her to train the squires and drill the men than she would expect him to design and stitch a gown. They had their pre-ordained roles and he had tried and tried to ensure she was comfortable and satisfied, but it was not enough and he did not know what else to do except walk away. He had no choice with the Flemings for the King had ordained it, and in truth it was a fine idea. But Nesta would fight him all the way, and even if he won, he would lose.

His heart heavy, he rose to his feet and prepared to continue with his tasks. Walking towards the hall, he met Marguerite de Barry coming from the opposite direction bearing a pile of folded linen for Nesta's chamber. He looked at her rosy, handsome face and her comfortable, solid frame and almost felt wistful.

Marguerite greeted him, and remarked what a beautiful little girl Angharad was. 'I wish I had a daughter,' she said, 'but God has not seen fit to grant me that joy – not yet anyway.'

Gerald gave her a distracted smile and her pleasant face filled with concern. 'Is something troubling you, my lord?'

He sighed and rubbed the back of his neck. 'Nesta is not best pleased with me. Sometimes I think we men cannot do right for doing wrong.'

'That would be more than sometimes if you heard my husband talk,' she replied with amused asperity.

'She objects to the Flemings settling here, but I can do little about it, and besides, their skills will bring prosperity to the area.'

'Yes, we have some tilling the land not far from Manorbier – they lost everything in the floods. But the man is a skilled weaver, and his wife spins fleece into yarn faster than anyone I have seen – her children too, and that includes the boys.'

'Will you speak to Nesta for me?' he asked hopefully.

Marguerite looked dubious. 'Do you think I will have better fortune than you?'

He shrugged. 'You could do no worse. Whatever happens I am set upon this course, whether she hates me to the bottom of her soul or not.'

Marguerite's expression softened and she patted his arm. 'Oh, she does not hate you, whatever she may have said.'

Gerald was not so sure. 'I am the vile Norman, trampling everyone down,' he said wryly, and then closed his mouth before anything else escaped him.

'Women who have recently borne children often suffer from unbalanced humours,' Marguerite said. 'Their wombs need time to adjust. I wept enough tears to sail a boat after bearing my William, and Odo threatened to leave me and go on crusade!' She chuckled. 'Nesta will come to herself by and by. She dislikes confinement, as we both know from last time – it's like trying to cage a lioness. But I shall speak to her as a friend if the opportunity arises. I suggest you send some of the Flemish to visit her and make supplication – the ones that make the best textiles. Let her see what they do. Let her become involved in their lives and business, and by that I mean properly involved. That way they become part of her world rather than an imposition forced on her by others.'

Gerald gazed at her in dawning hope, and his mood lightened. 'An excellent notion. If it were not inappropriate, I would embrace you here and now!'

Marguerite laughed and shrugged, but her complexion reddened until her face was the same colour as her cheeks. 'It seems like common sense to me,' she said. 'But if you want to regard it as great wisdom, I will not object!'

Nesta studied the bolts of cloth the Flemish merchant had placed before her. The quality was superb, thick and with a plush gleam in the late afternoon light. Of course, it was not as fine as the fabric from Italy, but still very good and would fetch a high price in any market.

Marguerite had suggested casually while they sat over their sewing that she might at least look at the Flemings' cloth to see if it was any good, and take her cut from it and make a profit. If the Flemish settlers were going to be here anyway, why not make use of them? Welsh, Flemish or Norman, she could rule them all. Put like that, Nesta had thought it worth a trial at least.

The merchant presenting her with the goods was in his middle years and stockily handsome, with curly hair, showing silver amid the strands, and a full beard, clean and combed. He spoke a smattering of recently learned Welsh words but was fluent in French and Latin. His name was William of Brabant and he represented the settlers in the area from Flanders and Brabant. A few of the textile workers had accompanied him, and stood at a respectful distance.

William of Brabant spoke of the weaves and dyes used in processing the cloth and revealed a deep knowledge of the textiles and the markets where they might be sold, and possessed an entire network of customers and contacts. Diffident initially, Nesta was impressed by his expertise, and found herself warming to him personally. He was dignified, but not self-important. He had humility without being obsequious and knew his own worth. Now she understood what Gerald had been saying, and why Marguerite had encouraged her, although it did not make her grateful. She was still not overjoyed that these people were settling on Welsh land, but she accepted that they were bringing increased opportunity and prosperity to Dyfed.

Gerald had been absent at Pembroke while she was conducting the meeting at Carew – being diplomatic, she suspected – but he returned in time to dine with the Flemings and continue the discussion of practical matters.

Later, when William of Brabant and his company had left, Gerald lingered in her chamber, leaning against the wall, arms folded, saying nothing; waiting.

Nesta was haughty at first and a little mutinous. William of Brabant had left her a gift of the fabulous wool cloth with the gleaming nap – enough to make a gown – and he had presented her with ribbons, laces and braid to trim it. She took the fabric in her hands now, unable to resist its feel, knowing it was bribery but still wonderstruck. When she spoke, she addressed the cloth rather than Gerald. 'You should still have asked me about the settlement and I am concerned about my own people, but I admit the Flemings will bring prosperity to the region. I am prepared to be civil and not stand in their way, providing they pay their just dues.'

Gerald unfolded his arms. 'Am I forgiven then?'

'I did not say that.'

'No, but will you say it now?'

'I will think on it,' she replied, hating to be pushed into a corner, hating to concede anything to her Norman husband. There was a dissonance within her. On the surface and day to day she could live with him, and even sometimes take pleasure in his company and the familiar routines. She could appreciate his gifts, and tenderness, even while thinking they were his way of laying crumbs into a trap of compliance. A dog, gold rings, wall hangings. He needed her and she did not need him, and had never wanted him, and that made him weak, and her strong, even while it took her nowhere. And yet, beneath the deep resentments, deeper still, lay emotions too difficult to process because she knew she would have to dive through fathoms of darkness to reach them, and was terrified of what she might find.

'I promise you will not regret it.'

She raised her head to look into his eyes. 'Never make promises, Gerald, it is too dangerous.'

'But a promise is a vow of intent, and a marker on the path. The only danger comes to the soul from not keeping a promise.'

'Your own promise, yes,' she agreed, 'but do not put your vow on how I will ever feel about anything.'

15

Palace of Carew,
Autumn 1109

Nesta gazed in awe at the bolt of cloth William of Brabant had sent to her as a gift. The woven wool was so fine it could have been silk, and it was dyed a deep mulberry colour without flaw. Following her meeting with him she had accepted the presence of the Flemish community, although she remained watchful. Her relationship with William was cordial though, and he kept it thus with regular gifts and appreciations.

'You could make a fine gown for the Christmas feast,' Gerald said. 'You suit the colours and no one else will have a gown so fine – not even Cadwgan's wife.'

'Do you think I care what Cadwgan's wife wears?'

'Yes, I think you do care to dress better than her as a princess of Dyfed.' He picked up six-year-old Gwilym and swung him round in his arms. 'Do you want to come and help me groom Taran? Henry too.' He nodded at his stepson, who was nearly ten.

'Yes!' Gwilym cried.

Gerald set him down. 'Go to the yard and find Dewi and meet me there in a moment. Walter's there too. I want a quick word with your mother.'

The boys ran off with Geri racing after them, and he watched them with a smile before turning back to Nesta. 'I have received a message from Cadwgan ap Bleddyn, inviting us to his Christmas court at Ceredigion. It is time I paid a visit to Cenarth anyway. We can stay there for a few days and attend the feast – if you wish to, of course. I can refuse him and we can feast here at Carew.'

Nesta narrowed her eyes. 'Why should Cadwgan invite us to Ceredigion?' Now she understood his mention of Cadwgan's wife.

Gerald shrugged. 'I suppose he is curious and we are neighbours as well as rivals. He will seek to draw things from me and test my strength, just as his son did when he came to Cenarth on that hunting trip. Of course, we can explore alliances too. Richard de Belmeis or one of his representatives will be there. You shall be the greatest lady in Wales, and I shall be proud to have you on my arm. Your prestige will be mine, and mine will be yours. Besides, the living chambers at Cenarth need your touch. You have made such a comfortable home here at Carew, I know you will do the same at Cenarth. You may furnish it as you choose and make it a fitting place to dwell.'

Nesta stroked the cloth. His cajolery made her want to snap at him. However, the fabric was wonderful and the notion of wearing a gown to outshine Cadwgan's wife and of visiting Ceredigion in all of her wealth and beauty was irresistible. No other woman would be as magnificent as she was. As Gerald had also pointed out, she would enjoy furnishing Cenarth to her taste. 'I think it would be a good idea,' she conceded graciously.

'Excellent!' He kissed her cheek and went to the door. 'It is October now – plenty of time to make arrangements. I had better go and join our sons before they grow too impatient.'

'My lord requests to know if you are ready, my lady?' Walter said, poking his head around the door. He had recently taken up full squiring duties for Gerald and would be leaving the household in the spring to train at Manorbier with Odo de Barry. His hazel eyes opened wide and his jaw dropped. Nesta preened, gratified by his response. She thought about saying that Gerald would have to wait a little longer yet, just to annoy him, knowing he was tapping his feet in the courtyard, but decided against it, for they needed to leave for Ceredigion now and she wanted to make a dramatic entrance without being too tardy.

'Yes,' she said. 'A moment while I put on my cloak, and you may take me to your father.'

Ceridwen and Eleri draped a thick blue cloak lined with fur around her shoulders and fastened it with two heavy gold clasps. Satisfied that no one was going to outshine her, Norman or Welsh, Nesta put up her head and gestured Walter to escort her.

Gerald looked up as Nesta emerged from the hall with her ladies, Walter walking before them, and could only stare. He had thought her beyond beautiful on their wedding day as his bride, but now he was gazing at a goddess. A coronet jewelled with rubies bound her gold-edged veil, and her gown, showing between the edges of the cloak, had a centre panel of embroidered birds and flowers. She had reddened her lips and done something to enhance her eyes.

He had to clear his throat before he could speak. 'My love, you look as if you have stepped from the pages of a Welsh tale.'

'That is my intent,' she answered. 'When the queen of another world walks into a chamber, all heads turn, and all wonder at her power.' She flashed him a brilliant smile. 'And as her consort, you are the most fortunate of men.'

'I am indeed.' Gerald bowed to her, not sure he felt fortunate. He was uncomfortable, almost afraid. The balance of power had shifted.

He offered his arm to escort her to her mare – one of Hera's daughters with a coat like grey sea undershot with gold. Even in their thick winter coats the horses were magnificent, and their polished harnesses rang out with the sound of silver bells as they set out to Ceredigion, their breath creating mist trails in the air, their hooves cracking the ice in the frozen puddles.

Nesta had never met Cadwgan ap Bleddyn, although her father had often spoken of him, usually with curses. Cadwgan's hair and moustache were badger-stripe grey. He was thin, but wirily strong, and his eyes were calculating even while he smiled in welcome.

He clasped Gerald's hand and spoke in Norman French with a heavy accent. 'Welcome to my hall and my Christmas feast, my lord. This is a time for peace and goodwill among neighbours. I am pleased you decided to come.'

Gerald answered in Welsh. 'I thank you for inviting me and my lady wife, the princess Nesta.'

Cadwgan bowed to Nesta. 'Word has spread far and wide of your great beauty, and word does not lie. Your father and I were not always allies, but we were distant kin, and I welcome you warmly to my home.'

Nesta curtseyed and swiftly straightened. She was a full hand's length taller than Cadwgan. 'I thank you.' She pitched her voice to be low and musical. 'I have not been to Ceredigion since I was a small child, when my father was still alive.'

The moment's uncomfortable pause was swiftly covered by a formal greeting to Cadwgan's wife, Emma, whose green silk gown revealed the high swell of another pregnancy. A heavy gold chain, flashing with a pendant in the style of Constantinople, hung at her breast, and an ornate clasp of Welsh gold pinned her cloak.

'I am glad you could come,' Emma said. 'As you see, my lord and I have been blessed, and we hope for a new son or daughter in the spring.' She rested her hand on her womb in emphasis, her smile feline.

'I am pleased for you, my lady,' Nesta replied. Since Cadwgan had several sons from a first, Welsh marriage, she wondered just what his Norman heirs would receive and if they would displace his other sons. Certainly Emma was capable of pushing for such an outcome.

They sat down to feast. The tables were covered with expensive cloths of sun-bleached linen. Nesta decided she would have the same at Cenarth and Carew, but with more embroidery, and perhaps some silver cups and a new hanging for behind the dais table. Richard de Belmeis, King Henry's governor on the Marches, was in attendance, and resplendent in the glittering robes he had recently acquired on being raised to the bishopric of London, but few other Normans were present.

It was so good to talk Welsh again and have it spoken to her in return as the first language of Cadwgan's court. The central hearth glowed dragon-fire red and lit the faces of the people gathered at the tables. The scent of the beeswax candles was heady and honeyed. Goblets clinked, and the rich aroma of roast meat wafted from the platters. Cadwgan's bards entertained the company with tales from Welsh folklore and the notes of the harp plucked at Nesta's own heartstrings with a bitter-sweet pain. This was *hiraeth* and belonging. This was what had once been, and for a few magical hours she could dwell in the past and imagine the future her path might have taken. She could almost forget about Gerald, who was alert and quietly observing, but in this vibrant atmosphere a vague outline in the background. The smoke rose in soft layers towards the louvres, adding to the other-worldly ambience, making everyone not only a watcher but a participant in the mythical tale unwinding from the harp strings.

The spell was broken by a sudden commotion at the hall door, heralding the arrival of a latecomer to the feast. Brushing flecks of snow from his cloak with impatient swipes of his hand, he strode up the hall, his wide shoulders made even broader by the sable lining of his cloak turned over like a collar. His hair was the glossy-black of raven feathers, and he had a glamour about him that drew every eye.

He paused theatrically before the high table and went down on one knee before Cadwgan. 'My lord father,' he said, bowing his head and folding one arm over his thigh. An embellished dagger hilt gleamed in the sheath of his waist belt. 'I am sorry to be late, but I had business to attend to, and then my horse cast a shoe, and it started snowing, but I am here now, and ready to do my filial duty.'

Cadwgan shook his head. 'When are you not a snag in my arrangements?' he asked, but he smiled as he left his seat to kiss his eldest son and raise him to his feet. Cadwgan was at an immediate disadvantage in height and breadth, and diminished by the other's charisma. 'Come and greet your stepmother and our guests.' He drew his son to the table. The newcomer dipped his head to Emma, who gave him a tepid incline in return.

Cadwgan introduced Owain to his other guests at the high table. Nesta was aware of Gerald's tension at her side, but her main focus was upon the newcomer; indeed, she could not look away.

Owain bowed to Gerald, who reciprocated with stiff courtesy. 'We meet again,' he said. 'I am pleased to see you at my father's court.' He turned his attention to Nesta. 'Welcome, my lady,' he said in Welsh. 'You grace us all with your presence and beauty.'

Nesta tilted her head to him and gave him an aloof look, although her heart had kicked in her chest. His gaze was admiring but did not stretch courtesy; but as she met his eyes, she recognised his fire and answered it with her own.

He took his place at his father's side and cast off his cloak to reveal a wine-red tunic encrusted with gold embroidery. Bracelets of braided gold and silver clinked on his wrists and heavy gold rings adorned his powerful fingers. He accepted a brimming cup and raised it in toast to his father, then took several deep swallows. Stroking red droplets from his moustache, he turned to Gerald.

'I saw some magnificent horses in the stables and the groom told me they were yours.'

'Yes, they are,' Gerald replied.

'They are from my father's stud herd with some blood from the Montgomery horses of Robert de Belleme,' Nesta said, bringing Owain's attention back to her.

'Ah, the storm-horses of Dyfed,' Owain said with a smile. 'I thought so. It is a fortunate man who has access to such stock. Do you ever sell them?'

He had addressed the question to Nesta, but Gerald answered with a shake of his head. 'Not often. We are building up the herd and King Henry has first call on any we do pass on.' He nodded to Richard de Belmeis who was listening with interest.

'That is a shame, for a man could turn a fine profit from selling such progeny.' Owain drained his cup, and a servant immediately refilled it. 'I have a likely young mare, due her first season this spring. Would you consider lending me your stallion to cover her?'

'I would be open to discussion at another time,' Gerald said without enthusiasm.

Nesta silently fumed. The horses were hers because they had been her father's and it was her right to say, not Gerald's, whatever he thought; but she bit her tongue, rather than bring an argument to the feast.

'Thank you, I appreciate it,' Owain said. 'I hear you have been busy at Cenarth since last I visited.'

Gerald shrugged. 'Strong border defences are essential.'

Owain grinned. 'Yes indeed, for who knows what liberties your neighbours might take if given the slightest chance.'

'Who knows indeed?' Gerald responded flatly.

Owain stroked his moustache. 'My father deals in diplomacy and war – as do I as his heir.' He shot a scornful glance at his pregnant Norman stepmother. 'But I am also a trader. I visit Ireland often with horses and goods to sell. Perhaps we could do business together?'

Nesta was immediately alert at the mention of Ireland. Here was another potential avenue for sending messages to her brother, although Owain and Gruffydd might prove to be rivals as well as allies. Even so, it was worth considering because it would not involve Gerald's scrutiny. The glances Owain kept sending in her direction were unsettling, but in an exhilarating way. Perhaps Owain and her brother might even make a pact and push the Normans out of Wales. What a day that would be.

Gerald nodded. 'I would need to know more specifics.'

Owain started on his second cup of wine. 'There is wealth to be had from Ireland, and soldiers as you know from being Constable of Pembroke. You have those Flemish weavers settled now, on your land, and more arriving – or so we hear. You could sell some of the cloth in Dublin to good advantage, and you could trade for furs and wheat. There are many opportunities if you know where to look.' Owain pushed his fingers through his hair, calling attention to the bracelets glinting on his arm.

Gerald's face was expressionless, but Nesta could tell he was considering what Owain had said. Her own emotions swirled with excitement. Owain was like a glittering dark jewel; a shard of firelit obsidian among plain pebbles.

Following the meal there was dancing, with men and women circling and interweaving. Nesta changed partners and clasped hands many times over. Gerald took part in a couple of the rounds, but then retired to talk to Richard de Belmeis, Cadwgan and Cadwgan's wife, who was not dancing because of her pregnancy. Nesta, however, threw herself into the entertainment with every fibre of her being, joyous as a girl, keenly aware of all the people watching and admiring her. And if she was the most outstanding lady present, then Owain was the man who matched her. When they clasped hands and turned in the dance the touch of his skin on hers was a lightning jolt, and when their eyes met they were spark and flame. She imagined kissing his mouth and having him between her legs, and it sent an exquisite sharp twinge through her belly and loins, and for the first time she knew pure, raw lust.

Gerald watched Nesta amid the dancers as he drank. Outside it was still snowing and settling, but inside the fire blazed, the walls were festooned with pine-scented greenery, and the mead was a taste of summer to keep the cold at bay.

He could see that Nesta was relishing every moment, and he watched her with poignant pleasure, for never had she thrown back her head and laughed like that with him. There was a sparkle about her tonight that drew every eye. His pride in her filled him up; there was not another woman in the room to match her. But her vivaciousness disconcerted him too – her strength, her passion, her Welshness. At Carew he had seen glimmers, but this was Nesta free and unfettered, and she took his breath away and choked his throat. He realised how much of an alien he was in this hall, and although he had been offered every hospitality, he was on his guard for sleight of hand or treachery, and on the lookout for whispers and secret conversations.

Owain left the dancing and joined Gerald to quench his thirst. 'Your wife is a fine dancer, my lord.'

Gerald returned Owain's coal-dark stare. 'I know my good fortune. Are you a married man?'

Owain shook his head and flashed his smile. 'Not yet. I am biding my time for the right woman.' He gestured with his cup in Gerald's direction. 'I meant what I said about trading prospects. They pay well in Dublin for Welsh and Norman goods.'

Gerald remembered the marks of a slave collar on Ifan's throat. Owain made income from capturing men and women and selling them to the Norse and Irish. 'I shall think on the matter,' he said neutrally.

'It would be to our mutual advantage, I promise you that.'

Gerald thought that he had had enough trouble from Nesta on the matter of promises. This man, he suspected, would only keep his word to his own advantage and an oath would only last the lifetime of the breath it was spoken with. 'We shall see,' he said. 'Will your cousin be part of your entourage?'

'My cousin?'

Gerald nodded in the direction of Madog ap Rhyrid who had drunk far too much and was trying to pick a fight with two other young Welshmen, but was being pulled back by his companions.

Owain curled his lip. 'He no longer rides with my warband. He courts other men he believes will offer him better reward, but he has an inflated sense of his own worth. He will learn soon enough the true value of his sword, and in the meantime, I do not have to pay him.'

Gerald said nothing beyond a grunt of acknowledgement. Welsh kinship ties were labyrinthine and volatile and someone was always at someone else's throat. If Owain was unpredictable, Madog ap Rhyrid wasn't, and had he been a Norman, someone would have hanged him by now.

Nesta had feasted well and drunk plenty but was still in command of her faculties. When Gerald went outside for a piss, Owain quietly took his place at her side. The hair rose on her nape, and heat flushed her face. He refilled her cup, and when he returned it to her their fingers touched and their eyes met. He dropped his hand as if the contact had been a mistake, but they both knew it was deliberate.

'You dance like a young doe,' he said. 'Where did you learn to step so nimbly – surely not at the Norman court?'

Nesta laughed bitterly and shook her head. 'I learned very little of this type of dancing at the Norman court. I remember the steps of the Welsh ones from when I was a girl.'

Owain's eyes gleamed. 'Surely that can be no time at all, for you are little more than a girl now. I would not even guess you were the mother of children. There is no woman in this room more beautiful than you – indeed I judge in the whole of Wales.'

Nesta laughed again, for his courtliness was so exaggerated that it was a form of jest, and the twinkle in his eyes compounded her impression. But she enjoyed his flirtation. Here was a Welsh prince of his people lavishing attention on her in a dangerous, exciting way.

Under cover of the firelit shadows, he took her hand and ran his fingers up and down her palm. 'In truth,' he said in a low voice, 'I do not think your husband understands or appreciates what he has.'

Nesta withdrew from his touch and looked down, but her breathing quickened. He had moved with such swift opportunity that it revealed his rashness in the face of danger – that he would dare to make the impossible leap across a chasm – but his recklessness made her feel reckless too. 'Do not underestimate my husband,' she murmured, and looked away, checking the room for Gerald's return.

'I do not,' Owain said. 'He seems to me a cautious and cunning man, for I admit he bested us at Pembroke with his ruse – although I am wise to him now.' He touched Nesta's arm in a more open gesture this time. 'You heard us speaking of trade and being of mutual help to each other, given my connections with Ireland and several merchant captains.'

Nesta lifted her head. 'Yes, I did. You could bear messages to my kin there if I asked you?'

'I would do so gladly,' Owain said with his quick smile. 'Whatever you want, I can obtain it for you.'

'For the right price.'

Owain dropped one eyelid in a near-wink. 'Yes, but let us not talk of price just now. There will be better opportunities.'

'Those horses are mine, not my husband's,' she said after a moment. 'You should ask me, not him.'

Owain raised his brows. 'My apologies, I misunderstood. Then perhaps you would be amenable to my request? To have the stallion cover one of my mares?'

Nesta glanced at him sidelong. 'Perhaps,' she said, aware of the nuances beyond a simple request.

Gerald returned and Owain bowed and moved away to

converse elsewhere. Nesta turned to Gerald with a forced smile, but she was still tingling from her encounter with Owain, and their brief conversation had only whetted her appetite. She could still feel the touch of his fingertips over her wrist and palm. It was dangerous, but he had made her feel alive and in charge of her own destiny – he had given her a choice.

The snow continued to fall and Nesta and Gerald changed their plans and stayed overnight in Ceredigion. Cadwgan found sleeping space in the hall for Gerald and his knights, and provided pallets and blankets. Nesta was given a bed in the ladies' quarters with Cadwgan's wife.

Gerald remained awake and watchful throughout the night. Although Cadwgan had been more than hospitable, he still felt unsafe, and lay with his back to the wall and his sword close to hand. Even if Nesta was secure with the lady Emma, and had clearly enjoyed the feast and festivities, he still felt as though they were bedding down inside a den of thieves.

In the morning, his head throbbing from lack of sleep, Gerald rose early and went outside to assess the weather conditions and decide if they could risk the return to Cenarth in daylight. The snow was deep and crumpy, reaching the top of his boots, but a horse would manage the five miles and the sky was clear all the way to the fading stars without sign of more snowfall. He made his way to the stables to speak to the grooms, telling them to make ready.

Gerald was still outside when Nesta came down to the hall to break her fast. Cadwgan's wife was resting in her chamber, but Nesta was too unsettled to remain there with her, and was irritated by her company. She knew they would be leaving today if Gerald had his way. It was a clear, bright morning and there was no reason to linger, for the snow, although deep, was navigable.

Last night had returned her to her Welsh heritage, and when she thought of Owain ap Cadwgan, it was like drinking potent, dark wine. He was still in her head; she could not stop thinking about him. Without the Norman invasion, the dynasties of Dyfed and Powys might well have united in marriage. In another life, she could have been Owain's consort.

She dined with a few other guests who were preparing to travel or were already about their business, and some who had never been to bed. She was not especially hungry, for she had drunk too much wine last night, but she nibbled on some bread and honey, fortifying herself for the journey but wishing she could stay longer.

Gerald's son, Walter, came to fetch her, saying that all was ready to leave, and Gerald was waiting. Nesta nodded and dismissed him, and as she fastened her cloak she noticed Owain arriving in the hall. He was attractively rumpled, with dark stubble along his jawline, sleepy eyes, and a smile for her.

'I heard you were making an early departure, my lady,' he said. 'I have arisen to bid you farewell, although I wish you – and your husband – were staying another day or two, so we could become better acquainted.'

Nesta felt the heat in her face. 'I too wish we were staying longer, but I cannot.' Meeting his eyes, she fancied she saw in them a recognition of her constraints as the wife of a Norman invader, and the unsubtle hint that she did not have to be. Last night she had feasted and danced among her own people for the first time in sixteen years, and the Normans had been the outsiders and it had felt magnificent. She didn't want it to be over.

'I regret that you must leave, but I am glad you enjoyed your visit. We do things differently here, but no less well than they are done in your own castles, although I suppose you are accustomed to a higher way of life with your fine Norman lord.'

Nesta shook her head. 'Your assumption is wrong. For the first time in many, many years I have felt at home and among kindred who understand me.' She turned away, for she had said too much and people were waiting for her.

Owain secured his cloak and prepared to accompany her outside. 'I am glad to hear of your pleasure, my lady, but it pains me to think of you being unhappy when you return to your other life. I hope we may meet again soon.'

She dipped her head without answering, while her blood surged.

'I shall be visiting your husband to arrange a trade deal and hoping to hunt when the snow has cleared enough. Make a list of what you need and I will give you anything you desire – anything.' His disarming smile was filled with mischievous innuendo and her body tingled.

Once outside, Nesta picked her way delicately across the snow to Gerald and the horses. She could tell from the way he was standing that he was impatient to be gone. She curtseyed to Cadwgan and thanked him warmly for his hospitality. Owain had escorted her out and stayed close, ensuring she did not slip, and the awareness of his proximity was like liquid fire in her bones.

As they rode out, she vowed not to look over her shoulder, but the temptation was too great. Casting a backward glance, she saw Owain still watching her, his heavy cloak thrown back, his hands on his hips.

'That was interesting,' Gerald remarked. 'It was good to meet Cadwgan ap Bleddyn face to face. Even if I dislike him, we are pragmatic men, and if de Belmeis can work with him, so can I.'

'Yes,' she replied. 'His son said he might ride over to Cenarth and speak with you further on matters of trade, and I said he was welcome.'

Gerald nodded, although his eyes narrowed in the way that they did when he was ambivalent about something – superficially agreeing but less certain beneath. 'He's interested in the horses, but he will have to come further south or send a representative if he wants to inspect them. The same with the cloth and the weaving.'

'He offered to help me with items for the chamber at Cenarth, and said he could bring me a set of Irish drinking horns.' She said nothing about the horses, but thought she would do all she could to make sure Owain's request was met.

'Let him visit,' Gerald said. 'He will succeed his father, even if the lady Emma has sons. I do not trust him as far as I could throw a spear, but it is best to know your enemy – I daresay he feels the same way about me.' He gave his wife a hard stare. 'Make no mistake, I do not consider Owain ap Cadwgan a friend, and even if I do enter into trade with him for mutual profit, we shall never be allies.'

They rode on, and Nesta's stomach continued to flutter, her mind filled with the image of Owain's glittering good looks, while she wondered how soon he would come to Cenarth.

Owain sat at a table, resting his elbows on last night's stained cloth stubbled with crumbs and wax. His cup was half full of leftover wine from the keg that had been broached to fete their Norman guests. He had developed a taste for wine, and traded it to the Irish when he could, although he was contemptuous of it too, because it was Norman.

His thoughts dwelt on Nesta and how fine she had looked the night before. Her flashing eyes, her laughter and vibrance.

The wife of a Norman oppressor, stolen from her own people and forced to bear his children. He hadn't wanted a woman so badly since the first desperation of adolescence. She was royalty, a princess, and despoiled by that clod Gerald. Despoiled too by that Norman weasel of a king. If only he and his father had arrived at Carew ahead of the Normans.

The humiliation over the siege at Pembroke was still an aching scar, and although he had smiled at Gerald yesterday and offered to trade with him, his gut was sour. Gerald possessed Nesta and enjoyed her body. He had built Norman castles on Welsh lands and settled those lands with Flemings and foreigners, thrusting deep roots into territory that was not his. Owain's hatred for the Normans was visceral. His father disgusted him. How could he have bound himself to their vile ways by taking a Norman wife and lying with her?

Cadwgan entered the hall, looked round with his hands on his hips, then walked up to Owain. 'Drink my hall dry, son, why don't you?' he said.

Owain gestured to the jug. 'There is plenty left. Do not worry, I won't be under your feet for much longer; I doubt either of us could stomach the experience. I have a merchant ship waiting for me at Aberteifi – I have a cargo to load for Ireland – and I have a few people to visit. You see to your business, and I shall see to mine.'

'Oh yes, what sort of people?'

Owain finished his cup and leaned back from the table. 'Our Norman guests. I thought I would ride over to Cenarth before I sail. Gerald FitzWalter may want to put a little trade our way, and I am interested in his horses.'

'Just his horses?' Cadwgan said with heavy inflection.

'Of course,' Owain responded, radiating innocence. 'He controls the reins – so to speak – of the storm-horses of Carew, and I would dearly love to add that strain to our own herds. Besides, it is always useful to know the strength of our neighbour's defences, especially on our borders. We should keep an eye on his doings.' He gestured with an open hand. 'Unless you want to ride over yourself and visit?'

Cadwgan shook his head and grimaced. 'I leave that to you. I don't want you underfoot in my hall.'

'You mean your wife does not want me underfoot in what she sees as her hall,' Owain retorted. 'She need not worry; the feeling is mutual. I am going to check the stud at Aber tomorrow. I will send you a message if I need to.'

Owain rose to his feet and left the hall, shaking his shoulders to rid them of tension. His father increasingly irritated him; his very presence stifled his ambition. He saw himself sitting in the great chair on the dais dispensing justice, a gold coronet encircling his head. He envisaged all of Powys and Dyfed under his control with the Normans and Flemings scoured from his homeland like dry straw in a blaze. A native Welsh wife would sit beside him, and she would be clad in a mulberry silk dress, dripping with gold and jewels. He would ride a storm-horse, and he would begin his campaign at Cenarth Bychan.

16

Fortress of Cenarth Bychan,
January 1110

Nesta was playing with Angharad, dandling her on her knee in the bower at Cenarth. Gerald had ridden out to patrol some outlying villages, but she expected him home before dusk. She sang to her daughter and cuddled her, but she was bored. After all the excitement and pleasure of the Christmas court at Ceredigion, she was stuck here in this raw fortress, with the winter wind whistling under the door. It was one thing to plan creature comforts, another to wait for their arrival.

She often relived in her imagination the feast at Ceredigion: the colours, the banqueting and entertainment by firelight, embraced by her native language, and her people. Most of all she dwelt on the beguiling attentions of Owain ap Cadwgan. He was a fever in her blood, and everyday life paled by comparison. She wanted excitement; she wanted to feel as she had done before the Normans came and took away her life, when her world had been wide open with possibility.

A messenger came to her chamber door. 'Madam, the lord Owain ap Cadwgan has arrived at the gates requesting admittance – what shall we do? I ask since my lord is absent.'

Nesta's heart kicked in her chest. 'Admit him and bid him welcome,' she said, feeling giddy and breathless. 'Tell him I shall greet him shortly and that my lord is due home later today. Go and bid the steward broach a new cask of wine.'

When he had gone, she gave Angharad to her nurse and changed her everyday gown for a more embellished tunic dyed a deep green, and swapped her plain shoes for an embroidered pair. She felt sick, excited, and struggled to contain her bursting emotions. She must be the dignified lady before Owain – a queen receiving a supplicant. She chivvied her women into tidying the room, added a spoonful of frankincense pieces to the brazier, and then sat upright in her chair, composed her body to regal stillness, and summoned him to her presence.

When he entered the chamber, she felt him like a flame, but strove to maintain an air of aloofness.

'My lady,' he said, and knelt on one knee, but looked up at her with a mischievous sparkle in his eyes. 'I had thought never in my life to be rewarded by such a vision of beauty.'

'You exaggerate, sire!' She laughed at his flirtatious effrontery. 'Stand up and be done.'

'I do not exaggerate; I tell the honest truth.' Rising to his feet, he placed his hand on his heart, before tucking his gloves through his belt. 'I have paid you a visit as I said I would.'

'And I am delighted to welcome you, but my husband has business elsewhere – although he is due home before nightfall. It is a pity he is not here to greet you himself.' Their eyes met and she knew neither of them thought it a pity at all. 'Will you take some wine?'

'That would be welcome, my lady.'

He sat down on the bench by the brazier and stretched out his legs, which emphasised his powerful thighs clad in leather riding hose. Nesta looked and then looked away, blushing, and knew he was watching her with predatory amusement.

'A fine castle your lord has built here,' he remarked. 'Doubtless he guards it very carefully – it would be difficult for an enemy to take.'

Nesta lifted her shoulders in a delicate shrug. 'That would be Gerald's business, but the defences are sufficient to prevent intruders from disturbing our sleep.'

Owain took the wine presented by Ceridwen. 'I would expect no less of such a puissant lord. I imagine the only way to take the castle would be from within – but I am sure that would not happen and that no one here has a chink in their loyalty.'

Meeting his gaze, Nesta saw that she had not mistaken his intent. 'Indeed not, for the safety of all is at stake.'

She looked round at her sons who were playing a game of strategy on the floor with toy knights. Henry, at ten, was being the dominant leader, but providing Gwilym, six, did not dispute his orders, was prepared to be magnanimous. Geri sat with them and now and again one or the other of the boys would throw a stuffed ball of rabbit fur for him to retrieve.

'Fine boys,' Owain said. 'I would be glad to have sons as strong and healthy as they are, but I would have to find the right woman to be their mother.'

Nesta looked down. 'I do not know where you would find such a woman.'

'I do, and she is not far from here should she make that choice for herself.'

Nesta swallowed. His eyes were alight, filled with daring and fierceness.

'It pains me to see the Welsh people trampled underfoot by

the Normans,' Owain continued, speaking quietly. 'If they have their foot upon our necks, it is only because we allow them to do so. If we resisted properly, we could drive them out once and for all.'

'That is dangerous talk!'

Owain shrugged. 'Why should we not talk dangerously? It is only dangerous because we are put upon. We must act and show them that we are not going to be cowed, that they shall not steal our land and use it for themselves, that we are not going to let them take our women and our birth right. What has happened to your family is the tale of us all. We should send them a message to say we shall stand for no more.'

Drawn in by his passion, Nesta was nevertheless anxious and looked round to see who was within earshot. The boys were absorbed in their game and too far away. Eleri and Ceridwen were sufficiently close, but she trusted both women not to carry tales; nor would Angharad's Welsh nurse. Owain was voicing thoughts she had harboured for a long time, but they were seditious, and complicated by contradictory threads that had been woven among them since. Yet the peril itself was seductive. 'You should be careful, even so,' she said.

'But surely as a Welsh woman, you will not betray me – you are my ally?'

Nesta looked down at her hands and turned her wedding ring on her finger. 'I am also a Norman wife, with children to consider,' she said. 'And I do not know you beyond a single feast and this moment now.'

'A single feast was enough for me,' Owain replied in a voice rough and soft at the same time. 'When I danced with you, when I spoke . . . when I saw you like a trapped bird set free for a moment at the fire . . .' He cleared his throat. 'I have never wanted anything so much in my life. If the women's chamber had not been barred, I would have come for you there and then. You do not have to be a Norman wife.'

Nesta met his fierce gaze and then had to look away, feeling shaky and disconcerted. When he spoke of the trapped bird freed at the fire, it was as if he had seen directly into her being – perhaps the reason she had been reliving the moments at the feast ever since.

Owain leaned forward, forearms along his thighs, hands clasped. 'This is your cause too. It is the cause of every Welsh man and woman, and we could lead it.'

'I warn you to tread carefully for your own good,' Nesta countered, speaking to him, but to herself also.

'Like my father you mean?' He curled his lip. 'Begging scraps from the English king's table for the right to hold feasts in his own hall?'

Nesta saw the fire flare in his eyes and was drawn towards the flame, by a flame of her own. 'Or perhaps *my* father's right.' She raised her chin. 'Ceredigion belongs to Dyfed, not Powys.'

Owain smiled. 'We could make a truce, unite our families and rule together. Whether we have just met or not, you cannot be happy living like this with a Norman – one of the very men who killed your father. I can set you free. I can make you a great lady of Wales, a true queen. I will take you away from all this.'

'So you say, but what guarantee do I have?'

'My word,' he said. 'On my oath, I swear this thing.' He unfastened the knife from his belt, a wooden-handled item in a sheath embossed with curlicues. 'On this knife I swear.' He set it down before her.

Nesta stared at it. Thus were oaths made in court. She had seen knives attached to charters in Henry's chamber, as an extra bond of faith. To swear on a blade was sacred.

'Send to let me know when it is safe, and I will come,' Owain persisted. 'Give me the means, and I will give you what you need.'

The sound of the horn winding from the gate, announcing Gerald's arrival, spared her from answering. 'My husband is here,' she said with a mingling of relief and regret. But she took the knife because it couldn't be left out in plain sight, and buried it beneath her sewing wools.

Owain eased to his feet, loose-limbed as a lion. 'Well, I shall speak with him, because trade is trade, and I hope I can find rare and beautiful things to adorn your bower – although perhaps a bower of a different making to this.'

Nesta wiped her palms on her gown. 'If you are bound for Ireland, will you take a message to my brother and tell him I am well and I hope for his return with all my heart?'

'Of course, you can depend on me – whatever you desire.' He tilted his head and smiled. 'Or you could come to Ireland with me and tell him yourself.'

The notion was so enormous that Nesta's turmoil tipped over into numbness.

'Think on it,' Owain said. 'But whether you will or not, I will carry your message to him.'

On entering the public hall, Owain immediately switched his attention to Gerald with expansive gestures and bonhomie. Gerald eyed him with wary surprise but was polite. Nesta followed, more subdued, eyes lowered.

'Your good lady has already furnished me with wine and confirmed her order for a set of Irish drinking horns for the high table,' Owain said. 'The Irish would be mad for any of your horses – MacMurchada of Leinster would pay a king's ransom I know.' He glanced at Nesta and gave her a concealed, teasing wink.

Gerald shook his head. 'As I said at Ceredigion, they are

seldom for sale. They are always more in demand than I am able or willing to supply.'

'I understand,' Owain said, bowing, 'but I hope you will not begrudge me another look at your stable while I am here.'

'Of course.'

The courteous host, Gerald took Owain away to see the horses. Nesta observed Owain talking easily to Gerald, drawing him in, encouraging friendship, but also glancing round at the defences, taking them in. The boys – Walter, Henry and Gwilym – accompanied the men, and she saw Owain pat Henry's shoulder in camaraderie. Walter, fifteen, walked at Gerald's side, head up and chin jutting.

She looked round the hall, unconsciously still twisting her wedding ring on her finger. Two of Owain's senior soldiers had gone with the stable party, and a couple of Gerald's, but the rest had remained in the hall. Owain's words churned inside her, running between her stomach, her heart and her loins. He was daring her to do something about her situation. To defy the subjugation of Norman rule – to strike a blow for each wrong she had suffered. He was offering her the chance of a life with her own people. And had she not sworn vengeance many times over?

She retired to her chamber and paced, wringing her hands and thinking first one way and then the other, except she was barely thinking at all. She could just stay here, pick up her embroidery and not come down to bid Owain farewell.

Geri trotted up to her and sat on his hind legs, begging for a treat. She fed him a piece of cheese from the platter that was still on the bench and picked him up. He wriggled, trying to lick her, and she buried her face in his curly white coat.

Whatever she wanted, Gerald gave her, except remove the thorn that lay deepest in her heart. The wound had been inflicted long before her marriage, and her flesh had grown over it. Perhaps Owain would be able to dig it out and help her to heal, but at what cost? Without following him she would never know, and remain forever locked in the gilded cage of her bower with her clothes and sewing and her pain.

Drawing a deep breath, she went to the door and down the stairs. Each step made her think about turning round and retreating to her chamber without bidding Owain farewell and without crossing a line. It wasn't too late; it wasn't too late. The moment between going forward and turning back grew shorter and shorter until the point of no return arrived and she paused on a pinpoint, and then walked forward.

Owain's troop was ready to leave. Seeing her, Owain left Gerald's side and came to make his obeisance. 'Thank you for your hospitality, my lady,' he said, bowing.

'You have been welcome,' she replied, trying not to sound breathless. 'I wish you success of your endeavours.'

'I hope for success too,' he answered with a smile. 'I shall obtain those drinking horns for your table, and those other items you mentioned. Anything you need, send me word and I shall endeavour to satisfy your desire.' He bowed again and flicked her an upward glance imbued with meaning.

He rode out without looking back. Nesta wished he would, and because he did not, the tug was all the keener.

Gerald grimaced. 'I am not sure it is a good idea to become involved with Owain ap Cadwgan in any form. In the interests of diplomacy and peace I will venture a little way, but I am very glad he has gone.'

Nesta murmured a bland reply and returned to her chamber. She sat down to sew but could not concentrate. Before, when her mind had dwelt on Owain, it had been a restless daydream; but now he had offered her the chance of a different, Welsh life

– a new start. He wanted her to elope with him, defy the Normans and pay them back for everything they had done to her and her kin.

If she thought of Gerald only as a Norman, one of the hated oppressors, the matter was simple: she would leave now, without a second thought. But Gerald the man was a different prospect – her lawful husband who gave her gifts and gowns, who sang to her and was tender and thoughtful, who loved his children and swung them in his arms and sang lullabies to them. The notion of betraying him made her queasy with fear and doubt. The conflict inside her was terrible, and she had no one to talk to.

Her women were quietly pecking away at their needlework, heads down, not daring to look up.

'I trust you to stay silent and say nothing of what you have heard or seen,' Nesta said. 'This is a private matter.'

'Of course, my lady,' Eleri said, and Ceridwen nodded vigorously too. 'Our loyalty is to you . . . but if you will permit me to say so, I think you should be very careful.'

Nesta pressed her lips together. Her life was a constant trail of being cautious, being careful, watching every move she made. 'The lord Owain has gone,' she said curtly. 'We shall not speak of it again.'

The women reiterated their loyalty and Nesta was reassured, but it did not ease her dilemma one whit. She could see the edge of the knife sheath peeping between the balls of coloured wool in her sewing basket, and she pressed it down, and covered it with several squares of cut fabric.

In early March, Gerald announced that they had been long enough at Cenarth and that in a fortnight's time, providing the weather was not too wet, they would return to Carew and Pembroke to prepare for Easter.

The news dismayed Nesta, for she was still sitting on her decision about Owain, vacillating between taking matters further or drawing back, sick with desire, but afraid of the precipice.

'I shall leave packing the baggage and organising the household in your capable hands,' Gerald said, and kissed her cheek. 'I shall be away next week, reporting to Richard de Belmeis before we return to Carew.'

He went off about his business and Nesta returned to her chamber. She took a gold ring from her jewel box and summoned her scribe, then dictated a letter to Owain, informing him of her imminent departure from Cenarth and saying that if he could deliver the goods he had promised before then, she would be indebted to him. She added that Gerald would be gone the following week and that Owain should change his visit to Carew if he wished to speak with him. The ring was proof of herself as the sender.

The messenger departed on his errand and Nesta pressed her hand to her stomach, sick with excitement and guilt at what she had just done. Fear too. The die was cast, let it fall where it may. The messenger might not find Owain. If he was still in Ireland or a far-flung part of Powys he would not be in time and she would have the utter relief and vast disappointment of a failed arrow shot at fate. Even if he did receive the message he might choose not to come, or he might not read between the lines. Everything was in God's hands, and she could wash her own. If it came to fruition then it was His will.

However, God helped those who helped themselves. After much deliberation, she went to the stables and sought out Dewi, for she trusted him with her life. He served Gerald equably enough, but he was still her family's man, and his loyalty was to her and Gruffydd, not Gerald, and not Owain.

'My lady,' he said, bowing to her outside his small hut at the side of the stable enclosure, and looking a little surprised.

'I have come to see the horses,' she said. 'I was thinking about them today.'

She moved along the stalls until she came to Taran. He was more than twenty years old now, and Gerald had brought him to graze with the mares at Cenarth. He was still strong and spirited with hopefully a few more seasons in him as a sire of fine foals, but his days as a warhorse and even a palfrey were over. Tymestl, born on the day her world had changed, was sixteen and in his late prime. Gerald still rode him but had a younger stallion in training, another of Taran's progeny, six years old, with a coat of dappled grey and gold. Gerald had named him Storm, and he was his pride and joy. Her own mare, Anain, was busy at her hay net as usual.

'I have something to tell you,' she said, turning to Dewi. 'Something with which I am going to entrust you, and if you break that trust it will be my downfall.'

Dewi's expression scarcely altered beyond a minor twitch of his brows. They were bushy silver now, and his cheeks had sunk where he had lost teeth, but he still had his strength and his eyes were bright and shrewd. 'You have always been able to tell me anything, my lady. I have kept your secrets – ever since you were a little girl stealing cheese from the dairy.'

Nesta made a face. 'This is a little more than stealing cheese.'

Haltingly, she told him about Owain, and speaking his name, felt her stomach flutter. 'He says he will drive the Normans out of Wales – that I will be his lady and we shall be avenged on the Normans for all they have done to us. He is going to come for me at my word.'

Dewi gave her a troubled, pensive look. 'That is a great step to contemplate, mistress. Perhaps you will be jumping out of the pan straight into the fire.'

'Perhaps I will.' She jutted her chin. 'But if I dare nothing now, then I never will. I have neither forgotten nor forgiven what happened to us at Norman hands. I made a vow and I shall keep it.' Her voice shook. 'Every day in my mind's eye I see my father's body being brought into Carew over the back of a horse, and I can never wipe from my memory what happened to us all after that. My children have a Norman father – a good father – but what if they had been Welsh? I shall bring the horses with me. They are my heritage – my birth right.' She spoke fiercely, convincing herself. 'I want you to help me.'

Dewi's gaze filled with sorrow but there was understanding and knowing also. 'My loyalty has always been to you, my lady, and always shall be.'

'Thank you.' Her eyes stung with sudden tears. 'Am I doing the right thing?'

Dewi lifted and dropped his shoulders. 'That is not for me to say, mistress. You have your reasons and you have been sorely wronged, but only you can make the choice, and rightfully so. You have my service and my loyalty whatever you do. I am growing old and I have seen much, and will doubtless see more before I go to God, but I have learned that if you walk into the sea or dance in the fire, you should know you have a way back lest you drown or burn. That is my advice to you.'

Over the next few days, Nesta saw to packing the baggage ready for their return to Carew. She quietly prepared a separate leather bag of her best gowns and jewels – just in case, she told herself. It was difficult to sit with Gerald in the bower, knowing that Owain was coming for her, and feeling the anticipation on one side and the dark weight of guilt and betrayal on the other.

When Gerald left to make his report to Richard de Belmeis, he rode Tymestl and she thought it a pity, but there was nothing to be done. At least Taran and Storm were still in the stables, as well as other good horseflesh. She bade him Godspeed and forced a smile onto her lips as she watched him mount.

'I will bring you a gift from Shrewsbury,' he said. 'I hear there is a new jeweller, and I shall look at his wares.'

Nesta swallowed. 'You should not spend your money on me.'

He gazed at her in surprise, then laughed. 'You would soon complain if I did not, and besides, it gives me pleasure to give you delight.'

She watched him ride out, and bit her lip, wondering what she had done.

Nine days after Gerald had gone, Nesta climbed to the top of the tower and looked out over the landscape, wondering if Owain would come. Her body yearned for him, knowing he was somewhere out there beyond her sight, but surely close. Unless the message had not reached him. Unless he had chosen to ignore her.

Tense and on edge, she visited Cenarth's small chapel to light a candle and pray. Kneeling before the altar, her hands clasped and head bowed, she sought the calmness to wait for what would be. She remained torn, one part of her vowing to do whatever was necessary to avenge her father and her family. That desire had eaten her for sixteen years, and was now mingled with a newer, more immediate longing.

The other part was a churn of fear, regret and guilt. Gerald had always treated her well, and given her the life of a great lady. As his wife she had credibility and status among the Normans, even if she loathed them. If Owain made good on her summons, she would destroy it all in an instant. But then she thought of how Gerald had been present at her father's death, might even have struck one of the blows that felled him. He had served the Montgomerys as he now served Henry. He gave trinkets and gifts to keep her quiet and then did as his overlords commanded. Balanced on a knife edge, she would cut herself whichever way matters turned out.

Towards dusk, she was returning to her chamber when the guards called out from the gate. Her thoughts flashed to Owain like lightning, and her heart started to pound, but instead it was Gerald who rode through the twilight towards her and she could only stare in horror for he was home early and should not be here. For a moment she was too shocked to do anything but stare at the men in their glittering grey mail, but then she rallied and went forward to greet them. Dewi emerged from the stables to help with the horses and briefly caught her eye, before dropping his gaze and shaking his head.

Nesta prepared a bowl of warm water for Gerald's ablutions, and behaved as a dutiful wife, removing his boots, washing his feet and providing him with clean clothes while the boys dealt with his armour. This was her answer from God in the chapel. Owain had let her down. He was too late, and Gerald was her path. Her hands were trembling.

'We finished our business sooner than I expected,' Gerald said as he drank wine and ate a platter of bread and cheese. 'De Belmeis is pleased with the way matters are progressing and will report to the King that all is well. We can set out for Carew tomorrow if the weather is good. How is the packing going?'

'It is done, my lord.' Nesta could barely get her breath and turned away.

'Good.' He caught her waist and pulled her round to face him. 'I can always rely on you.'

He made to kiss her and she ducked her head so that his lips brushed her forehead instead, then leaned her head against his chest and closed her eyes. Dear God, only let this moment pass.

Sitting down at her sewing, she began stitching an area where

she did not have to concentrate. Gerald finished eating and turned
to work on some parchments he had brought with him from de
Belmeis, dictating his replies to his scribe, but after a while he
began to yawn, tired after the long ride, and went to lie down.

Nesta saw the children to bed, returned to her sewing, and
fretted.

A commotion of banging and shouting outside made her lift
her head. Going to the narrow window, she looked out and saw
a burst of flame in the ward and, against it, figures running,
fighting, falling.

Woken from sleep, Gerald staggered out of bed, blinking.
'What's happening?'

Nesta, dry-mouthed, was unable to speak.

Screams and shouts carried up to them, some in Norman,
some in Welsh. A serving maid ran into the chamber. 'The
Welsh!' she cried, eyes wild. 'The Welsh have broken in and are
firing everything! A whole army of them!'

'Bolt the door!' Gerald commanded. He grabbed the cheese
knife off the platter on the table and waved it at Nesta. 'Get
behind me.'

Suddenly, in the midst of chaos, her own thoughts were clear
and decisive. There was only one way out of this if she did not
want Gerald's blood on her hands on Judgement Day. 'What
good will that do?' she snapped. 'You are in naught but your
shirt, with a cheese knife for defence. You will lose your life for
nothing – you cannot protect me if you are dead. You must let
me be your shield. They will not harm me, for I am Welsh
royalty, but they will cut you to pieces.'

'You do not know what they will do!'

'I know they will kill you!' she retorted. 'You have to hide if
you are to have a chance of surviving!'

The screams and shouts were closer now. There was a scuffle, a shriek, and then fists banging on the chamber door, bellowing for them to open up. The door would not hold for long. Angharad was screaming, and Gwilym was standing wide-eyed in his night-shirt. The older boys too had risen from their pallets.

Nesta pointed at the door to the latrine. 'Hide in there. They will not find you, and the shaft goes down to the rocks. I will not tell them; I will cover your tracks and say I have not seen you.'

'No!' Gerald's eyes were bright with furious denial.

'You would rather be slain at my feet? Do you want that to be my last memory of you? Do you want to leave your wife and children that final sight as their legacy? Use your head, you fool, while it is still on your shoulders. It is your only chance to survive, and for once let me deal with the matter!'

Against the door came the whump of an axe attacking the latch, and the wood started to splinter. Gerald hesitated for an instant longer, then grabbed her by the waist, and pulled her against his body, kissing her hard on the lips. 'I will come for you, I swear. Be strong, and do not doubt me.' He thrust her away, ran into the latrine and slammed the bar across.

'Mama, what is happening?' Henry demanded, staring at the chamber door as it continued to splinter. Angharad was screaming at the top of her lungs despite Eleri's efforts to calm her. Gwilym ran to Nesta's skirts and gripped them. Walter licked his lips, gazed over his shoulder at the latrine and then back at the door. Geri jumped up and down in his dog bed, yapping hysterically.

'None of you say anything!' Nesta hissed at the maids and older boys. 'I shall deal with this. Say nothing for your very lives.' She gave them all a fierce look. 'Stand back from the doorway.'

The last splinter flew from around the latch and Welsh soldiers kicked their way into the chamber, led by Owain, clad in a mail shirt and helm, so that he looked no different from a Norman reaver. Terror flashed through Nesta even as she drew herself to her full height.

'I bid you good evening, my lady.' Owain flourished her a bow with one hand, his blood-stained sword in the other. 'I would stay to accept your hospitality, but as it is, you must come with me and be a guest to mine.' He cast a sharp gaze around the room. 'I understand your good lord and master is at home. May I be pleased to encounter him too?' A snarl dwelt in his smile and he reached for her. 'Where is he?'

'Leave my mama alone!' Gwilym thrust forward, his eyes blazing, fists raised.

'Gwilym!' Nesta turned against Owain's arm, feeling the bruising grip of his fingers. 'What did I say about obeying me? Be quiet and do as you are told.' She looked to Ceridwen, who grabbed him and pulled him away from Owain's reach. 'Gerald is not here,' she continued to Owain. 'Yes, he returned, but he . . . he fled when he heard the commotion and knew we were under attack.'

'"Fled" eh?' With another wolfish smile he gestured at the latrine with the hilt of his sword. 'Llew, Tegwin, search in there. You, my lady, and your children and servants had better come with me for your own safety.'

Nesta met his stare with a fierce challenge, giving fire for fire as Owain's men threw their shoulders against the latrine door. 'For my own safety? Until a moment ago I was perfectly "safe" in my own bower!'

'Obviously you were deluded if you thought such a thing,' Owain replied. 'But then we all deal in lies and half truths, do we not, until someone faces us with reality.'

She glared at him, and he laughed, and she felt the glow in the pit of her belly.

'Nevertheless, I shall take you under my protection, and I promise no harm shall come to you or to your children. Let us not stand here and talk about it, but make haste. Do you have your cloak?'

Nesta turned to pick up the one with the rich vair lining she had left waiting on top of her baggage. 'Put on your cloaks,' she ordered the youngsters and her maids.

Owain's two soldiers smashed open the latrine door, weapons raised to bludgeon, but on the instant turned about. 'He's gone down the shaft, sire, too far for a spear, what shall we do?'

A broad grin widened beneath Owain's moustache. 'Go down to the base and greet the turd when he comes out – and be quick about your work.'

The men hastened out of the room.

Owain seized Nesta's arm but she shrugged free and indicated the prepared baggage. 'If you are any kind of man, you will let me bring my things.'

'Hah, I am all the man you will ever need,' he replied with a hard grin. 'Bring them if you must, but make haste.' At a gesture, another soldier seized Nesta's baggage and she experienced a qualm at their rough handling and the thought of all her finery going astray, but there was nothing she could do about it.

Eleri lifted Angharad in her arms. Henry shrugged off the grip of one of the soldiers who reached for him. 'I am the son of a king!' he cried indignantly.

'Then you will have the wit to do as your mother bids you and come now,' Owain growled, and put his own heavy hand on the boy's shoulder. 'Princes can die as easily as anyone else, and I say that as a prince myself.'

Henry scowled, but adjusted his cloak and protested no more.

When Nesta made to scoop up Geri, Owain shook his head. 'Leave the cur. I will buy you a dozen such if that is your wish, but I'll not have that mop yapping in my ear as we ride.'

Nesta put Geri down, but felt a spark of disquiet and resentment. She ought to be able to bring her dog if she wanted.

Once out into the night, the frozen air bit Nesta's face and hands. Her fur-lined mittens were still in the room above and, like Geri, had to be left behind. The bailey buildings were on fire and bodies strewed the ground amid the clash of fighting and mayhem. Dewi had brought the horses from the stables and they were saddled and ready; not just Taran, but all the decent horseflesh so that there would be no chance of pursuit. Owain boosted Nesta up onto his own dun, and she felt his strong hands on her body under her cloak, and shivered with fear and anticipation. She wondered how he had entered the castle with Gerald in residence, for she had given no order, but clearly others had.

Owain's men came running back from poking at the bottom of the latrine. 'We cannot reach him, sire!' the senior man said with a disappointed grimace. 'We reckon he's in the middle like a stuck turd and there's no reaching him.'

'Well, let him stay up there,' Owain said curtly. 'We cannot spare the time to stay and fight. We have what we want. Are all the fires set?'

'Yes, sire.'

'Then let us go.' He reached to his saddle bag and produced a large chunk of rancid bacon, which he jammed onto a spear and thrust upright into the ground before the open gates of the fortress.

They set off at a hard trot into the winter night with the stars glittering above them and the air crystalline and icy. Owain threw back his head and uttered a falsetto wolf howl of exultation before turning round in the saddle and kissing Nesta hard on the mouth.

A starburst of exhilaration shot through Nesta. The feel of Owain's lips on hers, the cold air on her face, the smooth motion of the horse beneath her, the stars wheeling over their heads, Owain's spine pressed to her body, and behind them the smoke and flames billowing from the buildings of Cenarth Bychan. The first was delicious and dangerous, the second, vengeance for her father and all her bloodline.

They rode on through the frosty night, covering the miles swiftly in washed grey light until they arrived at the gates of Ceredigion and were admitted within the compound. 'My father is not here,' Owain said as they dismounted. 'He has business in Powys and my stepmother has gone to relatives in the Marches for her confinement, but we are safe here and you shall have every comfort.' He swung down from the blowing horse, in clouds of misty breath, and, lifting her down, set Nesta on her feet. 'All that I can provide, you shall have.'

Servants came to take the horses to the stables and Owain led Nesta and her household inside the fortress.

'Are we your hostages?' Henry demanded, throwing back his shoulders, still high-handed.

'I don't know yet, boy, it depends how much that tender hide of yours is worth,' Owain responded. 'I told you before to mind your tongue. One more outburst and I might just test how tender that hide is with the end of a horsewhip. Your father may be the King of England, but I have no love for him either. It is only regard for your mother that stays my hand.' He issued a terse instruction to two of his men who began shepherding the household in one direction, while Owain led Nesta in another.

Henry resisted the soldier dragging him away. 'Where are you taking my mother?'

'Enough, Henry!' Nesta said sharply. 'The lord Owain has promised our safety. Nothing will happen that need concern you for now, but I need to speak with him. Go with your brothers and sister, and be brave for me. I will come to you later.'

'You have raised a strong-willed boy,' Owain said, leading her up some outer stairs and into a chamber she had not seen at her last visit, but which was clearly personal to him. There were few furnishings, just a bed with blankets and furs, a table with a jug and bowl, and a single carved chest.

'He is his father's son. You would do well to remember it.'

'And I shall,' Owain replied. 'But the sons you shall bear to me will be better by a hundredfold.' He kicked the door shut, grabbed her to him and began kissing her, pressing his body up against hers, gasping as if he had run the race of his life. 'Ah God be praised; I have waited for this since I first saw you at the Christmas feast. If I wait any longer, I shall burst!'

Nesta thought she would burst too and uttered a soft moan.

Carrying her to the bed, he threw her down on the coverlet. He was ablaze with lust, and her blood was on fire, for no man had ever been so desperate for her as he was in this moment, and he had promised her a new life and vengeance for the old. Gerald was always controlled, and politely considerate. Henry had been methodical and brutal, exerting control and spilling his seed as just another bodily function to deal with. But Owain's frantic desperation was because of her, and made her feel immensely powerful and bold. Every sense heightened, she was open and ready for him, with no thought beyond the triumphant blaze of the moment.

She clutched him fiercely as he rucked up her skirts, and she clasped her legs around his pumping buttocks. The flicker of his tongue in and out of her mouth echoed the motion of his hips. Her feet felt the coldness of his skin from the ride, and the leather of his hose. He pushed again fast and urgently, head thrown back, and suddenly let out a triumphant roar that resounded against the walls. Feeling him pulse inside her, she cried out as she tumbled into her own pleasure, squeezing him deep within.

He dipped his head and pressed into her neck, gasping, and she held on to him while the burn subsided to gentler flickers. She was still hungry, but the first, ravenous edge had been sated.

'I am sorry,' he panted. 'I wanted to last longer, but I promise you more tonight and tomorrow and for the rest of our days.' He withdrew from her and adjusted his clothing, then kissed her again. 'I have to go and attend to the men and other matters, but I will return as soon as I can. I will have someone bring food and drink to you.' He pulled a fur cover over her body. 'Rest now, *cariad*, you will need your strength for later, I promise you!'

He left the room, in quick strides, banging the door shut, where Gerald would have done so quietly. Nesta lay under the furs gathering her thoughts and recovering her senses. Eventually she rose, went to the jug and poured water into the basin. She washed her face and hands, and wiped herself between her legs. She could have done with Eleri or Ceridwen to help tidy her hair, but it was unwise, and she was aware of a prickle of shame and then resentment that the shame was there.

She wandered around Owain's chamber, touching this and that. It was the space of a man seldom at home with few and plain furnishings. She threw back the lid of Owain's clothing chest. The garments within were scattered with bright kingfisher feathers to dissuade the moths. She picked up a soft, short cloak and held it to her nose, drawing in his scent, and concentrated her mind on him. There was no Gerald – there could not be now. He was in her past. She had to cast him as a Norman, and not think of him as an individual man, because then she would feel ashamed and disgusted with herself for this. She had to submerge herself in Owain, a Welshman and her saviour. He would protect her and they would raise children to rule all of southern and central Wales – Dyfed and Powys combined to re-form the ancient kingdom of Deheubarth. She had been a prisoner and now she was free. A spark of anxiety told her that she had been abducted before and caged, that this might just be another cage of a darker, different kind, but she refused to heed the message.

A servant, eyes lowered, arrived with food and drink, set it out, and departed. Nesta ravenously devoured the bread and cold chicken. Every part of her was alive and on edge, every sense keen. It was as if she'd grown a new skin that was exquisitely tender. A butterfly with damply crumpled wings.

Owain returned as she was wiping her lips on a napkin, and she poured a cup of mead for him. He took and drank it with gusto and she avidly watched the rippling of his throat as he did so. He did everything with the strength and vigour of a lion and she wanted that power at her command.

'I have set extra guards on the walls,' he said, 'but no one will be coming after us this night. The men of Powys have their orders to polish their weapons and make ready. We are going to strike the Normans so hard that we shall erase them and their castles from every corner of Wales for ever.' Sitting on the edge of the table, he picked up a portion of chicken and tore into it with powerful teeth. 'This is the beginning, my love. I shall make you the lady of every kingdom in Wales!'

Nesta watched him with shining eyes. She wanted and needed to hear this, and the more emphatic the better to make her believe in a new reality that was still unstable and only half lit.

He washed down the chicken with more mead, and wiped

his hands. 'I have allies in Gwynedd, and my men of Powys. More will come from Ireland. My father will join us when he sees the lie of the land. He only holds back from weakness and fear. He should retire and leave the business of ruling to me, for he is a spent force. You shall be my consort, and we shall be the greatest rulers Wales has ever seen.'

He took her in his arms and again she submerged herself in the heat of his powerful, muscular body, and in the words that warmed her soul. She would not think beyond this moment, beyond this flame that had been kindled. Fire was ephemeral and greedy. It had to be constantly fed, and destroyed everything in its path, but it was all she wanted in that moment. Her and Owain. The flame and the fuel, the fuel and the flame, and bridges to safety did not matter.

17

Fortress of Cenarth Bychan,
March 1110

It had been a perilous descent as Gerald inched his way down the slimed, stinking channel, searching out hand- and footholds, his spine to one wall, feet against the other, his nostrils assailed by the stench of ordure, until finally he reached the base of the chute and staggered out onto the rocks beneath, covered in filth. He stooped over, gagging and retching, his eyes stinging, his body shuddering with fatigue and disbelief. His thoughts flew to Nesta. God alone knew what might have happened to her and the children already. Self-disgust rolled over him for escaping down that shaft and abandoning her to her fate. A real man would have stayed and fought with honour to protect his family, even to the death.

Stumbling over the slippery, soiled rocks at the foot of the latrine, twisting his ankle into the bargain, he made his way to the compound where the buildings were on fire and smoke belched from the thatched roofs. It resembled a scene from hell, with strewn bodies and people staggering in the smoky flame-light. Inside the gateway, a lump of meat had been thrust onto a spear. For a horrified moment he thought it was part of a human body before realising it was a chunk hacked from a bacon flitch with the words in Welsh 'Chew on this' carved into the rind. Pain and rage became a red glow inside him, and doubled him up again, but only for a moment before he forced himself to stand straight.

A surviving soldier, Matthew de Reivers, approached him, limping but not badly wounded. 'Sire, we thought you surely dead!' He coughed and covered his nose.

'As you can see for yourself, I am not!' Gerald snapped. 'Get everyone together. Bar the gate and douse those fires. How did they get in?'

'Through the postern, sire. It . . . it was unbarred . . . they were on us in an instant. Someone let them in.'

Gerald clamped his jaw. His anger was a heavy cloud in his head, but raging at his men would only be an outlet for fury at himself. If they had been off their guard, then it was because he had been lax, and while he wanted to call down the lightning, it would not help him regain control of the situation.

His body shuddering in the March cold, he barked instructions to the men who had minor injuries or were unharmed. 'Get this place in order. Shore up and douse those fires. You, tally the wounded and organise tending for the worst injured. Matthew, find out what is missing and report back to me. I am going to wash off this mire and put on my armour, and then we shall see what is what.'

They had not fired the tower, there had not been time, and he was thankful for small mercies. He took the stairs swiftly to the chamber where only a short while since he had been sleeping, thinking everyone safe for the night. Off his guard. He would never be off his guard again. He was prepared to find his children slaughtered and Nesta the victim of rape or murder, but the hacked door stood wide on an empty, ransacked room. The rich hangings had been ripped from the walls and all the coffers plundered or taken, including the strong box. Angharad's cradle was empty.

'Nesta.' He whispered her name. Then he roared it. Going back out, he found one of the lower maids cowering on the stairs. 'Where is the lady?' he demanded. 'Where are the children?'

She shook her head. 'I do not know, sire. Taken by Owain ap Cadwgan. Her and the other maids and children.'

Gerald dismissed her with a vigorous wave of his hand. He stripped off his soiled shirt and washed himself in Nesta's bowl on the coffer, but the stench still clung in every crevice and he knew it would never leave him and he deserved it, for he had not protected Nesta or the children. What message would it send to them, that their father had left them to their fate and saved his own skin by hiding in a latrine shaft?

Grimly he dressed in a clean shirt and tunic. He would have to tell de Belmeis, who would then write to Henry, and the King might be so enraged at Gerald's incompetence that he would take everything from him and demote him to the rank of a common soldier. A hollow man, with nothing but dishonour to his name, and he would deserve it. He looked round the room – at Gwilym's toys still scattered on the floor, at an overturned stool, at the embroidery loom set up with the needle hanging from it by a fine thread of scarlet silk, red as blood. Everything felt empty and loose and his eyes stung with tears.

His squire arrived from wherever he had been hiding. 'Sire, are you—'

'Leave me!' Gerald snarled. 'Go and bring my knights to the guard room – and find my armour. Go!'

The youth bolted and Gerald exhaled hard. He dug his fingers through his hair and then grimaced, for it was sticky from the latrine shaft. Taking a step, he felt something snap beneath his shoe, and looking down saw that he had trodden on the jewelled ivory comb he had bought in Shrewsbury, intending to give to Nesta. The gemstones glinted like small tears along the comb's spine, which was cracked in half. He stooped and picked up the pieces, swallowing hard on grief, for the trinket could never be mended, but even broken it was still beautiful. He rubbed his thumb over the carved ivory and the coloured droplets, then shouldered past the broken latrine door and pitched the little comb down the shaft.

A whimpering noise from the chamber made him spin round, and when it came again, he traced it to the bed. Lifting the trailing edge of the coverlet, he discovered Geri cowering beneath, his tail tucked between his legs, and his eyes showing their whites.

Gerald picked up the trembling dog and stroked and soothed him, thankful that the Welsh had not bludgeoned him to death. Finding the female servant again, he handed the dog to her, for he could hardly go to his men with his wife's lapdog in his arms. Facing his men at all was going to be bad enough.

'Sire, it was Owain ap Cadwgan, his warband and some hangers on,' said Juel, one of his Flemish soldiers. 'They knew what they were doing; it was all planned. The horses have gone from the stables – we cannot pursue them until we can obtain more. Dewi the groom has gone too, and his apprentice.' He licked his lips. 'The harness has been taken, and sacks of fodder.'

Gerald almost choked with the effort of controlling himself and not overturning the trestle in rage. Taran, Tymestl and Storm – all his best horses. Nesta and the children abducted to

God knew what fate, and Cenarth raided and fired. Owain ap Cadwgan had planned this. The invitation to the Christmas feast was where it had begun. He had been lulled into a false sense of security and cooperation by the welcome and the talk of trade, when there had been no intention to trade at all. He should have been on his guard and he had been duped. His family, his wealth, his horses, his honour. What a laughing stock Owain had made of him. Gerald, the man who hid in a latrine while the Welsh robbed his castle and stole his wife and possessions.

'Cadwgan could be behind this too.' His anger was raw and visceral. 'He invited us to his Christmas feast. Even if his son carried out the attack, the father must have been complicit.' Clenching his fists, he sought control. 'Let everything be shored up, repaired and rebuilt. I will write to Richard de Belmeis, for, however much it pains me, he must have the details of the raid. This deed will not go unavenged and I will have my wife, my children and my horses returned at the first opportunity.'

For the rest of the night, Gerald concentrated on repairing Cenarth's vulnerable defences. He put the guards on double duty, even the wounded ones, lest there be a second attack and he had letters written ready to be sent at first light on foot, since they didn't have any horses.

Finally, there was nothing left to be done. The men either went about their duties or retired to snatch a few hours' sleep. Gerald paced his desecrated stronghold, his stomach burning. In the under croft, he paused to stare at the empty shelves. A smashed jar of honey; spilled oats leading in a trail to the door. All the cheese had gone, and the barrels of mead.

'Sir, you should take some rest and sustenance,' said Odo de Barry from the doorway.

Gerald suppressed the urge to snap at him to go away and leave him alone. He didn't want to rest because the moment he stopped, his mind would flood with images of what might be happening to Nesta and their children. Odo's advice was sensible though, for without rest he would eventually cease to function. 'Very well, in a moment. Have someone clear up this mess in the morning and itemise what we have left.'

Leaving Odo, he went to the kitchens and sat down at the cook's chopping trestle. The Welsh had tried to fire the place but the quick-thinking cook had used a barrel of water to douse the flames. There was some singeing round the edges, but everything could be scrubbed clean or easily replaced. The cook himself had hidden in a storage recess under the floor until Owain's men had gone. Gerald gruffly praised him for his foresight, and sent him out of the room because he needed to be alone.

He forced down some half-stale bread with mutton dripping, and drank a cup of ale from a jug that the raiders had overlooked. He had never felt less like eating, but knew he must. Chewing and swallowing, he tried to take stock of the situation.

He could not imagine how it would be even if he did regain Nesta. The landscape would be very different, but at least he did not need to visualise it this instant. First, he had to get back his family from the Welsh and he couldn't achieve that without weapons, horses and supplies. The latter must be done at once to show how quickly he was capable of recovering, otherwise he would be the one dangling on the rope.

He would also send a messenger to Cadwgan demanding the immediate return of everything he and his son had taken, on pain of retribution from the entire Norman force on the Marches and from England's king, who was the father of one of the abducted children. He had to show that the lion had been poked, but the injury, rather than being a mortal blow, had roused the beast's fury.

He desperately needed to sleep, but the thought of doing so in his own chamber without the company of Nesta and the children was untenable. Besides, he stank. Instead, he went to the guard room and rolled himself in his cloak, with his dagger close to hand, and through sheer exhaustion eventually succumbed to a restless slumber.

Nesta watched Owain from the bed as he pulled on his tunic, appreciating his broad shoulders and his animal vitality. They had only recently made love but she wanted him again in order to make the world go away. When he held her, when he told her what would be, he filled a deep void inside her. She craved the stories he wove of driving out the Normans and laying Wales at her feet, and it was even better if he was inside her when he said it.

Owain turned to look at her. 'I am sending the horses to my stud today. Do you want to ride with me?'

She smiled and stretched languorously. 'I will go anywhere with you.'

'Make yourself ready then, and I will meet you in the hall.' He gave her a long kiss then drew back reluctantly. 'I could spend all day abed; you are too much of a temptation.'

She gave him an arch smile. 'Are you saying I am too much for you?'

He laughed darkly. '*Cariad*, no woman is ever too much for me, but strangely I cannot get enough of you. That Norman husband of yours, he has no notion at all about you, does he? Are you as wild for him as you are for me? I doubt it.'

Nesta felt a shard of unease at his words, which were not of love but of posturing and prowess, but she tossed her head and, leaning back, gave him a scornful, provocative look. 'I shall say nothing.'

He grinned, and made a half lunge towards her, but stopped, took a back-step and looked towards the door where Nesta's son Gwilym stood watching them.

Nesta immediately drew the covers above her breasts, and wondered how long he had been there, and just how much he had heard and seen.

Owain went to the door and ruffled Gwilym's fair hair. 'Where's your nurse, young man?'

'She's dressing my sister,' he replied, and took several steps back from Owain. 'I want to see Mama.'

'Your mama is busy. Come with me and we shall find another lady to take care of you.'

Gwilym danced further away from Owain's reach, and Nesta intervened as she saw Owain's shoulders start to tense. 'It is all right. Gwilym can talk to me while I am dressing, and I shall take him back to his nurse.'

'You indulge the boy,' Owain said with a snort. 'How will he become a warrior when you coddle him? Do not be long, my love, I want to be on the road soon, and I won't wait for women and children.'

He strode from the room, and Nesta swiftly pulled on her chemise and called for Eleri. Then she beckoned to Gwilym, who approached her with the stiff walk of a nervous dog. His hair stuck up in tufts, lacking the care of a comb, and his hazel eyes were filled with caution.

'I don't like it here,' he said. 'When are we going home to Papa?'

She regarded him with dismay and more than a little guilt. 'Why do you not like it? Ceredigion is bigger than Carew or Cenarth, and you have plenty of places to play. You have your brothers and sister. It is not as though your father was with you all of the time. This is your new life now.'

Gwilym shook his head. 'I don't like it,' he repeated. 'Henry and Walter keep going off without me and you are always in the room with the Welsh lord, and kissing him.'

Nesta's cheeks grew hot, but she drew him into her arms and hugged him. 'Well, that is because he is keeping us safe and protecting us. There are going to be many changes, and you will grow accustomed.'

'I won't.' Gwilym pushed out his bottom lip. 'I don't like him. I want my papa!'

'Oh tush, the lord Owain will harm none of you!' Nesta said crossly, but with a frisson of unease. 'Here now.' She gave him an apple to eat from a silver bowl on the table and he sat on her bed while Eleri helped her to finish dressing. Had she really chosen the right path for herself and her children? The heat of the moment had been an all-consuming fire inside her, but what happened when the flames died down?

Gerald watched Richard de Belmeis wipe his hands on a napkin and nod to an attendant to remove the remains of the salmon in herb sauce on which the men had recently dined. The Bishop's private chamber in Shrewsbury Castle was closed against the failing light and the bitter, rain-filled wind gusting against the shutters.

'Your news is grave indeed.' Richard took an apple from the platter in the centre of the table and cut it into slices with a thin-bladed knife. 'My clerks will write to the King immediately. I share your anger and grief – this disgraceful deed oversteps all bounds.' He looked pointedly at Gerald. 'I suspect many of the Welsh will be up in arms themselves when word gets out. We can exploit the divisions between them while we set this to rights and benefit ourselves at the same time. Cadwgan and his son have many enemies as well as allies among their neighbours and kin. Owain's cousin Madog ap Rhyrid will gladly bring his spear to the table in exchange for reward.' De Belmeis pointed his fruit knife at Gerald. 'Madog has little interest beyond violence and booty as well you know, but he's a useful tool to cause rifts among the Welsh.'

Some of the burden dropped from Gerald's shoulders. De Belmeis was a shrewd, astute and ambitious man of the world, born here in the Marches, and well aware of the dynamics involved. He was not sentimental and any dealings with him had to be about what was best for him and the King. He possessed the authority to remove Gerald from Cenarth for his laxness.

'I have summoned my Flemings from Pembroke,' Gerald said, 'but I am grateful for your support and intervention.'

De Belmeis set his knife down. 'We have known each other since our days in the Montgomery household. I am a good judge of men's characters, and that is part of my value to the King. I do not criticise you too harshly for what has happened, although I admit – as I am sure you do yourself – that you have been foolish.'

Heat crawled up Gerald's neck and tingled his scalp. 'I do admit to my error. I took my eye off Owain ap Cadwgan and his father for a moment, but I shall never do it again.'

'I am sure you will not, for it would be your last act as Constable of Pembroke and Lord of Carew, but you do not need me to tell you. I see your shame and anger even though you keep it reined. Every man is permitted one mistake in his career. Let us hope my own is not giving you that leeway.'

Gerald looked down. He deserved this castigation and worse. Indeed, he welcomed it as his due.

De Belmeis folded his arms and leaned back. A shadow of

blue stubble grazed the beginnings of a double chin. 'Cadwgan ap Bleddyn is Lord of Ceredigion at King Henry's pleasure and if he wishes to survive there, he will bring his son to task. Owain has been a thorn in everyone's side for too long and this latest act will give us the sanction to pluck him out. Seizing the King's own son will not be tolerated. You shall have your wife and children back safely, I promise you, and you shall have your revenge.'

Gerald nodded stiffly. 'Thank you, my lord. I am glad of your support.'

Richard acknowledged him with a brusque wave. 'Take what you need in the way of supplies and horses; you can pay me back later. I would not want to see you lacking resources for what you must do.'

Dismissed from the Bishop's chamber, Gerald retired to the hall to bed down with his men. He felt better than he had done at the outset of the interview, and grittily determined. He would regain Nesta and his children; he would weather the storm and deal with the repercussions. And whenever and wherever he encountered Owain ap Cadwgan, one of them would die. There could be no other outcome.

18

Owain ap Cadwgan's stud, a day's ride from Cardigan, March 1110

Nesta watched Owain ride Storm around the training field at the back of the stud. Owain looked magnificent on the horse, his raven hair gleaming, his expression vibrant and fierce. They had been here a week, but were returning to Ceredigion tomorrow to await the arrival of several Welsh lords and their warbands.

Owain knew how to ride like a Norman, but he was much harder on the horse than Gerald and the stallion pranced and sidled, bloody foam flecking the bridle. He had been giving Henry and Walter riding lessons and was showing off to them. Nesta was wryly amused at his boyishness, his need to pose in front of her, seeking admiration.

At length Owain dismounted, tossed the reins to a tight-lipped Dewi, and going to Nesta, engulfed her beneath his cloaked arm. Together they walked to the hall and a meal of hot mutton stew and bread. Although spring was only a breath away, the light was dim and the good candles had been used up, leaving them with weaker, smokier tallow. She remembered her chamber at Carew with a momentary pang, but pushed it aside. They would soon be returning to Ceredigion and where she dwelt should not matter as long as she had Owain. She had moments when she felt she was living like an outlaw's concubine rather than a future queen. Owain declaimed his grandiose plans every night when they were in bed together, and they still worked their alchemy, but the brightness had begun to diminish from its first brilliant flare and she had yet to see evidence beyond words.

They were finishing their stew when a soldier hurried up the hall and bowed before their table. 'Sir, your lord father is here.'

Nesta looked at Owain and drew a sharp breath. They had been expecting to meet with Cadwgan but on their terms, and not quite so soon.

Owain pushed aside his cup and stood up, but before he could gather his wits Cadwgan stormed into the room.

'I have just received a letter from Gerald of Pembroke demanding that I return his wife and chattels and children,' he snarled, casting his riding gauntlets on the board. 'What have you been doing in my absence, boy?' He fixed Nesta with a furious gaze. 'I could not believe it was true – I did not think any son of mine could be so stupid!'

Owain drew himself up to stand a full head taller than his father. 'I did it for us and for Wales, because you will not!' His voice rang with pride and contempt. 'Look at the tribute I have won for you. Stores and horses and valuable hostages. We can rouse all of Wales and be princes again in our true right!'

Cadwgan's thin features twisted in disgust. 'I see very well that you have brought ruin on us by your folly. By Christ, what were you thinking? You have kicked a wasps' nest so thoroughly that we shall be stung to death before it is over. I was always too lenient with you, boy. I should have whipped you until I striped some sense into that thick hide of yours. This is not some petty raid where you can take your booty and sell it afar. This woman has been the mistress of the English king and borne his son – whom you have stolen too. This is far more than gaining vengeance on a petty Norman lord and satisfying your tawdry lusts!'

Owain bared his teeth. 'Tell me, Father, when did you become such a coward? I did it for us – for Powys!' He thumped the table with his fist, making the bowls leap on the board, and Nesta gasped at his words.

'Hah, you did it for common lechery. I know you – led by your cock up every passing alley and snatch. There are far better ways of proving your manhood than sticking it in Gerald of Windsor's wife!' He made an air-punch in Nesta's direction.

'What would you know of manhood?' Owain sneered. 'At least I still have my cock and balls. You have allowed your own manhood to be thieved by the Normans. You fawn on them even to the point of taking that bloodless little milksop for a wife and wasting your seed inside her on children that will amount to nothing. At least my woman is of Welsh royal blood!'

'But she's your concubine, not your wife, while her husband lives!' Cadwgan snapped. 'You have never followed through on *any* of your deeds!'

His hand flashed to his sword and he half drew it from its sheath while Owain pressed forward, chest thrust out, daring his father to go all the way. Cadwgan was the first to back down, trembling with emotion, his eyes glistening.

'You have always been the apple of my eye and you have betrayed me,' he said. 'All I have worked through the years to achieve, you have brought down in this single act of lustful folly. You think that the Welsh are going to overthrow the Norman yoke? You are living on dreams, boy, and they are about to become everyone else's nightmare.'

Owain snorted in contempt. 'You are becoming weak and fearful in your dotage. Let Gerald of Pembroke whine for what he has lost. We do not answer to him!' He cast a blazing look at Nesta and she stared back, huge-eyed, her stomach sucked in with shock, for Cadwgan's reaction was the opposite of what Owain had led her to expect.

'I am neither weak nor fearful,' Cadwgan seethed. 'At least I have the common sense to deal in facts, not create mythical fantasies from acts of petty rapine. Gerald of Pembroke on his own we can deal with, but he is not on his own. Richard de Belmeis has ordered our own Welsh enemies and kin to attack us. He has told your cousin Madog that he can have Powys if he brings you down. Gerald of Pembroke is bringing his Flemings and vassals from the south and has aid from Tancred of Haverford. De Belmeis has sent word to King Henry that you have seized Gerald of Pembroke's wife and children, including the King's own son, and de Belmeis has implicated me in this too. We are in danger of losing everything for what you have done. They are coming, and if they arrive and we are still here, then we will die.'

'I will fight them all,' Owain said defiantly, although he had paled.

'You won't, not here, and neither will I.' Cadwgan turned to Nesta. 'Pack whatever baggage you have, my lady. I do not wish to know the circumstances by which you are here, but you endanger us all.'

Nesta's first inclination was to defend Owain against his weasel of a father, and spit that she was here of her own free will, and that she had faith in Owain. However, that faith no longer stood on solid foundations, and her own survival depended on keeping matters ambiguous. She needed time to digest the full implications of what Cadwgan was saying – time she did not have. 'Then you should return the children to him,' she said, thinking on her feet. 'It will keep them safe. Holding them hostage now will not increase your power to bargain, only make matters worse.'

She saw Owain's scowl, and looked away. She had discovered already that he would only listen to those who agreed with him and praised his idea.

'As you will,' he said with an impatient shrug. 'The children are a hindrance anyway, and we might be able to bargain a sum for them as hostages.'

Nesta bit her lip at the contempt in his tone.

'We will leave here the moment you have assembled your baggage,' Cadwgan said to his son. 'I advise you to go into exile. Make yourself scarce, for you will be hunted down and killed for this, and whatever you think, you are not strong enough to stand against your enemies.'

Owain curled his lip. 'I will say when we leave.'

'Then decide soon, because I am offering to help you now, but that offer will not last beyond sunset.' He stalked from the room.

Owain cursed, picked up a cup and dashed it against the wall. He kicked over a stool and began pacing up and down.

Nesta was suddenly afraid of him. The wild beast was in the room, and she was no longer its match, even though she was still attracted to him with sick fascination.

'My father knows nothing!' Owain ranted, storming about the room. 'All he wants to do is suck milk from the Norman teat. We still have allies.'

'I should go and make the children ready,' Nesta said. 'Whatever happens, they should not be a part of this – indeed, I should never have brought them.'

He whirled on her. 'Are you going to betray me too, like my father?'

'No, never that! I am with you, you know I am!'

'Do I?' He curled his lip. 'Yet you allowed your husband to live. And it wasn't you who opened the gate for us at Cenarth, was it?' He made a throwing gesture at her, his fist clenched. 'Your message said he would be gone, and he wasn't!'

'That was none of my doing. He returned a day early, believe me or not as you will.'

'Hah!' Owain pushed his fingers through his hair. 'I do not know what to believe with you.'

'It is the same for me. What are promises worth – a handful of nothing! I shall go to the children and make them ready. As you said, they are only a hindrance.'

Owain swore and grabbed her arm. She tried to fight him off, but his grip tightened, and a thrill of fear shot through her. His lips came down and he kissed her hard, and squeezed her bottom up against him so that she could feel him half hard and rising through his hose and tunic. 'Get them out of the way then. Better to sell them back to your husband than barter them in Dublin, eh?' Nesta gasped and would have clawed his face, but he held her fast, his chest heaving. 'Do not push me any further, I am warning you.' She glared into his coal-glitter eyes, answering him without words. He released his grip and gave her a shove. 'Just go,' he growled.

'Willingly.' Turning on her heel, she felt as though the ground had shifted under her feet and opened a huge chasm in front of her.

'The lord Owain has decided that you are to be returned to your father,' Nesta told the children as she set about packing their baggage. She could not prevent the tremble in her voice.

'Are you coming with us?' Henry asked. His face wore an expression much older than his years – hard and shrewd, judgemental too – as was Walter's.

She shook her head. 'I am to remain for now, but you are going to safety. That is the bargain.' She realised now she should never have brought the children, but then she had believed she was taking them to a new and wonderful life. The dream was very different from the hard reality.

'You still want to be with him,' Henry accused. 'You would rather be with him than with us.'

She forced herself to meet the hostility in her oldest son's gaze. 'I am doing what is best for everyone. The situation is dangerous and I do not know what is going to happen next, that is the truth, and I need to protect you.'

Turning to Gwilym, she took him in her arms. 'Tell your father when you return to him that I am well.' He flung his arms around her and, almost overcome with guilt and remorse, she hugged his sturdy small body, while a deep, sore part of her wished she was going with them. Then it was Angharad's turn, and she held her daughter, wrapped in a blanket of furs, and kissed her brow. 'Goodbye my little girl, safe journey – safer than I could give you.'

The children departed in a cart under escort of Cadwgan's men, bound for Shrewsbury and the initial custody of Richard de Belmeis. Nesta swallowed gut-wrenching guilt and grief as she watched the cart roll out of the entrance. She had failed as a mother to these children, so taken up in the blaze that was Owain, so consumed by lust and a festering need for vengeance that she had given no attention to what was really important, and now she was paying the price – and so were her offspring.

She tried to assuage her pain by telling herself they could now move more swiftly. If matters were as dire as Cadwgan warned, the sooner they took ship for Ireland the better. They could seek her brother Gruffydd's help and he would be a tie to rein in Owain's wilder tendencies.

With the children gone, she packed her own baggage. Owain had gone off somewhere to work off his frustration, and the room felt spacious without him, but emptier too, as if the hearth had gone cold. Her Welsh warrior; her untamed lion. Lurking among all her other volatile emotions, she harboured the terror that he would be brought down, exactly as her father had been – that the feast she had been expecting was in reality one of dead men's bones and the ashes of dreams.

The next day, they set out for the Irish ships waiting at Aberteifi at the top of Ceredigion Bay. Cadwgan rode with them, guarding Owain's much smaller warband and the booty seized from Cenarth. The horses came too, Owain having decided not to leave them at the stud.

When Nesta tried to ride at his side, Owain ordered her back to the baggage train.

'You were eager enough to have me ride on your saddle when you took me from Cenarth,' she said furiously. 'And you promised me everything.'

Owain scowled. 'This is no time to be difficult. You know nothing of warfare, and I need to be free to think without distraction.'

'I seem to remember a time very recently when you were very willing to be distracted. You laid your grand plans at my feet, and said that we would rule together.'

He snorted impatiently. 'And so we shall if that comforts your feelings, but for now you will ride where I say. Do not question me again before my warband.'

Shocked, Nesta retreated. She could feel Owain's men

watching her with hard-eyed contempt, and even satisfaction at seeing her put in her place. She realised with dismay that this was exactly how Henry had treated her – a commodity to be used and transported at his whim.

Gerald would never have treated her like this, but then in her blindness, she had believed him weak. But there were different ways of being strong. Owain was a taker, not a giver, and would drain her and leave her with nothing. Yet still that very fierceness and fire held a dark attraction. A life with such a man would never be dull . . . but was the excitement worth it? Confused, entangled, she gazed at her horse's mane and gnawed her lip.

They followed the coast, riding as swiftly as the terrain allowed. She could hear the muted roar of the sea on their left, washing into the bite of the bay. The air was sharply cold and a thick sea-mist enveloped their party. A silvering of hoar droplets dewed their cloaks. The men riding immediately in front of Nesta were greyly visible, but at the head of the troop, Owain and his father were faded ghosts. She shivered, remembering the tales her own father had told her of the Wild Hunt, the Cwm Anwn – a phantom army destined to wander the world for their sins, forever damned.

A flock of sheep bleated past them, herded by a tense shep- herd, head ducked low. The cold invaded Nesta's bones and her fingers and toes grew numb. She wanted comfort, attention and warmth. All the things that had been hers to command as a cherished child at her father's knee. All the things she had had with Gerald and that she had held at naught. And now, despite the physical attraction and the magnificent words, she was having doubts about Owain being a good exchange. She had sacrificed her secure life for him and he needed to acknowledge that, not send her back to the baggage train as an afterthought.

They covered many more miles at a swift pace until her body ached in the places it was not numb. The day was drawing to a close and the visibility had decreased so much that the horses had started to stumble when at last they arrived at a low building with stables attached. A few servants emerged in surprise, bearing tallow lanterns. One of Owain's soldiers helped Nesta from her horse.

'Where is this?' she asked.

'One of Lord Owain's homesteads,' he replied. 'We shall shelter here for the night and move on in the morning.'

Shaking out her skirts, Nesta entered the building while Owain remained outside, posting guards and talking to his men. A servant was stoking up the fire in the main room, and someone else was setting up a cauldron on a tripod stand. She paced the chamber, the hem of her cloak trailing on the beaten earth floor. The sputtering lights smelled of mutton fat and the place was little better than a hovel.

Owain and his father walked in, and the atmosphere bristled with tension. They had clearly been arguing, although whatever they had been saying had been silenced at the door. However, the way both men regarded her made it plain that she was their bone of contention.

Once they had eaten some greasy broth and bread, Nesta retired to a small chamber behind the hall that had been hastily cleared out and a pallet put down for her. She was bone weary but her mind was like a shower of sparks, and she knew sleep would be slow to arrive. Owain and Cadwgan were talking again in the hall. Knowing they had waited again until she was absent, she realised bitterly that rather than acquiring power, her status was becoming that of a diminished chattel.

It was late when Owain eventually joined her, dragging another pallet close to hers and covering them both in his fur-lined cloak. He put his hand on her waist. 'We have an early start in the morning, I hope you are up to the ride.'

'I am not fragile,' she said tautly. 'I am stronger than you will ever know. I am the daughter of Rhys ap Tewdr of Dyfed, and let no man forget it, even you.'

He chuckled softly. 'And I am no meek little lapdog like "Geri" to be ordered about by a woman, whatever her bloodline.'

He leaned over and kissed her, and she felt his heat and strength and once again she leaped into the fire, in desperation. They were fully clothed because it was so cold. He pushed up her skirts and she felt his heat on her thighs and then he was inside her. The pallet was lumpy and uncomfortable and his thrusts were full and fierce, making her gasp, but still she strove to bring him deeper into her, wrapping her legs around him, capturing and holding him there in a vice. His breathing grew harsh and he roared in triumph as he surged to his limit and pinned her, even as she trapped him. And then it was done, and he collapsed on her.

She held him to her as he bent his head against her neck and his breathing filled her ears. With the glory fading, her discomfort returned. He was lying on her so heavily that she could barely breathe, and at last she had to push at him until he rolled off with a grunt.

'Ah God, that was good,' he said. 'I swear I have given you my child just now.'

Nesta felt the cold residue on her leg where he had slid from her body. She pulled down her skirts. 'If you have, may that child be your heir, and may you do right by it and me.'

Owain turned on his side, taking the cloak with him. 'You know I will look after you,' he said. 'Go to sleep.'

She curled up beside him and he began to breathe deeply with a slight snore. Nesta wanted him to hold her and speak of tenderness and glory, but he was insensible, and eventually she put her arm around him for warmth in the draughty room and to comfort herself, before finally falling into a restless sleep.

She was woken up by Owain jolting violently against her, and her eyes flew open to see Cadwgan standing over them, kicking his son. It was barely dawn and cold grey light filtered through the window openings onto their pallet.

'Get up,' Cadwgan growled. His eye sockets were bruise-blue with exhaustion. 'Messengers are here. The March has been raised against us as I feared – we have to leave now.'

Owain pushed aside the cover and stood up, groggy and sleep-rumpled. 'Who?' he demanded.

'Who do you think? Your cousins Ithel and Madog.'

'I do not fear them,' Owain said belligerently, and reached for the piss pot.

'And Llywarch ap Trahairn, and Uchtred ap Edwin,' Cadwgan continued grimly. 'All have been promised rich reward by Richard de Belmeis. They have been told to take what they want with impunity and with the backing of the English crown. There are mercenaries heading from Shrewsbury to Ceredigion too. This is all your fault.'

Owain sent a torrent of steaming urine into the pot. 'I will defeat anyone who comes against me; I fear none of them.'

'Your words have as much value as your piss,' his father spat. 'Listen for once instead of playing the dunghill cock. Uchtred has sent a message saying that for the sake of old bonds he will hold off long enough for us to take our leave. We must ride for Aberteifi now, or die.'

Nesta left the bed and stood up, rubbing her arms. Cadwgan shot her an impatient look. Owain didn't look at her at all, but scowled and bit his thumb.

'I told you, you have kicked over a wasps' nest and those wasps are too numerous to crush underfoot – many of them are our own,' his father continued. 'De Belmeis and his Marcher levies will come down on us like a mighty rain of stones. Do not say I am being a coward or a man who licks Norman arses for an occupation. I see the world as it is. You need to be on that ship bound for Dublin while I do what I can to limit the damage.' He palmed his face. 'Owain, you are my firstborn son. I do not want to see you cornered and cut down for the love I bear you throughout all. You cannot fight your way out of this, not without more than you have.'

Owain glowered at his father and let out his breath in a sound of disgust. 'Very well, to please your weak stomach. I shall sell my gains in Dublin and recruit men to return with me and scatter all before us.'

Cadwgan waved his hand impatiently. 'Do as you wish, but make haste. We cannot be caught like this. Uchtred has given us fair warning, but they are on our heels nonetheless.'

Once more Nesta found herself bundled onto a horse, and now they were racing, in real fear of pursuit. Yesterday's ride had chafed her thighs and they were raw against the saddle as they chivvied her along, with barely a word spoken.

That evening, exhausted, they came to the estuary of the Teifi where a Norse trading ship tossed at anchor in the starlit evening, mast down, sails furled, waiting for the tide. The crew had pitched their tents on the shore and were tending and mending, awaiting their cargo. Owain was on familiar terms with the ship's master and they clasped hands and slapped backs as old friends and associates. The master, Magnus, plied his trade between Dublin and Wales. His hair was white-gold, and his beard flame-red. A hefty paunch bulged over his belt, but he had strong arms and a wide, powerful chest.

'What have you brought me this time?' he asked once they were all sitting round a fire with bowls of fish stew. 'I see you have some fine horses, even if you have worked them hard to get here.'

'I am bringing them with me,' Owain said. 'I am asking for passage on your ship. I have some superb bolts of cloth, silks and damasks, that will more than pay my way, and I shall be recruiting men when we arrive in Dublin. I have the silver for it.'

Magnus picked his teeth and regarded Nesta and her maids. 'No slaves this time? I could find you willing buyers for the right merchandise.'

Owain shook his head. 'No, but I will have some on the next voyage. The ladies are not accompanying me, but will be leaving with my father for England.'

Nesta lifted her head and stared at Owain in angry shock. He avoided her gaze, turning his head away.

'A pity,' Magnus said, turning to look out to sea. 'The tide will be turning around midnight. The skies are clear, no mist, so we'll use the stars to navigate.'

'I am coming with you,' Nesta said furiously to Owain. 'And the cloth is mine!'

Frowning, he took her arm and drew her away from the tents until they stood alone under the deep-blue starlight with the fire a distant flicker on their left.

'I have sacrificed everything for you,' Nesta said before he could speak. 'You made your promise, and now you are abandoning me and running away to Ireland, taking all my worldly goods with you. Dear God, you have played me false!'

'You cannot come,' he replied, curtly, as if ordering a child.

'It is too dangerous and you will slow me down. I shall be going places where I cannot keep you safe, among men who would take and trade you the moment they set eyes on you. You have seen how it is with Magnus. In Ireland it would be ten times worse.'

'But you must have known that before you made your promises!' she snapped. 'You have used me for your own ends, and now you leave me to a fate far worse than had you let me be!'

'That is not true. I wanted the best for us—'

'You wanted the best for yourself!' she hissed. 'To slight your enemy by taking his wife and then casting her off. I see it clearly now!'

'I have told you, I cannot take you!' he answered with exasperation. 'I need to be light on my feet and you will slow me down. You will be safe with my father until I come for you. I promise I will return and set you free.'

'I am done with your promises because you have not kept a single one. God knows, Owain, I would have walked this path of fire with you to the ends of the earth, but it seems that you will not walk it with me, or for me. You swore to cherish and protect me if only I would come with you. You swore you would make me your consort and queen and give me Wales. Now you are fleeing to Dublin with my goods, and abandoning me to your father, who you yourself have called a weak reed and a spent force. What kind of a man are you? What kind of coward?' She spat the last word, tears running down her face.

He gripped her shoulders and shook her. 'If you were a man, I would strike you dead for such words. I will return for you. Your cloth and the silver shall buy me warriors. You say you have risked all for me; well, I have done the same for you. I feel the betrayal of others in my heart, even my own father, yet I have to rely on him. If I do not go now, then all of us are lost.'

She stared at him in fury and grief. When she ran with him from Cenarth she had carried a sack full of hope and possibility, and now it was an empty, deflated thing at her feet.

'It is different for women,' he said. 'I have taken you once. It will be simple enough to claim you again. Have faith and wait for me.'

'I am done with waiting,' Nesta said, her lip curling in disgust. 'Either take me with you now, or never again. You betray me. You could take me straight to my brother for protection, but there is more to it than that, isn't there?'

Owain drew himself up, and pulled back at the same time.

'You are giving me into your father's custody but you have no right to make that decision. Your father says he will make everything right with Henry, and it does not take a fool to see that it will be much easier with the wife of Gerald of Windsor in his hands to barter for that goodwill.'

Observing a red flush creep up Owain's throat and into his face, Nesta realised how far he had betrayed her. Sold for a price like a piece of merchandise.

'Go then.' She turned her back on him. 'Take it all, and if I never see you again, it will be too soon. Dear God, you have played me for a fool!'

'In Christ's name, woman, I am doing my best for both of us!' he bellowed.

'You are doing the best for yourself!'

She kept her back turned, waiting for him to grab her and crush her to his body. She wanted him to say it was all a mistake and that she should board the ship with him now. She heard his harsh breathing, as he came to the brink, but then he cursed, and she heard his feet tear the grass as he walked away.

Nesta folded her arms inside her cloak, frozen to the soul. Her heart had cracked across the middle but she did not believe that Owain's heart had suffered any such damage. Perhaps some minor cuts that would scab over soon enough. He believed his own lies so strongly that for him they were the truth.

'My lady?'

Dewi had arrived at her side, and she hastily swiped her cuff across her face.

'What?'

'My lady, the lord Owain is taking the horses. I am to go with him to care for them – he has just instructed me – your mare also.'

Fury swept through her at this further evidence of Owain's perfidy. Dewi's leathery face wore an expression of worry and hangdog shame.

'I have to go with the horses, my lady . . . but it is wrong. I am not the lord Owain's man, I am yours, and the horses do not belong to him. He will sell them, and then he will sell me too.'

'He shall do no such thing!' she said grimly. 'Take the horses to my brother. Do not let the lord Owain sell them to the Irish or the Norse. Go at night if you must, but find the lord Gruffydd and seek his protection. The horses are his by right. I charge you with this task. Let my brother know what is afoot and what has happened as far as you know. Tell him that I continue to hope for the day when he returns to Wales.'

Dewi bowed, and when he raised his head again, his anxious expression held a glimmer of hope. 'I will do my best, my lady, I swear.'

She gave him a bleak smile. 'You are one of the few men I know who keeps their word. I fear that I have leaped from the fireside into the fire. I do not know what my future holds, but it is not the one I imagined.'

'You will survive, mistress, and find a way through, I am certain.'

Nesta shook her head. 'I am not so sure I will, but I have learned a great deal.' That the last person she should trust was herself, and the taste was especially bitter.

Dewi bowed and departed to see to his equine charges. Rubbing her arms, Nesta inhaled the scent of the Irish Sea and the camp-fire smoke. Even though her heart was full of anger towards Owain, she was going to miss him like a severed limb. But just how much would he miss her?

Gerald would have died for her at Cenarth, had she not forced him to escape. It had been her choice, and he had capitulated. Had she truly desired to have her revenge on all Normans, she would have stood back and let Owain kill Gerald. By now she could have been Owain's wife, not his concubine. But she had not followed through; perhaps Owain had sensed her ambivalence. Fresh tears filled her eyes. Gerald was safety, Gerald was the everyday fabric of life that she had cast away down a latrine, never appreciating its value until now.

At midnight, the ship's master and crew prepared to sail as the tide turned, drawing away from the Welsh shore and curling in white crests towards Ireland. The tents were all dismantled and packed up, and the cargo loaded onto the vessel, including the horses. Nesta's stomach twisted as she watched her sacks of cloth being carried on board. All the best pieces, some of which had been gifts from Henry and were irreplaceable. So much lost for so little gain.

Owain came to her again just before he boarded. Contrition had replaced his anger. 'I will return, I swear I will.' He took her arm. 'I will bring soldiers and we shall drive the Normans out of Powys and Dyfed, and we shall be married. I admit it was too soon this time. I should have waited, but you were a fire in my blood.'

'Were,' Nesta noted. And she was given the blame for being the fire. 'Go,' she said wearily. 'Do what you must, and make me no more hollow promises.'

'And will you wait for me? Say you will, or my heart will break.'

This time she was not taken in. He might mean the words, but they lay on the surface and had no depth. She thought of Dewi and the message she had given to him for her brother. 'Yes,' she said. 'I will wait.' But waiting meant waiting to see and building her defences in the meantime. Her own heart had already broken, and she had to begin the work of patching it together and hardening its shell.

He made to kiss her but she turned her head so that his lips only found the edge of her mouth and her cheek.

'I will return, you will see – for you and my child.'

He left her then, leaping with agility aboard the ship. In the torchlight she saw the gleam of his features for a moment and the light along the sable edge of his cloak. He didn't look back, and she turned away. The ship cast its mooring and the men rowed out across the starlit water and set the sail. They were swiftly lost to sight, although their shouts and cries carried on the breeze for a longer time. She listened for Owain's voice calling her name, and did not hear it.

Standing beside her, Cadwgan grunted. 'Let us hope he stays out of trouble long enough to mend this coil,' he said. 'I often wonder if he is more trouble than he is worth, although I would rather him than the likes of his cousins.'

'And you would rather the Normans too?' Nesta said coldly.

He looked at her with disfavour. 'From where I stand, alliance with the Normans has brought me better rewards and security than with my fellow kin and princes. I must do what is best for myself and my dependants. Owain thinks I am almost in my dotage, but living to achieve my dotage is a sign of successful strategy. I often wonder if he will live to achieve his. Dying in one's prime is only glorious for the bards, not the man who loses his life, for what will he know, even if his memory and myth are taken up in songs?'

Nesta said nothing, for what was there to say? In essence Cadwgan was right, even if she disliked him.

'Take some sleep,' he said. 'We leave for the Marches at first light.'

He walked off, and Nesta turned to stare across the waves. Her eyes were dry because she had used up her tears, and there was no point in weeping over what she could not change. Better to gird herself for what was to come.

19

Fortress of Cenarth Bychan,
March 1110

At Cenarth, Gerald continued to shore up and strengthen the defences. He had still not discovered who had left the gate open for Owain. When interrogated, the Welsh servants had all provided plausible denials, and no Norman would ever have left the postern unfastened. His only conclusion was that it had to be someone in the missing party, and that would include Nesta, her ladies, and the groom Dewi. Whoever it was, the main issue had been to tighten up the patrols and security so there would be no opportunity for further betrayal.

This morning more troops had arrived from the south. Flemings, Normans and even some Welsh with axes to grind against the house of Cadwgan, and Gerald had been busy deploying and assessing them.

He looked across the compound to where Walter and Henry were engaged in their swordplay lessons with Odo de Barry. To one side, Gerald's youngest was using his small wooden sword to strike at the pell-post, practising his moves, but in reality he was just bashing the wood with hard, haphazard blows, full of rage.

'What is this?' Gerald caught his arm. 'You are not battering your enemy into submission with a club. What have I shown you?'

Gwilym looked up at him, breathing hard, his little face red and flushed under his mop of fair-brown hair. He said nothing, but his hazel eyes were bright and fierce. Gerald's heart strings tugged, for he recognised the emotion, and had often given way to such fury himself of late, by punching the wall or kicking over stools. But that was in private and he had tried not to let it spill out into his daily life, especially around the boys, who had already endured God knows what at the hands of Owain ap Cadwgan and needed stability and steadiness from a man in control of himself.

Gerald removed the sword from his son's small hand and struck the pell in formation in the correct manner. Criss-cross, forehand–backhand, feet positioned, steady. 'One, two, three, four.' He handed the sword back to Gwilym. 'You have to practise until you can do this blindfold. It will come to you, but you will exhaust yourself and damage your weapon if you attack like that.'

Gwilym took the sword back from his father and scowled. 'I was pretending it was Owain ap Cadwgan, Papa. I hate him. I want to kill him.'

Gerald's chest tightened. He felt the same, and it would never go away: the wound was too deep. 'Even more reason to practise your craft. You must be sure of your own ability. Never be overcome by your anger, for it can drive you over a very dangerous edge. Come now, show me.' Gwilym raised his arm and began striking the pell again, and Gerald watched him with hands on hips. 'That's better.' He wondered what Owain had done to him, and what Gwilym had witnessed, to make him say such things.

Gwilym stopped and looked at his father. 'Will Mama come back?'

Gerald stood upright. 'Of course she will.' He gave Gwilym a reassuring shoulder pat. 'You were just sent back first, that is all.' He tousled his son's hair, and as Gwilym returned to his task at the pell, he glanced again at the older boys. Henry had been belligerent and rude since their return, and Gerald knew it was because he had failed in the lad's eyes and been made a laughing stock. However, he and Walter had provided him with a few important details.

They had told him that Nesta had been separated from them almost immediately and had slept in a different room, and that Owain was with her. That told Gerald all he needed to know – and too much. He was afraid for Nesta and of the danger to her from a man as volatile and dishonourable as Owain ap Cadwgan. If she turned out to be with child from this, then that child would have to be given to the Church, but the first thing to do was get her back, and go on from there. If he allowed his anger, his jealousy, his feelings of betrayal and inadequacy to overcome him, he would not just rage at the pell like his six-year-old son, he would burn down the world. A cleric in his middle years riding a bay cob arrived at the gates and the guards questioned him, then signalled him through. Gerald did not recognise him, but the man carried a document satchel and Gerald's breath shortened, for he knew it must contain news. There was no other reason for him to be here. Leaving the boys, he crossed the ward, and as the man dismounted he waved away the steward who was coming to attend to him.

'God's greeting,' he said.

The cleric dipped his head. 'The same to you, sire. I am seeking the seigneur Gerald FitzWalter.' He spoke fluent French and his accent was English, not Welsh.

'Then you have found me. What is your business?'

'I have come from the manor of Sai with a letter from the lord Cadwgan ap Bleddyn, concerning your lady wife. I know what is written and am also bidden to answer whatever you ask.'

'I see,' Gerald said. 'You had better come within to my chamber.' He raised his hand and beckoned Odo de Barry to join him. 'There is news,' he said. 'Finish the lesson and come with me.'

'You are not a Welshman,' Gerald said to the cleric once the men had settled in the chamber with a jug of wine.

'No.' The man's ingratiating smile revealed crooked front teeth. 'I am a chaplain attached to the household of the lord Cadwgan's father-by-marriage, Picot de Sai. It was deemed better diplomacy to send me.' He produced a letter from his satchel from which dangled Cadwgan's seal.

Gerald took it, but left it unopened. 'And what does the lord Cadwgan have to say to me that he does not expect to be answered on the edge of my sword?'

The cleric swallowed. 'He wishes you to know he had no part in the raid at Cenarth. It was all his son's planning and intent. He will swear an oath on holy relics to the truth of his statement, and he deeply regrets the situation. He vows to try and put it right with all the injured parties including yourself and the King.'

Gerald raised his eyebrows and looked at Odo de Barry, who stood with folded arms and a deep frown on his face. 'And just how does he intend to do that given the gravity of the situation and the insult offered?'

'The lord Cadwgan is dwelling on his wife's dower property

in England – he is taking no part in the troubles created by his son's ill-judged actions. Owain has fled to Ireland on a trading ship. The lord Cadwgan prevailed on his son not to take your lady with him, just as he prevailed on him to return your children.'

Gerald blenched, for he could imagine Nesta being eager to go with Owain and join her brother.

'He is striving to be a voice of reason,' the cleric continued, 'and he wishes to return your good lady safely to you.'

The words buzzed inside Gerald's head like a swarm of bees. 'So she is with Cadwgan?'

'Yes, sire, and safe and well. He wishes you to know he has rescued and protected her from his over-zealous son and he desires to make peace with you in order that she might return home as soon as all can be arranged to the satisfaction of both parties.'

'Meaning?' Gerald narrowed his eyes. Cadwgan had a reputation for being as slippery as an eel in a bucket, and despite all the fine words about him wanting to preserve and protect Nesta, he knew it was only a cover for piracy and that Cadwgan, no less than his son, desired to profit from it. He was deeply ashamed about the manner in which he had lost Nesta, but fooled once did not mean being fooled twice. 'What price does he wish to exact for my wife's restoration?'

'That you will not pursue him as your enemy, and that once your wife is returned, it will be the end of the matter.'

Gerald snorted at such brazen effrontery.

'There shall be a truce between you and Cadwgan. He has taken an oath to forswear his son and has promised not to aid him by any means should he return to Wales.'

'"Promised"?' Gerald almost choked. 'What are promises from such a man except as rags to clad his lies? Just how will he prevent his son from doing as he wants? There is only one way to stop a rabid wolf.' He compressed his lips; his main objective was to have Nesta restored. 'What of my horses and the valuable goods that were stolen at the same time as my family? Are they to be returned too?'

The cleric flushed. 'My lord gave me no instruction on that matter.'

'I am sure he did not.' Gerald threw up his hands. 'I will draft you a reply for Cadwgan ap Bleddyn, and in the meantime, my own chaplain will find you refreshment and sleeping space.'

'Thank you, sire.' The cleric started to rise from the bench.

'Have you seen or spoken to my lady wife?' Gerald was driven to ask, but felt diminished to do so.

'I have not spoken to her, sire, but I saw her with the lord Cadwgan's lady.'

'And how did she seem?'

'She was well, my lord, and being treated as an honoured guest.'

'And a most valuable one,' Gerald remarked sharply.

He was glad to hear that Nesta was unharmed, but that did not tell him what had happened beforehand. One part of him wanted to know every damning detail, although he would never ask. Had she colluded with Owain and gone willingly with him? Had they had their will of each other or had she been coerced? He owed his life to her, but had been utterly humiliated by what he had been forced to do to survive. He tried to keep the cool, rational side of his mind uppermost and subdue the other dark, unworthy feelings, but it was a struggle.

He saw the cleric to the door and bade Walter, who was attending on squire duty, to take him to his own chaplain, and then he closed the door, sat down heavily on the bench and put his face in his hands, his composure crumbling.

Odo de Barry came over to him and gripped his shoulder. 'Steady,' he said.

'Ah God.' Gerald cuffed tears from his eyes. He could have Nesta home in a matter of days, but he had not planned how it would go from there. He loved her beyond his own life, and feared her rejection, for he knew she did not feel the same about him. Over time she had grown gentler like a tame wild bird, but what if it was Owain's hand she answered to? He had to rise above this crushing jealous despair and somehow find the strength to start again. 'Do you think I am mad?'

Odo hesitated, and when he spoke, cautiously measured his words. 'I think you should be careful. You must do what is best for your standing and your position in Dyfed. However much it pains you, you must treat with Cadwgan, but keep your eye on the other players too.'

Gerald raised his head from his hands. His mind was filled with wool, and for the moment, Odo had the clearer vision. 'If you are telling me to treat with Owain ap Cadwgan, your advice will go unheeded. I vow to bring about his downfall, however long I have to wait.'

Odo shrugged. 'Then have patience, and do not rush into retaliation. Richard de Belmeis has given Madog ap Rhyrid and others the opportunity to run wild through Powys, but I doubt he intends to give them free rein for longer than it suits him to punish Cadwgan for losing control of Owain. They'll serve their purpose and then be dealt with. Cadwgan will pay a fine and return to his lands. He is bound to do so, for he is the greater Norman ally. He knows if he does not curb his son, he will be deposed – he has been given fair warning. Since Owain has fled to Ireland, he is not currently a problem. When he returns, as we know he will, it will be a different matter.'

Gerald slowly absorbed Odo's words, and saw the logic.

Odo, standing apart from the situation, had better clarity than he did.

Odo poured them both some wine and sat down across from Gerald. 'But do not ask me how you are going to handle your wife when she returns. That is beyond my knowledge and advice.'

Gerald took a drink and grimaced. 'It is beyond mine too.'

Last night's rain had made the ground soft and Nesta held her skirt hem above the ground and stepped carefully in her wooden overshoes, trying to avoid the worst of the mud. She had left the bower for some fresh air and to escape the cloying, judgemental presence of Cadwgan's wife, but there had been little gain to her foray. The manor was fortified with a stockade and well guarded. In a horrible way, it reminded her of her life at Caus following her father's death. There was that same heavy atmosphere, that air of being constantly watched.

The lady Emma treated her with cold disdain and mostly did not speak, blaming her for the fact that they were mouldering on this small English manor instead of dwelling in Ceredigion with all the wealth of Powys at their disposal. When Nesta had first arrived, Cadwgan had confiscated all of her good clothes and jewels and given them into his wife's custody, and Emma had locked them away in the strong box, making it very clear that Nesta was more of a hostage than a guest.

A woman was scattering food for the poultry and two others stood talking at the well, hands on hips, seeming to her like human hens, pecking at scraps of gossip. Beyond the constant smell of dung, a green glint of spring wafted on the air, though it was still damp and chilly. The women were left in one another's company which Nesta found tedious and unpleasant. She was certain that Emma de Sai was of a similar mind. Cadwgan was spending most of his time in Shrewsbury at

Richard de Belmeis's court, attempting to mitigate the damage wrought by Owain, and find a way to extract a pardon and have his lands restored. Nesta had gleaned that he would probably have to pay a hefty fine of a hundred marks – the same sum any baron would pay to have his lands after a hiatus. As part of the bargain, he was to repudiate Owain and swear not to assist him should he return from Ireland. The deal was still being negotiated, but was drawing to a resolution.

She had spent a great deal of time thinking about Owain since arriving here. Indeed, there was little else to do except sew and think. It was like having toothache and constantly exploring the pain with the tongue. She still yearned for him with a hollow ache, but part of that ache was acknowledgement of folly. When her monthly bleed had arrived at the appointed time and she knew she was not carrying his child, she had wept with relief and loss. Like every possibility with Owain, it was a failure that had bled away, leaving her bereft. She longed with remorse to hold and kiss the children she did have, and tell them how sorry she was.

She crossed the ward and entered the small garden surrounded by withy fences, and knew the guards were watching her. Her every move was observed, and although Cadwgan insisted she was a welcome guest, in reality she was a prisoner, lacking only the shackles. She was a means by which he could worm his way back into favour, goods to be exchanged – soiled goods that had to be brushed off to present as unsullied, when nothing was further from the truth.

The garden looked bare, only just starting to stir after a long winter. Grey clouds scudded across the sky, scattering to show patches of faded blue. A pair of blue tits chased in the branches of an apple tree – a male and a female flirting with each other. She watched them for a moment and her feelings of desolation increased.

Sensing a presence at her back, she turned swiftly and found Cadwgan watching her. He had clearly just got back, for he still wore his shabby riding garments, with the fur-lined cloak of his rank pinned high at his shoulder.

'I was told you were in here,' he said.

Nesta puffed out her breath. 'Everyone sees everything I do. I can barely visit the privy without the matter being reported. Do you wish to speak with me?'

Cadwgan shifted to ease hips sore from long hours in the saddle. 'I have some good news inasmuch as good news can be derived from this sorry state of affairs.' She regarded him haughtily, and Cadwgan curled his lip. 'Your looks are wasted on me. You have no cause in your situation to be anything but humble. I have been in communication with the King of England through Richard de Belmeis, and I have also spoken to your husband via an intermediary on the matter of your return to him.'

Her stomach clenched. She had been trying not to think about this moment.

'As you may imagine, negotiations have been both robust and delicate. Your husband is desirous of your return, as I am sure you are. But certain guarantees and conditions have had to be agreed first.'

'Conditions?' Nesta's voice caught in her throat.

Cadwgan tugged on his moustache. 'Of truce and peace-keeping. Your return to your husband will be my gesture of goodwill, and your husband's gesture will be to withdraw and let all be as it was before – as if no stone had ever been thrown into the pool. The King will restore my lands once you are safe in your husband's keeping.'

'And when is this to happen?'

'In a week's time,' Cadwgan said. 'We are meeting on the great border dyke a mile south of Knighton to make the exchange.' He lowered his hand and set it on his knife hilt in an unconscious gesture. 'I have done all I can to keep the peace within my realms, but others constantly seek to disrupt it. My son has called me a coward for not resisting the Normans, but I am the one standing in the storm and facing reality. He will understand one day if he lives to learn wisdom and master his base impulses. It grieves me that you are one of them. We both know what we have lost through recklessness and betrayal and trusting too much, and perhaps the price is too high.'

After he had gone, Nesta closed her eyes and felt the cool wind on her face. What would it be like to return to Gerald? She might not have entirely burned the bridge behind her, but the crossing back to familiarity no longer existed and the road would be strewn with stones. Perhaps Gerald would lock her up. Perhaps he would make her a brood mare and keep her constantly with child. He would probably hate her, and never trust her again, and she would deserve it.

On Nesta's return to the manor, the lady Emma regarded her with hostile eyes, and it was clear she had heard the news.

Nesta lifted her chin. 'I am to return to my husband. I will require the return of my jewels and the other items you confiscated.'

Without a word, Emma went to her coffer. The keys jangled on her chatelaine's hoop as she unlocked it and removed the roll of cloth in which Nesta's rings and brooches were wrapped. There were jewelled belts too, and an ivory mirror case. Emma handed them to her with a gesture that only just fell short of throwing.

Nesta unwrapped the cloth to check the contents, and Emma watched her with arms folded over her advancing pregnancy.

'I thought you would be glad to be rid of me,' she said. 'Once

I have been restored to my husband, you will be able to return to Powys and your fine chambers at Ceredigion.'

'Yes, I am glad,' Emma replied coldly. 'And I am glad too that you have shown me the difference between gold and dross. What you and Owain have wrought upon Cadwgan and upon your own husband is a stain for ever. Go home and pretend to be the great lady and princess in your fine hall with all your wealth and your beauty, but I will always know you have less than nothing, and so will you. I used to envy you, but no longer.'

Nesta re-wrapped the jewellery and suppressed the urge to slap Emma. 'Why would you want to envy me in the first place?' she replied. 'My beauty is no gift for it has brought me to the attention of men who take what they want and all for themselves. If I receive silks and jewels in exchange, it is no reward. They buy their pleasure and do what they will – you should know what it is like after all. You are right that even in the midst of riches I have nothing, but why should it be a reason for you to sit in judgement? There go all of us, and the grace of God does not always save us from our fate. I shall say one thing, and that is I would not trade my life for yours.'

Emma flushed and turned away to her sewing, and Nesta went to pack her jewellery into her own chest. A toxic silence settled between the women. Life with Gerald could be no worse than here, Nesta thought, and at least she would have her own chamber and household to command.

20

Fortress of Cenarth Bychan,
April 1110

Gerald had given Henry and Walter some harness pendants to clean and polish, and was doing the same himself, so that the lads had a task to occupy their hands while he spoke. He had already talked to his youngest son about Nesta's return, but that had been easy, and Gwilym had been accepting of the news that his mother would be home very soon, and that life would return to normal. But it was not the same for the older ones with their greater awareness.

After they had settled into their jobs, Gerald said casually, 'Your mother – your stepmother, Walter – will soon be returning home. Arrangements are in hand.'

Henry raised his head and narrowed his eyes. Walter continued his polishing with increased vigour. They had told Gerald what had happened in terms of where they had been taken and how they and Nesta had been treated, but spaces sometimes remained between words, and were perhaps even better left as such.

Henry said, 'I wouldn't negotiate with any of them.' He thrust out his jaw exactly like his royal father. 'I would bring an army and destroy them all.'

'But first you would have to gather that army, and then supply it, and you would need a strategy,' Gerald answered. 'The Welsh are cunning fighters and would melt away into their forests and hills. Fighting the Welsh is like fighting shadows, and you have to find other ways and choose your battles.'

Henry gave a one-shouldered shrug, as if he knew it all.

'For now, it is a matter of negotiating and having your mother returned safely.'

'She might not want to return,' Henry said sullenly. 'She was ready to go to Ireland with Owain ap Cadwgan and she spent most of her time in his chamber – and a lot of the time I doubt they were talking.'

Gerald felt the cutting sharpness of the boy's words. Walter's face was set; he was not going to say anything. 'You have to understand that your mother was in a difficult situation, as were you.' He spoke firmly, building a wall to hide what he dared not think about, and gave them the version he was choosing to believe himself. 'What you saw and heard might not necessarily be how she felt. Women in such situations have no power. They have to concentrate on what they must do to stay alive.'

Henry's eyes remained narrow, but he nodded a grudging acceptance.

Gerald raised his hand in warning. 'No matter what has happened – and I mean no matter – we must be united and strong, without dissent from anyone. We have to walk side by side. Whatever your mother has or has not done to survive, we have to move forward. Both of you have an important part to play in keeping her safe and in making her know that she also has a part to play in our lives. She must know we are loyal to her and that this is where she must put down roots. What else are we to do? Leave the younger ones without the comfort of a mother? Is that what you want?' He fixed the boys with a hard stare, making them acknowledge his will. 'When she returns, I expect you to welcome her with compassion and courtesy, is that understood?'

The youths murmured their assent and Gerald went to pour them all a cup of wine, so that they were men together. Taking his drink, Henry regarded Gerald with new respect, but still with lingering curiosity. 'But what about Owain ap Cadwgan?'

Gerald lifted his cup. 'He is a dead man,' he said.

Nesta approached the cart that Cadwgan had arranged to transport her to Gerald. A canvas awning had been stretched over the top to protect the traveller from the weather, and the bench was lined with fleeces stuffed into linen cushions. Cadwgan had insisted that she wear her finest gown of mulberry wool, with her jewelled belt and fur-lined cloak. His wife looked on, her cheeks sucked in as if she had been drinking vinegar. Nesta ignored her.

'I hope you will tell your husband that you have been well treated in my custody,' Cadwgan said, giving her a meaningful stare.

'Indeed, I shall,' she replied with a false smile. 'The accommodation has been all I expected.'

She climbed into the cart and arranged the folds of her cloak. A roil of conflicting emotions made her queasy. She had gone round in a circle and come back to the start with nothing gained and she was empty.

Cadwgan cleared his throat. 'The less that is said, the sooner we can mend this.'

'Do not worry,' she said bitterly, 'I will play my part even as you play yours.'

The cart rolled out of the manor and Nesta took a last look through an arch of pale canvas. Smoke drifted from the louvres in the thatch of the low roof, and poultry pecked in the yard. There was a brief swirl of bright wool skirt as the lady Emma turned on her heel and vanished from sight through the hall doorway. Then the gates swung shut and they were on their way to the rendezvous.

Nesta steeled herself as they covered the miles. She kept thinking of things to say to Gerald and then discarding them. Successive waves of guilt and shame swept over her; resentment and fear too. Thinking about it was hard enough, but she also had the children to consider and their reactions. What would they think and say? What had they already said to Gerald? Dear God.

The scouts came trotting back to report to Cadwgan. Listening through the cart's arch, she heard them say that Gerald was waiting at the rendezvous point with his entourage. She crossed herself and offered up a silent prayer, asking God for mercy and not to let this be too terrible, and felt as if she was going to her own execution.

They arrived at a small hillock with a gnarled oak tree standing stark against the sky, the leaf buds on its dark branches yet to unfurl. A band of Norman soldiers waited around it, mounted and armed in their mail. Gerald sat astride a brown destrier from Pembroke, and her stomach wallowed, for here was the hard Norman warlord and she could tell by his posture and the set line of his mouth that his mood was grim. She shrank back in the cart, glad of its cover, not wanting to meet his granite stare.

Cadwgan drew rein.

'Ten men,' said his scout. 'As agreed.'

Cadwgan nodded and warily dismounted. So did Gerald, and

walked forward, bidding his men stay back. Cadwgan turned and beckoned to Nesta. 'My lady, will you accompany me?'

Nesta summoned her courage and, gathering her skirts in one hand to avoid stumbling, stepped down from the cart, wishing to be anywhere but here in the midst of this silent storm. Cadwgan held out his arm for her to take formally, and leaned in to murmur, 'I am relying on your cooperation, my lady. We both need this exchange to be smooth and successful, with no blood spilled and no swords drawn.'

'That is my wish too.'

She straightened her spine, stood taller than Cadwgan and put on the face that was her mask to the world – the imperiousness of a queen, covering anxiety and terror – and because of that she was able to look directly at Gerald rather than hide behind lowered lids. He had removed his helmet and his face sent a pang of familiarity through her, striking emotions of remorse and fear, but also a discordant sensation of recognising that here was rescue and protection. His expression was neutral, but a flush had crept up his throat into his cheeks and brightened his eyes.

Cadwgan halted several paces away from Gerald. 'God's greeting, my lord,' he said. 'I am glad that we could meet on peaceful terms.'

Gerald did not answer, and Nesta realised that despite his outward calm he was struggling. She saw him swallow several times, and then he just nodded and made a brusque gesture, both acknowledging and dismissing the niceties.

'As agreed, I have brought your wife safely to you, and as you see for yourself, she is unharmed and has been our honoured guest. I have kept her safe and guarded her honour and I hope you will acknowledge my goodwill in this and that we may return to being neighbours and bear no grudges.'

Gerald gave Cadwgan a cold stare. 'I thank you for your care of my wife,' he said icily, 'and I shall honour whatever truce Richard de Belmeis requires us to make in these Marcher territories. You, I shall not touch. But your son has offered irreparable insult. Should he ever return to these lands, then his life is forfeit to my sword.'

Nesta stifled a gasp. She had expected Gerald to say no less, but hearing the words was still a shock.

Cadwgan flexed his jaw and responded stiffly, 'That is understood, my lord. Indeed, I have banned him from all of my domains, and sworn an oath never to entertain him in my halls again. He is no longer a son of mine – I disown him. It is a hard thing for a man to sever his own flesh and blood, but when a limb has grown diseased, what else can he do?' He turned to Nesta. 'Go to your husband with my goodwill, and I ask you to commend me to him and tell him that I speak the truth.'

Nesta inclined her head graciously to him; despite their enmity, they understood each other and had the same goal for now.

She reached Gerald's side but his face was closed, and he beckoned to Odo de Barry, who came forward to lead her into the midst of their protection, leaving Gerald alone, facing Cadwgan. He fixed him with a long, silent stare, and then turned his back on the Welsh prince in a gesture of bold contempt.

Odo escorted Nesta to her own horse, a sturdy brown gelding, again from the Pembroke stock; all the fine horses from Carew were gone. Odo helped her mount, his gaze sliding from hers. There was the minimum required by courtesy and no words of welcome.

The saddle was an ordinary one, not a ladies' chair saddle, and she had to straddle the horse and then arrange the folds of her gown and the cloak. Eleri and Ceridwen were assisted onto two cobs. At Gerald's command, the troop set out, turning onto the track that led from the dyke and into Wales.

Gerald rode at the head of his men and said nothing, and Nesta could not go to him because of the protocols. She studied his back as he rode and saw him take a deep breath and rotate his shoulders to dissipate tension. Compared to Owain he was slightly built, without the vibrant charisma. He could be one of his own men at arms, and that was one of the reasons she had overlooked him before, or thought of him as of less consequence. He was no prince, but a soldier for the King. No glamour shone about him, and no one would mark him out in a crowd, but he was calm and steady – the boundaried river rather than the all-engulfing fire. She had jumped into the fire without a second thought and been badly burned. Now she faced the river, and leaping into that deep water daunted her as the fire had not.

The sun shone and the clouds, although grey, were high and streamered with blue. Sheep grazed at the side of the track, many with new lambs afoot, and the shepherds leaned on their crooks to watch the troop pass, eyes wary. They ventured deeper into Wales, heading westwards for the rest of the morning until, towards noon, Gerald called a halt by a stream that ran close to an empty shepherd's hut. He turned his stallion and rode back along the line to her, bringing the horse in close to her side. His expression was intense, but when he spoke, his words were mundane. 'We shall stop here to eat and attend to ourselves, and then press on. We should reach Llandridod before nightfall.' Before she could speak, he reined away and rejoined his men, leaving her unsettled and disturbed.

Dismounting with help from one of the knights, Nesta relieved herself behind a stretched-out barrier of cloaks with the soldiers turned the other way. Gerald's squire brought her water from the stream to wash her hands and she sat on a spread cloak to eat the food provided.

Gerald ate on his feet, alert and on guard. He was plainly not going to speak with her in front of his men, even though they were his trusted inner cohort, and she realised what a task she had before her to bridge the gap between them. Now and then she caught his gaze as they ate. Once she tried smiling at him, but he did not respond and turned away to his knights, his shoulders taut, and she began to feel very afraid.

On the fourth day, they arrived at Cenarth. Nesta gazed at the palisade. New sections of paler sharp stakes had replaced damaged areas. A new door stood open to admit them, re-inforced with iron bands. Beyond, within the ringwork, stood the various service dwellings, some patched and some new. Guilt washed over her for none of this would have happened without her infatuation for Owain. She was still mourning his refusal to take her to Ireland, even while realising that their passion was corrosive and that she would have lived the existence of a camp follower and concubine – and perhaps that was all she deserved.

Gerald dismounted in the courtyard and the grooms took the horses to the stables. Then for the first time he held out his arm for her to take formally. 'My lady wife,' he said, 'may I escort you to your chamber?'

Nesta inclined her head and let him lead her up the tower stairs to the chamber from which she had fled with her baggage on a dark evening between winter and spring. He opened the new door and she hesitated before stepping over the threshold, the hair rising on the nape of her neck. The shattered latrine door had been replaced too and was firmly closed. Everything was tidy, swept and polished. Gerald's harp leaned against his stool. Her sewing frame still held the piece she had been working on, although the needle had been carefully set in the fabric and she knew she had not left it like that.

Gerald closed the outer door and the thud was like a heartbeat inside her chest. Her stomach clenched until she felt as though it would touch her spine. He could do anything in this moment – beat her, rape her, lock her in here and make her his prisoner.

'I suppose you are pleased to be home,' he said.

Nesta swallowed. She did not know where home was. The physical setting was the same, but putting herself back into it was beyond her. She searched frantically for a way out, but nothing came, except submissive appeasement. 'I am thankful and grateful that you have taken me back,' she said. 'I thought of you long and often.' She reached her hand to him, but he did not take it, and fear swept through her. 'I swear I will be a good and true wife to you for all of my days. I will do anything to make this right.'

Gerald shook his head and said softly, a little wearily, 'Nesta, you do not have to say any of this. The last thing I want is a cowed wife, speaking what she believes I desire to hear.' He fixed her with his steady grey gaze. 'Let us be as we were, and let none of what has gone before interrupt our life together as man and wife. I freely take you back, and it does not matter. Let it be as if you have just walked from one room to another, and there shall be no more between us than that. We shall never speak of this again. It is done and discarded.'

Nesta stared at him in disbelief. How could either of them close the door on something so enormous? By Welsh law, and Norman, Gerald was entitled to kill Owain for the insult. How could he say it did not matter? How could he not revile her or think of her as soiled and defiled? He should be raging, but he was as calm as a still rock pool.

Stepping forward and taking her hand, he raised it to his lips like a courtier. The gesture increased her feelings of guilt and unworthiness. Any other man would have struck her, and she would have welcomed the pain as atonement.

'I say again, it is finished,' he said. 'You are my wife in honour and nothing will ever change that – nothing.'

She shook her head, overwhelmed and without words.

'Come,' he said. 'The children are eager to see you.'

She gave him a stricken look. She badly desired to see them too, but the older ones would judge her, and perhaps hate her too. 'No,' she said in a thin whisper.

'I have spoken with them and they understand,' Gerald said quietly. 'You have nothing to fear.'

Nesta thought she had everything to fear.

Gerald led her to the chamber he used when conducting business. She hesitated at the door, her stomach churning.

'I cannot do this!' she whispered in a tight voice. 'I cannot!'

Gerald rubbed the top of her arm. 'Go on, it is all right, I promise you – and I keep my promises, always.' He set his hand to the ring in the door and, as he turned it, kissed her cheek in encouragement.

Nesta drew a deep breath and walked into the room. The children were gathered at a trestle table and looked up as she entered. Gwilym was the first to leap to his feet and run to her with a cry of 'Mama!' He flung his arms around her and laid his head against her body. She hugged him close, a torrent of love and shame washing over her.

'Oh, I have missed you!' she exclaimed tearfully. 'And I have been so worried about you! It is so good to be home, and to see you safe!'

The two older boys rose from their place to greet her. Henry kissed her cheek and Walter bowed, although his eyes were wary. However, neither youth rejected her. Nesta took Angharad from her nurse's arms and cuddled her. Looking at Gerald over the top of their daughter's wavy brown hair, she mouthed a silent thank you.

'Come now,' Gerald said, 'let us eat. It has been a long journey for your mother and we are all in need of sustenance.'

'You, all of you, are the only sustenance I need,' Nesta said, but allowed them to bring her to the board and place her with ceremony at the head of the table. She perched Angharad on her knee, and as the child ate bread and cheese in her arms Nesta did not mind the crumbs and half-chewed morsels that dropped onto her gown because the things that had mattered so much only recently were as nothing now. Geri wagged around her feet and rolled over to have his tummy rubbed.

Once they had eaten, the older boys went to play a board game. Angharad returned to her nurse and it was Gwilym's turn to sit on Nesta's knee. She smoothed his fair hair back from his brow with a tender touch and continued to battle a murky sensation of guilt.

'He is a resilient little boy,' Gerald said. 'They all are, and I am proud of them. I thought I had lost everything, and I am blessed to have so much restored.'

Nesta looked down at their son. 'I feel blessed too.' And cursed. Her eyes filled with tears. Gerald watched her with concern, taking in every nuance with intensity, until she felt like a creature in a trap. 'I should like to retire,' she said. 'It has been a long and difficult day.'

'Of course.' He rose and extended his hand.

Nesta's stomach began churning again. Henry and Walter looked up from their game and she saw the knowing in their eyes and felt judged and ashamed. She kissed Gwilym. 'I need to sleep now,' she said, 'but I shall see you in the morning.' She bid a stilted farewell to the older boys who replied formally, and the missing connection was like a slipped cog.

Gerald escorted her up the stairs to their chamber. The brazier had been lit while she had been with the family, and the charcoal was imbued with the aromatic scent of frankincense, but rather than being an enhancement it took her back to her days as Henry's concubine. She closed her eyes and tried to quench her fear. Gerald's chivalrous demeanour was surely a front. No one could be this calm and considerate after what had happened. He must suspect something at least. He had said that the incident was behind a closed door and they would not speak of it again, but how could they not speak of something so enormous? There was precious little room to have a normal conversation around it.

Owain would have backed her against the door and they would have made love with rough, hot fire. She would have been tangled up in the moment, without time for anything but the lust. But now there was too much time, and her thoughts were a tangled web.

She followed Gerald's gaze to the bed, to the pristine covers, all neatly made and tucked in – a direct contrast to the fur-covered tumble of Owain's. Gerald methodically removed his tunic and shirt and drew her into his arms. Kissing her, he slowly undressed her, stroking and renewing his acquaintance with her body, reclaiming it for his own by mapping it with his hands and lips and tongue.

Nesta was passive. She could not feel; she was numb. If she yielded to the feelings he was rousing on her skin she was afraid she would lose herself for ever. With Owain, losing herself had been swift and fiery with no time except to be in the moment. But this was like having the water level rise in slow increments until it threatened to cover her head and fill her lungs. She would drown. His tenderness terrified her. She had not expected him to lie with her in case she was carrying Owain's child and she had thought to have at least a little reprieve.

She bit her lip and fought back tears as eventually he entered her. He was gentle and slow, whispering that he wanted her and that he wanted to make her feel loved, but that made it more difficult to bear. How could he love her after what had happened? And what was love? She let him do as he willed, and put her arms around him, just to have something to hold on to, hoping it would soon end. He had not repudiated her but welcomed her home, and she was in his debt. But it shouldn't be like this.

He did not spill his seed inside her, but withdrew at the final moment and bowed his head against her neck, breathing hard, the first sound almost a sob. Eventually he got up, fetched a cloth from the wash bowl, and cleaned them both. 'A precaution,' he said. 'I need to know you are not carrying Owain ap Cadwgan's child.'

Nesta swallowed and swallowed, but the tears still ran down her face. 'I am not,' she said, 'but I do not expect you to take my word.'

'Come now, no tears. I love you – I always will.'

She shook her head. It was impossible to be so forgiving and she would rather in some ways that he had turned against her and locked her up. But then perhaps the weight of guilt was to be her punishment.

'I will leave you to sleep, but I will be here when you wake, I promise,' he said. 'I will always be here.' He kissed her temple gently and left the room.

Nesta closed her eyes and turned over. She could not bear this, but she had no choice. When left to choose for herself, she had made the wrong decision. She looked at the candle he had left burning and then she wondered what Owain was doing in Ireland, and whether he would return as he had said he would. Even now, she was conflicted.

Exhausted, she fell asleep, and when she woke later in the

night she saw Gerald rolled in his cloak on a mattress at the bedside. She could hear by his breathing that he was awake, and he must have sensed her own awareness, for he turned and sat up.

'I did not want to disturb you by coming to bed,' he said, 'but I wanted to be on guard and protect you.'

Nesta also sat up. 'If you stand guard over me every moment like a serpent coiled around its treasure, you will stifle me. How can the past be a closed door if we live like this?'

Gerald slowly rose to his feet, and looked at her with troubled eyes. 'I need to protect you because I failed before. Had I kept better watch none of this would have happened and the outcome and consequences would have been very different. I am glad you are here. I will always be glad, and I will give you the time that you need. If you wish, I will go and sleep in my chamber.'

She would have liked nothing better, but she shook her head. 'No, stay,' she said, as part of her own atonement. 'You are too good to me, Gerald. I do not deserve your love.'

'That is for me to decide,' he said. 'It is not in your gift, but mine. As I have said, the door is closed and we are in a different room now. Come, I shall play my harp and soothe you to sleep – and then I shall go.'

He went to his low chair and picked up the instrument. Rippling the strings, he adjusted the tuning, then began picking out the delicate notes of Stella Maris – in praise of the Virgin Mary. Nesta lay down and curled up on her side away from him, and the tears rolled silently down her face as the tune undulated like gentle waves running along the shoreline. The last note died away and she heard Gerald leave, softly closing the door.

21

Palace of Fearns, Leinster, Ireland, May 1110

Gruffydd ap Rhys sat around the fire with his companions in the hall of Donnchadh MacMurchada, King of Leinster. A hog was being roasted over the fire to reward and celebrate a successful wolf hunt and the succulent, mouth-watering smell of roast pork rose on the smoke to the roof louvres. Gruffydd raised his drinking horn, took a swallow of mead and tasted honey at the back of his throat. Under half-lowered lids he was watchful, observing the open-mouthed laughter and jests, and men's expressions, ruddy in the firelight. It was the fighting season and there was an edge to the conversations like the blade of a sharp axe. Sap coursed through his own veins. He had been seventeen years in exile, was twenty-one now, and the time was fast approaching for him to leave his Irish hosts and assert himself again in Wales as a Welsh prince.

He watched as Owain ap Cadwgan of Powys carved himself a substantial portion of meat and fat from the roast. To

Gruffydd's eye he looked edgy and piratical, although with the bearing and charisma that effortlessly drew men into his circle. Gruffydd had occasionally seen Owain during his childhood, when Owain had come to Donnchadh's court recruiting men, or with slaves to sell and other goods seized during raids on his neighbours. Gruffydd had heard other rumours too, more personal and disturbing, that made him wary. There was no love lost between their bloodlines, and while they were mutually opposed to the Norman invaders, the rivalry remained strong and deep. They would conciliate with each other if it suited their purposes, but Owain would as soon stick a dagger in him as help him, and he the same.

Owain lifted his head and met Gruffydd's scrutiny, and the men silently appraised each other across the flickering firelit room. Then Owain flashed a wolfish grin and joined Gruffydd with his glistening bowl of pork. He held out his free hand and Gruffydd took it. Owain's grip was hard and bone-crushing, deliberately forceful. Gruffydd squeezed back with a young man's tensile strength, but Owain had all the power of a mature warrior.

'This is excellent,' Owain said, indicating his bowl. 'I haven't had decent pork for a long time.'

'Indeed, King Donnchadh keeps a fine table,' Gruffydd replied, and watched Owain put a strip of meat in his mouth, chew, and then lick his fingers. 'I had heard from others that you had landed in Ireland.'

Owain shrugged. 'Yes, came back on Magnus Sigurdsson's *Esnecca* from Aberteifi with a good cargo.' He gazed around the room, keenly observing its occupants and, unlike Gruffydd, not being circumspect about it. He didn't care who saw.

'This is the first time I have seen you though. I will be glad to know news from Wales and especially any of my sister.'

Owain stopped chewing. Eventually he swallowed and looked at Gruffydd. 'I do not know what news has come to Ireland of late and how much you already know.'

'This and that,' Gruffydd said cagily, 'but I think you are in a position to tell me more.'

Owain dived into his food again and Gruffydd knew full well he was giving himself time to think.

'Your sister is a fine lady of the Normans and the Welsh,' Owain said at length. 'I saw her and that husband of hers at my father's Christmas feast in Ceredigion.' He paused again. Gruffydd waited with implacable patience. 'Her husband has built a new fortress right on the border of my father's territory at Cenarth and I paid a visit where she and I laid a plan to remove her husband and rouse up the Welsh people against the Normans.'

Gruffydd raised his brows. He had no objection to any Welshman taking up arms against the Normans, indeed intended to do so himself once he returned to Wales, but Owain struck him as a chancer and an agitator, incapable of holding such an uprising together. Imagining Nesta plotting the same took an even broader stretch of the imagination.

'We failed,' Owain said, waving his hand to sweep away the details. 'Partly because her husband was a wily coward. Would you believe, he climbed down a latrine chute to escape my sword? But I will deal with him once I have raised troops here, and I shall return and finish what I have started. I shall free your sister. Vile pretenders like Gerald of Windsor should not be allowed to flourish on our lands, but should be cut out like canker to save the tree.'

Gruffydd eyed him calmly and nodded, while wondering just what kind of tale Owain was spinning and if he actually expected Gruffydd to believe him. He was young, but he had learned early to be steely and pragmatic, to ignore boasting rhetoric and to judge by deed, and just now he was not impressed by the deeds of Owain ap Cadwgan.

'I agree with you,' he replied, 'but I would know more, for I think you are telling me as little as you can, and mostly what I wish to hear. News has come ahead of you about what has been happening in Wales. We have heard that there has been insurrection and that your father and the King of England have become involved, and that the lands of Powys have been given to your kin, Madog ap Rhyrid.'

Owain gave him a glittering look. 'If you have heard, then I do not know what more I can say.'

Gruffydd returned his stare. 'But much of what I hear is rumour and not to be trusted. I would prefer to hear what you have to say, especially about my sister.'

Owain put his bowl aside and took a silver toothpick from his purse. 'I was protecting your sister from her Norman husband. You do not know the life she has led with him. A fair lady of her status should not be forced to serve as a brood mare for such a man, and live under his rule.' He waggled the toothpick between his front teeth and spat out a shred of meat. 'It is not right that her lands, and yours by right, should be subject to that rule. She begged me to liberate her, and I tried, but my enemies conspired against me and I narrowly escaped with my life. Your sister agreed that I should come here to recruit men, while I sent her with my father for safety. My father's wife is Norman and your sister will be safe until I come for her.' He smiled at Gruffydd. 'She is a lady of high esteem among the Welsh. Are you not both children of the great Rhys ap Tewdr of the line of Hywel Dda?'

Gruffydd arched his brows, disgusted rather than flattered by Owain's efforts to ingratiate himself. Who did this man think he was? 'I do not need a reminder of my lineage,' he said curtly.

'Indeed not, but I was speaking of the great insult to your sister that she should be wed to a Norman foot soldier – indeed, he used to serve the lords who killed your father and doubtless took a part in his death.' Owain clapped a heavy arm across Gruffydd's shoulder, taking on the role of mature mentor. 'I will avenge what has been done, I promise. I know you are coming to manhood and I know you would wish this yourself too.'

Gruffydd drew back, insulted by this man who had usurped his own position in the matter of vengeance and was now belittling his age. His subtle suggestion that Gruffydd had done nothing and it had been up to him to take the fight to the Normans was like a dagger in the ribs. Just what was the relationship between his sister and Owain? Had he bedded and despoiled her as the rumours suggested? Gruffydd refrained from asking outright, but suspected he knew the answer.

'I am the head of my family,' he said, 'and I shall decide what is to be done about my sister. You say your father will keep her safe, but from what I have heard – and of course it might be more hearsay – he has had to retreat to England and has been forced to disown you to save his own skin. Indeed, I learned only this morning, so perhaps it is fresh news to you, that Nesta has been returned to her husband, so I do wonder what has been the point of it all.'

Owain flushed. 'Whatever you have heard it is a temporary thing. All campaigns suffer setbacks. I am here to recruit men in order to take back my land and reclaim your sister. Join me if you wish. You would be welcome in my warband. My father is becoming a spent force. When I return, I shall treat with the King of England personally and make it worth his while to make peace with me rather than having me for his enemy.' He expanded his chest. 'We are princes and we are better than any of them; why should we bow our necks?'

Gruffydd dipped his head in agreement but thought no better of Owain. Yes, he hated the Normans, but he had no intention of joining the warband of this man who acted on impulse and was reckless. High courage and charisma were not enough. Owain was a chancer, a man who fed on glory having formed it from his own inflated view of himself and his deeds. The only sincerity in the man was his belief in his own lies and exaggerations. Daring and pushing to the front were useless without careful planning, and Gruffydd understood this well, even if he had not long been able to grow a beard. Gruffydd had watched Owain move among the Norse and Irish, taking orders and down-payments on goods and slaves. And if these items were to be raided from Gerald's territory, then it was from his territory too, and why should he impoverish them or be a part of those raids? If he joined Owain, he would be under Owain's command and domination, and at risk from an 'accidental' spear throw or arrow.

He drank his mead and looked around the room at the raucous company. 'I wonder why you did not bring my sister to me rather than entrusting her to your father?' he said.

'I had to make the decision on the spur of the moment and I deemed it safer than bringing her among rough battle camps on my way,' Owain replied glibly. 'I have taken her once from her husband and it will be easy to do it again. If anyone is at fault, it is my father for handing her back to the Normans.'

Gruffydd looked sceptical. 'And you did not think he would do that at the first opportunity?'

'He is finished.' Owain skipped the question. 'I will deal with matters once I have recruited men.'

'I hope you do. If one hair of my sister's head is harmed, I will make you pay for it. I am not inclined to join your warband – I have my own business to conduct – but I shall keep abreast of your progress, you may be certain.'

Owain's eyes sharpened but he continued to smile. 'As you wish. I can understand that you might not yet be ready for such an undertaking.' He stroked his chin to emphasise Gruffydd's beardless immaturity and left to go and join Eirik Olafsson, a Norse slave trader with silver arm bracelets up to his elbows.

Gruffydd walked off to rejoin his own group. 'He wants me to accompany his raiding party, but I turned him down,' he said to Morgan, grimacing.

Dewi's son, who had taken him into exile when he was four years old and was now an experienced man in his early middle years with crease lines around his eyes and a receding hair line, grunted. 'A wise decision,' he said. 'You would not benefit from such an alliance. You are your own man after all, and Owain ap Cadwgan is not trustworthy.'

'I agree. All he wants is my extra influence and any resources I can bring, but all for him and none for me.'

'Did he speak in the matter of your sister?'

Gruffydd's frown deepened. 'Yes, although not to my satisfaction. He made a raid on the new castle at Cenarth and that was all it was – an opportunity to plunder and rub the Normans' noses in it. I think in his head he believes it was more, but it wasn't. He came away with loot and my sister, but left her husband alive when he should have made sure to kill him outright. It is what I would have done. He has likely despoiled her too, and now his father has bartered her back to the Normans to protect his own hide. I shall deal with this in my own time and that time shall be the right time. I have no intention of letting Nesta come under Owain's "protection" ever again.' He looked at Morgan. 'He might prove convenient though. We can use him as an agitator. Let him try his hand, but I doubt he will get far.'

'And the husband?'

Gruffydd considered. 'It remains to be seen. From what we know, Gerald of Windsor is a cunning man, a survivor, and my sister has borne him children. I would wish it not so, but would I rather him than Owain? A man must have allies to succeed, and he must deal with what is in front of him. For now, we wait, but I shall not put my trust in Owain ap Cadwgan.'

Owain departed the following morning, heading for his next settlement to recruit warriors and raise funds. Gruffydd was glad to see him go, for Owain had increased the tensions at Donnchadh's court, and the only difference between an embrace and a knife in the ribs was Owain's whim. Even as the Normans had overrun his family lands and slaughtered his kin, Owain would do exactly the same given half the chance.

Pondering the situation, Gruffydd went to the stables to visit his mount, an Irish gelding called Pobble, stocky and strong. Pobble was lazy too and would have eaten hay all day and dozed on a hitched hip if not prevented by his owner. Gruffydd stood by the horse and affectionately insulted him for his greedy indolence while scratching his neck and checking him over.

Hearing the sound of horses entering the compound and the warning honk of the guard-geese, Gruffydd looked round, hoping Owain had not suddenly returned. But this was a small, older man with a complexion liked seamed bark. He was riding an elderly but still handsome golden-grey stallion. Another stallion in full maturity followed on a lead rein and by the coat colour was related to the first. There was an old mare too, and a younger cinder-grey one with fluid lines.

Gruffydd watched the man dismount. His clothes were travel-stained but of good quality, and showed evidence of recent hard wear. A pair of grooms emerged from the stables to help him and as he spoke to them, one looked round and pointed to Gruffydd.

Seeing that he had been singled out, Gruffydd walked over, driven by curiosity.

The newcomer removed his cap and bowed deeply. 'My lord.'

Gruffydd gazed at him. 'Do I know you?'

'No, my lord, you do not, nor do I know you as a man, but if you are indeed Gruffydd ap Rhys and these gentlemen have not directed me amiss, I knew you as a child before you were taken to Ireland, and I served your father faithfully. My name is Dewi ap Einan and my sons Geraint and Morgan are the ones who got you away. I was the head groom at Carew until your father died. I have served several different lords since then, but I have always gone with the horses as their caretaker.'

Gruffydd stared at him in wonder. 'Forgive me, but how do you come to be here?' He stepped slowly to one side, his movements deliberate so as not to alarm the horses, and the better to study their conformation. They were as far beyond Pobble as the stars were to the earth.

'The old ones, the mare and stallion, were seized by the Montgomerys,' Dewi said. 'Taran was your father's mount.' He stroked the old stallion's arched neck. 'This one, Hera, bore many foals to him, including Tymestl.' He indicated the other stallion. 'The grey is your sister's, bred from Taran and a Montgomery dam. Your sister's husband took on the horses when the Montgomery lords fled to Normandy. Owain ap Cadwgan raided Cenarth Bychan and brought them to Ireland to sell.'

Gruffydd stiffened. 'Did he indeed? And is that why you are here now? To sell them to me?'

Dewi looked horrified. 'No, my young lord, never that! I have been biding my time. Your sister told me to bring the horses to you and keep them safe until she should see you again. She bid me say she has always remembered you and prays for you and she will welcome and support you in any way she can when you return. I have done this without the lord Owain's permission or knowing – although he will be aware by now.' Dewi stood tall. 'These horses were sent to you by your sister and they are yours by right. The lord Owain may say what he wishes, but they do not belong to him.'

'Indeed not.'

Gruffydd approached the animals for a closer look. They were immaculately groomed, and their pricked ears and alert expressions showed curiosity without fear. The old stallion must have been a sight to behold in his prime, and Gruffydd's eyes filled as he thought of his father riding him. The second stallion was one that any prince would be proud to ride, and the younger mare's dark-dappled coat and black legs were striking.

'She is the swiftest,' Dewi said proudly. 'Even the stallions cannot outrun her. My lord Gerald was hoping to breed her this year to his hunting stallion. He already has a two-year-old filly from her who will go into the breeding herd.'

Gruffydd noticed that Dewi spoke about Gerald of Windsor in a natural, even admiring way, and he was curious, because Owain had vilified Gerald. He needed to know more. Personal relationships were important within the political ones, and he had learned to play the long game.

'Come,' he said to Dewi. 'We need to find stabling and fodder for these fine creatures, and we shall talk. I will employ you from now on. Owain ap Cadwgan will not be pleased, but there is nothing he can do short of stealing them from me and he will not do that for he is not foolish enough to compromise himself at the court of Donnchadh MacMurchada.'

He took Dewi to the stables and they found room in a barn

at the end for the horses. Gruffydd sent a servant for bread and mead and, once Dewi had ensured his charges had settled, the men sat down on a pair of upturned pails.

'Tell me about Gerald of Windsor and my sister,' Gruffydd said as Dewi hungrily tackled the food. 'What manner of man is he, and what manner of ties does my sister have with him? You do not need to tell me that he is a Norman and an invader, but what is he like? Be fully honest with me.'

Dewi wiped his mouth and took a swallow of mead. 'He is a measured man,' he replied, after a pause to muster his thoughts. 'And a diligent one. He listens as well as hears and is a practical and cunning soldier – ruthless to his own ends, but fair and not cruel. Your sister he treasures, and he loves Wales. Indeed, he has taught himself to speak our language.' Dewi grimaced. 'Of course, he speaks with the accent of the Normans and sometimes it does not sound well in his mouth, but he tries, and he sings well.'

Gruffydd nodded. Gerald of Windsor, as a knight in Arnulf de Montgomery's pay, had probably been involved in the death of Gruffydd's father, and had been part of the force when Nesta and his mother had been taken to England as hostages. The thought was like a hot stone in his belly. 'What of my sister? Does she treasure him in return?'

Dewi rested his elbows on his knees. 'My lady has had a difficult life, as have we all since the coming of the Normans. You must be aware of much of it, my lord, but the effect of my lady's treatment at their hands is hard to judge, and I do not know the whole of it – none of us do. You ask does my lady treasure her Norman husband . . . that is difficult to say. Sometimes she is accepting and affectionate, and sometimes she turns her face from him, but she knows she must keep the peace in order to survive. What she really feels for him in her heart, I know not.'

'Is she loyal to him?'

Gruffydd watched Dewi look away and then down.

'You would have to judge that for yourself, my lord.'

'Did she go with Owain ap Cadwgan of her own free will, or did he abduct her by force? Answer me truthfully and look me in the eyes.'

Dewi raised his head. 'My lord, she was smitten by him – indeed many of us were, who should have known better, myself included, and I regret my part in it.'

'Go on,' Gruffydd said.

'He promised he would make her his lady and force the Normans out of Dyfed and Powys. His words were fire, but it was an idle flame. She saved the Norman from certain death by persuading him to hide down the latrine chute. The lord Owain had planned to kill him and she foiled that, but she accompanied the lord Owain willingly and gave him her heart and her trust – I am sorry to say. When she realised her mistake, she entrusted me with the task of bringing the horses to you. That is all I know.'

Gruffydd grunted. He was contemptuous of Gerald for hiding beneath a woman's skirts, but then the man had lived to fight another day and Owain had made a fatal mistake. Cadwgan's position was precarious, and he had a Norman wife which meant he would want to keep the peace with his volatile and powerful Norman neighbours. Even if Owain returned with an army, Nesta would not be his for the taking. From what he had seen of Owain's efforts to raise troops, he would be embarking with a band of pirates intent on plunder and rapine, who would care little except to slake their appetites. There had to be a long strategy in place, and Owain thus far had only shown a desire to live in the moment and talk big words rather than engage in solid deeds and statesmanship.

Measured against the other players on the board, Gruffydd did not find himself wanting. Life in Ireland had taught him that personality and emotion were essential to understand others before making a commitment and meant the difference between success and ruin.

'So, if I returned to Wales and had to choose between Owain ap Cadwgan and Gerald of Windsor?'

'I think you already know the answer to that, my lord,' Dewi said.

The old stallion snorted and Gruffydd went to stroke his neck crest with its heavy fall of iron-gold mane. The time was not yet ripe, and he would observe Owain and see where his actions led, but he had plenty of food for thought.

22

Palace of Carew,
late Summer 1110

Nesta opened her eyes as she heard someone moving about outside the cocooning bed curtains. The taste of last night's wine lingered in her mouth, and her lips were dry and sticky. A low headache pounded behind her eyes in further evidence of how much wine she had consumed before tumbling into oblivion, and it had still not been enough to banish shadows.

She waited for Eleri to ask if there was anything she wanted, because it was how the mornings often began. Her maids knew to leave her to surface and would usually bring a fresh flagon of wine. After two cups she would lethargically rise and prepare to drag herself through another day. But sometimes it was too difficult, and she would turn her back on the world and tell Eleri to bring a fresh jug, and go away.

The movement ceased, and then the bed curtains swept back, sending a crash of blinding light across the bed, making Nesta cry out. She sat up in her wine-stained chemise and, through eyes filled with pain at the brilliance, peered at the figure standing over her.

'It is a beautiful day and you should be getting up to enjoy it,' said Marguerite de Barry, wife of Gerald's vassal Odo, who had come to keep her company. She turned away and said something to Eleri, who murmured a reply. Marguerite gave her a sharper order, and moments later the shutters were unbarred and full daylight flooded the room, adding to Nesta's discomfort. 'This has gone far enough,' Marguerite continued. 'You should be coming back to those you love.'

Nesta turned her head away for she did not want to read the impatience in Marguerite's eyes. 'I am not well,' she said. 'You should let me be.'

'Ah, I would be no kind of friend if I did that,' Marguerite said. 'Come, Eleri has brought a bowl so that you may wash and dress. I shall make you a soothing tisane, and we can sit and talk awhile.'

'The only tisane I need is wine,' Nesta replied, slumping against the pillows.

Marguerite made an exasperated sound. 'I doubt that, but I know when the men have been drinking of a night, more wine in the morning sets them straight.' She brought Nesta a brimming cup and waited while she drank it, and then went to sit by the window while Eleri saw to Nesta's toilet and helped her to dress.

At length Nesta joined her. It was plain from the way in which Marguerite had solidly planted herself on the bench that she had no intention of moving. Nesta sat down facing her, the fingers of one hand spanning her forehead, the other holding a second cup of wine.

'Come now,' Marguerite said gently. 'I know you are deeply troubled. You can tell me and I will not repeat a word of it to anyone, I promise.'

'Nothing is wrong,' Nesta snapped. 'I wish people would leave me alone.'

Marguerite snorted. 'Do not lie to me. Your face is grey and you look as though you have not slept, even though the maids tell me you have been abed since early yester-eve. You are as thin as a rake, and I hear you eat next to nothing. When you returned from . . . from your ordeal, you were as bright and sharp as a knife, and I feared for you, but now I fear even more. And for your husband and children also.'

Nesta shook her head in the face of Marguerite's simple, wholesome forthrightness, and felt as though her bones were made of metal shards. 'I cannot tell anyone, least of all myself.'

Marguerite put an arm around Nesta's shoulders. 'What can be so terrible? You have your life here. You have your husband, your children – you have me,' she added with a smile and a squeeze. 'I know it has been hard, I understand that.'

Marguerite's sweet voice was like a sword in Nesta's wounds. 'You understand nothing! It will never be the same again!' Grief surged up from deep inside her and she began to sob.

Marguerite prised the cup from her hands and folded her in a full embrace like a mother with an injured child. 'But not so much that it is impossible to mend, surely. Your husband is a good man and what has happened holds no slur against yourself. He is desperately worried about you – everyone is.'

Marguerite's pragmatic sympathy made Nesta cry all the harder. After a moment, Marguerite drew back to look in her face.

'What is it?' she asked. 'What is it really? I know there is something more.'

Nesta shook her head. 'I cannot tell you, let it be. The burden is mine alone.'

Marguerite rose and, with a sigh, went to plump the bed

pillows. 'No burden is anyone's alone unless they choose it to be so. I do not think you are being truthful with yourself, or with me.'

'Then go away!' Nesta waved her hand. 'Go, like all the others!'

Marguerite slowed her plumping. 'I have no intention of leaving you to wallow.'

Nesta looked away at the window. 'You would if you knew. Indeed, you would shun me.'

Marguerite turned her back to the bed, frowning. 'It's Owain ap Cadwgan, isn't it?' she said suddenly. 'He is the cause of all of this.'

Nesta gasped and began to sob again. It was as though she had been holding back a leaking dam ever since her return, and now it had been breached and the flood released.

'I thought as much.' Marguerite returned to Nesta. 'You fool, why didn't you tell me?'

'Because I couldn't!'

'Oh, my dear, of course you could!' Marguerite took Nesta in her arms again, but held her loosely now. 'I would not have spoken of it to anyone else; you can trust me. Weep and be done. Today is a new beginning. You do not have to be bound by the past unless you will it so.'

Nesta allowed Marguerite's well-meaning platitudes to wash over her, while she sobbed for all that was lost and would never return. For all the betrayals and broken dreams. For every heartache and grief of her whole life.

At last, as the storm eased, Marguerite briefly left her to send for bread and broth. Returning, she attended to Nesta's toilet, wiping her face with a soft cloth dipped in rose water, and then unfastening and letting down her hair and plaiting it afresh with red silk ribbons. She had tremendous sympathy for Nesta, imagining herself in a situation of abduction, and rape. She did not know how she would have coped. Both Nesta and Gerald in their own ways had been broken by the event, and somehow it had to be mended.

The food arrived and Marguerite dismissed the servant and brought it to her. 'Drink the broth, it will make you feel better. You need sustenance other than wine.'

Nesta sipped and slowly came back to herself. She was exhausted, wrung out, but calm, like a flat shore left behind by a massive storm.

'How did you know it was Owain?' she asked.

'Because of what you have not said. Because I whittled down the possibilities of what the trouble might be, and in the end, there was only Owain ap Cadwgan, and what he did to you.'

Nesta was certain that while Marguerite had realised that Owain was the root cause of her anguish, she had no notion of the reason. The passion, grief and betrayal. She could now be in Ireland if Owain had not reneged on his promises and proven to be the fire without the substance. 'I was not unwilling,' she said at length. 'Indeed, even the opposite.' She waited for Marguerite's shock and outrage, perhaps even for her to walk away in disgust, but the look in her friend's eyes was compassionate, if a little exasperated.

'It was a way of taking control of a difficult situation,' Marguerite said. 'Being a queen, not a pawn. You had to do it.'

'Do they not say that people who play with fire get burned?' Nesta said hoarsely. 'It was more that fire met fire. Owain and I, we are the same element, now left in smoking ruins.'

'Then you must rise from those ruins. You cannot let one moment of madness destroy you and others for the rest of your lives. Your husband is a good man, and your children miss you. Do not let your misery become theirs.'

303

Nesta gave her a bleak look. 'I do wonder if your faith in me is ill placed.'

'I hope not, not only for your own sake, but that of your husband and children.' Marguerite continued to speak forthrightly, but calmly. 'What kind of future are you making for them by taking to your chamber like this? You need your allies, and from what I have heard and what you have told me, Owain ap Cadwgan is not one of them.'

Nesta shook her head. 'I knew that even as I burned my bridges.' But it had made no difference, not when she was in the fire.

Marguerite sighed again. 'Let me speak plainly, as your friend, and as the wife of one of your husband's vassals. If you cannot turn to face the life you have, then someone else will replace you, or else your life will continue as a midden pit, and not only yours. Do you want your children to grow up seeing you like this?'

Nesta shook her head, and hot tears crowded her eyes again. 'No,' she whispered, 'I do not.'

'The remedy lies in your hands. But first you should grieve properly for what has happened, and then put it behind you. You must offer something more to your husband and children than tears and guilt or you will destroy them too. Rest for a few days and I will keep you company and say to everyone you are much improved but still recovering. You may tell me as much or as little as you wish.'

Nesta swallowed. 'I do not deserve—'

Marguerite set her hand over Nesta's. 'None of that. We are friends. Nothing you say will go beyond this room. You can have a good life here with Gerald, but make it soon, for everyone's sake, including your own. Where there has been fire, the ashes create ground for new green shoots in time. Remember that.'

* * *

Nesta sat at her weaving with Eleri and her women. The September morning was bright with sunlight flooding through the window splays and striping her chamber floor. Somewhere outside, she could hear the shouts of children at play. Plying the thread and shuttle left her mind free to wander. Under Marguerite's tending, she had begun gradually to relax and find a new equilibrium and sense of self, but Marguerite had returned to Manorbier four days ago, and now she was on her own and feeling vulnerable.

Those cold March nights on the run with Owain and sharing his bed seemed now like a tale told before a dark fire, a tale in which she had been deeply entangled, and pulling free from its thorns had left raw and painful scars. She still thought of Owain, but with a dark, viscous energy that left her sickened though still desirous.

She wondered how he was faring in Ireland and what he was doing, and knew that if she had gone with him, all that fiery, volatile emotion would have destroyed her. She prayed that Dewi had found her brother and given him the horses, but there had been no word, and the silence felt like the still heat before a gathering storm. Cadwgan had been reinstated at Ceredigion after paying a steep fine. Madog ap Rhyrid had been deposed and had fled to Ireland. Everyone was waiting on the next move, for Ireland was just a bolthole for the renegades, a place to plot and regroup.

Gerald had continued to be kind to her. At first, she had been so consumed by self-loathing that she had stiffened at his approaches, wondering how he could still love her, and thinking perhaps he was mad. All the men to whom she had been close, willingly or otherwise, had taken what they wanted, including her father, and until Gerald it was what she had understood as manhood. Gerald's controlled gentleness baffled her. He had resumed lying with her in full, but his tender consideration left her numb and guilt-ridden. She accommodated him and thought of other things until it was over, and of late he had become increasingly reticent in his approaches. Although she was trying, she did not know how to come back across the bridge she had almost burned when she fled with Owain. A new crossing had to be constructed, but where to start when the way was so strewn with wreckage?

Looking up from her sewing, she became aware of Gerald standing in the doorway regarding her pensively, and she tensed. 'Is something amiss, my lord?'

He shook his head. 'No, but I would like a moment to talk with you . . . no, there is no need to send your ladies out.'

She set aside her weaving and looked at him. His hand was behind his back. Perhaps it was an important letter from the King, after so much disturbance. Her instinct was to look for bad news, but Gerald was flushed and his eyes were bright, like a sunlit winter sea.

Taking a deep breath, he brought his hand round to the front, and she saw that he was holding a box of carved walrus bone. Kneeling on one knee, he offered it to her. 'I have had this made for you as a gift,' he said.

Nesta took the box, opened it, and gasped. The sight of the twinkling jewels caught in a hair covering of gold mesh took her breath, and beside it a set of slim gold lozenges that would fasten together to make a circlet. Even at the royal Norman court she had never seen anything finer. Her eyes filled with tears. She did not deserve this from him, but she could not stop herself from picking up the headdress, with its tactile gold thread and tiny glinting jewels.

'It is yours to do with as you will,' Gerald said, 'but I hope you will wear it in honour when we dine in the hall. I told you about that jeweller in Shrewsbury. I commissioned this after your return, but it has taken a while for him to craft.'

She gave a short nod, too choked to speak. The gemstones in the mesh blurred to glints of colour. He could have spent the money on swords but he hadn't, and inside her, something was moving and changing.

'I was thinking of the Book of Proverbs in the Bible,' he continued. '"Who can find a virtuous woman? For her price is far above jewels. The heart of her husband doth safely trust in her, so that he shall have no need of spoil. She will do him good and not evil all the days of her life."'

Nesta swallowed against the painful lump in her throat and looked at him. It was as if he had suddenly been illuminated in her vision like a beam of sunlight, and the feeling was as overwhelming as his gift. 'Gerald . . .'

'This is what attaches to this gift,' he interrupted. 'This is the trust I place in you, that everyone shall see it. Wear it in the hall, as I have said – for me and for yourself.' He kissed her again, almost awkwardly, nodded, and left the room, closing the door behind him.

As shaky as a new lamb, Nesta replaced the hair net in the box and stared at the sparkling threads, overcome. For now, she did not have the wherewithal to assemble the circlet.

Gwilym, who had been playing in the bower, came to look. 'Papa has made you a queen,' he said.

'Much more than that,' she whispered. She had been a prince's plaything and borne his child, and he had given her away when he tired of her. Owain's jewels were all in his head and presented on dangling gold chains of broken promises that were not gold at all but glamoured dross. But Gerald's gift would show to all that whatever the past had wrought, it was indeed the past, and that she was of the highest worth and virtue to him. This was so much more than a gift of jewellery and she owed Gerald the greatest debt of her life.

Dinner was late that day for the cooks had been busy making extra fare. A haunch of venison had been prepared for the high table, dressed with greenery. Fresh salmon from the river glistened in silver and pink, surrounded by clams and mussels in a piquant sauce. The best white napery covered the trestle tables, and at Nesta's place stood a silver cup, its base embellished with rubies.

Gerald escorted her into the hall on his arm, walking proudly, freshly barbered and wearing his court tunic. Nesta's red silk gown matched the gems in the hair-mesh and the hinged circlet, glinting as she walked. The hair covering was such an unusual piece that it would have been a talking point on its own, but the news of its giving had spread throughout Carew and all craned to see it.

Once everyone was settled in their places at the high table, a damask canopy draped behind their chairs, the chaplain blessed the food, but before the feasting began Gerald stood up and raised his horn. 'This day, I want to toast my wife, Nesta ferch Rhys, for all that she is – Lady of Carew, Princess of Dyfed, mother of my heirs, and lady of my heart. Let every individual present honour her as I do.' He had earlier primed everyone with strict instructions, and they rose as one without hesitation to raise their drinks.

Nesta blushed. The accolade soothed a sore place inside her, but increased the friction of guilt, rubbing on that sore place. She suspected that many folk had risen because Gerald had commanded it, but at least it had created a platform for a fresh start. Marguerite de Barry had returned for the occasion and was smiling at her warmly, and her raised cup was a genuine toast that gave Nesta courage.

'Thank you,' she whispered to Gerald as they settled to dine.

He polished his eating knife on a napkin. 'I hope to have done some good. You are rightly adorned and you sit in pride of place as my wife. I have given you my honour as a protection and no one will gainsay it. Every person in this hall, be they Welsh, Norman or Fleming, will obey your command, whether I am here or not.' He took her hand and raised it to his lips. 'This is our court and you are its lady, and your place is to shine.'

Warmth filled her like sunshine, and she smiled at him and entered into the role he had made for her anew.

After the banquet, as night fell, Nesta retired to see the younger children to bed and kiss them goodnight. She felt light and warm as she entered her chamber. Gerald was busy elsewhere discussing some military details with his men and making farewells to others. A cool breeze blew through the window, but she left it open so she could admire the stars. The brazier gave off a glow of heat.

She stood on the sheepskin rugs at the bedside as her maids removed her layers of clothing and carefully hung them over poles. When they made to remove her circlet and hair net, she stopped them. 'I will do it, you may retire,' she said.

The women curtseyed and left, and Nesta was alone. She stood in the breeze from the window and her nipples hardened. She ran her hands lightly down her body, and felt a sense of anticipation, almost hunger – an erotic charge that had seldom been present when she thought about Gerald. She wanted him with a dull ache low in her pelvis. Turning to the warmth from the brazier, she draped her cloak around her shoulders and raised her hand to touch his gift. How well he knew her. She thought she had known him too, but that was untrue. Fire was simple. It took and it consumed and the embers before the ashes were fiercely hot. But water had so many changing layers that you could never know its full depth.

She gazed at the bed, the same bed in which she had lain with him ever since their marriage. Where Gwilym and Angharad had been conceived, and where they had slept together in separation, and she went to lie down and wait for him, careful of her headdress.

He was a long time, and she was dozing when he returned from his errands. He tip-toed quietly, but she heard the soft clink as he removed his belt and the hiss of fabric leaving skin as he undressed. And then he was lifting the covers and climbing in beside her. She held her breath and waited for him to approach her, but he was silent for a long time, and when he did move, he leaned over and kissed her cheek before turning to his own side of the bed with a sigh. She considered initiating intimacy herself, but because of what had happened with Owain, she held back. There was a gap where they had to meet in the middle, but she did not know how to bridge it.

His breathing eased into sleep and, leaving the bed, she put her cloak back on and restlessly paced, before pausing by the brazier, trying to warm the cold place inside her.

Gerald stirred and sat up. 'What are you doing?' he asked, the candle light making deeper lines of his frown.

'I could not sleep.'

'Why not?'

She bit her lip. 'Don't you know?'

Gerald shook his head. 'Women are a constant mystery to men, but I suppose that is part of their allure. I might guess that you do not feel safe, or that your mind is troubled by something I cannot remedy – or that you do not wish to sleep at my side. And of course, all those guesses might be wrong.'

She was heavy with longing, perhaps even a little desperate, because this was either the way forward or a final dead end. 'But you can indeed remedy the situation, and I do wish to sleep at your side.' She sent him a look across the dim light, willing him to understand, willing him to know her. 'We have a son and a daughter. We should have another child to secure your bloodline – and mine.'

'That is what you want of me?'

'If you are willing.' She saw his breathing quicken and her own increased in response.

'If I am willing?' His voice rose on the last note.

She looked at him and then down, for her hunger had become a flame. Like Owain, she was fire and she needed Gerald to stoke the flame, not put it out.

Leaving the bed, he came to her by the brazier. His face was almost grim with desire, taut and fierce. He unfastened her cloak with swift decisiveness, let it drop on the floor at her feet and pulled her body against his, cupping the back of her head under the gold net as he kissed her. She felt the heat of his body, his readiness, and threw her arms around his neck, responding full measure. When he tried to bring her back to the bed, though, she resisted him and lay down on the cloak on the floor. 'Not tonight,' she said, 'there has been too much misunderstanding. Let us be ourselves when we make this child between us.'

Gerald's practical side would rather have made love in a comfortable feather bed, but there was raw desire in her eyes that had never been there before, and as she knelt and kissed his thighs and then lay down upon the furs, his rational mind yielded to instinct and with a groan he joined her, and was immediately, slickly, inside her, for she was open and ready for him. Her legs rose and clasped around him and she sought his mouth, a partner with him in the moment.

He closed his eyes and shuddered, and heard her cry of release as she bore down against him and rocked to completion.

The night breeze cooled the sweat on Gerald's body while the stars blazed in the arch of the open window. At last he raised himself up enough to cover her face in small, nibbling kisses. 'My love,' he said. 'My lady, my Welsh princess, my heart.'

She smiled up at him and stroked his face, and then said shyly, 'My true husband . . . now we can go to bed.'

In the Dublin lodging he had hired, Owain looked up from his conversation with his guest, a Hiberno-Norse mercenary called Einar Yellowbeard, and observed his cousin Madog cross the room towards them, his cloak drenched with rain, and his hair hanging around his face in rats' tails.

Madog reached the trestle where Owain was sitting, performed a brief nod of obeisance, then raised his head, an ingratiating smile on his lips.

'You have a nerve turning up here,' Owain said icily. 'No one would blame me if I put out your eyes or cut off your ballocks.'

The Norseman at his side grunted with amusement, and his eyes flicked between them in assessment.

Madog spread his hands in an open gesture somewhere between apology and self-exoneration. 'You should not believe everything that comes to your ears. I would hardly be here if I had wronged you so badly that you would want to do such things to your own kin.'

Owain snorted. 'I know you for a two-faced weasel who would drink out of his own mother's skull if there was profit in it, and deny the deed in the next moment to save his skin. You have no loyalty to flesh and blood. You are here because you have nowhere else to go and you are desperate.'

Madog shrugged, but his grin remained. 'You recognise me because we are the same. Would you have refused land if it was offered to you on a platter by the King of England's viceroy? You were being forced to flee – what was I supposed to do? Have you not thought that I was holding the land for your return? I did my best, but your father made a bargain with the Normans and I was betrayed and discarded – you know how that feels. I lost some good men along the way, but I still have a few with me. I have come not for succour but to offer you my spear and my warriors. When have you ever turned down those?'

Owain fixed his cousin with a hard stare, but Madog stared back with equal steel. There was something unbalanced about him. Owain could be rash and wild, but Madog was a law unto himself. He was honourless, and even if he swore an oath, the words evaporated as they were spoken. However, he was his cousin, and for now they had similar goals. Madog was the devil he knew and, providing he didn't turn his allegiance, a fierce and ruthless fighter. His news, too, would be recent.

'I thought of you first when we arrived in Dublin,' Madog said, 'but if my company is not to your taste, perhaps Gruffydd ap Rhys will be more amenable to hear me sing for my supper.'

'Gruffydd ap Rhys would slit your throat.'

'Not if I slit his first. I could do that for you – for both of us.' Madog cocked his head like a willing dog.

'I am sure you could, among many other acts of stupidity.' Owain indicated the trestle. 'Sit,' he said. 'Get yourself some mead and bread and we'll talk.'

Madog skipped around the trestle with startling alacrity and immediately availed himself of the food and drink, setting to with a ravenous will. He pointed his piece of bread at Owain's companion and said through a mouthful, 'So you're hiring then?'

'Negotiating,' Owain replied.

'Always good to negotiate. Your father's back in Ceredigion although it cost him a hundred pounds, but I reckon you could take Powys from him. He's on borrowed time with the English king.'

'Is that so? Well, he still managed to gain it back from you.'

'Hah, I didn't have a French wife and that kind of coin in my purse, did I? But the Normans won't wear it a second time.' He swilled mead around his mouth. 'Stir up an ants' nest is what I'd do; let your father take the blame, and then replace him. There are always deals to be struck to have peace after bloodshed.' He looked meaningfully at his eating knife before plunging it into the cheese.

Owain had been thinking along similar lines himself, although he had not yet finalised his plans, but he wasn't going to give his weasel of a cousin any kind of encouragement.

Madog tossed a piece of cheese into his mouth. 'You should have killed Gerald of Windsor when you had the chance. That was your mistake. No point in abducting the woman and not killing the man. Where has that got you beyond a warm nest for your cock? The woman didn't matter. You should have killed her husband before you did anything else.' Chewing on the cheese, he gathered his dripping hair and squeezed the water out of it onto the floor.

'We couldn't reach him and there was no time,' Owain seethed, furious that he was being held up to scrutiny by his feckless cousin and even more furious with himself for answering with excuses.

Madog wiped his wet hands on his tunic and shrugged. 'If you say so, but I would have made the time. You were wise to dump the woman once you'd had your way. Sure as anything she betrayed you. The Norman would not have hidden in the latrine of his own accord – I bet you a gold ring that it was her idea.'

Owain sat up tall. 'Use your mouth to eat while you still have teeth in it. I find the benefit of your wisdom as appetising as a turd. If you have nothing more to say, then you will be a wise and fortunate man.'

Madog shrugged again. 'Fair enough. I was done talking anyway, and you know what you know.' He raised his cup in toast to Owain and his guest, who was staring in silence. 'Count me in for the next raid.'

23

Palace of Carew,
August 1111

Nesta leaned over the cradle to look at her new son. Born six weeks ago, his hair and eyes were dark like her own. He had been baptised Dafydd at the font for the patron saint of Wales and he had begun smiling yesterday. He gave her one now. Captivated, Nesta tickled his chin. 'Nothing shall ever hurt you, little man, I swear it,' she said softly. 'You are a prince of Wales and your life shall be magnificent.' She turned to Angharad, who had danced to her side, clutching her doll. 'And you are my princess.'

Angharad had hazel-brown eyes and dark-blonde hair with fairer wisps at the edges. She had Gerald's steady nature and outward calm, although, like her father, it did not preclude an active imagination. 'Will I marry a prince?'

Nesta stroked her head. 'Who knows what the future holds for any of us, my heart, but you shall be well settled, I promise. Now is not the time to think of such matters. Now is the time to play without such cares. Come, let us dress your hair with ribbons and then I shall build a tent for you and Hunnyd out of some spare cloth I have.' Hunnyd was a maid's daughter, the same age as Angharad, and the little girls were close companions.

Nesta combed Angharad's hair while singing softly to her in Welsh. All the children spoke fluent Norman and Welsh, as well as a smattering of English. They were also learning Latin, although it was a slow process for Gwilym, who would rather be at sword practice than studying with his tutor.

Nesta tied Angharad's hair with red ribbons and went to her fabric store to sort out a bolt of grey woollen cloth for the tent. The moths had got into it and she was intending to give it to Gerald for a horse blanket. She had commissioned William of Brabant to provide her with some more good woollens for the household and hoped that he could prevail upon his merchant contacts to obtain her a length of Venetian silk. Gerald needed to speak with him too, for Brabant was a carrier of news and had his fingers in many more pies than trade.

Ceridwen returned from the herb garden where she had been cutting lavender to strew over the floor. 'Your lord has arrived from Pembroke,' she said. 'I saw him dismounting in the courtyard.'

Nesta nodded. She had been expecting him. Gerald divided his time between Carew and Pembroke with occasional forays up to Cenarth. In routine fashion, they would dine together, discuss the day's business, and he would return to Pembroke by dusk, unless he decided to stay the night, which she thought he probably would. She had been churched four days ago, and abstinence had sharpened appetite. If he did stay, she had plans.

Gerald entered her chamber wearing his new mail shirt which fell to the knee and had long sleeves below the elbow. It was the latest military kit, and he was as proud as a young knight with his first hauberk. Gwilym dogged his heels, clamouring for attention. The older boys followed him into the room, from which she knew that Odo de Barry was among Gerald's escort. Walter, at nearly seventeen, was growing like an ear of wheat in June. A downy line smudged his upper lip; his hair gleamed like dull bronze and the girls were beginning to cast looks in his direction. Henry, almost twelve, was still a boy, but not for much longer, and the day was soon coming when he would leave them to join either Richard de Belmeis at Shrewsbury, or be sent to his father. She dreaded the summons, but it was the way of the world and it would happen. Time might pass without word or interference from Henry, but it did not mean he had forgotten.

Gerald kissed her and then went to look in the cradle. Dafydd crowed and showed his new smile to his father, and Gerald stooped, picked him up and gently held him high above his head. 'Hey, my little seagull,' he said in Welsh. Behind his back, Nesta saw the older boys making faces at him taking such interest in a baby, and was amused.

'He has just been fed,' she said. 'On your own head be it – truly – if you waggle him about like that.'

Gerald promptly handed Dafydd to Eleri.

'Will you remove your armour?' Nesta asked, and smiled to see reluctance warring with practicality in Gerald's expression. Nevertheless, he unlatched his sword belt and had the youths help him remove his hauberk, warning them to be careful. Gwilym looked on wide-eyed. Nesta took Gerald's hunting knife and put it well out of the reach of little fingers. Gwilym had been a little too interested in blades ever since the incident with Owain.

Divested of his armour, Gerald sat down to drink a cup of wine, but having had a moment with the children, and a little time to relax, his expression grew serious.

'I have news,' he said. 'I spoke with Tancred de Rhos yesterday. Owain ap Cadwgan has at last returned from Ireland and is plundering along the coast with his cousin Madog.'

Hearing Gerald speak Owain's name churned Nesta's stomach. She noticed that the older boys had pricked their ears, even though their backs were turned.

'Do not worry, he shall not get past my guard this time,' Gerald said grimly. 'I have set up extra patrols and the word has gone out for all to be on guard. Ifan came to Pembroke last night and told me Owain has taken up residence in Ceredigion with Madog and is raiding from there as he pleases.'

'But I thought Madog was his enemy.' Nesta's stomach continued to churn. Owain back on Welsh soil? Had he come for her? Had he returned to fulfil his promise?

'Well, he is not now,' Gerald answered. 'After de Belmeis used and then discarded him when King Henry restored Cadwgan's rule, Madog went to Ireland and reunited with Owain. If there's profit to be had, then bad blood can wait another time.' He finished his wine. 'Thank God I strengthened Cenarth again, and I have sent orders to double the guard. I shall write to de Belmeis this minute. I do not believe Owain will raid as far as Carew, but he may enter the Forest of Twyi, and I cannot take that chance. I'm doubling the guard here too.' He shook his head. 'This is the end for Cadwgan. If he is not in league with his son, which I doubt, it shows he cannot control him. Whatever the reason, he has broken his oath to have nothing to do with him, and when such oaths are made to the King . . .' He broke off, grimacing.

'What will happen then?'

He shrugged. 'If Owain and Madog are only here for plunder, then de Belmeis will deal with it, but if they oust Cadwgan, then the King will become involved. Whether Welshmen like it or not, Henry, for now, has the power over who reigns in Ceredigion and Dyfed.'

'And if Owain makes a truce with Henry?'

Gerald rubbed the back of his neck. 'Then it will be Henry's task to contain him.' Rising to his feet, he abruptly left the room.

Nesta sighed. Remembering her last parting from Owain, she wondered again what would have happened if he had taken her to Ireland. His forcefulness still burdened her like a weighty cloak. What would she say to him if she saw him again? Would he exert the same draw on her as before? Thinking of Owain was like having small thorns in her clothes and no matter how many times she believed she had pulled them out she always missed some, and they would multiply until there were as many as before. What if he did raid Carew as he had raided Cenarth? How then would she greet him? And if it came to a fight between him and Gerald, who would she choose? The thought frightened her, for even now it was a fine balance.

That night she and Gerald lay together and she urged him on when he held back.

'I do not want to hurt you,' he gasped against her ear. 'You have not long been churched.'

'You won't,' she whispered. 'I would tell you. But I need you. I need you now, and I need . . .' *Oh God, I need you to be more than Owain, to send him away.* She clasped her legs around him, and she pulled his mouth down to hers.

He pushed into her and she welcomed him, arching and crying out at her moment of crisis, and she heard his voice too, and then the sudden stopping of his breath.

When he rose from her, he smiled and stroked her hair. 'You are incomparable,' he said. 'I could sing a thousand songs about you, and none of them would capture you as you are, but your name is written on my heart.'

She stroked his face. Was his name written on hers? Owain's was, but as a scar. 'I do love you,' she said, because it was true, whatever else complicated their path.

He kissed her again. 'Then it is enough,' he said, and lay down beside her.

She stroked his hair and heard his breathing grow slow and steady. She put her hand on her belly and wondered if they had already conceived another child tonight. When her mind tried to show her a vision of Owain, she moved closer to Gerald and put her arm across him.

Rhian, Nesta's new maid, had a particular skill with cosmetics and adornment. Kneeling on a cushion at Nesta's feet she buffed her fingernails, which she had lightly stained with madder dye earlier that morning and was now polishing off to leave a subtle, gleaming pink. Nesta was relaxing in the moment, her mind wandering, until Rhian said softly, 'My lady, rumour has it that the lord Owain has been seen in the country again.'

Nesta opened her eyes, suddenly alert, unsure why Rhian would mention such a thing. 'Yes,' she said. 'I am aware.'

Rhian flushed. 'My uncle travels, selling ribbons and thimbles. He saw him landing from some ships with his men.' She bent her head over her task, but flicked Nesta a swift upward glance. 'My uncle is here now if you wish to talk to him and view his wares.'

Nesta pursed her lips. 'Bring him to me and I shall hear what he has to say, but finish what you are doing first.'

'Yes, my lady.'

The girl completed her task and Nesta held up her hand to study the effect while she considered the matter of loss and gain, loyalty and betrayal. She wanted to know as much as she could, but it was like pushing her tongue against a sore tooth. While the matter remained unresolved, it would only continue to unsettle her life.

Rhian's uncle arrived with his shoulder basket of goods and bowed to Nesta. Thin as a broom handle, he had the weathered skin of a man constantly on the road, and crafty eyes with yellowish whites.

'Show me what you have,' Nesta said imperiously.

He opened the pannier and laid out hanks of silk ribbons in a jumble of colours. Silver pins, thimbles and needles and little shears. Cheap alloy jetons, and combs of carved antler and bone.

'Your niece tells me you have seen the lord Owain,' Nesta said as he assembled his wares.

'Yes, my lady – and he sends you greetings and trusts you are well.'

'He knows you sufficiently to speak with you and entrust with personal messages?' She eyed him with disfavour and a jolt of fear. Her home, her very ground at Carew, had been infiltrated. That was how easy it was despite all of Gerald's assurances.

He gave her a wary look. 'My trade takes me to many places. It is only natural that I bear information for many.'

She did not believe a word. Here, under her nose, was one of Owain's spies – two if she included Rhian, which was a pity, since she was so skilled with cosmetics. She picked up the jumble of ribbons. 'What else did the lord Owain say to you?'

His eyes sharpened craftily. 'He begs your attendance, my lady, for the love that is between you and for the promise he made to return.'

Nesta's stomach clenched. She heard a short intake of breath from Eleri.

'Well then, tell the lord Owain that he should seek my husband's permission first if that is the case. But I do have something to give to him as a keepsake.'

The pedlar's expression was wary now. Nesta reached into the sewing basket at her side and took from it a leather sheath holding the knife Owain had given her. She had kept it because for a while it had represented freedom and had tied into her longings and dreams, but now the sight of it made her queasy, and her hand shook as she tossed it into the middle of the pedlar's wares. 'Tell him to give me no presents of this type ever again, and no gifts or words, save that he should speak to my husband first who will advise him. Let that be for you also.' She looked pointedly at Rhian. 'And may you take your niece with you too, for I will not have any spies in my household. If the lord Owain believes that the way to my heart is through slaughtering and enslaving my people, he is deluded, and this knife is all I have for him. He will know what it means. Go now, and be glad for your lives.'

The pedlar took the knife, gathered his pack together and without lifting his gaze from the ground backed from her presence, a flushed Rhian sheltering at his side.

Nesta shivered. Although she had acted decisively, she was unsure if she had done the right thing.

'Will you tell Lord Gerald?' Eleri asked.

'I will have to,' she sighed. 'I risked everything for Owain ap Cadwgan and he failed me. Now he thinks he can come back and dangle his bait to see if the fish will return to the hook, but the fish is wiser now.' She looked at Eleri. 'Keep your eyes and ears open and tell me if you hear or see anything untoward.'

Gerald arrived a short while later as the women were settling to their spinning and sewing. 'I saw that new maid of yours leaving through the gate with the pedlar, and she was carrying her bundle. Has she done something wrong?'

'I have dismissed her from my household,' Nesta replied primly. 'She cannot be trusted. The pedlar is her kin, so let him look out for her now.'

Gerald folded his arms, waiting.

'I have dealt with it,' she said shortly. 'There is nothing more to say, but you should instruct the guards at Pembroke to look out for them and not admit them through the gates.'

'Spies?'

'Travellers with information,' she said. 'There is no point in chasing them down. They are not worth your bother.'

Gerald frowned.

'They will not return to Carew, I promise you that.'

'Did they come from Owain?'

'They were a fishing expedition,' she said. 'I did not take their bait.'

Gerald compressed his lips. He was in half a mind to go after them and cast them into the keep prison. He was not happy that Nesta had seen fit to let them go, perhaps carrying a message for Owain. 'I am glad to hear it. If they are seen anywhere between here and Pembroke, I will have them arrested, for even if they did not take your bait, others might do so, and we can do without fires starting all over Dyfed. I am sure that is at least part of their intent.'

Nesta said quietly, 'You can trust me.'

'I do,' he said. 'With my life, the lives of our children. For myself I do not know, but what is the life of Owain ap Cadwgan when weighed against those of innocent babies?'

'Exactly.' Nesta's hands were clammy but a prickling sensation of heat ran through her body. 'I would put none of that at risk.'

Gerald departed abruptly. She suspected he would send scouts out after Rhian and her pedlar uncle; whether they escaped or not was in the lap of the gods. She had discharged her duty to them as her own Welsh people by letting them go, and that was the end of the leeway.

Her stomach suddenly roiled into full revolt and she had to run to the latrine hole to be sick, retching up bile, feeling wretched. Eleri ran to her in concern, but there was nothing to be done until Nesta had finished dry-heaving and could stand up straight.

'Madam, shall I send for the physician?'

Nesta shook her head. 'No,' she said. 'I do not think he would have a remedy for this. I have not bled since bearing Dafydd, and I do not think I shall for some time to come.' She thought of the night she and Gerald had made urgent love and knew she had probably conceived then even before she had had time to bleed following Dafydd's birth. 'Let me lie down awhile and rest.' Suddenly she was exhausted, could barely remain upright, and was glad to lean on Eleri. Even as her head touched the pillow, her eyes were closing.

When she awoke, several hours later, it was well past noon, and her first sight was her own hand curled beside her on the pillow, and her gleaming, pink-stained fingernails. Immediately she remembered what had happened and muttered a soft oath. How dare Owain do this – dart back into her life and send her hard-won equilibrium tumbling.

She sat on the side of the bed and reached for her shoes. As she was slipping them on, Eleri quietly parted the curtains. 'Are you feeling better, my lady?'

'A little,' Nesta answered. 'The sleep has settled my stomach.' Her eyes were still heavy, but she was no longer exhausted to death.

'William of Brabant is here and talking to my lord in the hall.'

Nesta immediately brightened. She was fond of the Fleming and he always brought her gifts of cloth and trinkets. She loved talking to him about fabrics and dyes while Gerald's eyes glazed over, and haggling with him was one of her secret joys. She swiftly changed into a fresh gown and had Eleri dress her hair and arrange her veil, then went to join the men in the hall.

Gerald and their guest were sitting at a trestle sharing a dish of cooked mussels in broth with plenty of bread. Nesta's stomach curdled at the smell of shellfish and she opted to eat just bread and sip on a cup of buttermilk. The men had been deep in conversation, but that had ceased abruptly as she joined them.

Gerald looked at her with a question in his eyes as a servant set a platter down before her. 'No mussels? I thought they were your favourite.'

She shook her head. 'Not for the moment.'

Gerald's brows rose and she blushed and answered his silent query with a slight nod.

'Your maid said you had been unwell and were sleeping,' William said with concern in his eyes. 'I hope you are feeling better now?'

'Yes, thank you, and not unwell, just tired. I suspect God has blessed us again, and you are one of the first to know, Master William.'

Gerald took her hand and raised it to his lips.

The merchant lifted his cup in toast. 'I am delighted for you and your lord, and I wish you good health in the months to come. I have brought some linen from Ireland in my pack, of the very finest. Perhaps you will be able to make use of it for towels and swaddling and other clothes.'

Nesta thanked him.

His brown eyes twinkled. 'I might also have in my pack some of the new woad-dyed wool we spoke about last time – certainly enough to make a pleasing gown for a lady in the full bloom of her power and beauty.'

Nesta looked coy, and Gerald chuckled. 'I expect your winning ways are a great asset to your business.'

William wiped wine droplets from his moustache. 'I only speak the truth.'

'If that is the case, what were you talking about before I joined you?' Nesta enquired, looking at Gerald. 'And do not say "nothing to bother your head about" or "men's business" or that you were exchanging pleasantries about the weather.'

Gerald cleared his throat. 'Only about the situation pertaining to the return of Owain ap Cadwgan and his raiding from Ceredigion. I was warning William to be careful and offering him some extra men for escort.'

It was a sensible reply and mostly satisfying, but William's peregrinations and trading contacts made him a purveyor of information and Nesta knew Gerald used him in that capacity. 'Indeed, you should be wary,' she said. 'He is bound to know your movements.'

William waved away her concern. 'I am old, but not yet in my dotage. I have enough experience to avoid trouble on the road. After this, I am bound north to report to Richard de Belmeis and then to spend time with my brother and his family. I will be careful, I promise. Cadwgan has offered me protection. I know you will caution me against accepting such aid, but he is beholden to King Henry, and he walks a knife edge. If he slips, he is finished, so he is bound to cooperate.' He smiled at Nesta. 'Enough of this talk. I will take the necessary measures and all will be well. When I return from making my report, I hope to have some Venetian silk for you, and more news.' He had adroitly changed the subject, bringing it round to talk of cloth, and proceeded with a few amusing anecdotes of his life on the road, thereby burying the threat posed by Owain: a donkey that had eaten several straw hats before they could be sold in Rhos; the perils of ferrying pack horses across a river in spate.

They saw him off on the next leg of his journey in the late afternoon. He had ten miles to cover and was confident of arriving before dark. Gerald sent three extra soldiers with him, all experienced men, one of them a skilled archer.

'I hope he will be all right,' Nesta said. 'Next time he must stay longer; I enjoy his company.'

'Indeed. He beat me at chess last time and I owe him a return game.' Gerald looked at her with amusement as the gates closed behind their guest. 'You were determined to hate him at the outset.'

'Perceptions change,' she answered, giving him a sidelong look.

Gerald slipped his arm around her waist. 'Another child?' he said. 'It will be less than a year.' He rubbed his hand up and down her side to show his concern. 'I do not want you to be a brood mare, but if God has seen fit to give us this gift, I am glad.'

Nesta was not certain how glad she was either to be facing another nine months of carrying a child in her womb so soon after Dafydd's birth, but as Gerald said, if it was God's will, then so be it, and she could be more careful in future.

Nesta stood on the beach at Manorbier and watched the sea unfold onto the shore, white crests rolling over pebbles, green and grey and warm red. The day was mild for mid-October and the sea breeze not too bracing. The salt smell and the fresh air filled Nesta's lungs and brightened her mood. She had brought the children to visit Marguerite de Barry, while Gerald and Odo were occupied with military matters concerning the protection of Dyfed.

Marguerite's oldest boy, Guillaume, and Nesta's sons were busy building a dam with twigs across the fork of a fresh-water stream that glittered down to the sea. The children's voices piped on the wind. Angharad was collecting shells and arranging them beside the women who had carried fleece rugs from the castle and sat on the beach, protected from the breeze by a canvas tent awning. Marguerite had brought wine and bread, and Nesta was enjoying the novelty.

'The children come here most days,' Marguerite said. 'Even in winter. It is a safe haven for them to play and it gets them out from under my feet.'

Nesta looked out over the sea. She enjoyed visiting Manorbier; it was only five miles from Carew, and no distance. She was still at the nauseous stage with the new pregnancy, but over the last week it had subsided a little – enough for her to travel.

Angharad carried some of her shells over to the boys and gave them to Guillaume, who directed her to arrange them at the side of the dam, including her in the project without losing face with the other boys.

'The children get on well together,' Marguerite said.

'Yes.' Nesta eyed Marguerite with interest, for her neighbour never made conversation for its own sake.

'Perhaps one day our families might share a closer bond. Angharad is very sweet.'

'Perhaps.' Nesta watched her daughter and young Guillaume de Barry. It might be no bad thing. The de Barry household ran smoothly with few frictions, and Angharad's life could be rich here without turmoil. Manorbier was strongly defended, with access to the sea, should sudden escape be required. Odo and Marguerite were quietly ambitious for their children, and Nesta owed Marguerite an enormous debt for her loyal friendship and care. Nesta mitigated her unqualified reply with a smile to show it was not a rejection. 'Who knows what the future will hold for our offspring? I never guessed my own when I was Angharad's age.'

Sensible enough not to pursue that particular line of exchange, Marguerite folded her arms around her knees. 'What did you think it would be then?'

Nesta sighed. 'I used to dream of sitting on a throne with a man exactly like my father at my side. We would rule all of Dyfed and be the greatest family in Wales. I would wear silk and eat sweetmeats every day, and bards would praise our dynasty every night in the feast hall.' Marguerite lifted her brows and Nesta laughed wryly. 'I was young and naive.' Her amusement died. 'The Normans came and smashed everything. I became the unwilling concubine of the King of England and my mother died in an English convent. When I returned home to the lands my father once ruled, it was as the wife of a Norman soldier.'

'That must be very hard for you at times,' Marguerite said.

Nesta managed a bleak smile. 'It is better than it was.' She watched the playing children, then picked up a red pebble gently warmed by the sun. Turning it in her hand, she said, 'I have learned some difficult lessons. I am still not sure that my heart is ready to accept them, but I try to count my blessings.'

Marguerite said nothing, but touched Nesta's arm, and after that the women sat in silence, each with her own space and thoughts, until Gerald and Odo arrived to join them and share the food that Marguerite had brought from the keep.

Nesta walked down to the shoreline and stood just beyond reach of each rolling wave. Gerald joined her, and picking up a handful of stones, began casting them individually into the surf.

'I love this land, troubled as it is,' he said after a moment, 'but that trouble is only caused by the ways of men, not the land itself. This is my home, everything I love is here. This is where my bones shall rest and I shall be at peace.'

'You should thank God that you were not born a Welsh lord.'

She stirred her toe in the sea-washed grit of the shoreline. 'You would find it difficult to keep possession of your birth right if such was the case.'

'I know that,' he answered sombrely. 'I do thank God for his great bounty, and you, that my sons and daughter have Welsh blood in them.'

Nesta thought about commenting that she was glad their children were part Norman, because it preserved their advantage in the world, but she bit her tongue, for the remark would have served no purpose.

He threw the last stone and turned to pick up some more, but stopped and straightened as he saw Odo beckoning to them. Standing at Odo's side was his scout, Ifan.

'There is trouble.' Gerald wiped his hand and started away from the sea, Nesta hurrying at his side.

Ifan bowed as they arrived. 'My lord, my lady, I bear grave tidings. William of Brabant has been murdered on the road from Brecon to Carew, and all of his goods have been looted.'

Nesta put her hands to her mouth. An image of William of Brabant filled her mind: his shrewd, twinkling eyes, his curly silver beard. She remembered waving him off from Carew, bidding him a safe journey.

'We must hunt down whoever did this and deal with them,' Gerald said grimly after a moment's shocked silence. 'We cannot have robbers ranging through our country like this, killing innocent travellers on the road at will.' He looked at Ifan. 'What else?'

The scout gripped his belt. 'It was Madog ap Rhyrid and Owain ap Cadwgan with a band of Hiberno-Norse and Powys men, and it was deliberately planned. They had been watching the road. The men you sent with him are dead too. I caught their informer though and slit his throat. He had this on him.'

Ifan indicated a straw basket with carrying straps that Nesta immediately recognised as the one owned by the pedlar who had approached her about Owain. 'No letters,' Ifan said, 'but he had ribbons tied together in varying patterns, which probably had a meaning to Owain and Madog.' He tipped out the contents on the sand to demonstrate what he meant.

Nesta saw the wooden-handled eating knife tumble out in its leather sheath and shuddered. 'No!' she whispered. 'No!'

'Do not worry,' Gerald said, misconstruing her distress. 'I will deal with the matter; I promise I will keep you safe.'

'Do you think it keeps me safer not knowing and leaving everything up to you?' Nesta snapped, lashing out from her own guilt and pain.

Gerald met her gaze and then looked away, and she knew she had struck a blow under the belt, and in so doing kicked open the door to what had happened at Cenarth.

'On my life,' he said harshly, 'for that is what it will come to – my life or his.' He turned to Ifan. 'Put these things back in the pack and we shall look at them at the manor. You bring us dark tidings, but you have done well. Go and take some rest and refreshment and I shall speak to you in a while.'

Ifan bowed. Gathering up the gauds and ribbons he had spilled onto the beach, he added, 'No one is safe, Welsh, English or Fleming, until they are stopped.' Shouldering the pack, he started back towards Manorbier.

'We need to consult with Richard de Belmeis,' Gerald said. 'I will have masses said for William of Brabant and will send succour and condolences to his family.'

'They will think Gerald cannot keep the peace,' Nesta muttered to Marguerite as they made their way back to the safety of the fortress. 'They will think he is incapable and that Owain is running rings around him – and it would be true. Owain can move and disappear as swiftly as morning mist in the trees. He excels at ambushes and raiding, and Gerald is not equipped for that. It is like trying to kill a fast rat with a hammer.'

'But in murdering William of Brabant they have overstretched themselves again,' Marguerite pointed out.

Nesta paused to ease the stitch in her side. 'What do you mean?'

'When Owain ap Cadwgan abducted you, it caused a stir throughout Wales and the Marches. Cadwgan lost his land and had to buy it back for a hundred pounds and Owain had to flee. Now Owain and his cousin have taken over Ceredigion and killed an important Fleming, indicating that they can raid the trade roads at will. What do you think will happen to them now? You speak of hammers, but Richard de Belmeis will come down upon this with more than just a hammer – he will have to. They have sown their own undoing.'

They began walking again, and Marguerite touched Nesta's arm. 'Do not worry about Gerald. No blame accrues to him, for he did his best, and William of Brabant was murdered on Cadwgan's lands, not ours.'

Nesta hoped Marguerite was right, but she knew what Henry was like with men who fell short of his own exacting standards of control. She was also desperately sorry for the loss of someone who had become a good friend, a man of deep knowledge, kindness and humour. That she would never sit with him again over wine and hear him speak with love of wool and linen and silk, that he would never again unfold a bolt of blue broadcloth for her approval and cajole her into buying an extra length, made her wish she had never heard of Owain ap Cadwgan, much less lain with him in the heat of unthinking desire.

24

Palace of Carew,
May 1112

Nesta watched the newest addition to her family settle to sleep in his cradle. Maurice had entered the world almost a month early to her reckoning, but although small, he possessed a lusty cry and a voracious appetite. She had had to employ a wet nurse after the first few days, for he guzzled milk like a sailor hitting a tavern after months at sea. At six weeks old he had a quiff of sandy-gold hair and dimples in his cheeks. 'Oh, the women are going to love you, I can tell already,' she said, stroking his cheek as his eyelids drooped. 'How many hearts will you break along the road? Too many I guess!'

She turned from the cradle and watched Branwen the wet nurse folding fresh swaddling clouts by the open window. Gerald had gone to Shrewsbury to report to Richard de Belmeis, as he periodically did, and had been absent for several days. He had been at Carew for her churching, but they had not shared the bed afterwards, for her body was still healing, and neither of them wanted to risk another child within a year of this one. She sometimes pondered the situation at the royal court. Henry's queen had only given him a son and a daughter in eleven years, but he had more than a dozen bastards by a succession of women. Perhaps Henry and his wife did not share a bed very often, although it was obvious that Henry was continuing to indulge in his familiar pattern of pastures new.

Her own days at the Norman court sometimes seemed like a lifetime ago, yet at the same time, very near. It was still too easy to recall the visceral fear of that first night when Henry had summoned her to his chamber and used her as a vessel for his release with no more thought than eating a meal.

William of Brabant's death had created repercussions throughout the Welsh Marches. Richard de Belmeis, acting under instruction from Henry, had seized Ceredigion and given the lordship to a powerful Norman baron, Gilbert de Clare, Lord of Striguil. Cadwgan had been ordered to remain in England on his wife's manor. The King had furnished him with an allowance of twenty-four pence a day – little more than the wage of a household official – on which to live and run his household, until Henry had time to come to Wales and sort matters for himself. Owain and his cousin Madog had been summoned to appear before de Belmeis and answer for their actions, but both men had retreated to their Irish bolthole again. They had not gone empty-handed, but with a booty-laden ship of slaves and goods. On leaving Ceredigion, Owain had stripped the fortress of every last saleable item and shipped it all to Ireland.

There had been no word during the winter months when crossing the Hibernian Sea was hazardous. Even the improving weather and daylight of spring had brought precious little information. Gilbert de Clare patrolled the coastline on constant watch for landings, and Gerald liaised with him in the interior while Cadwgan remained confined in England on his pension. Tension was rife in the Marches where the line was so blurred that a man could be predator and prey at the same time.

Hearing the sound of the horn at the gates, heralding Gerald's return from Shrewsbury, Nesta sent one of the squires to tell him where she was and set about organising food, drink and washing water. When he arrived, she sensed his tension, although he smiled and greeted the children, ruffling hair, lifting Angharad and giving her a kiss. But he wasn't really smiling at all. He kissed her too and asked how she was faring, but she could tell his mind was elsewhere. She dismissed the servants and had the children's nurses remove them from the room.

'Tell me,' she said. 'And do not say that I do not need to know, or that all is well, for quite plainly it is not. What has happened?'

'It is not good news,' he said sombrely.

'I suspected not. Has Owain returned again?'

He shook his head. 'Not yet, but he will, and before too long – because Cadwgan is dead.'

His announcement stunned her. 'I do not believe it! How?'

'Owain's cousin Madog,' Gerald replied, grimacing. 'He returned from Ireland alone to make his play for Powys. It seems that he and Owain parted company and their former association was no more than a raiding alliance.'

'Madog has killed Cadwgan?' Nesta was still struggling with disbelief.

Gerald nodded grimly. 'Ambushed him at Trallwyng and slaughtered him and his guard. Cadwgan was apparently across the border visiting allies and Madog had been waiting his opportunity and set upon and killed him – just as he did with William of Brabant. Now Madog is demanding that Richard de Belmeis recognises him as ruler of Powys. I saw the letters myself when I was in Shrewsbury.'

Nesta's jaw dropped at the audacity and at the notion that Madog ap Rhyrid could rule anything without it descending into violence and chaos.

'Owain is bound to respond, for Madog now has Cadwgan's blood on his hands and is trying to steal his birth right.'

Nesta shivered and rubbed her arms. 'What did de Belmeis say?'

Gerald looked at her ruefully. 'That it was too weighty a matter for him to decide of his own accord, even if he did represent the King. Madog has his own lands from his father and de Belmeis has ordered him to go and dwell on them while Henry is informed and makes a decision. De Belmeis will send messages to Owain too, and require both him and Madog to come before the King at an arranged time.'

'De Belmeis said nothing about the attack on William of Brabant?'

'Madog put the blame squarely on Owain in his letter. I have no doubt that Owain will say in his turn that Madog was responsible, and the outcome, whichever way it goes, will be a hefty fine.'

Nesta frowned. All this was no business of Henry's, but in practice he held the balance of power and had the resources to enforce his decision.

'It is a moot point as to whether either man comes,' Gerald continued, 'for by the time the letters reach the King, he will be leaving for Normandy and may not return for months – certainly not until after the Christmas feast, perhaps longer depending on what is happening in Normandy.'

'Then why doesn't de Belmeis make a decision now?'

Gerald sighed and rubbed the back of his neck. 'He said why should he be in a rush to settle matters when the Welsh are all busy killing and betraying each other after their manner? It suits him to have Powys fragmented between smaller areas of loyalty.

Madog has served him before, and by keeping him neither in nor out of favour he can exert control over him. When Owain returns, which he will, then de Belmeis will do the same with him. He will exact promises and money from both men, and satisfy neither, for it is not in his interests to do so. As long as they are at each other's throats, why stop them? If the Welsh were capable of uniting with each other instead of pursuing petty kinship feuds and tearing each other to pieces, they would be a force to be reckoned with.'

Nesta's mouth twisted. 'It is to your advantage, then, that we fight. But your own people are hardly paragons.'

'No,' he agreed. 'There are rebellions and feuds in Normandy and England too, but not as intense as in Wales. The King's word is law and rivals are swiftly dealt with. That is why the Welsh lords make alliances with Henry – as they did with his father. He has the power and the military strength to support his decisions. He may change policy and remove that support at times, but it is still better to ally with him than a neighbour who will cut you down the moment you look away.'

What he said was true. Her own father had once met William that some called the Bastard and made a peace treaty that had kept them secure until William died, and his son Rufus had given free rein to the Montgomerys.

Cadwgan dead – it was inconceivable, like all the autumn leaves dropping on a single day.

'I should go,' Gerald said. 'I need to speak to the men about what was said in Shrewsbury. I will return later and we can talk more.'

'Perhaps it is time for my brother to return,' Nesta said that night when Gerald was back from dealing with the garrison and sorting details for the protection and security of their lands. He was sitting on his favourite stool with the comfortable leather seat and tuning his harp, because playing the instrument always soothed his mood. She curled up at his feet and ran her finger over the embroidery on his leg binding. 'If Henry is prepared to recognise either Owain or Madog and give them their entitlements, then he should recognise my brother also. Perhaps the other Welsh princes might prefer negotiating with a son of Rhys ap Tewdr to either of those two.'

Gerald continued tuning, plucked a handful of notes, then set the harp aside. 'Your brother has been exiled since he was a child. Perhaps he would rather make his life in Ireland.'

'It will do no harm to find out though. He is your kin as well as mine now, and uncle to our children.'

Gerald snorted. 'Since when has kinship been a recommendation for alliance among the Welsh? He will not necessarily be an ally.'

'If the boundaries are set, he will understand them.'

'As Owain understands them? As Madog understands them?'

'My brother is neither of them,' Nesta said, growing irritated. 'You do not know him.'

'I do know that if we are his allies, he will leave us alone because we have given him the foothold he needs to return. His aim will be Powys, not Carew and Pembroke. He will protect us against inroads from Powys. This is his homeland and he should not have to live the rest of his life in exile. If we ally with him, the Welsh would be more cooperative with you.'

Leaving his harp, Gerald rose to pace their chamber.

Nesta said softly, 'You need more men, not just Normans and Flemings who can tramp a swathe and never see into the trees.' He shot her a sharp glance and she continued quickly, 'I know you are proud and you say I should not trouble myself, but you are constantly in the saddle and barely at home. This is the first time you have sat with me and picked up your harp in an age and you will be off again in the morning. Your younger children barely know their father. Gruffydd would take some of that burden as a Welsh ally and your kin.'

Gerald paused and let out a hard sigh. 'The likes of Owain and Madog weave their vines and send them out in all directions. I am a straightforward man. I have a goal and I remain focused on it. For some, my honour may seem like naivety. For some, I may seem like easy pickings and someone of little consequence. "Oh, never mind Gerald, he has no teeth. He has no courage. He could not protect his own wife but had to skulk in a latrine while a Welsh pirate abducted her and their children and burned down his castle. Never mind Gerald, you can raid his lands with impunity, burn his homesteads, murder the travellers on his roads. Never mind Gerald, he's a cuckolded, brainless idiot with a soft sword in his scabbard!" I am shamed, but the shame is theirs for their own dishonour.' The last word emerged like a flung stone, and half moons of tears glinted in his lower lids.

Nesta stared open-mouthed at his outburst. She had no idea that this massive tide-surge had been existing inside him. In a way it was exciting, to see this different person exposed under all the quiet cladding. The storm at sea had finally hit the shore.

'There is no shame due to you,' she said. 'You are right, you are an honourable man, and I esteem you for it. I know you – I see you.'

'Do you?'

She rose, took his face in her hands and looked into his eyes. 'I know what I have, and what you have given me. I did not want to marry you, I freely admit. Why would I when the Normans had taken everything from me and I was being ordered to obey by the man who had taken my innocence and forced me to be one of his whores?'

Gerald winced and recoiled, but she stepped into his space again.

'You brought me home to Wales and you showed me that even in Normans there was decency and honour, even if I hated all of you. Indeed, I resented you even more, for if I felt my heart softening towards you, then it seemed that I was betraying my own kin. When I turned away or slighted you and you were still kind, then I loathed myself even more because you would not punish me and it was what I deserved, and I thought you weak for not doing so. You have given me consideration and honoured me throughout. You have loved me through thick and thin – and I give the same back to you now, freely. You told me once that we should not speak of Owain and what happened at Cenarth ever again. Then hold to your word. Let tomorrow be another day – one without a bitter story behind it; one without memories. That is how we must try to live if we are to survive.'

Of her own accord, she kissed him. Gerald uttered a soft groan and, grasping her shoulders, returned the kiss, hard, before burying his face against her neck. She felt him shudder. Then he pulled back, wiped his eyes, and gazed at the moisture on his fingers almost in surprise.

'Are we not both fools?' he said hoarsely.

'No,' she said, and smiled. 'I would admit to many things, but never that.'

He swallowed and shook his head. 'Very well. Send for your brother.'

'We shall write the letter together,' Nesta replied in a soothing voice, controlling the urge to dance and sing in triumph for she recognised this was not a moment of triumph for Gerald, rather one of resignation. 'Thank you. You will not regret this, I promise.'

He shook his head. 'My father used to say the more you pay,

the more it's worth, so I judge this turn of events as priceless.' Going to the chamber door, he called for the scribe, and when he returned to Nesta his expression was set in its customary lines of pragmatic calm.

Standing on Pembroke's palisade, Gerald watched the party from Ireland approach. They numbered about a hundred Welsh and Hiberno-Norse, and he was not entirely comfortable about admitting them inside his defences, but he had to go out on a limb and extend a modicum of trust to Nesta's brother. Gruffydd could hardly launch a massive insurrection with so small a warband in heavily dominated Norman and Flemish territory. Besides, the messages that had flown between them over the last several months had been cordial ones of alliance and family. Still, he remained wary. He had learned the hard way that closing the door on the past did not work unless you removed the issues blocking that door. He and Gruffydd had a common bond in Nesta, and a common enemy in Owain ap Cadwgan, but common bonds only stretched so far before they snapped. There was the matter of what Richard de Belmeis and the King might feel about Gerald giving Gruffydd a stepping stone in Wales.

'Open the gate,' he commanded the serjeant standing at his side. 'Welcome our guests and let no man offer insult by either word or look for these people are allies and kin and my bread is their bread.' He adjusted his cloak, shook his shoulders, and went down to greet his guests.

Nesta's brother rode into the compound on a handsome young chestnut stallion and dismounted with the lithe bounce of young manhood. He had dark hair and eyes like Nesta, although the latter were narrower and longer in shape. His nose was sharp and fine, his jawline firm. A rich blue cloak draped his shoulders and beneath he wore a tunic of red wool, embroidered in blue with intricate interlacing. He bore no sword, but a hunting knife in an ornate scabbard rested at the back of his belt with the hilt within easy reach. Fixing his gaze on Gerald, he stepped forward with a wide smile the image of Nesta's.

Gerald advanced too so that they met in the middle. 'Welcome, my wife's brother,' he said formally in Welsh. 'Will you take some refreshment and accept my hospitality before we ride to Carew to greet your sister?'

Gruffydd inclined his head. 'Thank you, it would be welcome, although I am keen to see her.'

'Pembroke's function is military; Carew is Nesta's and with more comfort and space for guests,' Gerald replied. 'It is less than an hour's ride. She has been preparing your welcome for weeks now.'

Gruffydd looked round, assessing the stalwart defences with a warrior's eye, and Gerald experienced a frisson of unease. Gruffydd smiled, recognising his trepidation.

'I had not expected you to speak our language so fluently,' he said.

'I judged it useful to learn,' Gerald replied. 'That way I do not need to depend on an interpreter and there is less scope for misunderstanding. I am sure I do not do it the justice it deserves, but it serves me well.'

'Better than well.' Gruffydd regarded Gerald in the same way that he had been regarding the structure of the fortress. Then he said, 'I have a gift for you to mark such an auspicious occasion.' He gestured, and an elderly man came forward from the back of the troop, leading three horses.

Gerald's eyes widened in astonishment. 'Dewi?'

The little Welshman bowed deeply, then straightened up as much as he could. He had aged considerably from when Gerald had last seen him over two years ago and now sported a distinct stoop. 'My lord, I am glad to be home on Welsh soil too.'

Gerald gazed beyond him to the horses. Here was Taran, elderly but still strong in the haunches. And Tymestl, and Nesta's leggy black mare that he had last seen at Cenarth. His heart swelled, and as he approached them Taran nickered at him and pawed a forehoof in greeting. His coat shone like sunlit shingle, and even as old as he was, he was still in magnificent condition. 'How . . .?' Gerald said, and swallowed.

'Dewi brought them to me when Owain ap Cadwgan arrived in Ireland and they have been in my stable ever since,' Gruffydd said. 'I return them to you as a gift to you and my sister.'

'I did not know what was going to happen to them with the lord Owain,' Dewi said. 'He is unpredictable and only cares for what he owns when he has the whim. He might as easily have had them slaughtered and sold for dog meat, or killed to wreak his revenge. They were not his, they were never his, so I brought them to my lady's brother, the lord Gruffydd.' He made a face. 'I am sorry that I was unable to bring Storm; the lord Owain still has him.'

'For the moment,' Gerald said. 'I will get him back.' He clapped Dewi's shoulder. 'I am in your debt for this, as is your lady, and I shall say nothing more on the matter of how you came from Cenarth to Ireland. I know your first loyalty is to the horses for as long as you live.'

Dewi said nothing, but bowed and touched his forelock.

Gerald turned to Gruffydd. 'Thank you. Even if you had brought chests of treasure, there could be nothing more precious than these horses.' Indeed, it felt like having his manhood restored.

He took Gruffydd and his men to the hall where wine and food had been set out, and sent a messenger to Carew to inform Nesta they would be arriving before dusk.

Gruffydd looked around the chamber, still absorbing every detail. 'I remember hearing tales of how you held this place against the men of Powys, including Owain ap Cadwgan.'

Gerald shrugged uncomfortably. It would not be the only tale Gruffydd had heard and the most recent must have caused a deal of mirth around the Irish camp fires, especially with Owain present in person to exaggerate them. 'I did what I had to do. I knew if I did yield, I was finished. Even if I had not died in battle, my life would have ended. As it is . . .' He opened his hand. 'God's plan is never clear, except to God.'

'That is true,' Gruffydd said. 'I never thought this day would come, but it has. So many years of exile. I barely remember the time before and I must rely on others to tell me.' He rinsed his mouth with a swallow of wine. 'Still, there is no point living in an idyllic past that is but a trick of the mind and does not help to deal with what is now.'

'Indeed not,' Gerald agreed.

'In other circumstances we would be deadly enemies, but we share a common foe in Owain ap Cadwgan.'

Gerald dusted crumbs from his hands and regarded Nesta's brother. Now they came to it, to the grit in the oyster. 'The raids along my borders cause constant damage. By the time we receive news of their latest one, they have melted away, having taken their plunder and burned the settlements. If it's a Norman or Flemish settlement then the Welsh are cheerful, and if it's a Welsh settlement then I am blamed for being unable to protect them. I cannot win, but I will not give up.'

Gruffydd had listened intently, and now set his cup down. 'Owain and his cousin turn fine profits in Dublin from the plunder they acquire when raiding. For what he has done to my father's lands, and to my kin, he is a greater enemy than any Norman – for now.'

His smile was supposed to be a jest, but was greeted with unease and exchanged glances among Gerald's men.

'Our argument with the line of Bleddyn has a long history,' Gruffydd continued. 'My father slew two of Cadwgan's brothers in battle long before I was born, and in their turn Cadwgan and his kin have long trespassed into Dyfed and will not cease unless forcefully tackled. I do not intend to return to Ireland – Wales is my home. I shall do everything I can to bring down Madog ap Rhyrid and Owain ap Cadwgan, and any of their kin who stand in my way.'

'Madog is governed by his passion for violence first and strategy second,' Gerald said. 'Owain has more intelligence but they are still of a kind – but you must know that already, from Ireland.'

Gruffydd rolled his eyes. 'Indeed. Owain tried to tell me he was going to rule all of Wales with my sister at his side, and this was immediately after his arrival in Ireland after fleeing from his rash exploits.'

Gerald tightened his lips and Gruffydd kept his expression neutral.

'You will have to tread carefully,' Gerald said after a pause. 'Richard de Belmeis is King Henry's viceroy and an expert at playing one side against the other. You should beware of stirring up an ants' nest. Do not underestimate de Belmeis and the King, for they are formidable men, Henry especially. He is ruthless in ways that Owain and Madog and you cannot begin to know. You must be careful, for the game is much larger than a single board.'

Gruffydd smiled tightly. 'I have not waited all this time in exile in Ireland to lose now, but I swear on my life that whatever happens, I will bring no danger to you and my sister.'

'I hope that is true, for I welcomed you here to lighten our load and help protect our borders, not to endanger us.'

'That is understood.' Gruffydd was sombre now. 'I promise I shall not assault any land under your jurisdiction, and I shall be cautious when it comes to the English king and his viceroy.'

Gerald nodded but felt uneasy and unconvinced. It was simple for Gruffydd to say the words, but deeds were always the proof and he had learned not to trust anyone, including the young man sitting at his board, Richard de Belmeis and the King. Perhaps Nesta too, but he buried that thought like a stone.

Nesta smoothed her red silk gown and patted the meshed head-dress and circlet to reassure herself. She was so tense with anxiety that she had almost been sick. Preparing to greet her brother again after so long apart was almost like being with child.

The messenger had arrived to announce that Gruffydd was at Pembroke and would be here before dusk. She had started readying a chamber for him the instant he had accepted their invitation. Yesterday she had had to change the coverlet because it had rained and Geri had rolled about on it and left a bone on the pillow, but all was orderly now. The children were spruced and wearing their best clothes, the hall was swept and the floor had been strewn with new rushes and sweet-smelling herbs. She had prepared the high table with a seat of honour for Gruffydd and the kitchen servants were toiling, although she knew Gerald would already have offered Gruffydd and his men refreshment at Pembroke.

Nothing remained of their parents' possessions, but she had done her best to make the hall look as it had in their childhood. Gruffydd had been such a little boy he might not remember, but she did, and she wanted to recreate it. She could not have her past returned, but even the ghost of memory was a kind of consolation.

Her hands were clammy as she wondered what Gruffydd would be like now. She could barely remember the four-year-old boy she had kissed farewell. So many losses and so much heart-ache and harshness to mould them both. Would she know him? Would he know her – not in the flesh, but in the essence of family? He would be aware of what had happened to her, but what would he think of her relationship with the King of England? And of what happened at Cenarth with Owain? What if he regarded her as a whore to the Normans?

Hearing the horn blow at the gate, she swallowed her fear and gathered her courage. Assembling the children, she took them out with her into the courtyard. Her heart pounded like a fist on a drum. Henry was watching her with a look she recognised from his father – coolly assessing. Gwilym was excited to see his uncle, Angharad too, hopping from foot to foot, her doll tucked under her arm. Dafydd stood by his nurse on the wobbly legs of a recent walker, and Maurice was asleep in a sling tied at his nurse's back.

The gates opened and the troop paraded into the courtyard behind two banner-bearers, one belonging to Gerald and the other to her brother. Gerald was not riding his usual bay, but Tymestl. She saw Dewi astride Taran and realised with a flood of mingled emotions that he had succeeded in his mission to deliver the horses to her brother. However, both these sights were sidelined as she focused her attention on the young man riding in on a glossy chestnut stallion. He drew rein and dismounted with the lithe arrogance of a prince. She could have been looking at her father, the resemblance was so strong, and her legs almost buckled from the shock.

Gerald dismounted too, handed the reins to his squire, and hurried to her side to support her.

Gruffydd came forward, bowed, and took her hands. 'My sister,' he said in a constricted voice. 'I have dreamed of this moment and waited almost twenty years exiled in a foreign land for this reunion. It is the family that matters, and what has brought us together again, and I swear my oath of loyalty to my kin by blood and by marriage.' He shot a glance of acknowledgement to Gerald.

Nesta looked at him through a blur of tears then threw herself into his arms and hugged him fiercely. 'I have dreamed of it too. Every moment of every single day since we were parted. I have hoped and prayed for this day. You look so much like our father – so much!'

'I am here to stay; I am never going back to Ireland, whatever happens,' he said fiercely. 'I will not flee back and forth like a rat to a hole. That time is finished. I have my father's sword and I shall use it.'

Pride surged through her, and fear, for his stance was dangerous as well as bold. She looked at Gerald to gauge his reaction to the speech, but his expression was the bland, still-water one he used to conceal his thoughts.

She presented the children to their uncle. Henry regarded him with a glint in his eyes, assessing, challenging and interested – measuring himself against him.

'A fine brood,' Gruffydd said, sharing a smile between the children. 'I have gifts for all of you and I am proud to call you kin.'

Angharad danced forward and shyly put her hand in his.

'Angharad will show you into the hall,' Nesta said, amused.

Gruffydd laughed without embarrassment or awkwardness, and Nesta warmed to him even more.

'Come then, young lady,' he said, 'show me within. I lived here when I was a little boy.'

The rest of the day and evening was spent in forging family bonds out of fragile threads. Gruffydd regaled them with stories of his life in Ireland as they ate around the fire in the hall and dusk darkened into night. There were wafers and sweet cakes served hot from the griddle, and bowls of mutton simmered in wine with garlic and herbs, accompanied by fine white bread. Fresh honey from the comb with wild strawberries and thick yellow cream.

Angharad had to be told off for gorging on the strawberries and was taken away by her nurse to have all the sticky juice wiped off. Gruffydd chucked baby Maurice under the chin and held Dafydd in his lap for a while, letting the child play with an amulet on a cord around his neck. Watching him, Nesta felt sad with stirrings of her own lost childhood and what might have been. This was a brief moment out of the stream, a starting point rather than a homecoming, and soon Gruffydd would leave and face danger, away from all this warmth and affection. He had not said how long he would stay and she dared not ask him.

Eventually, Gerald rose and threw a fresh log on the greying embers. 'You have much to say to each other that is best between you alone,' he said. 'It is a fine night; I will visit my horses again, and then retire.' He bowed to both of them and left, taking Henry and Gwilym with him, and instructing the nurses to remove the younger ones to their beds. There were still servants around in the background, but none near enough to eavesdrop, and the knights and soldiers in the hall, belonging to Gerald and Gruffydd, had retired to their own areas.

For a short while brother and sister sat listening to the soft crackle of the new log on the fire. Then Gruffydd looked across the flames at Nesta and she poured more mead into their cups.

'Well, sister,' he said, 'what of your story?'

Nesta handed him his drink. 'What of it? I daresay you have heard most of it. I have survived, but it is not something I wish to revisit. Gerald says that once each day is past, we close the door behind us, for a new one waits to be opened, but it is not as simple as he would have it.'

'It would seem like wisdom on the surface,' he agreed, 'but like you, I am not so sure, and neither, I think, is Gerald in his heart. Rather it is a comfortable thing to say, or wishful thinking. Even if you close a door, what lies behind it does not go away.' He looked into the fire. 'When I heard what had become of you at the hands of Henry of England and again when he married you to this man, I killed both of them in my imagination for their great dishonour. It was not the destiny you should have had.'

Nesta clenched her hands together in her lap until her rings bit against bone. She glanced around but there was no one within earshot to hear his words.

Then Gruffydd shrugged his shoulders. 'I have changed since then, because I know I must be practical and because I now think as a grown man, not a child. It seems to me that your husband, even while he is unworthy of you, is at least an honourable man and he treats you and the children well.'

'He does.' Nesta's tension relaxed, but not her wariness. 'We have our differences, and he is still a Norman who obeys his king, but he loves me, and he loves Wales.' She touched the mesh headdress and circlet. 'This is mine, to do with as I will. He gave it to me after I returned from . . .' She made a gesture to serve for the rest of the words. 'It was to show everyone in the household how much he honoured and valued me – not as a prize possession, but as a wife. He was reluctant to send for you, but for my sake he agreed – and because the gamble that you would be his ally was worth the risk.'

'Do you love him?'

She bit her lip. 'Yes, I do, but as you said about closing doors, it is more complicated than that. What I feel for my husband has been a long time developing and it is far from perfect, but then what is? If you are asking me if I will cleave to him if it comes to a contest between you and him, then I cannot answer you and I beg you not to lead me to that choice.'

'And Henry, the King?' Gruffydd's eyes narrowed and he gave no commitment.

She took a long drink of mead. 'Henry took everything from me. I was little more to him than a source of release at the day's end, and a hostage with whom to trifle on a whim. He enjoyed his power over me. Do not tangle with him, for you will not win. Whatever you think you have gained will only be what he permits, and if he chooses to take it away, he will. I have no influence with him.'

'But he left you his son to raise.'

Nesta made a face. 'He will be going to his father to finish his training when Henry returns from Normandy. You might call it a sign of favour that he left him with me when I went to my marriage, but Henry is not sentimental in that way. Although I have raised his son to be Welsh, I am sure Henry will educate him otherwise. He will do what best suits his policies and destroy anyone who gets in his way. He can be your enemy, he can be your ally, but only ever on his terms, and you will not win.'

Gruffydd nodded thoughtfully. 'What you say confirms what I have heard said about him in Ireland. Do not worry, I shall cut my cloth accordingly.' He contemplated his cup. 'And what of Owain ap Cadwgan?'

Nesta tensed again. Owain was another of the shadows in the room, always there, stealing the light, and at the same time offering an enticement of darkness. 'What of him?' she asked defensively.

'What does he mean to you?'

She shivered. 'He means danger. You must be as wary of him as you are of King Henry. When the Normans seized our land, Cadwgan and Owain were waiting to snatch whatever they could, and even if Cadwgan is dead, that still pertains.'

'I have met Owain in Ireland and I know what manner of man he is – and his cousin Madog,' Gruffydd said with distaste. 'I know what he wants and what he would take given the slightest opportunity. He thinks too well of himself and he overestimates his own abilities.' He paused. 'If the Normans had not come raiding, if the kingdoms of Wales had been left to their own affairs, then you might have been Owain's wife.'

The words struck Nesta like lightning and she had to look away for a moment. 'Yes, I have thought upon it before,' she said eventually. 'There was even a moment at the time of the raid at Cenarth when I thought it might come to pass, but it was a fever dream.' She looked at Gruffydd. 'Even though I went with Owain, I made a choice that night, and it was to save Gerald. That is why I say that matters are complicated.' She stared into her cup and it was empty, but when Gruffydd made to refresh it, she shook her head. There was no answer to be found in mead as she had learned to her cost. 'Had I married Owain, I would not have survived with him – we were too fierce, too wild. I have counselled you to be wary of King Henry, but even more so beware of Owain, for Henry is logical and pragmatic and you have a chance for reason if you play chess with him. But Owain just sweeps the board off the table and crashes the pieces against the wall – all of them.' Her mind filled with the image of Owain walking up the hall at Ceredigion at the Christmas feast when she had first laid eyes on him. So elemental, so vibrant, so beautiful . . . and so destructive.

'Owain will not get the better of me even if he throws the

board at the wall,' Gruffydd said implacably. 'I am not here to play games but to restore our family to its rightful place, and no one will stand in my way.'

'I do not doubt that,' Nesta said. 'And I will help you all I can, but just be wary.'

Gerald and Nesta travelled up to Cenarth with Gruffydd and his men. Over the last two months, Gerald had come to enjoy the company of Nesta's brother and his entourage. Gruffydd was an easy guest in the solar, a teller of tales. He was intelligent and shrewd, a man who listened to others rather than talk about himself. Indeed, on that score he was enigmatic and not forthcoming.

The time had come for him to leave and seek hospitality and patrons elsewhere and Gerald was ready for him to go: much as he liked Gruffydd, he could not sustain him and his warband indefinitely, and he risked the displeasure of Richard de Belmeis and the rest of the Flemish and Norman communities if he allowed Gruffydd to get his feet too far under the table. He was tolerated as an opponent of Owain ap Cadwgan and as Gerald's brother-in-law, but such tolerance had a limit. So now Gruffydd was bound for North Wales, to Gwynedd, to the hall of its prince, Gruffydd ap Cynan, who had been his father's friend and ally once. Gerald was escorting him as far as his own borders.

Arriving at Cenarth, Gerald felt uneasy. Although it was stoutly defended with solid fortifications and guards on the lookout boards, tension still stiffened his neck and spine.

'Only four miles from Ceredigion,' Gruffydd said, looking round.

'Yes, and guarding our border and protecting Gilbert de Clare's interest there.'

'My ancestors were once lords of Ceredigion. Perhaps they may be again. Who can say what will happen on the turn of Fortune's wheel?'

Gerald sent him a warning look. 'I would advise against setting your sights on Ceredigion, for if you did I would have to oppose you. I could not turn a blind eye.'

'I would not expect you to,' Gruffydd said with an easy smile. 'Do not worry, I shall not attempt targets that will necessitate you taking up arms against me.'

Gerald said nothing. The King and de Belmeis would order him to fight as they saw fit, but for now there was no point in raising the issue, for Gruffydd's current targets were his own Welsh enemies.

That evening, Nesta and Gerald held a farewell feast in Gruffydd's honour with toasts and stories, and they stayed up until the small hours, burning the candles to stubs. It was close to dawn when they finally retired to bed.

Gerald put his arm across Nesta's waist as they lay down. 'I am going to miss your brother,' he said. 'It would be unwise to bid him stay, but I admit I shall be sorry to see him leave.'

Nesta turned in his arms. 'He will visit again as often as he can, given the constraints. You should have invited him long before now.'

'I am not so sure,' he said ruefully. 'He has it in him to run rings around all of us, but providing he sticks to his bargain, all will be well.'

She shrugged against his chest. 'He has no reason not to; we have done the right thing.'

Gerald made a sound of acknowledgement, and kept his doubts to himself.

Gruffydd departed with his men shortly before noon, laden with food and gifts and affectionate farewells.

'Be careful,' Nesta said, hugging him close as he prepared to mount his horse. 'It would break my heart to lose you again.'

'You will not lose me,' Gruffydd said with all the sunny confidence of youth. 'You will not break either, my sister – you are too strong for that.'

She watched him ride out, and when he had gone, she returned to her chamber. It seemed darker somehow, as though his leaving had taken a bright presence out of her life; and even if she was strong, she was fragile too.

25

Shrewsbury Castle, Spring 1113

Nesta approached Richard de Belmeis and curtseyed to him. When he extended his hand, she kissed his amethyst ring of office.

'Welcome, my lady,' he said. 'It is a rare pleasure to receive the wife of one of the King's constables. I am pleased to greet you after so many years.'

'And you, my lord Bishop.'

Having already made his obeisance, Gerald stood at her side, stiff with tension but maintaining a bland expression.

Nesta's memories of Shrewsbury Castle held dark images of a frightened girl taken into Norman custody and coerced by Henry into becoming his unwilling concubine. De Belmeis then had been a servant of the Montgomery family, just like Gerald. She had no liking for him, but she respected his power, both as a churchman and as Henry's representative in the Marches. His influence was everywhere. He had the resources to bring to any situation. He was urbane, benign, friendly – and utterly ruthless.

'And this is Henry.'

She beckoned him forward. Her other children were at home with their nurses, but Henry was here to be handed over to begin his training under de Belmeis and then to go to his father when he returned from Normandy at midsummer.

Henry knelt to de Belmeis in proper obeisance as he had been taught.

De Belmeis gestured him to his feet and looked him up and down. 'A fine young man.' He tipped up the boy's chin on his index finger. 'You are the image of your father.'

Henry stood a little taller and looked proud.

'Let us see what we can do with you before his return, hmm?'

'He has already begun his training,' Gerald said. 'I am pleased with his progress in all disciplines, especially that of sword and shield.'

'I am sure, knowing you, my lord, that he is well accomplished in all you have been able to show him,' de Belmeis said smoothly, 'but now is the time to give him the polish that can only be achieved at court. Although of course he shall always belong to Wales as well.' He smiled at Nesta.

Nesta returned the Bishop's look and wondered if he was crediting her input in her son's raising, or was he saying that Henry's Welsh blood would hold him back from promotion? With de Belmeis there was no knowing.

De Belmeis summoned an older squire and told him to take Henry around the castle and show him his sleeping quarters. And then he called for wine and wafers and sat down to talk with Nesta and Gerald, crossing one leg over the other, acting as if he were at full leisure, although Nesta knew he was intently focused beneath the urbane exterior.

'I heard you have been entertaining kin recently,' de Belmeis said as the servant poured wine and then departed.

Nesta clasped her hands modestly in front of her. 'My brother returned from Ireland to visit us. I had not seen him since . . . since he was a small boy. He is no longer with us as he wished to travel and visit friends.'

De Belmeis smiled but his gaze remained hard. He turned to Gerald. 'It is generous of you to welcome your kin by marriage, but I believe there is danger too. Some might say you are being foolhardy.'

Gerald folded his arms across his chest. 'It depends what you mean by foolhardy, my lord. What weapon would you use to counteract the depredations of Madog ap Rhyrid and Owain ap Cadwgan? Gruffydd will prove a useful ally.'

'That remains to be seen,' de Belmeis said. 'I suspect he may just be more fuel on the fire. The Welsh lords fight among themselves like dogs over a bone. They make an alliance for as long as it suits their purpose and then break it to form another with the man they have just been trying to kill. There is no reasoning with them. You may think you have everything laid out in a neat line, but next moment you discover that they have made a pact with the Irish, or with a neighbour who has a mutual desire for booty. I am sure that your brother-by-marriage is not just dwelling pleasantly in Wales visiting friends.'

Nesta pressed her lips together, wishing she could scratch the supercilious smile from de Belmeis's well-fed face.

'My lord, I know this, and I do have long experience, but I believe this is the right course,' Gerald replied steadily. 'We need to reach the ordinary Welsh folk and Gruffydd is better placed to do it than I am. He has no desire to see Owain ap Cadwgan and Madog ap Rhyrid flourish. And better as my ally where I can see him.'

De Belmeis frowned. 'I counsel you to leave well alone. Let the King deal with the struggle for power in Powys on his return.

You should go back to Pembroke, my lord. Look to your walls, be prudent, and not too swift to support any faction until we see which way the wind blows. Remember, your foremost loyalty is to the King your own lord.'

'Yes, sire,' Gerald said calmly, although a muscle flickered in his cheek. 'And part of that is keeping my land safe from predators on limited resources.'

'Then I trust you to know what you are about. In the meantime, rest assured that I shall take very good care of your stepson before I send him on to his father.' He smiled benignly and rose to his feet. 'You will excuse me for now, I have matters awaiting my attention, but stay and dine as my guests and spend a little more time to bid farewell to your son.'

Nesta turned to Gerald with flashing eyes once the Bishop had gone. 'I didn't like him before and don't like him any more now. He treats us like underlings.'

Gerald shrugged. 'But he has the power and the rule of law, and he is the King's representative. Richard de Belmeis is better an ally than an enemy, believe me.'

They went to dine in the hall a short while later and Henry joined them, enthusing about the number of hawks in the mews, and how he had been watching some of the young knights at their training. He had been ready for some time. Nesta had cherished each moment that the summons had not arrived, but he needed this, and she was proud to see him already testing his wings, eager to fly, if sad for herself. This was what it was to have sons.

Richard de Belmeis had afforded them a position at the high table and Nesta was pleased that at least he had seen fit to acknowledge her rank. Several of the Montgomery retainers and knights who had transferred their service to de Belmeis were present and Nesta knew some of them from her days as a hostage. None addressed her, and as a defensive shield she adopted the regal air of a queen, and in her turn ignored them.

Gerald had just served her with a portion of salmon from the dish set before them when an usher came to the dais table and stooped to speak in de Belmeis's ear. The Bishop stopped chewing in mid-rotation, dropped his napkin and excused himself from the table. Nesta noticed a man being escorted along the side of the hall – a Welshman with a bloody, bandaged arm – and he was taken aside to de Belmeis's chamber. Her thoughts flashed to Gruffydd. What if something had happened to him, or he had done something rash? There was danger, but from which direction she did not know, only that it was sufficient to drive Richard de Belmeis away from his dinner.

Her appetite vanished and the salmon's deep-pink flesh, flecked with dark-green herbs, made her feel nauseous. She saw a scribe hurrying to the chamber with his satchel of parchments and other equipment, and hard on his heels a pair of messengers.

Eventually de Belmeis returned and, making his apologies, sat down to resume his dinner. But after a couple of mouthfuls he sighed and put down his knife. 'Owain ap Cadwgan has returned and seized his cousin Madog,' he said. 'This changes the balance decisively.'

'Madog ap Rhyrid is dead?'

De Belmeis shook his head at Gerald. Pushing up his sleeves, he held out his hands and a servant poured water over them from a brass jug in the shape of a centaur. 'No, but he will not be fighting again. Owain has gouged out his eyes in revenge for Cadwgan's death and has laid claim to Powys. We all know where we stand now – although it is still for the King to decide and Owain has still to answer for the death of William of Brabant and other infringements.'

Through her shock, Nesta realised that she should have expected such tidings. The thought of Owain back in Wales and having eliminated one rival filled her with turmoil.

Gerald shook his head. 'I doubt there will be peace along any border in Wales if you give Owain free rein.'

'Who said I was giving him free rein?' de Belmeis responded sharply. 'I shall do no such thing. The man may have entitlements of heritage, but nothing is resolved, and shall not be until he kneels in person to King Henry. My duty is to hold everything steady here. It is like having a dozen horses pulling on the reins all trying to go in different directions and fighting each other at the same time. The best you can do, my lord, is keep to your own jurisdiction and govern well. I do not want you to be one of my problem horses. Remember, every man is expendable. And before you take offence, let me say that I value your friendship and your good sense. I need you to help me hold the reins, not take the bit between your teeth.'

'I think we understand each other,' Gerald said. 'But let me say this clearly too: in order for me to help you, you must support me also.'

'And I shall,' de Belmeis said firmly. 'You have my word.'

Nesta unnecessarily adjusted her son's cloak as she prepared to depart and entrust him to the care of Richard de Belmeis. With every fibre of her being she wanted to take him back to Carew and protect him from the dark adult world he was about to enter, but then again he had tasted a vestige of it already.

'I shall miss you every day. Do not forget your Welsh blood, or what your stepfather has taught you. Be honourable and true, and I shall hope to hear well of your progress.' She touched his cheek, still soft with the last bloom of boyhood.

'Yes, Mama.' He planted his legs wide and squared his

shoulders, reminding her of his father. He had so many of Henry's mannerisms that she worried for the future.

A frown forked his brows. 'Do not worry about Owain,' he said. 'I shall speak to my father about him. I will tell him what I know.'

Nesta swallowed, wondering just what he might say to the King. 'I think it better that you let the past lie for our family's sake,' she said. 'Your father has all the information he needs from other sources.'

He nodded to satisfy her but pressed his lips together, and she knew he would do as he chose.

'If you do speak to your father, then tell him of your uncle Gruffydd and his desire for an alliance.' She kissed him. 'I love you. You are a son of princes, always remember that.'

He puffed out his chest and stood proud. 'Always, Mother.'

Gerald helped Nesta to mount her mare and together they rode out. 'I won't look back,' she said, and blinked tears from her eyes. 'God help me I will not.'

Gerald reached across and squeezed her arm. 'We shall see him again.'

'But he will be changed.'

'Yes, but it is the way of life. When I went to be a squire, my own mother grieved, but I saw none of it; I was ready to go, and my parents had prepared me well. When I returned, the love was still as strong, but changed, because the boy had gone for ever. I hope she was proud of my manhood, although I think she never quite grew accustomed to the fact that her youngest son was capable of growing a beard!'

He was trying to make her smile, but her unease remained.

'I am worried about Gruffydd too – about what will happen to him.'

Gerald was silent for a while, settling into his riding, one hand loose on the reins, the other at his hip. 'Gruffydd is a grown man,' he said eventually. 'What he does is laid at his own door. I can only do so much to protect him for you. I am not his keeper. Indeed, if the King is to be involved in this then you are the one with the persuasion since Henry is his son, and Gruffydd is your brother.'

'He would not listen to me.'

'The best we can do is return to Carew and Pembroke and strengthen our boundaries. Owain will be our neighbour.'

She dropped her gaze. The thought of Owain was a discomfort, like rich, dark wine that had made her dreadfully sick but there was still a brimming cup at her side waiting to be picked up.

'How shall we ever be safe?' she asked. 'How shall our children ever live lives not steeped in blood?'

'We shall teach them well,' Gerald said with grim determination. 'They must have guile as well as strength. They must learn to bend in the storm and not break. God alone knows, we have enough experience ourselves – they can learn from us.'

26

Windsor Castle, Christmas 1113

'My lady mother.'

Nesta gazed at the youth on one knee before her and wondered how so much could have changed in a little over six months. He rose, having performed his respects, and he was almost as tall as she was. His chin was lightly whiskered and she remembered Gerald's comment about his mother and her son's beard.

'Who is this man who calls me mother?' she asked in a tremulous voice, wanting to embrace him but constrained.

He drew himself up, and she saw his pride and the masculinity that was taking him away from her, deeper into a world where she would be his past.

He flashed her a smile. 'My father says I am progressing well, and he is going to give me more duties and privileges.'

'I am pleased to hear it.' She had to force the words. She knew what duties the squires were given, and that included waiting attendance at night.

King Henry had chosen to hold his Christmas court at Windsor with his queen and their eleven-year-old son. Their firstborn child, a daughter, Matilda, had been sent away to a marriage in Germany. Nesta and Gerald were attending the gathering and visiting Gerald's kin at the same time. His parents were no longer living, but his older brother William was the incumbent constable. Nesta had never been to Windsor, not even as Henry's concubine, and she was still assimilating the fact that this wealthy royal fortress was where Gerald had been born and spent his boyhood. It made Carew look like an insignificant manor by comparison, and when she saw how smoothly the castle functioned, like a well-greased wheel, she realised where Gerald had obtained his manners, his polish and his formidable administrative abilities.

Gwilym and Angharad came running to greet their older brother. Gwilym, coming up for eleven, was next year going for training to Tancred, Constable of the castle of Rhos in Haverford, and was eager to talk to Henry who embodied all of Gwilym's aspirations. Angharad, six, demanded a kiss. Then Henry hugged the younger ones: Dafydd, two and a half, and eighteen-month-old Maurice.

'Where is my stepfather?' Henry asked, glancing around.

'Here he is now,' Nesta said as Gerald entered, talking to his brother, William. Gerald's son Walter was with them, handsome at nineteen with sandy-fair hair and chiselled features. He and Henry embraced with a certain reserve. They had been bower-companions but not close at Carew. Now Walter was the experienced squire on the cusp of knighthood, but Henry held the higher rank and position in the world. However, they had a smile for each other in front of parents.

Henry greeted Gerald and tensed when Gerald called him 'son', and Nesta could tell that he considered that part of his life finished and was distancing himself from reminders. He left shortly after that, summoned away to his duties by one of the other boys.

Gerald watched him go, then gently touched Nesta's hand. 'Are you all right?'

'Yes,' she said, but felt sad. 'He is growing up too fast, and the court is already changing him.'

'He is becoming a man.'

'Yes,' Nesta said, thinking it not necessarily a good thing – not at the Norman royal court.

At a late formal meal in the hall, Nesta and Gerald were afforded a place at a trestle to the side of the high table, the latter being occupied by the King and Queen and an inner circle of prominent nobility. The Queen sat in quiet dignity beside her husband, sombrely dressed in fine-quality wool of darkest blue, her face framed by a wimple of white silk. A gold cross glinting with rubies lay on her breast, and she might have been mistaken at first glance for a prominent lady of the Church rather than a queen. Henry deferred to her, treating her with decorum and grave respect.

Queen Matilda had borne a son and a daughter early in the marriage and fulfilled her duty. Nesta had heard gossip that a physical relationship did not exist between them, that the birth of their son had been difficult and that they kept to separate chambers. Whether it was true or not, Henry went his way with other women, and the Queen spent much of her time in prayer and religious observation.

Between the several courses of food, a variety of tumblers, dancers, minstrels and story-tellers entertained the company. As the wine sank in the flagons and the noise level increased, the Queen quietly retired with her ladies and the King bade her farewell with courteous attention.

With the meal formally ended, people were free to seek out friends and relatives, engage in conversation, and relax. Some gathered to play dice, tables, and other board games. Nesta inveigled her eldest son into a game of chess before he could abscond with his friends to play dice.

'I might see you again before long,' he said. 'My father will be coming to Wales after Whitsuntide.'

Nesta paused, her hand on a pawn. 'Will he now?'

'He's going to summon Owain ap Cadwgan – I know that much.'

She had been expecting such an announcement, but her stomach still lurched.

'He's not going to return Ceredigion to him,' Henry added. 'De Clare's garrison is staying. I think de Clare means to sit hard on Owain.'

'How hard?' she asked.

Henry shrugged. 'He just said he would deal with him, nothing more, but it was the way he spoke. He asked me about Owain, what he was like.'

'What did you say?'

'That you never knew what Owain would do next and that Owain himself didn't know either.'

'Did . . . did your father ask about me in connection with Owain?'

'Yes.' He gave her a keen look. 'I said what my stepfather said – that you did what you had to do in the circumstances. I didn't tell him any more than that. I know when to say nothing – for my own honour.'

Nesta flushed, feeling guilty and chagrined. 'Thank you,' she said.

They finished the game and Henry won easily, for Nesta could not put her mind to the strategies.

'Do you wish that Owain had taken you to Ireland?' he asked, fixing her with a hard stare.

Nesta shook her head. 'Not any more.'

'But you did once?'

Meeting his gaze, she saw the judgement and accusation. 'I thought I did, but sometimes our thoughts misguide us and lead us down roads we should never have travelled. It may be difficult for you to understand, but for the first time in my life I had a choice, and it was like rare wine. I made a mistake and trusted too much, and I have regretted that choice ever since.'

He began setting the pieces up again without comment. She watched him, but knew she could not play another game. 'Perhaps if I had sailed with him and gone to your uncle Gruffydd it would have been different, but Owain made it clear he was out to save his own hide, and that I was an encumbrance. If I had gone with him, I would not have been safe.' She looked at the chess board and the light gleaming on the pieces. 'Owain ap Cadwgan put his own life first, whereas your stepfather would die for me.'

'He didn't at Cenarth,' Henry pointed out with a curl of his lip that indicated what he thought of Gerald's actions.

'Because I would not let him. I had a choice then too, and I entreated him for my sake to save himself. He did it at my behest, not his own.' The words sparked within her, kindling a new level of awareness about her feelings for Gerald.

She could tell that Henry did not understand, for what did a woman's plea matter in the face of a man's will?

One of the King's senior squires came to the board and bowed to her. 'My lady, the King would have words with you in his chamber,' he said.

Nesta looked at him in alarm and her breath locked in her throat, preventing her from answering.

'Mother, I will escort you,' Henry said, standing up.

Nesta pushed to her feet and took his arm. She was grateful for his support, but he was a fourteen-year-old boy and what could he do to protect her? What could Gerald or anyone do against the King who would take what he wanted?

'No,' she said, 'go and join your friends. You are not on duty.' She forced a smile. 'I shall not be long.'

He gave her a doubtful look, but one of his friends called across to him, waving a dice cup in his hand.

'I will be all right,' she said. 'Go.'

He nodded at her insistence and hastened over to the group of youths, although he did look over his shoulder at her once, and she kept the smile on her face. This was a game already in play, and she had to leave room for manoeuvre.

The duty squire conducted her from the hall to the King's chamber and she had to walk past Gerald who was talking with his brother. He looked at her with brows raised, and she shook her head. 'It is all right,' she said, 'I will speak to you later.' She walked on, nauseous with anxiety. Pressing her lips together, she told herself that before she had still been little more than a child; now she was twice that age, mature and experienced in the ways of men, a mother of five children. If she could not hold her own now, then she never would.

The ante chamber was busy with courtiers when she arrived, and an usher directed her to sit on a bench and wait. A group of nobles stood talking together, cloaks rippling as they gestured. Richard de Belmeis stood among them and she caught his eye and forced him to acknowledge her, even though he tried to look away. When she stood up and started towards him, he murmured an excuse to the group and joined her.

'My lady,' he said courteously enough, but with a hint of exasperation.

Nesta curtseyed, kissed his ring, and came straight to the point. 'My lord Bishop, if you have any respect for me or for my husband and our loyalty to the crown, then I ask you to safe-guard my honour, for I am here at the King's request. I would not have anyone misconstrue that invitation, not least my husband and his kin who are our hosts.'

He lifted his brows. 'You are in no danger, my lady, I assure you.'

'I am glad to have that assurance, especially from a man of the Church.' She continued to nail him with her gaze.

The royal chamber door opened and a balding man in a plain brown tunic emerged and went to talk to one of the clerks working at a table. Nesta knew him as one of Henry's spies from her time at court, although he had had fewer wrinkles and a full head of hair then. He cast a glance in her direction and the side of his mouth curled up. Then he caught the Bishop's glare and lowered his eyes.

'That is what I mean,' Nesta said grimly.

De Belmeis sighed and inclined his head. 'Do not worry, my lady, I shall address your concerns.'

'But I do worry,' Nesta said brusquely, 'with every cause.'

An attendant came to the chamber door and beckoned to her.

'I am depending on you, my lord Bishop.'

She curtseyed again to de Belmeis and entered the royal inner sanctum with dragging feet. The attendant who had summoned her bowed to the King and went out, closing the door behind him, leaving her alone with Henry.

Feeling sick, Nesta placed her spine against the wood. Henry was sitting on a padded bench beside a brazier. Beyond him loomed his bed, piled with pillows and furs. The memories assaulted Nesta, as vivid and sharp as blood welling from a cut.

Henry patted the bench, indicating she should join him. 'Come,' he said. 'I will not bite.'

Swallowing bile, Nesta took a few steps into the room, then stopped.

Henry eyed her. 'It has been a long time,' he said, 'but I have often thought of you.'

'A very long time, sire.'

'But not so much that I do not remember how sweet you tasted.'

Henry brushed his hand over his groin, smoothing the cloth so she could see the shape of his penis and be immediately reminded of the solid force of him on top of her. She looked back towards the door.

Henry gave an amused snort. 'You always were a doe I had to hunt, and so innocent then. Now you have maturity, but you are still lovely – if less innocent.'

'I was looking at the door because I was thinking about our son,' Nesta said. 'We were playing chess when you summoned me.' She hoped the detail would give him pause for thought. 'I am glad he is doing so well at court.'

Henry narrowed his eyes, evaluating her. 'I am pleased with him. He is a strong boy, and quick to understand what is required of him and how the court functions.' He spread his legs and pushed his hips forward to emphasise the contents of his braies. 'Perhaps it would be no bad thing for you to give me another to match him.'

Nesta stared at him in horror. 'Sire, I am a married woman and my husband is here at Windsor!'

'The presence of your husband did not stop you from absconding with Owain ap Cadwgan, so I hear,' Henry said nastily, 'right under your husband's nose while he was hiding in the latrine chute. You do not deny that?'

She did not answer, because whatever she replied would damn her, and he knew it.

'Do not refuse me. You were my girl then, and you are still my girl, however many men you have had.'

Nesta wanted to rake her fingernails down his face, but reminded herself that she was playing for her survival. 'Sire, I fear I am no longer your girl in the way I was before. I bore your son, and have given my lord four children since then. Indeed, I am still bleeding from the birth of my lastborn and I am unclean. I would not conceive for you if you took me now. Indeed, it would compromise your own health to lie with me, for who knows what damage my womb-blood might cause to your future potency. I am sullied by childbirth and my physician believes it may be a lasting affliction.'

Henry scowled with displeasure. 'I am sorry to hear that. I shall have my own physician examine you if that is the case, for you are still a young woman and these things can be rectified. Your husband should have more care of your wellbeing.'

'Shall I go then, sire?' Nesta tried not to sound eager.

'No.' Henry's eyes narrowed with intent. 'Come and sit by me. Even if you are discommoded, you can kiss me for the memories, and for your loyalty above all to the King of England.'

Nesta shuddered, but did as he said, knowing if she refused further he had the potential to be vindictive. She perched on the edge of the bench, one foot pressed down ready to leap away. Leaning towards her, he pinched her chin in his fingers, and kissed her, thrusting his tongue back and forth in her mouth – a substitute copulation. Taking her hand, he placed it on his braies, over his erection. Nesta whimpered in her throat and Henry grunted and pushed his hips. He tugged off her circlet and hair net and, breaking the kiss, buried his face in her throat, biting and sucking, while his hands dug forcefully into her hair.

With a loud knock, and a cleared throat, Richard de Belmeis entered the chamber. Nesta used the moment to wrench out of Henry's grasp and leap away from the bench, panting.

'Get out!' Henry shouted at de Belmeis, his face reddening.

The Bishop stood tall and said in a level voice, 'Sire, I am sorry to disturb you but messengers have arrived from Normandy and I thought you would wish to see them.'

Henry stood up, brushing down his tunic. 'So important that you need to interrupt me, my lord Bishop?'

De Belmeis said pointedly, 'I did not believe what you were doing was important, sire. If I was wrong, I crave your pardon.'

'Bid them wait,' Henry snapped. 'I will deal with them in a moment.'

De Belmeis bowed, giving Nesta a look that said he had done his best, and exited the chamber. He drew the door almost closed but did not drop the latch and left it a crack open.

Nesta raised her head. 'I beg your leave to go, my lord.' Her voice trembled, but she imbued it with volume.

Henry returned to his seat on the bench and spread his arms along it. 'Well, so many twists and turns in the hunt,' he said, giving her a humourless grin. 'I know you set that up with Richard de Belmeis, and I do wonder about the claim of your women's ailments too, but let it rest for now. There are, after all, many more deer in the herd and younger, sweeter meat at that. You have earned your reprieve. But you are still my girl and I can take away all you have with a single instruction.'

Nesta curtseyed. 'I shall never forget it, sire, and I thank you for your understanding and mercy.' She snatched her circlet and hair net from the bench.

'Be gone, before I change my mind.' He flicked his fingers. 'Tell de Belmeis to come back.'

She fled the room, her heart hammering against her ribs.

De Belmeis raised his brows at her as she stopped in front of him. 'The King wishes to see you,' she said, adding, 'Thank you, my lord, I am in your debt, as are my family.'

'Indeed, you are, my lady,' he replied, looking less than pleased at being backed into a corner. 'Your husband is loyal to the King and I do not wish to see that loyalty tested beyond endurance for any of our sakes, but I warn you, I shall dare no further on your behalf.'

'That is understood. I shall not be caught unawares again.'

Leaving him, she walked through the ante chamber with her head held high as she had done on so many previous occasions when summoned to Henry as a girl, and she gave every man who looked at her a stare of frozen dignity that kept her pride intact while shaming them.

When she arrived with Henry's squire at her chamber door, her ladies exclaimed in shock at her appearance but Nesta waved aside their cries. 'Be silent,' she snapped, and gave them her hair net and circlet. 'Put these away, and tidy my hair.' She dismissed the squire with a curt nod, stalked into the room and held herself together with a will of iron.

Eleri brought her new veil and Ceridwen prepared a bowl of rose water to wash her hands and face, and gave her a pot of marigold salve for the bite marks on her neck. Gerald arrived, and with an oath of 'Christ on the cross' came to her, hands outstretched. She instinctively recoiled, and saw his eyes fill with pain, and then rage as he saw the marks on her neck.

'I will gut the whoreson and hang him with his own entrails for doing this to you,' he said through gritted teeth.

'You will do no such thing!' Nesta retorted. 'If you strike out at the King, none of us will survive. My position will only be made worse for you will be dead. You might say better dead than dishonoured, but what will happen to our children, especially Angharad? Look what became of me when my own father died. I will not have that fate come to our daughter!'

He turned away, fists clenched. 'It is intolerable,' he said, his voice gravelly with revulsion.

'He did nothing.' Her own voice was tight with all that she was holding back.

Gerald swung round. 'You call this nothing?' he shouted. 'He rumples your clothes, he leaves marks on your body. Just what did he do to you? Tell me, am I to raise another of his bastards under my roof?'

Rage and misery flamed like hot coals in Nesta's belly. 'I told you, he did nothing – or nothing beyond what you see. And in the scheme of what he has already done to me, it is indeed nothing!' She bared her teeth. 'I told him I was still bleeding from my last childbirth and that he should not risk contaminating himself in that way.'

Brought up short, Gerald stared at her open-mouthed.

'I will deal with this, and get us out of this bind. Leave it to me, for in this matter a woman's guile will serve more effectively than any sword. I shall go to the Queen and say I am not well and seek permission to leave the court and recuperate in peace. She has influence with the King and will want me gone from here because she will know of my past and support me as one woman to another. It will be the best course of action for everyone.'

Gerald shook his head and said bitterly, 'For a second time I cannot protect my wife and she must save us both at her own expense while I do nothing.'

Nesta rolled her eyes. 'Dear God Gerald, swallow your pride! If you have a better idea then say so. It is nothing, I tell you – nothing!'

He muttered and paced the room, chewing his thumb, but at length he stopped and exhaled hard. 'You are right. And I do not like that you are right, but there is no other way to keep us all safe. Very well, seek permission of the Queen and I shall make sure we are ready to leave as soon as you have it.'

Nesta knelt before Queen Matilda, in her personal chamber. She had dressed for the audience in her plainest gown and a wimple of thick white linen, with some simple wooden prayer beads tied at her waist. Gone was the jewelled and exotic Welsh princess, and in her place was a quiet, devout matron of modest attitude. Nesta thanked Matilda for granting her the audience and she was sincere, for there had been no certainty that she would do so. Indeed, she could have proven openly hostile.

Matilda welcomed her with calm courtesy and directed her to sit on a stool at her feet. 'What may I do for you, my lady?' she asked.

Nesta folded her hands in a prayerful attitude. 'Madam, I crave your permission to leave court,' she said. 'I have suffered ever since the birth of my fifth child, and I find myself indisposed in the way that women sometimes are after such events.'

The Queen eyed her shrewdly, and Nesta's cheeks burned. By now the court gossips must have told Matilda what had happened between her and Henry, probably a salacious version.

'That would be for the King to decide,' Matilda said neutrally.

'Yes, madam, but I hoped you might intercede on my behalf. I know he pays heed to your wise counsel. I do not wish to offend him or put my husband in difficulty.'

A knowing look entered the Queen's eyes, but compassion too. 'I am sorry to hear of your affliction,' she said. 'I understand and sympathise with your need to retire from the court, and I shall do what I can to assist you. You shall have a safe conduct immediately, and I shall speak to the King and ensure you are not hindered in that endeavour.' She beckoned to a scribe and gave him instructions, and he departed forthwith.

'Thank you, madam, thank you with all my heart!' Tears of gratitude filled Nesta's eyes. 'You are very gracious – I did not know where else to turn.'

Matilda clucked her tongue in a way that said Nesta was making too much fuss. 'I will always help those in genuine need,' she said, and directed one of her women to provide Nesta with a cup of wine. 'I appreciate your prudence and wisdom in coming to me.'

My desperation too, Nesta thought, lowering her gaze.

The scribe soon returned with a parchment bearing a document with the Queen's seal dangling from a woven ribbon. Matilda took it from him and presented it to Nesta. 'Go with my good wishes, and may God protect you on your journey.'

'Thank you, madam.' Nesta rose to her feet and curtseyed deeply. 'I am in your debt.'

Matilda waved her hand. 'No talk of that. But I advise you to avoid visits to court in future given your delicate condition, for I will not always be there to succour you.'

'Madam, I take your advice to heart.' Nesta bowed her head. 'I was only present this time to see my son, and visit my husband's kin. And it was at the King's behest.'

'I believe he will understand from me why it would be unwise for your health to summon you again,' Matilda said. 'You may go.'

Weak with relief, Nesta made her obeisance and backed to the door.

'I have a safe conduct from the Queen,' she said once in the safety of the family chamber, and showed Gerald the letter with the Queen's seal attached. 'I told you all would be well. Now we can leave. The Queen says she will speak to the King and that he will not send for me again.'

She sat down abruptly as her legs gave way, and put her face in her hands.

Gerald hastened to enfold her in a tender embrace. 'You fill me with awe, my matchless wife,' he said. She lay passively against him while he murmured reassurances, too exhausted from the ordeal and the relief to do anything else. Her eyelids were leaden. Gerald carried her to the bed, placed her gently down and covered her with a blanket. She curled up, hugging herself, but before she fell asleep, as her eyes were closing, she saw him slump on the bench and put his face in his hands, his shoulders shaking.

Gerald and Nesta arrived at Carew nine days later after a tiring midwinter journey. On the first night they had stopped at Gerald's manor of Moulsford, thirty miles from Windsor, and from there it had been two days to Bristol to cross the Severn and a day's stop at Gilbert de Clare's castle at Striguil before continuing on into Wales. The weather was frosty, and although they were beset by the bitter cold, the tracks were at least firm to ride along.

Gerald hunched his shoulders as they approached Carew. He should have been relieved to be home, but instead he was beset by a sense of anger and futility. What was all this striving for when he was mocked at every turn? He needed a reprieve; to be able to stand tall and not have other men look at him with derision and scorn. His feelings were like a pit of bubbling tar inside him. People thought him weak – a man who hid in his wife's skirts. He felt ashamed, jealous, and deeply angry. Some of that anger even spilled out towards Nesta and made him disgusted with himself, and he withdrew into his shell, shunning contact.

When he built Pembroke, when he took Nesta to wife, he had possessed the respect and envy of other men. He hadn't regarded himself as a dupe, taking the King's leavings; rather he felt as though he had been given a precious jewel to care for. He still viewed Nesta in that way, but now he understood that Henry had never truly relinquished his grip and thought that he could have what he wanted whenever it was convenient.

Gruffydd was at Carew to greet their return. Gerald had entrusted him with the manor during their absence as a test of Gruffydd's loyalty and commitment to family.

'I thought not to see you for another week at least,' Gruffydd said, a little annoyed, for he had been enjoying his role as lord and master. 'Did your faith in me waver?'

'Of course not,' Gerald said curtly. 'We had finished our business at Windsor, that is all.'

'Mama wasn't well,' Angharad piped up.

Gruffydd turned to Nesta and she shook her head and touched her stomach. 'Women's matters,' she said. 'I am much better now.'

His expression said he was unconvinced, but he held his peace.

Later, when Nesta and the children had retired, he sat down before the fire with Gerald and they shared a jug of wine.

'What really happened in Windsor?' Gruffydd asked.

'You do not need to know,' Gerald said flatly.

'It was Henry, wasn't it?'

Gerald took a swallow of wine. 'Be wise and do not pursue that avenue. And before you get any notions into your head, I am not in rebellion against the King and I faithfully serve the crown. Do not think you can slide your knife into the side of a crack and widen it.'

Gruffydd regarded him with a pained expression. 'You are my kin. I would never do that.'

'Good, then we understand each other,' Gerald said curtly, thinking that Gruffydd's protest was somewhat sideways of the truth. He sighed, and palmed his face. 'The King is coming to the Marches after Whitsuntide, to settle the matter of Powys and the other principalities, and he will be bringing a full army with him. It seems likely he will grant Owain ap Cadwgan his father's lands. It behoves you to do nothing untoward that could imperil our own situation.'

'Are you warning me?'

'Yes I am. If the King comes after you, I am duty-bound to obey his will. Do not give him cause to turn his attention your way, for it will jeopardise us all. I mean it.'

'I will make sure to stay away from Carew,' Gruffydd replied calmly. 'And I will bear your words in mind.'

Gerald finished his wine and stood up. 'Do so. I do not want to face you with a sword in my hand, for your sister's sake as much as my own. I will bid you goodnight; it has been a long road.'

Leaving Gruffydd at the fire, Gerald made his way to his own chamber, feeling dispirited and full of trepidation.

Nesta was wearing her bed robe and sitting in his chair. Her hair was loose down her back, black and heavy as midnight. The sight of her jolted him, for he had not expected her to be here tonight.

'I thought you would be asleep with your ladies,' he said.

She shook her head. 'I thought so too, but when it came to the moment, I wanted you beside me.'

'I do not know why, for I am not good company.' He sat on the bed and rubbed his hands over his face.

'I do not know why either, but I do. Will you sing?'

He dropped his hands and grimaced. 'Ah Nesta, I do not think I have a song within me just now.'

'Do it for me, and I will listen.' She picked up his harp and brought it to him. 'Comfort me. Comfort us both.'

Gerald shook his head, but took the instrument from her hands. It needed tuning and he set about the task, turning the pegs, plucking the notes, and all without conscious thought because of the long familiarity.

'Even if we cannot close this door, it will pass in time and the distance will stretch away from what happened at Windsor until it is but a smudge on the horizon.'

Gerald felt the words he had used so glibly returning to haunt him. What had happened at Windsor was indelible. As was Cenarth. He looked at Nesta sitting beside him, utterly beautiful in the candle light, and knew he was unworthy.

'Play for me,' she encouraged again. 'I have missed your voice. Henry may be the King but he cannot sing a note worth a bean.'

'Can Owain sing?' Gerald asked with welling bitterness.

'Not in the way that you do.'

He looked away. He knew songs to reflect his mood – one about a skull and another about a sword, yet another about betrayal – but they would not please her. At last he sighed and sang about the breeze, his voice wavering over the first lines but gradually gathering strength.

Seagull, you come from the zodiac,
Tell my wife, my courageous love
For as long as I may live,
I am her faithful plaything.
Nothing I am without her,
If truly she is not untrue,

Fly high and you shall see her beauty
Fly low and find a road of sky
Go to my raven-haired mistress,
And give her all my breath.

The last line ended on a sudden choke of tears. Nesta removed the harp from his hands and, kissing him, reached to his belt buckle. 'Come to bed, Gerald,' she said. 'I will take all your breath and give it back to you in mine, and let there be no doors tonight.'

27

Fortress of Cenarth Bychan, Summer 1114

Nesta watched Gwilym striving to contain himself as he waited for a groom to bring his horse. Now and again he performed a little dance from one foot to the other. Today he was going to become a squire to Tancred de Rhos, Lord of Haverford. She was unsettled at having a second son leave her care to join another household where he would be subject to other influences, but he was ready to leave the nest. He had been restless for some time and was accompanying Gerald to the King's great muster at Trellech, joining Tancred along the way.

Nesta embraced him, then stepped back. 'Remember your mother,' she said. 'Always ask yourself before you do anything if it is the honourable and right thing to do.'

'Yes, Mother,' he said, his complexion ruddy with embarrassment, his glance flicking around to see who was watching.

'Know who you are, and be proud.'

In due time, he would rule as Lord of Carew and Constable

of Pembroke. But he needed first to learn and mature and become a man. At Carew he had been taught the laws and customs of his Welsh ancestry and spoke the language fluently. She did not want him to enter a Norman household but she was pragmatic. To be successful he needed to assimilate both cultures, and at least Haverford was not far from home.

Gerald emerged from the stables leading a horse for Gwilym, a five-year-old storm-dun with a white blaze, bred from Tymestl and a Welsh mare. 'Care for him well,' he said gravely as he handed Gwilym the reins. Gwilym had been eyeing up the young gelding for a while among the Carew horses and while Gerald had remained noncommittal to the hints and sighs, he had taken private note.

Gwilym's complexion brightened with pleasure. 'Thank you, sire, thank you!'

Gerald clapped his shoulder and smiled. 'I thought he would be to your taste.' He watched Gwilym for a moment, proud of his eldest son, then turned to bid farewell to his other offspring before finally taking Nesta's hands and facing her. 'I will see you before summer's end. Take care of yourself.' He lowered their clasped hands to her waistline in a deliberate gesture. Last night she had told him she thought she might be with child again. She had missed her flux at the end of March; it was now early June and still no blood. She had been feeling queasy and her breasts were sore. Thank Christ that it had not happened in January, lest anyone think she was carrying the King's seed.

'I shall do so, and God speed you. Be wary of everyone,' she said, 'especially the King.'

Gerald stroked her cheek. 'I will do what I must to keep us whole, no more, and no less. I trust Gruffydd to keep his head down and to do and say nothing to jeopardise the situation.'

'I will go surety for him,' she said. 'He will not cause trouble.'

He nodded, and turned to Tymestl, who was past a score years now, but still strong.

She climbed to the wall walk to watch them ride out and her eyes followed the entourage of soldiers, servants and sumpter horses until they were lost from sight.

She and Gerald had weathered the storm after the events at Windsor, but there were still moments when he went off alone or grew quiet and morose. There were moments too when she would return to being in that room with Henry, feeling his hands upon her, and his mouth working at her throat, deliberately marking her for all to see, and all she could do was lie beneath a blanket and shiver until the moment passed.

But she and Gerald had survived. Taking long walks together side by side had been a great remedy in the darkest days. There was nothing to say that would ever make it better, but the experience had drawn them closer in understanding. Even if they could not leap with joy, they were walking a level and united path.

In Shrewsbury, Gerald left Tymestl with Dewi and went to his tent, pitched in the castle's outer bailey. It had been a sweltering midsummer day; his mouth was parched while the rest of him stewed inside his armour and padding, for even in the late afternoon the sun was still a furnace.

They had been riding on patrols and sporadically skirmishing with the Welsh. Henry was now in Shrewsbury, having arrived from further north dealing with Prince Gruffydd of Gwynedd, who had been succouring Owain ap Cadwgan. The weather had simmered and so had Wales, but Henry had thus far controlled the situation. One by one the leaders of the various principalities had come to him to make peace.

Gerald ducked into his tent, removed his helm and sighed with relief as his squire helped him out of his armour. His mail shirt and under-quilting had chafed the tops of his shoulders, and his feet were gently throbbing. The youth brought him water for washing, fresh clothes, and a jug recently filled from a clean stream. Gerald poured a cup, drank it down as fast as he could swallow, and repeated the action. He wrung out the cloth in the bowl and wiped his torso, then stood bare-chested to let the breeze dry his body. The coolness was delicious and he took a moment to enjoy the sensation. He would have to report to the King in a moment, but Henry could wait a little longer.

Odo de Barry arrived from his own tent, wearing a clean shirt and hose and carrying his tunic. 'News,' he said as Gerald began dressing. 'Owain ap Cadwgan rode in to make his peace this noontide while we were on patrol. He's with the King now. Tancred's just told me.'

Gerald hitched up his braies and rolled the belt around the waistband. 'He is here because he has no choice. I would not trust any peace of Owain's further than the distance between my hand and my knife.'

'Neither would I, but that is in the King's remit. He has dealt with Gwynedd, now for Powys.'

Gerald donned his tunic over his fresh shirt. Nesta and her ladies had made it from a bolt of indigo silk that had been a gift from William of Brabant. His hose were a paler-blue linen, with embroidered leg bindings secured at the top with small hooks of Welsh gold in the shape of horse heads. And then a belt, with a buckle of engraved walrus ivory. He noticed Odo raising his brows and said gruffly, 'Nesta would expect me to do her full honour in the King's court as the consort of Welsh royalty.' Besides, he needed the bolster of fine garments to go before other men and face the King and Owain ap Cadwgan. 'We should be there in the hall. We need to know what Owain is saying and what twists and tricks he has up his sleeve.'

The men left the tent and walked across the inner bailey and up the hill to the castle. At the door, an usher stopped them and bade them wait outside until the King had been informed, but eventually they were brought to the hall which was crowded with the nobles and barons of the Welsh Marches. Gerald nodded to Robert Corbet and Picot de Sai, also Tancred of Haverford, who had been patrolling a different area today. Gwilym stood nearby waiting to attend, and Gerald caught his eye for a swift, tense smile.

The King sat on a decorated chair near the open hearth which was swept and empty today. Owain ap Cadwgan sat beside him, garbed in jewel-red silk, with rings on his fingers set with rubies like clotted blood, and a cloak of deep forest-green pinned high on one shoulder with a brooch of Welsh gold. He brimmed with a vital, heavy energy that drew every eye. When he saw Gerald, a grin curved under his moustache. He leaned in to speak to Henry, who arched his brows and put his hand across his mouth, perhaps concealing a smile of his own.

Despite his fine clothes and his determination not to be intimidated, chagrin crept up Gerald's spine. Setting his jaw, he knelt to Henry, a bitter taste in his mouth, for it also meant he was kneeling to Owain, and Owain knew it for his grin was sharp as a knife.

'I trust you are well, my lord,' Henry said.

'Yes, sire,' Gerald replied stiffly.

'And your lady wife too? Has she recovered from her ailment?'

Gerald saw Owain's smirk. He considered telling the King that Nesta was with child, but the best way to protect his family was to drink the poison and stay silent. 'Sire, she is as well as can be expected, but she still has certain issues to which women are susceptible.'

'Well, you must give her my wishes for her good health when you return,' Henry said with a wave of his hand, and his gaze flicked briefly to some women sitting in a corner of the room, among whom were several pretty younger ones that Gerald knew had been hand-picked for the royal delectation. Nesta, it seemed, was former business, not worth pursuing.

'Now,' Henry said, the formalities accomplished, 'you know it is my intention to settle affairs on my borders. Tomorrow, before dinner, I shall announce that the lord Owain is to receive his father's lands in perpetuity – free from all tribute, and from the raising of further castles on his soil. I shall expect all men to acknowledge this agreement and obey my will.'

'Yes, sire.'

Gerald's heart sank to the floor. Owain would never dwell peacefully on his lands and his presence would be like a stone dropped into a pool with ever-widening rings of consequence for himself and the other Marcher lords. He wondered what Owain had agreed in return; or perhaps Henry was buying off a troublemaker because of his imminent return to Normandy. And Owain had perhaps realised, like his father, that being an ally of the King of England was better than being his enemy.

Dismissed, Gerald went to speak with other men in the room. Gilbert de Clare, who had castles at Ceredigion and Aberteifi, accepted him into his circle, which included Tancred of Haverford. Gerald managed a wink for Gwilym, even if he felt sick. These men too must accept Henry's decision regarding Owain ap Cadwgan. He said nothing, but his face betrayed him, for Gilbert de Clare said, 'I will not ask your opinion of this business, but it must be difficult for you.' Gerald still said nothing, but stood a little taller and tightened his jaw. De Clare nodded and took no offence. 'Well, we shall see. The King is no fool, and Owain ap Cadwgan would be wise not to play him for one.'

* * *

A meal was served in the light summer evening with long trestles laid out and covered with white cloths. Gerald was not
placed near the high table where Owain was dining with the
King, but at one of the side trestles arranged for the general
Marcher lords who had answered the summons.

Owain occasionally glanced his way and even raised his cup
in a smiling toast that Gerald recognised as not-so-subtle
mockery. Several times Owain made asides to Henry that Gerald
was certain were about him. His appetite vanished, but he
chewed on the bread anyway, in order to work his jaw.

Owain showed off at the high table, telling jests with flourishes,
making people laugh. Watching his bonhomie and ebullience,
forced to be civil, Gerald's hatred intensified. He imagined
Owain pursuing Nesta and turning her head. He thought of
him lying with her, and the wine soured in his belly.

He left his place at the board to visit the latrine and empty
his bladder, and decided he had had enough and would return
to his tent rather than keep this kind of company. He finished,
arranged his clothing and set off, but had gone no more than
half a dozen paces when he encountered Owain, who was
already freeing his penis for a piss. Gerald stopped, square-
shouldered, in Owain's path. Owain grinned at him, although
his eyes were glittering and narrow. Gerald wished he had his
sword with him.

'Well met, neighbour,' Owain declared. 'You do seem to have
a liking for latrines. I might begin to think they are your natural
home.'

A red mist encroached on Gerald's vision. 'You will stand
aside,' he said with rigid control. 'I am leaving, and you are
entering. Piss on my piss if it gives you satisfaction. But I warn
you, come near me or mine ever again, and I will kill you.'

'I will bear that in mind,' Owain responded with a supercilious smile. 'Give my regards to Nesta when you see her. She is a rare woman, as we both know.'

He stepped aside with an insulting flourish. Gerald mustered every last iota of control and pushed past him with a shoulder-barge. Behind him, he heard Owain chuckle.

Stamping back to his tent in the deepening twilight, fists clenched, he came upon a scuffle of fighting squires. Two had ganged up on a third, who was putting up stiff resistance but being pummelled. Gerald thought to leave them to it, for the language was Welsh, but then recognised Gwilym's voice, and he was the one being set upon by the other boys. He was giving at least as good as he got, and had just kicked one lad in the testicles with a well-aimed and forceful foot. The other one cursed and drew a knife.

'Enough!' Gerald roared, striding forward and disarming the Welsh lad with a sharp blow across his wrist. The youth turned and fled into the twilight, jeering an insult over his shoulder. Gerald hauled the kicked boy to his feet by his scruff. The lad ducked and twisted out of his cloak, leaving Gerald holding the garment like an empty sack as he pelted after his companion. The cloak was of good Flemish wool, he noted, with an intricate bronze pin. Gwilym yelled after his assailants and shook his fist.

Gerald stooped to retrieve the knife. 'What was all that about?'

'Nothing,' Gwilym said, immediately clamming up.

'A lot of nothing for one of them to draw a knife on you.'

Gerald put an arm around Gwilym's shoulders and took him back to his own tent. His hands shook slightly at the thought that if he had not happened by, Gwilym could have been stabbed to death. He poured them both wine from a jug standing on a low table.

'You landed some good punches there,' he said. 'Who were they?'

Gwilym curled his lip. 'From Owain's camp. The one that pulled the knife was with Owain when we were his hostages.'

'I see.'

Gerald waited out the pause until Gwilym sighed and looked past him so he did not have to meet his eyes.

'They were saying you were a soft sword unable to defend your own castle and that you . . . that you were not a real man. That you hide underneath a woman's skirts and are too cowardly to come out.' His eyes brightened with indignation. Now he had started, the words flowed out of him like blood from a nicked vein. 'They said my mother . . . that she needed a real man to show her who was in charge. They called her a slut. They knew I was listening. They started throwing stones and calling me a bastard.'

Rage rose in Gerald's breast but he forced it down. 'I hope you did not believe any of it. Their words and deeds reflect dishonour on them, not you. You are as far above them as the stars are from the gutter.' He put a firm hand across his son's shoulders. 'You are swiftly coming to manhood, and part of that manhood is knowing how to handle yourself. Sometimes leaving the sword in the scabbard is a more difficult test of character than drawing it, and does not mean a man is a coward. Do not become known as someone swift to react with violence. Some men might fear and respect you, but in the long journey it will benefit neither your standing nor your soul. Be the master of your anger and not the other way around.'

'So, I should have let their insults go unchallenged?' Gwilym demanded hotly.

'Indeed not. You were defending your family honour, and I understand why you responded to their taunts. I confess that I almost rose to their master's insults tonight when we encountered each other outside the hall. Be in control of yourself, that is all, and remember that the game is much longer than the moment. Your time will come.'

In talking to his son, Gerald settled himself too, although controlling his own anger had certainly not given him a feeling of mastery.

'Come, I will escort you back to your lord. He need know nothing of this save that you were paying a visit to your father.'

'I wasn't afraid of them,' Gwilym said stoutly as he finished his wine. 'I mean it.'

'I know that, son.' Affection tightened Gerald's throat. 'I am proud of you and of the man I know you will become.'

He returned Gwilym to Tancred's camp and made sure he was taken in by one of the knights. Then he went to the kitchen quarters and approached one of the Welsh urchins lurking near the door, waiting for scraps from the main table. The boy was bare-legged and hollow-cheeked. 'Here,' Gerald said, giving him the cloak. 'Wear this to keep you warm, or sell it if you will.' The boy stared round-eyed at such bounty, and even more so when Gerald gave him a silver penny. 'Remember the house of Dyfed in your prayers,' he said.

Returning to his own tent, he attended to his own prayers and then reached for the flagon his squire had refilled before departing to join his friends. His men sat outside around the camp fire, but he did not want to join their group. He wished with hindsight that he had organised to have Owain killed long ago, when he was in Ireland. He could have arranged it.

He was drinking his second cup when Richard de Belmeis arrived without attendants, wearing a plain cloak and dark cap. Gerald looked up in surprise as the Bishop entered the tent, then hastily knelt to kiss his ring. De Belmeis gestured for him to rise, and went to sit on the camp chair across from Gerald's.

'Would you care for some wine?' Gerald indicated the jug on the table. 'It's still almost full, no dregs yet.'

'Were you going to drink it to those dregs on your own?' de Belmeis enquired.

Gerald had been intending precisely that. Evading the question, he fetched a second cup and poured for the Bishop. 'I was not inclined to company tonight, sire, although of course you are welcome to join me.' But what was de Belmeis doing here? His visit was not exactly clandestine, but neither was it official business, for then the Bishop would have sent for Gerald and had him come to his own quarters with servants in attendance.

'I can understand your wish for a little solitude to digest today's news,' de Belmeis said. 'I realise that having to breathe the same air as Owain ap Cadwgan is distasteful to you, but it is the best for peace.'

'Indeed, my lord, as you say,' Gerald answered tonelessly. 'I would not question the King.' He took a long swallow of wine.

'I am certain you would not,' de Belmeis responded blandly. 'Not openly anyway. Your own thoughts on the matter are yours to manage, but your loyalty to the King's wishes are my concern.'

'I can assure you of that loyalty,' Gerald said, forcing out the words as if pushing a block of granite, and wondering if de Belmeis was here to assess his loyalty and double-bind him to the King. Perhaps because of Nesta's brother too, but he would not raise that issue unless de Belmeis did.

'I am glad to hear it.' De Belmeis smoothed his robe over his knees. 'For the moment Owain ap Cadwgan is to receive full possession of Powys, although the castles already occupied by the King's men shall remain garrisoned.' He looked shrewdly at Gerald. 'Do not think the King is ignorant of your situation, or that he has been taken in by Owain ap Cadwgan's charm. He sees straight through it, and whatever Owain says about you makes no difference to the King's regard. Thus far you have proven steady and loyal, whereas the King barely knows Owain ap Cadwgan, and what he does know suggests he is untrustworthy. Whispering insults behind his hand in public about other men is not the sign of a mature or wise man.'

'And yet the King still favours him and fetes him at his table.' Gerald was unable to stem his bitter contempt.

De Belmeis sighed with amused exasperation. 'That is because a man should keep his enemies close to his bosom. I came to tell you that the King is keeping Owain ap Cadwgan at court and will be taking him to Normandy. The man is too volatile to be let loose on the Marches during the King's absence. He will not be plaguing your borders for many months to come.'

Relief flooded through Gerald, although it fell far short of euphoria and only brought him back up to the level. It would be good to be rid of Owain and to return to his lands and have peace, but the other side of the coin was that Owain would have access to the King's ear and an opportunity to learn more of Norman ways and modes of warfare. At some point too, Owain would return; this was only a temporary reprieve. 'That is good news, sire,' he said without enthusiasm.

De Belmeis continued to eye him shrewdly. 'It will serve for now. I would find reasons to count your blessings rather than curse your circumstances.' He finished the wine and set down his cup. 'Go and join your men. Tell them they can go home. The King will not require you or them for any further business he has to conduct – and that is not a mark of insult, but of trust. I am certain you would rather not be at court just now. I assure you again that the King has the measure of his man, and so do I.' He pressed Gerald's shoulder and made to leave the tent, but turned at the entrance. 'I am counting on you – do not let me down.'

As the flap dropped behind de Belmeis, Gerald sat down heavily on his chair, utterly wrung out. At least for now Owain would not be his problem even if the issues had only been kicked into the long grass.

Eventually he rose and went to his men at their camp fire.

'We are returning home tomorrow,' he announced. 'Make a night of it if you wish. The King has no more need of us on this campaign.'

He hooked up a vacant stool and accepted a piece of toasted bread one of the men had been browning over the fire. He was aware of them looking at him askance but they did not know what he did about Owain and doubtless thought they were being dismissed under a cloud. They were already furious at the warm reception Owain had received from Henry and that he had avoided punishment for the death of William of Brabant. Any one of them would have willingly slipped a knife between Owain's ribs given the chance.

Gerald looked round the firelit circle at his men. 'The King has plans in place to contain and deal with Owain ap Cadwgan.' One knight gave a derisive snort, and Gerald silenced him with a glare. 'Some of you may have noticed the Bishop of London visiting my tent tonight. I cannot tell you what he said, but we are not being sent away in disgrace, far from it – we are still needed. We are to strengthen our borders and remain vigilant.' He held out his cup to be filled and raised it in toast. 'But for tonight, pass the jug and let's have a song.'

28

Palace of Carew,
April 1115

Gruffydd stooped over the cradle of his three-month-old niece and smiled over his shoulder at Nesta. 'What a little beauty,' he said. 'Fair hair?'

Nesta came to his side and looked at her second daughter who had just had her swaddling removed and was pumping her little limbs up and down and waving her arms, fists clenched with the joy of movement. Her hair had begun to grow and was a soft sandy-gold glinted with red. 'She looks like our mother,' she said. 'It is one of the reasons we named her Gwladus.'

Gruffydd waved a rattle in front of the baby's face, and she followed it with her eyes and made a grab. Nesta laughed at the interaction between uncle and tiny niece. Gruffydd had visited them at Christmas while she was heavily pregnant but had not stayed long, and had been away until now in the north with Gruffydd ap Cynan, Lord of Gwynedd. Nesta had been delighted to see him ride in this morning.

'I suppose Gerald is at Pembroke,' he said.

'Yes, but he will be here tomorrow morning – and pleased to see you I am sure, unless you want to ride over and talk with him.'

Gruffydd looked up from the rattle. 'No,' he said, looking furtive. 'In fact I was waiting for a time when he was not at Carew.'

Her breath shortened. 'And why would that be?'

'I should not even be here, but I wanted to tell you . . . unless you already know?'

'Know what?' Her stomach knotted. She beckoned Gwladus's nurse to take charge of the baby and drew Gruffydd to a chair by the hearth. 'What has happened?'

His lip curled. 'Owain ap Cadwgan must have been whispering in King Henry's ear, for a price has been put upon my life,' he said. 'Gruffydd ap Cynan received a message from King Henry offering him a great reward if he would separate my head from my shoulders and send it to him as proof of a deed accomplished.'

'What?' Nesta stared at him, horrified.

'Gruffydd agreed, but sent me fair warning and I had to flee. I took sanctuary in the church at Aberdaron and managed to escape down the coast on a fishing boat. I have been on the run ever since, but many have given me succour and I have increased promises of support from all the Welsh after the King of England's request.'

'Henry demanded your head?'

'Yes, but encouraged into it by Owain – I have my contacts.'

'Henry is never swayed by the persuasion of others unless he wishes to be,' Nesta said flatly.

'Well, in this case he wished to be – why not? It is to his advantage to set the Welsh against each other. I knew Owain in Ireland and saw him for what he was. He thinks well of himself – better than he thinks of others. And whatever you say about Henry, Owain is good at persuading people – he charms them into peril like a ghost-light in the marshes. You of all people should know that, sister.'

Nesta flushed, for the echo of that charm still dwelt in her bones. 'Gerald will have to know. Indeed, he will find out in short order.'

'Tell him whatever you want when he comes tomorrow, for I shall not be here. I won't disclose where I am going, so you do not have to lie to him. I just wanted to see you and the children before I go . . . and also to beg a few supplies.' He looked slightly sheepish.

'Take what you need; I will make it right with Gerald.'

Nesta went to her jewel casket and opened it. For a wild moment she considered giving him her gold hair net to sell, but it was too much and she certainly could never make that right with Gerald. However, she took out the ring that Henry had given her with the large amethyst stone for the sight of it sickened her, and she had only kept it because of its value. If it would support Gruffydd and keep him from harm, then the sacrifice was worth it. She put it and some other pieces in a silk bag, costly in itself, and handed it to him. 'Take these, and use them with my blessing.'

'Thank you. I know what these mean to you. If I succeed, I shall repay you tenfold.'

'Just do not get yourself killed!'

Gruffydd gave her an edgy smile. 'I have managed so far despite the best attempts of my enemies.' He kissed her cheek.

'So far,' she qualified. 'Do not break my heart, Gruffydd.'

Gruffydd stayed at Carew for a meal with his nucleus of loyal men, and when he departed a few hours later he took Carew's pack horses with him laden with supplies from the under-croft stores. Flour, oats, honey, bacon flitches, apples. Sheaves of arrows and some spears. Tents, nails, rope. Watching him depart, Nesta knew it would leave them short for a while, but Gerald was an accomplished quartermaster and they could eke out what they had. She was not looking forward to the confrontation, but she would stand fast for Gruffydd just as much as for any of her children. The thought of Owain and Henry conspiring with each other to murder her brother made her sore inside. She would never forgive either of them.

Gerald arrived at Carew early the next morning. One of his own messengers had brought him the news from Carew late the previous evening and he was livid. Having dismounted, he strode to the stables and found the sumpter horses gone, and their tack. The stores looked as if a plague of locusts had been through.

He marched across the compound to Nesta's hall and found her sitting with her ladies at their sewing as if it was an ordinary day.

'Madam, a word,' he said. 'I ask you to dismiss your attendants, for what I have to say is for your ears alone.'

He well recognised the defiant look she gave him and the jut of her chin, but she gestured for her women to leave. He closed the door behind them and set his squire outside to fend off any disturbance. Then he faced her.

'I cannot believe you have emptied the under croft to supply that brother of yours in revolt,' he said furiously. 'You have involved us in providing a band of rebellious young men with the wherewithal to make war. You have put every single person in this settlement in jeopardy including your own children, and you have compromised my honour.' He struck his chest in emphasis. 'Either you are beyond foolish or I have to accept the unpalatable fact that you have betrayed me.'

Nesta rose and faced him. 'How dare you say I have betrayed you. I had to make a choice and I made it as Lady of Carew and was within my blood right to do so. Gruffydd asked for my succour and I gave it to him. Why did I do that? Because your king has paid for his death. He offered Gruffydd ap Cynan of Gwynedd favour and reward in return for cutting off Gruffydd's head.'

Gerald flinched.

'God help me, Gerald, the Normans killed my father, and my mother eventually. You know my tale – you were there, after all, with Arnulf de Montgomery. And now Henry, who destroyed my girlhood, comes for my brother to wipe him out too. Do you think I am going to stand by and do nothing about it? Yes, I gave Gruffydd supplies to tide him over and I do not need your permission for any of it!' She pushed her wrists out towards him. 'Put me in fetters, lock me up, beat me, do as you will, but I will not regret what I have done!'

He ignored her dramatic gesture. 'You might when Carew is seized by the King and our children disinherited. Christ!' He dug his fingers through his hair. 'Why would Henry turn on your brother now, unless your precious Owain has been pouring poison in his ear?'

'He is not my "precious Owain!" I hate both of them. I hate them for what they have taken from me and what they would still steal if they could. I won't let them, and I won't let you. I would die first, truly I would!'

He shook his head at her, torn between his hurt and rage, not just at her but at what had brought them to this pass. 'And do you hate me because I am part of this too?'

'No.' She shook her head and her anger deflated a little. 'Your hand has never hurt me even if we often take opposite sides. I am glad I helped my brother. I am not glad I am facing you now, but I would do it again.'

Gerald sat down heavily on the bench and dug his fingers through his hair with a sigh. 'Done is done. I shall have to find the means and wherewithal to replenish the supplies, and find soldiers so I can double the guard. Where is Gruffydd now?'

She shook her head. 'I do not know. He did not tell me so that I did not have to compromise him, or lie to you.'

He puffed air through his cheeks in exasperation.

She stamped her foot. 'I am caught in the middle! Do you not understand?'

'Of course I understand,' he snapped, 'because I am also caught. In your turn, do *you* not understand?' He raised and lowered his arms in a gesture of capitulation. 'At least since you do not know Gruffydd's whereabouts I am spared the dilemma of whether to pursue him or not. But in the name of Christ, next time do not keep me in the dark because I am the one at the sharp edge of the sword. Swear you will tell me.' He knew he was whistling into the wind, for she would only tell him as much as she wished – as she always had.

'I swear I will not lie to you.'

Which was not the same thing.

They heard an altercation outside, and Gerald's squire saying firmly that his lord and lady were not to be disturbed. Gerald turned from Nesta, strode to the door and flung it open to find the youth arguing with Dewi, who was grey-faced. 'Sire, my lady,' he panted, 'it is Taran. You must come!'

Nesta gasped. Gerald nodded to the groom, and taking Nesta's hand, hurried with her to the stables. Dewi hobbled after them, leaning on the squire's arm, while people in the yard stopped and stared.

Taran lay collapsed in his bedding straw, his breathing laboured. He had been quieter over the last few days and off his feed, although still eating sporadically, and nothing had indicated this sudden turn for the worse.

Taran struggled as Nesta and Gerald arrived but did not have the strength to get up. Gerald knelt before him and lifted the stallion's heavy head onto his thighs. 'Old friend,' he murmured in Welsh, 'be still, be still. Rest now. Go now to lush green fields and be with your mares and foals. Go now to your master, Rhys. Lightning-born, thunder-bringer, wind-racer, bold-jumper, battle-strider, spark-striker, finest steed.' He chanted the words softly, stroking Taran's cheek. Nesta looked on, her hands over her mouth. She dropped to her knees beside Gerald and laid her head on Taran's neck. The stallion's breath fluttered. A long shudder rippled throughout his body, and he was gone.

Gerald's voice fell to silence. He leaned over and kissed the stallion's nose, and cupped one pointed ear to murmur a farewell. Then he looked at Nesta, tears crescenting his lower lids.

She gazed at the horse, thinking of her father riding to war on his proud young stallion. Taran had been a connection with him, and now that connection was gone and she was bereft all over again. Grief expanded in her chest. She tried to stifle it against her hands but it was too vast and it burst from her in a wail. Gerald pulled her into his arms and she gripped him and beat her head against his chest and howled. He bent over her body, trying to comfort her, torn by his own grief, for this was the end of his young ambition. The horse that he had dared to ask the King for all those years ago.

'We shall bury him,' he said once he could speak. 'Not give him to the hounds, but treat him as a prince. He has left his legacy in our herds, in all his sons and daughters and their progeny. The storm-horses of Carew will live on with our own offspring . . . this is not the end.'

Nesta slowly drew back and, with tears streaming down her

face, stroked the still-warm hide. A fly settled on Taran's eyelash and she brushed it away. 'Yes,' she said. 'Build him a grave and grow sweet grass on the summit . . . and among all your memories, remember that it was my brother who brought him home to you.'

29

Palace of Carew,
May 1116

Nesta sat on Taran's grassed-over grave mound and listened to a blackbird trilling. She had come to be with him for a while under the rising sun of an early May morning. The bleating of sheep carried to her across the cool dawn air, and the shepherd calling to his dogs. From her vantage point she could see smoke twirling from the hall and bakehouse, and watch the poultry maid collecting eggs.

She ran her hand back and forth over the grass and daisy stars growing on top of the mound. Life had been difficult in the year since Taran had died. Gerald was absent on campaign, and although he sent regular messages, she had not seen him for a month. Gruffydd had made peace with Gerald and sworn he would do no harm to any of his tenants or territory. But the fact remained that Gruffydd had nowhere to go and no income unless he seized it as plunder. He had dwelt with them uneasily for a month in midwinter with just his bodyguard and had disappeared again, and neither she nor Gerald had asked where he was going.

Six weeks ago, Henry had instructed Gerald to take Gruffydd into custody. Owain would soon be returning from court to claim his lands, and Gruffydd had to be curtailed. All the Norman garrisons had been put on alert and patrols sent out. On the heels of the news about Owain's return, Gruffydd had assembled a warband of hot-blooded young men, had attacked Narberth and razed the castle. Then he had tried for Llandovery but had been seen off by its Welsh castellan after burning the outer works. An assault on Swansea had followed, before he swept across the country and plundered Ceredigion, gaining support with each act of insurrection. Gerald was under orders to find Gruffydd and either imprison or kill him, and hand him over, living or dead, to Richard de Belmeis.

Gerald had so far succeeded in appearing to be industrious about his task while only going through the motions, steering his men away from Gruffydd's raids so they were always that slight moment out of step, but it could not continue.

Sighing, Nesta rose to her feet, swept her palm over the grass to bid Taran farewell, and returned to the fortress, with nothing resolved in her mind.

In her chamber, she listened to Dafydd reading to her from a book of Welsh stories. At not quite five years old he was a precociously bright little boy, with her shining black hair and dark eyes. Already he spoke Latin better than any of Gerald's knights, and was fluent in Welsh and Norman. Maurice, who generally preferred to run around with a toy sword at the ready, sat and listened to his brother with his head on one side and his weapon resting across his legs. Angharad had brought her sewing to do while she listened, her doll sitting to attention too, and Gwladus perched on her nurse's knee, chewing a piece of bread into a soggy pulp.

The horn sounded at the gate in the sequence signifying Gerald's return. Nesta left her seat and hurried outside. The sight of the troop dismounting in the courtyard and handing over their horses to squires and grooms for tending sent anxiety swooping through her. Gerald slapped his stallion's shoulder, gave him to Dewi, and walked towards her. His mail shirt was stained and rusty from days in the field and his face was thinner with new lines graven into his cheeks. A pungent smell of hot horse and sweaty man emanated from him, and she sent a servant to set about preparing a tub.

The children came running to greet him and Gerald tousled their hair and smiled. Angharad backed away, wrinkling her nose. 'You need a bath, Papa,' she said.

Gerald chuckled ruefully. 'I do indeed, daughter. My armour could stand up and walk on its own just now.'

Dafydd's eyes widened at the notion; so did Maurice's.

Nesta leaned forward sufficiently for him to peck her cheek with a stubbly kiss, but no further. 'Your daughter is right,' she said. 'You smell worse than the midden. What have you been doing?'

'Let me bathe first,' he said, and followed the servant with the bath tub into her chamber. As the servants filled it with pails of hot and cold water, Nesta sent the children off with their nurses. She removed her over-gown so that it would not become wet and took off her wimple and pinned up her hair. Once he had stripped and stepped into the tub, she sat on a stool behind him to wash his hair with her own soap of Castile, and checked him carefully for lice. He took the cup of wine she gave him and drank deeply.

'Well?' she said when the attendants were out of earshot. 'Tell me.'

Gerald set the cup down at the side of the tub. 'The King

insists Gruffydd must be taken.' He looked round at Nesta. 'I have done my best, but it cannot continue. De Belmeis believes I have missed the target too many times, and he is right. I am putting myself in jeopardy – I can protect your brother no longer.'

Nesta bit her lip and turned away to a pile of clean towels. 'Do you know where he is now?'

Gerald gave an irritable grunt. 'He has disappeared into the forests of the Tywi and could be anywhere between Carmarthen and Brecon. I have sent Ifan and his son Rhodri to track him and report back to me.'

Her eyes widened in alarm. 'But you will not seek him out deliberately?'

Gerald grimaced. 'I shall act only when I must, but be warned. The next raid he makes may well be his last. We invited him here, and we are responsible. Rhodri is to find Gruffydd and warn him. I have been avoiding your brother, but now he must avoid me at all costs. I shall not seek him out while he lies low, but I dare not turn a blind eye if he raids again.'

He stood up in the now murky water. Nesta tipped another half pail over him to sluice him down, then handed him towels. He dried himself, dressed in the clean clothes she brought for him, and sat down to a meal of bread and smoked fish.

'You say nothing?'

'What is there to say?' she replied, numbly. 'He is my brother and he has every right to these lands, but he puts us all in danger, and never again do I want to be dragged from my home and imprisoned. Our daughter is nine years old, and what would happen to her? Whatever I do, some part of my life will be torn at the seams.'

'Come, sit down and eat,' Gerald said. 'There is nothing either of us can do to make the situation better.'

Nesta hesitated. Being alone with her turmoil would only turn it further inwards and she had already had that time with herself at Taran's grave, and to no purpose. Sighing, she came to the table, but she wasn't hungry. Gerald was eating with a hearty appetite, but he had been on patrol for days on end and had a strong stomach that reacted far less to tension than hers did.

'Your brother is a grown man and he will make his own choices,' he said. 'Do not set that on yourself. We have done what we can for him. Now we must do our best for ourselves and our children.'

'I know in my head that you are right,' she said. 'But a heart is less easy to reconcile.'

He gave her a sharp look, and this time he was the one to remain silent.

Sitting on the bed, Nesta watched Gerald and their daughter with a tender feeling close to pain as Angharad performed a woman's duty of combing her lord's hair – a task necessary for her role as a wife in the future. Gerald was spending the day at Carew with the men to rest and recuperate.

Angharad touched the hair over his ears. 'You have grey at the sides.'

'I don't think a lady is supposed to mention things like that,' Gerald said, looking serious but with laughter dancing in his eyes.

'Why not?' She tilted her head and her own hair tumbled on her shoulder, thick and silky brown.

'Because some people might see it as a mark of old age.'

'Are you old, Papa?'

Gerald folded his arms. 'I feel it sometimes, I admit, but in truth, I am just wise.'

Nesta snorted.

'So, if all your hair is grey you are either very old or very wise.'

'Or both?'

'What about Mama?'

'Your mother is a law unto herself.' Gerald grinned at Nesta, 'She gives me grey hair though, but since that is the source of my knowledge, I shall not complain. Now then, have you finished? I have to be about my duties.'

He looked up as Ifan was conducted into the room by Nesta's usher. The scout was sweating and out of breath, completely at odds with his usual quiet containment. 'Sire, my lady, I have news,' he panted. 'Owain ap Cadwgan and his ally Llewarch are sweeping through the Forest of Tywi to Carmarthen slaughtering everyone in their path, and they intend to find and kill the lord Gruffydd. They are acting on the orders of the King, and granting no mercy to everyone they come across.'

'Papa?' said Angharad as the silence fell.

Gerald gestured to Nesta's women. 'Take the children outside,' he said, then turned to his daughter. 'This is not business for you or your brothers and sister. You will know what there is to know in good time.'

He gave Ifan a strong look, but before he could speak further another messenger was shown in bearing a letter from Richard de Belmeis. Gerald took it, broke the seal and rapidly read the contents. 'I am commanded by the Bishop of London to bring my Flemings to Carmarthen,' he said, and looked at Nesta. 'I am to stand against Gruffydd should he make a further attack. Owain ap Cadwgan is bound for Carmarthen too in order to liaise with the King's son Robert FitzRoy who is commanding operations.' He nodded brusquely to the usher. 'Take this man and give him food and drink. I will have a return message written.'

The moment the door closed behind the men, Nesta sprang

to her feet. 'You have to protect Gruffydd!' she cried in panic. 'You have to save him! Send him back to Ireland, anything, but you must save his life!'

Gerald looked down at the letter. The young man was rash, over-confident and annoying in more ways than he could count, but he was kin and he neither wanted to fight him nor dress him in shackles. 'He should make himself scarce and lie low, but we dare not succour him here. I will do what I can, but I make no promises for I cannot be seen to defy the King's orders.'

'I have faith in you,' she said hoarsely.

'Do you?' He raised his brow. 'I have often thought that you do not.'

'You are my only hope. If I have doubted you before, I do not now.'

Her only hope of saving her brother, and she was clutching at straws. He dropped his gaze from hers and left the room, unable to deal with her beseeching look. The weight on his shoulders was immense: on one side his king, the other his wife. From Carew to Carmarthen was a day's ride, and from there he had to locate Gruffydd and deal with him without being seen to deal with him.

Once outside he issued orders to his men and called for the horses to be saddled. There were no baggage animals, and the soldiers had to burden their own mounts with their packs and travel light. He told Ifan to take food from the kitchens and ride Nesta's mare. A messenger was sent off at speed to Pembroke to fetch more Flemings from the garrison.

Nesta hastened to bid him farewell as he prepared to mount his horse. 'Be careful,' she said. 'Come back to me whole.'

'I intend to,' he replied grimly, 'but whether I do or not is in the hands of God. Look to our defences, and keep a close watch. I will return if I can, and as soon as I may.'

She put her arms around him and kissed him hard and he set his hands to her waist and pulled her tightly against him for a moment before setting her away and putting his foot to the stirrup.

Watching him leave, Nesta fought the fear that she would never see him again and prayed that he would succeed. She might well lose both him and Gruffydd. The dark, guilt-riddled thought turned in her mind that she might end up with Owain, as she had once wished. The notion horrified her yet still exerted a sickening pull, like an inexorable undertow, or standing giddily on the edge of a cliff.

The children knew something was wrong. How could they not when Gerald's scout had spoken in front of them? Angharad gripped Nesta's hand tightly as the gates closed behind the troop.

'Papa's coming back soon, isn't he?'

Nesta thought of herself as a girl not much older than her daughter, watching her father riding out from Carew never to return, and felt nauseous, but she forced a smile for Angharad's sake. She had to have the faith in Gerald she had spoken aloud. 'Of course he is,' she said briskly. Her gaze flicked to Maurice who had been fired up by the sight of the soldiers and was dashing about with his toy sword, yelling and challenging another small boy to a fight. Dafydd was watching solemnly with his arms folded and a frown on his face, already a typical priest. In other circumstances she would have been amused. 'We have strong soldiers to protect us and secure defences,' she said to Angharad. 'Come, we shall all go and say prayers for your father's and uncle's safety, that all may be well.'

Two thirds of the way to Carmarthen, Gerald and his soldiers made camp for the night in the forest. Gerald posted guards around the perimeter and sent Ifan to scout.

Odo de Barry eyed Gerald across the crackling camp fire. 'What happens now?' he asked. 'What if Gruffydd comes to Carmarthen again?'

'We will cross that bridge if we come to it,' Gerald answered. 'I hope he has the sense to turn back. He will have his scouts out the same as us, and they will know their craft with the same skill as Ifan and Rhodri.'

Odo put a pan on the fire and threw in some fatty salt bacon. As it began to sizzle, the tantalising aroma made Gerald's mouth water.

'Do I take it that Ifan and his son might just know where to meet one of Gruffydd's scouts?' Odo asked nonchalantly, poking the bacon around the pan.

Gerald shrugged. 'I could not say.'

Odo's nod said more than words. He cracked four eggs to cook beside the bacon.

'We are balancing on more than one knife-edge,' Gerald said. 'You have been my friend and ally for many years. I hope you know me well enough that while I take risks, I always consider the odds, and I never step into the unknown.'

'Yes, but I also know how difficult it is when we are pursuing your own brother-in-law. He is the apple of your wife's eye, and she is the apple of yours – while Owain ap Cadwgan and the King are not.'

'There you have it,' Gerald said as Odo finished his cookery and divided the eggs and bacon between two wooden bowls. Then he took some bread from a bag nearby and broke it, handing half to Gerald. Gerald's stomach growled for it had been a long day in the saddle. 'I am trusting my brother-in-law and relying on my scouts.'

They settled to their meal but were barely halfway through when they heard loud crashing sounds through the trees and shouts from the sentries. The soldiers leaped to their feet, reaching for weapons, wide-eyed, hearts thundering. Three cows, one with a calf at heel, blundered into the camp. The leading beast had massive widespread horns that immediately tangled up in a tent rope, bringing down the canvas on top of the men inside, who floundered and struggled while the cow bellowed in panic. As the men were trying to catch the beast and avoid being gored, two perimeter guards arrived escorting a man, two older boys and a woman with a toddler whose screams added to the racket.

The man dropped to his knees. 'Mercy!' he sobbed in Welsh. 'I beg mercy for my wife and children! Kill me, but do not hurt the baby or my woman and boys, I beg you!'

By now the cows had galumphed off into the woods and the occupants of the collapsed tent were thrashing their way out into the air.

'Enough!' Gerald roared in Welsh. 'I am not going to harm you or your children. What are you doing here? Speak!'

The man stared at Gerald wide-eyed, tears running down his cheeks. His mouth opened and closed without sound.

'We're fleeing from Owain ap Cadwgan,' the oldest boy said. 'He came on our herds and began driving them off. My uncle Malgwyn is dead. They put a spear through him, and my cousin Sion. We got away with our cows and the calf, but now we've lost them. They took the bull. We've been running ever since.' He sniffed loudly. 'Are you going to kill us?'

'No,' Gerald said. 'You are not my enemy and I have better things to do than make war on ordinary folk.'

The woman had folded to her knees and was comforting the toddler. Gerald gave the husband a cup of ale from the camp supplies and the man rallied from his initial shock. Gradually Gerald learned more of the story. Owain was moving through the Vale of Twyi, plundering and killing as he went, taking as a given that everyone he encountered was one of Gruffydd's supporters. The people were fleeing with their goods any way they could. The penalty for not being fast enough was either death or capture for future enslavement. Owain was ensuring that neither they nor their livestock and stores became part of Gruffydd's resources.

Gerald frowned. 'Do you know the whereabouts of Gruffydd ap Rhys? Are you his followers?'

The woman vigorously shook her head, but Gerald saw the father and sons exchange glances. 'No, my lord,' the man said with exaggerated emphasis. 'I would never be, I swear.'

Gerald raised his eyebrows. 'Well then,' he said, 'you may stay here the night, under our protection, and go where you will in the morning. But tell me where you came from.'

The man mentioned a destination to the north-east. 'But not with Gruffydd. We had to run because of Owain ap Cadwgan and his men.'

Gerald rubbed his chin. 'Make your way to Carew,' he said. 'The lady Nesta ferch Rhys will take you in and offer you succour.' He removed the woven scarf from around his neck and handed it to the man. 'Give this to the lady. She will recognise it as mine. Tell her everything you have told me, for she will want to know.'

At dawn Gerald sent the Welsh family on their way with some bread and hard cheese for their journey. The soldiers poured water on the camp fires and saddled up. There was no sign of Ifan or Rhodri as yet, but Gerald was not worried, knowing they would report as and when they had information.

Gerald and his troop rode in formation with archers on foot flanking, looking out for trouble. Nearing Carmarthen, they came across another group of refugees at a crossroads, Flemings this time. A father was carrying his son, a boy of about six years old with an arrow wound in his shoulder. The boy was white, shivering and barely conscious. The story they told was the same as last night's, and they had only managed to escape because the Welsh who attacked them had been laden down with booty and captives.

'Which Welsh?' Gerald demanded, sickened.

'I know not,' the man replied with a shrug. 'I only know a little of the language; they are all the same.'

'If they have booty and captives, it is likely to be Owain,' Odo said.

'If this is bringing peace and stability to these parts, I dread to see what chaos looks like,' Gerald said grimly. He turned to the father. 'Give me the child, I will carry him on my saddle. We are only two miles from the castle and there will be a chirugeon there who can help him.'

The boy barely made a sound as his father handed him over and the child's eyes rolled back in his head. Gerald feared he was going to die in his arms, and having instructed his men to take the other children and women up on their saddles, kicked the horse onwards.

Arriving in Carmarthen, Gerald took the injured boy in his arms, carried him through the compound to the castle and made his way directly to the chamber occupied by Robert de Caen, King Henry's bastard son and in command of the campaign on the Norman side. He ignored the demands to know his business, and people were so shocked at the sight of him carrying an injured child that they stood aside.

Robert was talking to one of his adjutants, but looked up in astonishment as Gerald strode up to him and put the little boy down on the table before him. 'Look,' he said. 'Look at this Flemish child with a Welsh arrow in his arm – shot by one of Owain ap Cadwgan's archers. His family are below, torched out of their homes. Is this the rule of order?'

Robert dismissed the man with whom he had been conversing and called for a servant to bear the senseless boy away to be tended by the castle chirugeon. 'Calm yourself, my lord,' he said to Gerald. 'Tell me what has happened.'

'Owain.' Gerald could barely speak his rage was so bright. 'He has taken matters into his own hands and is up to his old habits. Last night we encountered some Welsh fleeing from his troops in disorder. Now, this morning, the same again, but this time Flemish folk, and within a short ride from this castle. He has laid waste to a settlement and injured people who owe their allegiance here. Is this the way we enforce our law, or is it the way we create mayhem?'

'I will have you mind your tongue,' Robert said curtly, but in the next moment he sighed and held up his hand in a gesture of appeal. 'This is indeed a terrible thing, and I will deal with it, but at the appropriate time.'

Gerald stood rigidly to attention. Robert was smoother than Henry, but still his father's son. Nothing would be dealt with for as long as Owain was useful to the King. He met Robert's eyes, showing him that he understood very well what was being said, and what he thought of it.

'Pull yourself together, man,' Robert snapped. 'These things happen in warfare as well you know. Now you are here, I have work for you to do if you are up to it. If you are not, then I will employ someone else.'

Gerald clenched his fists. 'Sire,' he said, swallowing his anger.

'I want you to search the Llanegwad section for Gruffydd ap Rhys. Go and quarter the area.'

He was being pulled to heel with everything to lose if he refused. 'As you wish, sire,' he said flatly.

'I do wish. You and your men are welcome to eat in the hall before you set out.'

Gerald shook his head. He was too furious to think about food, and did not want to be here a moment longer than necessary. 'I should leave immediately, sire, but I shall take provisions to eat on the way. I ask the boon of you that the Flemings I escorted here are given succour.'

'I would do that even without your plea,' Robert said defensively.

Gerald bowed, and swept from Robert's presence, still seething. What did a privileged youngster like him know of the situation? Nothing. And nothing of Owain either. He collected his men from the hall, acquired the necessary provisions, purloined three sumpter horses and departed, pausing only to reassure the Flemings that they would be cared for. There was no sign of the wounded boy and Gerald assumed he was being tended to by the chirugeon.

He set out from Carmarthen, heading north-east. He had still not heard from either of his scouts and could do with their services now. He sent a couple of other men out in front as they left the town and fields behind and entered the woods. The dappled pale-green light of early summer filtered through the new leaves. Gerald was alert for every movement, every snap of twig, every rustle of bush and bird call. He ate some bread to fill his empty belly, even though he had no appetite.

They rode on further along a trail with trees arching either side in leafy vaulting. The smell of wild garlic was damp and powerful in Gerald's lungs, and the jingle of the harness seemed unnaturally loud.

Suddenly they heard hoofbeats galloping towards them from

further up the track. The soldiers reached for their weapons and Gerald's archers put arrows to the nock.

An instant later Ifan's son Rhodri burst upon them astride a sweating dappled horse. Two arrows had sunk deep into his saddle pack but not pierced his mount's flesh. Reining to a halt, he slewed the horse round and gabbled in Welsh, 'Thank God, my lord, thank God! Owain ap Cadwgan . . . I came across him and his men taking a respite and examining their spoils. One of his sentries saw me and raised the alarm and they came after me, but must have turned back when they saw you.'

'Can you lead us to him?' Gerald's heart had begun to pound like a hard, steady drum.

'Surely, my lord, they are barely a mile away. About ninety of them, but many are archers and light spearmen. They have booty and captives to hamper them.'

'Good, bring us there, a reckoning is long overdue.'

Owain's troop, warned by Rhodri's pursuers, who had turned back in haste at the sight of the contingent from Carew, were scrambling for their horses and weapons when Gerald arrived. A shout went up and arrows flew from Owain's archers. Gerald's own archers immediately retaliated.

Gerald fixed a steely focus on Owain, who was riding Storm. Gerald's whole body vibrated with rage, but that too was steely. This man had belittled him, trampled his honour, dragged his name through the mire. He had cuckolded him and mocked him at every turn – and now he had him, face to face.

Gerald drew his sword and spurred directly at Owain. He struck a vigorous blow that Owain warded on his blade, but Owain's defence was clumsy. He was red-faced and sweating with a double chin amid the folds of dark stubble. He had broadened out while absent in Normandy, and it wasn't muscle.

Gerald easily blocked Owain's retort. The forest might be Owain's territory, but fighting in mail on horseback was Gerald's.

'Traitor!' Owain roared. 'You would turn on your own side?'

'You are not on my side – you never have been!'

Gerald struck again. Owain counter-attacked and the men exchanged a flurry of silver blows, their horses plunging and stamping. Gerald's breath burned in his chest, but Owain was in a much worse state, drawing great sawing gulps of air, his complexion darkening until it was livid. He barely raised his arm for the next parry and Gerald slipped in under his guard. As the blade sliced home, an arrow flew past Gerald's ear and punched through Owain's quilted tunic into his chest. The air left Owain's lungs with a loud grunt. He rocked back against his saddle cantle, eyes wide, and then slipped sideways and sprawled on the forest floor. His chest rose and shuddered as he choked, struggling to draw breath, blood bubbling from his lips. Gerald dismounted and stood over him, his gaze on his enemy's face until the light left Owain's eyes and he ceased to move. Gerald kicked the body to make sure and it rolled against his foot like a dead seal on the shoreline.

Too much good living, Gerald thought. Too much self-indulgence at Henry's court. Too much complacency. Owain had lost his edge and paid for it. Beyond his outward dispassion, an enormous rush of triumph was gathering inside him. He wanted to roar his exultation and release all his pent-up emotion, but he couldn't, even though it made him nauseous, for there were too many other considerations.

'Who shot the arrow?' he demanded, looking round.

'I did, my lord.'

Ifan stepped forward. Gerald nodded curtly. His scout's enmity with the lords of Powys had given him right of retaliation, just as much as his own. Ifan set his foot on Owain's body, tugged out the arrow shaft, then spat on the corpse. 'For my wife and child,' he said.

The remainder of Owain's force had melted away into the forest, abandoning their booty and their dead lord, but the noise of their retreat had masked another arrival. Looking up, Gerald saw Gruffydd dismounting from his horse. His men were with him, but Gruffydd gestured for them to stay back, and Gerald made a similar sign to his Flemings. Gruffydd looked at Owain's blood-stained corpse, then at Gerald, with bright eyes. 'Well, that is a cat among the pigeons for sure.'

Gerald returned Gruffydd's look implacably. 'Owain's troops attacked mine first. I think you had better get out of my sight now. I never saw you, for if I did I would either have to kill you or bind you and take you to Robert de Caen, and I wish to do neither. Go now and go swiftly.'

Gruffydd remounted his horse. 'What are you going to do with him?' He nodded at Owain.

'Bear him to Carmarthen,' Gerald answered. 'It was self-defence; I have nothing to fear. If you want any of the booty, take it now while we look the other way, but I do not want to see you again – not until the dust has settled. Do not think of crossing into my territory. Stay away for the sake of your sister and nieces and nephews. Even if this was unplanned, you are still in my debt.'

Gruffydd saluted acceptance. A gesture to his men sent them to collect Owain's laden pack horses.

'Find somewhere to lie low and stay low,' Gerald reiterated. 'Somewhere out of my sight.'

Gruffydd bowed to Gerald from the saddle. 'It is a pity you are a Saison and not good enough for my sister, because I like you and you are a cunning warrior.' He reined about and rode off into the forest, following the trail that Owain's fleeing men had taken.

Gerald puffed out his cheeks and turned his attention to the matter of putting Owain's corpse onto one of the plunder carts. He threw Owain's fur-lined cloak over his body and arranged it. A man was known by how he treated his fallen enemies. The Owain he bitterly hated had gone. What remained was a shell of slack flesh. Besides, the more respect he displayed now, the better he would weather facing Robert de Caen at Carmarthen.

One of his Flemings brought Storm to him. The stallion's ears were back, and his hide twitched like a midge-pool in summer. He sidled as Gerald reached for the reins. 'Whoa now,' Gerald said softly. 'Whoa now, my beauty. You are in safe hands.' Stroking the horse's face and neck to steady him, he also steadied himself and damped down his churning emotions. It wouldn't be wise to ride the horse, not in this volatile moment, and even though it was a wrench, he put him on a lead rein. There would be time enough later.

He remounted Tymestl and set out for Carmarthen with Owain's body tied across a pack horse. First he would report to Robert de Caen, and then he would return to Carew and face Nesta, and volatile, unknown territory.

Robert de Caen turned from Owain's body, laid out in Carmarthen's castle chapel, and looked at Gerald. 'How did this happen?' he demanded. 'Give me the truth.'

Aware that everything he said would be reported to Richard de Belmeis and the King, Gerald was wary. The little Flemish boy was lying in the chapel too, for he had died from his wound, and for Gerald, Owain's death added an extra fillip of justice. 'One of my experienced scouts was set upon by the lord Owain's troops but managed to reach me ahead of their pursuit,' he said. 'We rode to investigate and Owain's archers attacked us.

Perhaps they thought we were going to steal their booty, or intended to draw first blood, I know not. We defended ourselves, and once battle was joined it had to run its course – there were too many grudges on all sides.'

'Including yours for Owain ap Cadwgan?' Robert said, narrow-eyed.

'I admit it was a factor, but I did not engage first – Owain did. The wound in his breast was caused by a Welsh arrow, put there by a man whose family he had once enslaved. I am not sorry he is dead, but it happened by chance, not design.'

Robert gave him a hard look, and Gerald knew he was not fooled at all.

'It may play to the King's advantage,' he added. 'Owain's lands will be divided between his brothers who are of lesser degree. There is no one to carry Powys forward.'

'And your brother by marriage? Might he fit himself for that role?'

Gerald shook his head. 'The men of Powys would not follow him, for they have been enemies of Rhys ap Tewdr's line since before we came to the Welsh kingdoms. But if your father was able to negotiate with Owain ap Cadwgan, then surely he can do so with Gruffydd ap Tewdr. My wife and I will keep the south under control, as will our heirs in time to come.'

'You are saying that everything has worked for the best?' Robert said flatly.

'I am saying that there are opportunities in the circumstances, even if those circumstances were unforeseen, sire.'

Robert sighed and opened his hands. 'I will report to the King and he will decide what to do. Before you leave, I will have you dictate a full report to my scribe that I will send to him. Certainly he believed that Owain ap Cadwgan had the right to impose his rule on these lands, and this act will not go unremarked, but in the meantime you will hold your office and not deviate further from my father's policy, is that understood?'

'Very clearly, sire.' Relieved that he was going to escape with a chastisement, Gerald knelt to Robert with his hands pressed together, rendering fealty. 'I promise you my sword in loyalty.'

Robert leaned over, set his hands over Gerald's and bestowed a perfunctory kiss of peace. 'Return to Pembroke, and for now, hold it as you have done before. Under no circumstances offer succour to your brother by marriage. If you do communicate with him, tell him to desist his depredations, for if he does not, he will die.'

'My lord, I think you will find that Gruffydd has been chastened by recent events, but I shall make sure that he knows the peril in which he stands.'

'Then we are done,' Robert said.

Gerald bowed and left the chapel, pausing before the bier of the Flemish boy to sign his breast and bow in honour. His hands were clammy with cold sweat, but he was heartened, for matters could have been much worse. He might have further storms to navigate, but at least he was still afloat.

30

Palace of Carew,
May 1116

Nesta stood with Dewi in the stables, looking at the colt foal that had been born a few minutes earlier. His coat was a storm-washed dun with a lightning splash on his nose identical to Taran's. He struggled and lunged while the mare whickered and nudged him. Entranced and tearful, Nesta looked at Dewi, remembering how she had stood like this beside him when Tymestl was born, the first of Taran's get. Now this foal was his last, there would never be another, and she looked on this precious, final gift with a mingling of grief and joy.

She swiped away her tears on the heels of her hands. Of late she had been easily stirred to emotion, caused by the weight of all that had happened throughout her life, and it felt like a heavy cloak upon her shoulders. She had heard nothing from Gerald or Gruffydd and the silence was an abyss that she had no bridge to cross.

The mare licked her new baby, encouraging him to stand. As he strove with might and main to obey the imperative rasp of her tongue, the horn sounded at the gate, and for a blind instant Nesta was a girl again, in the moment before her life changed for ever. She looked at the elderly groom in wide-eyed panic and he shook his head.

'It is the lord Gerald,' he said. 'It would be a different sequence for anyone else.'

'But he has sent no word – and it is too soon.'

She had horrible visions of him returning with Gruffydd dead over his saddle in a twisted repeat of what had happened years before. She sped from the stables, her mind flashing with images of disaster, but Gerald rode in with his troop, all in good order, with no signs of injuries or empty saddles. And then she registered the grey-gold stallion he was riding and covered her mouth. 'Dear God,' she whispered behind her fingers.

Gerald dismounted from Storm, saw her standing there, and strode vigorously to her side. Throwing his arms around her, he pulled her against his chest.

'What has happened?' she demanded, still not knowing if this was a triumph or disaster. The meshed rivet links of his mail shirt were cold against her cheek.

He held her away and his eyes gleamed winter-grey, his expression hard with tension. 'Owain ap Cadwgan is dead – he shall never darken our lives again.'

The words struck the surface of her understanding like a bird flying into a wall. 'Owain is dead?' she repeated, trying to make the words mean something.

'Yes, there is no doubt. He lies in his grave even now.'

Owain is dead, Owain is dead. The words were a faint call coming closer and closer until they smashed like a hammer on her heart, sending cracks through it like striations of lightning. She took a back-step from him. Beyond, the men were dismounting and the grooms and squires hurrying to their business.

'How?' she whispered.

'In battle,' he said. 'One that he started.'

Nesta shuddered. Seeing Gerald return riding Storm had reinforced the memories of the day she had learned of her father's death. The enormity of Owain being dead was too great to process.

Gerald pressed his lips together. The children came running out to greet him and Nesta excused herself. 'I will organise food and drink,' she said in a choked voice and fled from him, cuffing her eyes, but the more she tried to stem the tears the harder the waves of grief came. She managed to tell Eleri to prepare refreshments and washing water for Gerald, and then sought refuge in the cellar store rooms, running to the furthest recess at the back, where she collapsed on a pile of tent canvas and howled.

Her feelings for Owain had always been overwhelming – of destructive love and lust, of passion, of hatred and fear mingled as one in a massive storm cloud. To have him no longer in the world was a gulf too great to process, the shock too powerful. He was such a force of nature, and however briefly, he had been her taste of freedom and the possibility of another life. Even if it had all been lies and half truths, she had still been struck by the lightning and now it was blanked out. She wanted to curl up in her own darkness and never emerge. They would be looking for her, and she knew she had responsibilities, but her legs refused to move.

Curled in her corner, she heard the door open, a dog snuffling in the entrance and Gerald's encouraging voice, and realised he had set one of the scent hounds to find her. Wiping her eyes, smearing them with dust and making them sting, she watched man and dog approach through a watery blur and pressed her spine against the wall.

The hound lunged at her, baying, and Gerald grabbed its collar and jerked it away, then handed it to his squire. 'Take the dog,' he said. 'Leave us.'

When the youth had gone, he turned to her, breathing hard. 'I wonder,' he said, 'would you weep for me in the same wise? What would you have done if Owain had come riding to Carew's gates? Let him in as you did before?'

'I didn't let him in!' Her voice cracked. 'I am weeping because . . .' She shook her head. 'You would not understand.'

'Tell me, and we shall see. You cannot hide in the dark because none of this is going away.'

Without touching her, he stepped aside so that she could stand up and go out before him. She walked past him on unsteady legs, pulling in her body so that there was no contact, but when she reached the doorway she paused, gripping the post for support.

He removed his cloak and folded it around her dust-smeared gown. 'I have my pride,' he said. 'When my wife runs away in grief at the news of the death of her former abductor, what is seen and what is said afterwards may only be water off a stone, but it wears away that stone eventually and changes the channel for eternity. You are Lady of Carew and you are my wife, and mother of our children.'

Nesta swallowed, and with a wordless nod walked beside him. He took her to the garden rather than the public space of her chamber, and the way he looked at folk as they passed ensured that no one interrupted their progress. He closed the gate behind them and led her to a bench in the orchard where the apples were just beginning to set, small and hard-green.

'Now, tell me,' he said. 'Do not run from me in tears. We shall have this out once and for all and know where we stand.'

She looked down at her folded hands, then around at the

trees, and finally at him. 'You were the one who said we should close the door, go into another room and not speak of it again.'

'I did. I was wrong.'

Nesta shook her head. 'If Owain had come to the gates of Carew I would not have opened them for him, I swear I would not. I knew what he was; I knew what I had . . . I knew I could never go with him again.'

Gerald folded his arms and looked at her.

'But there was always the possibility, always the dream,' she said hoarsely. 'Like having a dark gemstone: I might never wear it, but I knew it was there in my jewel box nevertheless. And now it has gone.'

Gerald sighed heavily and made a weary gesture. 'I can never be Welsh by birth, but I love you, and I have loved Wales since I was a youth. Never once have I been untrue to you; always I have been steadfast. Men have looked at me askance and told me I am soft for love of you. Men have called me a cuckold, an unmanned fool, and there are times that I think they have the truth of it – but it is also true that it makes no difference, until my dying breath.'

Nesta started to cry again from what seemed like a bottomless well of tears.

'We cannot live on dreams,' Gerald continued. 'I thought I could, but I have learned the hard and bitter truth, for my dream was you, and I still have that jewel, bright as day, in my own box, but no key to unlock it.' He rose to his feet and turned away towards the garden entrance. 'You should know that Gruffydd is safe, and providing he lies low his head is no longer in jeopardy except by dint of his own folly. I shall eat and then ride on to Pembroke; there is much to do.'

Nesta sat rooted to the spot, struggling. He reached the gate.

'Wait!' she cried, and sprang to her feet. 'Gerald, wait!'

He turned, and every line of his face was taut, his body rigid. 'Please,' she said. 'I have something I need to show you.'

He hesitated, then gave a half shrug. He stood aside again for her to go before him and she was keenly aware of his body and how there seemed to be a layer of resistance between them. She took him to the stables where the colt foal was now on his feet and feeding from his dam, his neck crested with a fuzz of dark mane. The mare swung her head to regard the visitors, alert and prick-eared but not agitated.

'Taran's last offspring,' she said. 'He was born as the horn was blowing for your arrival. In time I hope he will carry you, or perhaps Gwilym or Maurice.'

Gerald stared at the foal. She could not read his thoughts for his expression was opaque, but she sensed that he was poised with one foot on a decision and the other still on the ground.

'Tymestl was born in this stall when my father came home,' she continued. 'Taran's first-sired foal, and now this is his last.' Tentatively she touched his arm. 'I don't want this to be an ending. I want it to be a beginning, and I want all the doors to be open.' Her voice quivered. 'I don't want to be in the dark any more. I don't want to be in the dungeon where Henry put me, or even at a camp fire with Owain. I needed you to find me. I cannot change what happened before – it will always be there – but I would rather be in the light than the darkness. I grieve for what might have been, but I want to go forward at your side. That is my greatest desire, and I hope it is not too late.'

Gerald's opaque expression brightened.

'You love me,' she said, 'in a way no other man has. Not my father, not my brother, not Henry and not Owain. What that means is as vast as an ocean, and as small as a grain of sand, and unseen because of its greatness and its smallness. You don't notice a mountain when it is always in your sight until it is no longer there, and the grain you would not see at all, yet it forms the very ground beneath your feet.' She swallowed and held out her hand in entreaty. 'Stay,' she said. 'Gerald, please stay.'

She heard a strangled sound in his throat and then he pulled her to him in a full, hard embrace. She gasped as the motion drove the air from her lungs, but her next breath took in the scent of him, and then his lips were on hers, and she felt the energy surge between them, fire and water.

'I could never leave you,' he said as they briefly drew back. 'Then indeed I would break. For me it is *am byth* – for ever.' And he pulled her close again.

Over food and wine, Gerald told Nesta what had happened at Carmarthen and the manner of Owain's death. The notion of him no longer being in the world was a raw wound, but she faced it, and was even aware of a feeling of relief, as though that wound had been drained of poison and cauterised, and now she could mend and allow the healing to truly start, even if there were scars. She concentrated on the fact that she had Gerald, and her children. Her brother, for the moment, still lived. They had weathered this storm, even if more were brewing on the horizon, but perhaps, between them, they could stave them off.

She took a drink from the cup Gerald had just refreshed for her. 'I want to go to Carmarthen.'

'What for?' His eyes filled with wariness, and she did not blame him. After what had happened, he might be justified in thinking that she wanted to go and mourn over Owain's body.

'To speak with Robert de Caen and ask his clemency and intercession with Henry on behalf of my brother.'

Gerald raised his brows but said nothing, merely folded his arms and looked at her.

'I knew him when he was a child, and I remember him fondly. His mother was kind to me and we held each other in affection. It may be worth his while to listen to me as a peace-broker, and at least have a truce. I want to be able to welcome Gruffydd to Carew again and sit with him around the table. All this hunting and hiding and fighting. If only we could make an end to it. Gruffydd cannot do it for himself just now, it would be too dangerous, but women have the power to intercede, a power that fighting men do not.' She reached across the space between them and took his hand in a gesture that both softened her words and added physicality to her intent. 'Robert might just listen to me, and Henry will take more notice of his favourite son than anyone else.'

Gerald looked down at her hand, then wove his fingers through hers. 'And what might that intercession entail?'

'A lasting truce,' she said. 'An agreement to let Gruffydd have a place to settle, in exchange for an alliance and an agreement not to go to war.'

'A lasting truce?' Gerald tried not to look too sceptical.

She grimaced at him. 'I am not naive. When I say this, I mean one that will keep for longer than a season, and perhaps many. My brother will value the opportunity to wed and beget heirs to follow in his stead, and my father's. I know he is keen to marry one of the daughters of Gruffydd ap Cynan. And who knows what alliances he will make with our own sons, for the benefit of all.' She squeezed his hand. 'It can do no harm. What is there to lose?'

He conveyed her hand to his lips and kissed her knuckles. 'I do not know if you will succeed, but we shall try,' he said. 'You are right: we have nothing to lose.'

Epilogue

Pembrokeshire coastline,
late Summer 1116

Nesta drew rein beside Gerald on the cliff tops near Manorbier, and sat with him in companionship to watch the sea roll into the curve of the bay. A warm breeze blew into their faces, smelling of salt and shore. Breathing deeply, Nesta watched the changing colours of the waves under sunlight and shadow. A single seagull wheeled above them, and Gerald raised his head to watch the bird ride the thermals, the sunlight turning its wings to blazing white. Nesta remembered from long ago a dream that had come to her in the days of darkness, when her father had said he would fly above her like a seagull and watch out for her, and she welcomed that portent now.

Two months ago she had gone to Carmarthen and spoken privately to Robert de Caen. There was much of Henry in him, but tempered by his mother's nature, and he remembered Nesta fondly from the time they had spent at Woodstock. Calm and pragmatic, he had heard her out on the matter of a truce with

Gruffydd, and after some initial reserve had agreed to negotiations. The discussions had been delicate and had involved messages to and fro between Richard de Belmeis and Henry in Normandy, for Robert had been thorough once committed and had sought a solid binding for the truce, which needed the support of de Belmeis and the consent of his father. Eventually an accord had been reached. Gruffydd swore to keep the peace and agreed to settle on lands to the north of Carmarthen, at the top of the Cothi river valley where it was said that the waters ran with gold. The boundaries he had been given might not contain him for ever, but it was enough for now. She could face the future with hope.

She smiled and reached her hand across to Gerald, and when he took hers there was something good and healing about the simple contact of entwining their fingers like strands of fate, Norman and Welsh.

'I was thinking of my father,' she said, and told him about the seagull dream. 'I wonder if he is watching over us now.'

Gerald raised his head to the gull as it continued to wheel. 'If he is, I hope he knows the love I have for his daughter, and for Wales.'

'I am sure he does.' She touched her heart with her free hand, and no words were needed.

At the sound of hooves, they turned to see Gruffydd trotting towards them, riding one of the grey-gold Carew horses. His cloak was vivid red, and Nesta's heart leaped, for with his dark hair and his smile he looked so much like their father. Drawing rein beside them, he saluted in greeting. 'Dafydd said I would find you here. I know you were not expecting me until Lammas-eve, but I thought a few days would not make a difference. I want to thank you for all you have done.'

Gerald shrugged. 'I am glad that matters are settled,' he said.

'It will be good to hunt together again, rather than hunting each other.'

Nesta swallowed, her throat tight with emotion. It seemed no coincidence that she had thought of their father in the moment before Gruffydd arrived. 'Stay for as long as you wish,' she said. 'You will always be welcome at Carew.' She would not think of the lost years, only those to come.

'Providing you do not stir up any more trouble,' Gerald qualified, but with a smile.

Gruffydd returned him a full grin. 'We have always understood each other. Do not worry, "brother", I shall never outstay my welcome – and I shall always ask from now on before I borrow the pack horses or raid your under croft.'

Gerald laughed and shook his head.

Seeing her brother and husband together, bantering with each other, filled Nesta with a deep, satisfying warmth. Had someone told her frightened, traumatised fourteen-year-old self that a day like this would come, she would not have believed them.

As they turned their horses back to Carew, she smiled, and thought that today was glorious and tomorrow would be fine too.

Author's Note

My decision to embark upon the story of Nesta ferch Rhys and Gerald of Windsor owed more to a gradual accumulation of awareness than a sudden spark. Numerous different strands quietly assembled themselves in my subconscious over a period of years.

I am a frequent visitor to Wales, enthralled by its beautiful scenery and its complex history. While researching earlier projects involving the de Clare, Marshal and Bigod families, I became interested in some of the other stories embedded in the places I visited. Several trips brought me to Pembroke and Manorbier, the latter with its castle sitting a very short walk from the beach. The famous chronicler of the twelfth and early thirteenth centuries Gerald of Wales was born at Manorbier and speaks of playing on the shoreline with his siblings. Gerald was Nesta and Gerald's grandson, born from the marriage of their daughter Angharad to William de Barry, son of Odo. I have called him Guillaume in the novel to avoid a plethora of Williams!

Visits to the castles of Carew and Cilgerran furnished me via their guidebooks with more details of Nesta and Gerald's story. It is interesting that both places claim to be the site of the infamous latrine scene and Nesta's abduction, willing or otherwise, by Owain ap Cadwgan. In the novel I have chosen Cilgerran (Cenarth Bychan) because it makes by far the most sense, being only five miles from Cardigan where the Christmas feast of 1109 was held. The palace of Carew is situated deep in the heartland of Dyfed, thirty miles from Cardigan; I doubt Owain the opportunist would have chanced his luck that far.

Another element that pulled me in to write Nesta and Gerald's story was my interest concerning Henry I and his many mistresses. Although begetting only two legitimate children by his wife Edith (who changed her name to Matilda when she married) of Scotland, he had at least twenty-one illegitimate children with a succession of different women. Some historians take the view that these women were cherished mistresses and even at times seductresses themselves. There is also the subtext view that Henry was some sort of super-lover whose bedchamber skills were irresistible and women fell for him on sight. A chronicler excuses Henry's promiscuity by saying he didn't indulge in these affairs because he was lecherous, but rather from a desire to procreate and have children. The medieval view of sexual intercourse was that it should only happen for the purposes of procreation so the chronicler was giving Henry the validation he needed on that front.

My own view is that Henry saw and Henry took because Henry could, whether the young women consented or not. The women would have had no say in the matter because they were generally either hostages, or put forward by their families in the interests of gaining royal favour (as in the case of Isabelle de Beaumont, whose time as Henry's mistress coincided with her brothers' return to favour after suffering Henry's displeasure). Most of the women had no option to refuse. Henry certainly took care of the numerous children begotten by these liaisons and many grew up to become important cogs in his ruling machinery, so in a way he was producing his own support group and that could well have been part of his strategy. The women themselves were often married off to men who would value a tie with the King and regard the link as a privilege and a useful part of networking. How the women themselves dealt with the matter, and their view of the situation, has never been investigated.

Henry kept a mini-harem (and menagerie) at the royal hunting lodge complex at Woodstock. Professor David Crouch has written an interesting article on the matter of the domicile at Woodstock and some of the political, social and sexual ties involved with the site. Woodstock continued to be a pleasure palace for later generations of English royalty. Henry II's mistress Rosamund Clifford was to spend time here for example, and Henry is supposed to have built a pleasure garden there for her.

What do we know of Nesta in history, and what can we extrapolate from digging around the edges?

There are numerous conflicting theories and the 'facts' change depending on the teller. An example would be the above-mentioned claim by both Carew and Cilgerran to be the site from which Nesta was abducted. The stories in their guidebooks are identical.

Nesta was the daughter of Rhys ap Tewdr, Prince of Dyfed (see map), which roughly equates to modern Pembrokeshire. Wales in the eleventh century consisted of numerous principalities and the rulers of those principalities spent a great deal of time warring with each other. The Welsh system of inheritance wasn't 'the eldest son takes all' but was based upon a division between the sons, which led to in-fighting and scheming, even while the strongest usually took the upper hand, and younger siblings, both legitimate and not, would unite or squabble as the shifting political scenery dictated.

Nesta's father, Rhys, was the enemy of Cadwgan ap Bleddyn of the neighbouring principality of Powys. Cadwgan had forced Rhys to flee to Ireland with his family for a brief period; Nesta would have been a small child at the time. When Rhys returned and regrouped, he fought the Powys lords and killed two of Cadwgan's brothers. Re-establishing himself, Rhys made a protection pact with William the Conqueror that lasted until William's death in 1089.

The Conqueror's successor, William Rufus, did not continue that pact and a new offensive on the Welsh principalities was launched, driven by ambitious, power-hungry Norman warlords who began extending their territories, building castles as they advanced. Arnulf de Montgomery was one such among several, and part of the powerful house of Montgomery, lords of the Welsh Marches.

In the spring of 1093, Nesta's father was killed in a skirmish near Brecon. His lands were overrun by the Normans and Nesta was taken hostage. Her younger brother Gruffydd was spirited away to Ireland under the noses of the invaders. Another brother, Hywel, not mentioned in the novel to keep the narrative flow streamlined, was held captive and possibly castrated. There is no mention of what happened to Nesta's mother after Rhys ap Tewdr's death and my placing her in the convent at Wilton is purely my invention.

Nothing is known of what happened to Nesta in the years following her father's death; all we have are possibilities. We do know that William Rufus and his brother Henry came to Wales on campaign in 1097, and that Nesta was very likely in the custody of the Montgomery family at that time. She may well have encountered Henry then and become his concubine. Some historians suggest a later date of 1114 for her meeting with Henry when he came to the Marches again to sort out Welsh affairs. I have gone with the 1097 dateline because Henry seems to have mostly preferred younger women for his conquests, rather than wives of many years' standing (there were exceptions, but on the whole it stands true), and it is unlikely, given his theatre of operations, that he would have had the opportunity to encounter Nesta, living deep in South Wales. Whatever the dateline, it is almost certain that Nesta bore Henry a son, who was given his father's name.

Somewhere around 1102, Nesta married Gerald FitzWalter of Windsor, Constable of Pembroke Castle.

What do we know about Gerald?

Although we have no date for his birth, he was a younger son of Walter of Windsor, so called because he was Constable of Windsor Castle in Berkshire, one of the most important royal fortresses in southern England. Gerald would have grown up here with his siblings and absorbed the modus operandi of running a great castle. He would have had access to excellent training in arms and the best equipment. Although a younger son and of the service nobility rather than the baronage, he would have been able to avail himself of all the tools for advancement.

Gerald came to South Wales with Arnulf de Montgomery as one of his hearth knights, and at some point after 1093 became Constable of Pembroke Castle and responsible for the general area. On first arriving in 1093, following the death of Rhys ap Tewdr, there was no castle at Pembroke and Gerald must have been present at its conception, and probably oversaw the building of the first timber tower and palisade. Certainly by 1096 it was sufficiently secure to withstand a siege by the Welsh. The incident in the novel where Gerald throws bacon flitches at the Welsh to show he has plenty of food in store and where he makes sure a letter to Arnulf de Montgomery, declaring he has supplies to last throughout the winter, is intercepted is reported in the Welsh medieval chronicle the *Brut y Tywysogion*, a source of Welsh history dating from 682 to 1332. Gerald's cunning saved the day and Pembroke was only one of two fortresses to hold out in South Wales during the Welsh onslaught on the Normans in 1096.

A few years later, the Montgomery family rebelled against the new King of England, Henry I, who had come to the throne after William Rufus's 'accidental' death while hunting in the New Forest. At this point Gerald was no longer Constable of Pembroke, but Henry reinstated him, and it is probably around this time that he married Nesta, presumably to give him the authority of the ruling Welsh house in that part of South Wales. Wedding into the blood of Dyfed's rulers also ensured that future generations had a claim on that bloodline. Pembroke Castle belonged to the crown, and Carew was the family caput. Gerald and Nesta's eldest son went by the title of 'William of Carew'.

Nesta and Gerald had five children in all: William (Gwilym in the novel), Angharad, Dafydd, Maurice and Gwladus. All were to make successes of their lives. William was to carry on the family line at Carew; Dafydd would become the Bishop of St David's and head of the Welsh Church for a time; Maurice would travel to Ireland and make a name for himself there with other relatives. Angharad married William de Barry, and her son, Gerald, became the famous raconteur and chronicler whose works are still in print today. Gwladus married into the de Cogan family, whose descendants also crossed to Ireland with Richard de Clare.

Nesta's son Henry FitzRoy was given lands in Wales by his father and was killed in battle in 1158, fighting the troops of Owain Gwynedd in Anglesey. His son, Meilyr, became King John's constable in Ireland, where he clashed with the great William Marshal (see my novel *The Scarlet Lion*).

Gerald had a son by an unknown mistress but we know nothing about him beyond that he may just possibly have been called Walter. In the novel I have given him that name, and provided him with a back story.

The incident concerning Gerald and the latrine escape is reported in the *Brut y Tywysogion*, which tells us that Owain's father Cadwgan held a great gathering at Ceredigion at Christmas – the year varies, but I have put it as 1109. Owain became very interested in Nesta around this time and, learning that Gerald was staying at Cenarth (Cilgerran) with his family and all his worldly goods, made a plan to raid the castle and do his worst.

The *Brut* tells us that he entered the castle by surprise at night and that Nesta, thinking quickly, ordered Gerald to hide down the latrine rather than be killed. Owain, meanwhile, plundered the castle and abducted Nesta and the children. The insult and outrage caused by the attack sent a storm throughout the Welsh Marches. Owain's father found himself implicated for failing to prevent his son's reckless behaviour and fled into exile in England while Owain hid out in Ireland. Presumably Nesta was restored to Gerald at this stage. The *Brut* makes no mention of the actual event. It does say, though, that the children were returned as a gesture of appeasement.

The *Brut* tells us that Owain had had 'connection' with Nesta – willingly or not on her part we don't know, but we do know that she and Gerald went on to have another three children after they were reunited, which suggests that the abduction was no block to marital relations.

Owain fled to Ireland following the abduction, leaving his father to deal with the brunt of the Norman anger. However, he returned at a later point and took to raiding his enemies' lands, burning, plundering and capturing people to be sold in Dublin, where the Hiberno-Norse at this time had a prospering slave market. One of Owain's raids resulted in the death of William of Brabant, who was an official of senior importance among the Flemish and Brabançon immigrant community whom King Henry had settled in Wales following catastrophic floods in their own lands.

To Gerald, Owain was now a marked man, and he eventually got his revenge in 1116, when Owain was on campaign, fighting for King Henry, attempting to rid the country of Nesta's brother Gruffydd ap Rhys. Gruffydd, now a young adult, had returned to Wales in 1112. For a time he stayed with Nesta and Gerald, before going north to former allies of his father. He began agitating against the Normans, although not in Nesta and Gerald's territory. Owain, meanwhile, returned from exile after his father was murdered by his erstwhile ally and cousin Madog ap Rhyrid. Having dealt with Madog by putting out his eyes, Owain made his peace with King Henry and set out to deal with Gruffydd.

Owain and Gerald were supposedly fighting on the same side, but when their troops clashed in the Forest of Tywi not far from Carmarthen, Gerald and his Flemings brought Owain down and killed him. The *Brut* says that Owain made the first attack, but was hampered by the plunder he had seized along the way as he raided and burned indiscriminately.

With Owain dead, his territories were divided among surviving male relatives and the strength of Powys was diminished. Nesta's brother Gruffydd settled down in the Cothi Valley, married the daughter of Gruffydd ap Cynan of Gwynedd, and raised a family – although on occasion he continued to cause trouble. He was never to rise to great heights, but his son Rhys stood on his shoulders and led the Welsh revival, ruling from Cardigan during his lifetime as 'the Lord Rhys'. He is still celebrated today for his great statesmanship and is one of the many giants of native Welsh history.

What happened to Gerald after the events of 1116 is one of history's unanswered questions. He disappears from the records after this point, and some historians place this as the date of his death and think that he might himself have been injured during his fight with Owain ap Cadwgan. However, we know Nesta remarried following his death, and the earliest mention of this is 1130 when she was the wife of the Sheriff of Pembroke, a Fleming called William Hait. She bore Hait a son, William, who appears in the records as Lord of Llanstephan. The marriage did not last long though, and Nesta married a third time to Stephen, the Constable of Cardigan, and bore him a son too – Robert, who was also part of the Cambro-Norman invasion of Ireland.

There was a Welsh uprising in 1127, and other historians believe that this is when Gerald may have died, which makes sense to me. Had he died in 1116, Nesta would have been remarried rapidly for the security of the territory, for Gerald's son and heir at this point would only have been in his early teens. A date nearer to 1130 for Gerald's death seems to fit more closely with the known history, by which time his eldest son would have been in his twenties.

We have no death date for Nesta herself, but it's presumed to be some time in the mid-1130s. I hope she outlived Henry I, who died late in 1135.

The King's Jewel only covers Nesta's first marriage to Gerald, which, if the 1127 date for his death is correct, lasted for at least twenty-five years and against many odds. Their descendants would affect the history of Ireland in depth, and in later centuries would cross the Atlantic to the United States of America and reach as far as the presidency. John FitzGerald Kennedy was one of those descendants.

As always, researching and writing *The King's Jewel* has been an amazing voyage of discovery for me. I have met some fascinating characters on my journey, and learned a great deal along the way about human nature – that it doesn't change, but is only coloured by social attitudes and technology.

For anyone wanting to know more about the lives and times of Nesta and Gerald, I have included a select bibliography that follows.

Select Bibliography

Barlow, Frank, *William Rufus* (Yale, 1983)

Carew Castle Souvenir Guide (Pembrokeshire Coast National Park)

Crouch, David, *Robert of Gloucester's Mother and Sexual Politics in Norman Oxfordshire* (Historical Research vol 72 issue 179 pages 323–333, 1999)

Davies, Sean, *War and Society in Medieval Wales 633–1283: Welsh Military Institutions* (University of Wales Press, 2004)

Davies, Sioned and Jones, Nerys Ann (eds), *The Horse in Celtic Culture: Medieval Welsh Perspectives* (University of Wales Cardiff, 1997)

Gerald of Wales (translated with an introduction by Lewis Thorpe), *The Journey Through Wales and The Description of Wales* (Penguin Classics, 2004)

Green, Judith A., *Henry I* (Cambridge University Press, 2009)

Hilling, John B., *Cilgerran Castle, St Dogmael's Abbey, Pentre Ifan Burial Chamber* (Cadw, 2000)

Johns, Susan M., *Gender, Nation and Conquest in the High Middle Ages: Nest of Deheubarth* (Manchester University Press, 2013)

Lloyd, J. W., *A History of Wales from the Earliest Times to the Edwardian Conquest, Vol II* (Longman, 1948)

Ludlow, Neil, *Pembroke Castle* (Pembroke Castle Trust)

Maund, Kari, *Princess Nest of Wales: Seductress of the English* (Tempus 2007)

Roberts, Sara Elin, *The Legal Triads of Medieval Wales* (University of Wales Press, 2011)

Stephenson, David, *Medieval Wales c. 1050–1332: Centuries of Ambiguity* (University of Wales Press, 2019)

Williams, John (ed.), *Brut y Tywysogion: The Chronicle of the Princes of Wales* (Cambridge University Press, 2012)

Acknowledgements

This is where I thank the wonderful people behind the scenes in my life and writing. Their support and comfort has grounded me during strange and difficult times, when we are all having to adapt to a different world. Their personalities, their laughter and stories – and their love – have uplifted me and kept me sane.

My husband Roger, as in many other acknowledgement notes is still doing the ironing, bringing mugs of tea to my study and being a steady rock at my side. A dedicated gardener, he also ensures we are three-quarters self-sufficient in homegrown fruit and vegetables. The love of my life is not a cliché.

My thanks as always to my dear friend Alison King for our journeys in time travel. Her extraordinary skills have allowed my ventures into historical research to be so much more enlightening and vivid than using reference works alone.

In publishing, I want to say a huge thank you to my agent Isobel Dixon, her assistant Sian Ellis Martin, to James Pusey and Hannah Murrell, and everyone at Blake Friedmann for their knowledge, dedication and professionalism. The same appreciation goes out to my lovely editor at Sphere, Darcy Nicholson, and also to editor Dan Balado-Lopez for his sympathetic and observant copy-edit of *The King's Jewel*. As always it's a joy to work with him. Thank you, too, to Millie Seaward, Ben McConnell and Jon Appleton at Sphere for the great job they do. And a special remembrance thank you to the late Thalia Proctor who was a true professional and the best editorial manager any author could have.

I also want to send out appreciation to my magnificent readers. Without you, I wouldn't have this wonderful job, and have made so many dear and knowledgeable friends. I greatly value the reading community and if I have brought entertainment, pleasure and knowledge to your lives through my writing, then it's a totally reciprocal thing.

Elizabeth

New York Times bestselling author Elizabeth Chadwick lives in a cottage in the Vale of Belvoir in Nottinghamshire with her husband and their three dogs. Her first novel, *The Wild Hunt*, won a Betty Trask Award and *To Defy a King* won the RNA's 2011 Historical Novel Prize. She was also shortlisted for the Romantic Novelists' Award in 1998 for *The Champion*, in 2001 for *Lords of the White Castle*, in 2002 for *The Winter Mantle*, in 2003 for *The Falcons of Montabard* and in 2021 for *The Coming of the Wolf*. Her sixteenth novel, *The Scarlet Lion*, was nominated by Richard Lee, founder of the Historical Novel Society, as one of the top ten historical novels of the last decade. She often lectures at conferences and historical venues, has been consulted for television documentaries, and is a member of the Royal Historical Society.

For more details on Elizabeth Chadwick and her books, visit www.elizabethchadwick.com, follow her on Twitter, read her blogs or chat to her on Facebook.